Chapter and Verse

Backslider's Ball

Chapter and Verse

Backslider's Ball

Mark Witt Mysteries

Frank Hamilton

ISBN-10: 0985810327

ISBN-13: 978-0-9858103-2-0

Published in the United States by Freeze Time Media

Cover design by Jeff Covington

This book belongs to all the thoughts that went into this writing — thoughts that entered my mind and seemed to take up residence. These thoughts ranged from ones of happiness, family and purity, to thoughts of evil and sinister happenings and ultimately to so, so many thoughts of sex and murder. In fact, some of these thoughts — say, for instance, the ones of sex, and in particular, certain hedonistic thoughts of rampant sexual acts with unknown, albeit beautiful and extremely welcoming women — appear to not only have taken up residence in my mind but also to now be landscaping, decorating and holding neighborhood watch parties. Forget about being a cathartic undertaking; this book will probably send me into therapy. One positive, though. Luckily for me the wife always breezes past this part and doesn't bother reading the dedications.

Also, an extra special salute and dedication to my two best buddies, the two best cocker spaniels a guy could ever know, Barney and Buffy. Miss you guys. Your paw prints are all over my life. And keep an eye out — I'll be coming to see you over the Rainbow Bridge when my time is done.

Chapter 1

Parked at the corner of Jefferson and Cockrell Hill Road, the squad car sat idling at the curb. As the car's exhaust hit the freezing air outside, it instantly became white fumes of smoke. Officer Richard Witt got out from the passenger side.

"Sit tight. I gotta check something out," he said to John Coleman, the rookie patrolman who sat behind the wheel. Witt closed the door and walked away, leaving the rookie alone.

It was mid-December 1988, and Coleman never imagined Dallas, Texas, could be so cold. With the car heater running inside, the light snow falling would hit and crystallize like shimmering diamonds on the windshield. But Coleman would find no treasure this evening while waiting for his partner.

A native of Youngstown, Ohio, Coleman had left the Rust Belt a year earlier searching for opportunity. Really more pressing than an opportunity, he had come looking for a way to feed his family. He decided on moving to Dallas to try and make his mark in life for three very good reasons: the local economy; his love for America's Team, the Dallas Cowboys; and a warm southwestern climate. So much for the warmth part, but at least his timing was good.

He found an affordable little house in Oak Cliff, and affirmative action helped get him hired by the DPD in quick order. Coleman made the most of the opportunity and graduated top of his class at the academy. He took to police work right off and liked it. But he didn't like this part of the job.

Before the windows and windshield became completely covered, Coleman watched Witt walk past two homeless men and into the Fairlane Apartments. Built at least thirty years earliwer, the Fairlane was the sort of low-slung apartments that were built around a courtyard with a type of old Vegas flair. Maybe back in Frank and Sammy's day it was a happening spot, but its day had clearly passed. Peeling paint and rotting stairs were all that remained from any possible past glory. None of this deterred Richard Witt, who moved with a purpose as he stepped over a sleeping homeless man and made his way up the sagging stairway.

As he reached the top, Witt turned to his right and headed for Apartment 232. He pulled out his nightstick and used it to knock on the door. "Who is it?" a female voice asked from inside.

"Dallas Police, open up," Witt responded sternly. He could hear rustling sounds from inside, and finally the door opened.

Doris, the woman who answered, looked like the Fairlane herself. Perhaps twenty years ago she, too, had been something, but time had exacted a heavy toll. "What do you want?" she asked, pulling a half-smoked Marlboro from her lips.

"Guess," was all Witt said as he pushed her aside and entered her apartment.

Very quickly the woman's robe was strewn on the floor, and Witt's uniform was thrown on the dresser. The sex that followed was primal, vicious—certainly not lovemaking. Heavy groans accompanied each thrust, and tenderness was not on the menu.

Doris and Richard's relationship was strictly business. If Doris was not a professional, she was certainly a talented amateur—an amateur who didn't require the cwharade of romance or even foreplay.

Down on the street, Coleman sat waiting in the patrol car. He blew into his hands trying to warm them and then looked at his watch. Behind him, a gray Buick Century turned onto the street and sped towards him. The Buick's driver hit the brakes and started to slide through the slush that covered the street from the previous day's hail and sleet storm. It stopped only inches from smashing into the squad car.

Coleman wiped the window clear to get a look at what was going on. Seeing the car so closely and knowing he had almost been hit, Coleman started to get out and investigate. Instead, he remained motionless as he watched a sturdy, twelve-year-old boy exit the car and enter the Fairlane.

The boy, too, walked with a purpose. Freezing in only pajamas and a loose jacket, he ambled up the creaky stairs, over the sleeping man, turned right at the top of the stairs, and then knocked on the door of Apartment 232.

"Who the fuck is that?" Officer Witt yelled from inside the apartment.

"How the hell should I know?" answered Doris, standing in the kitchen pouring a Johnny Walker Black. Unconcerned, she dropped another ice cube into the glass and took a long drink. Soon afterwards another knock followed, louder and more forcefully than before.

"Will you fuckin' check to see who's at the goddamn door?" bellowed Witt from the bedroom. "It might be my partner."

Doris made her way to the door slowly and looked out the keyhole. "It's not your partner," she said, turning her head towards the bedroom. "It's your son."

"Fuck. Well fuck, let him in!" Mark Witt heard his father say.

The door opened and Mark stood face-to-face with the first naked woman he had ever seen. Doris made no attempt to cover herself, and Mark could only stare as she tilted the glass upwards and drank down the last of the scotch. A bit of the Black Label attempted to slide down her lip, but she deftly used her tongue to prevent its escape. She performed all this while smiling devilishly at Mark. Soon his father came into the room, still trying to get the rest of his police uniform on.

"I'll call you in the morning," he said to Doris as he pushed Mark out the door. She shrugged her shoulders indifferently while closing the door behind them.

"Guess your mother's downstairs," Richard asked as father and son made their way down the stairs.

Anger was building in Mark, and he wouldn't give his father the satisfaction of responding. At the bottom of the stairs, when the same question went unanswered a second time, Richard grabbed the boy by the shoulder and Mark stiffened. He couldn't stand for his father to touch him. It made him angry. He hated his dad—hated him for what he did to his mother. The hatred was so palpable that even Richard couldn't miss it.

"Better settle your little ass down," Richard said, not letting go of his son. "And stop looking at me like that. One day you'll be doing the same fuckin' thing. Same goddamn thing I just did."

That was never going to happen. It would just be another in the long line of lies his father told him. Mark was not going to be like this man. No matter whose blood was running through his veins, he was never going to act like his father. The hatred was too consuming. It would never go away.

Downstairs the scene became a blur. Mark's mother, Rebecca, jumped from the car at the sight of Richard. Screaming, the two of them instantly went at it. Little brother, Cubbie, was crying, and Mark tried to shield him from the battle. Officer Coleman quickly got out of the squad car and attempted to calm things, to no avail. Soon the altercation reached the point of all their conflicts; Richard had heard enough from Rebecca and backhanded her. Before he was able to hit her a second time, Mark reached his mother and took her place. The force from his father's now closed fist sent Mark crashing to the ground.

As his eyes flew open, he realized he had been having a nightmare. His heart was pounding and he was drenched with sweat. How he hated relieving the fear, pain, and anger from his childhood. He was thirty-five years old, with two children of his own. Why couldn't he escape that memory of readying himself to withstand yet another thunderous overhand right from his father?

Upset and shaken, Mark turned to Yolanda, his beautiful wife sleeping peacefully next to him. At least this time the reaction to his dreams hadn't awakened her too. He glanced at the bedside digital alarm clock and saw it flashing 4:28 a.m. He knew his sleeping was over for the night. Dammit. He hated that his father was still keeping him up at nights.

He knew that if he stayed in bed next to Yo-Yo (the pet name he had given his wife), other memories would deluge him — other more upsetting memories. So Mark got out of bed, put his headphones on and started his daily hour run on the treadmill.

Chapter 2

When the police-issued cell phone lying on his night-stand awakened Homicide Detective Lt. John Coleman on Sunday morning, it wasn't yet 5:00 a.m. Before he even answered it, John knew it couldn't be anything good.

Homicide Detective Ray Smithson, on the other end of the line, was ex-military and devoid of imagination. But he knew the rules and followed them. Smithson told Coleman another body had been found. A guest at the Stoneleigh Hotel near downtown Dallas had complained of loud noise from the room next door. Management went to check on the situation and found forty-three-year-old Matthew Michaels dead in the bedroom.

Smithson told Coleman the man had been repeatedly and brutally stabbed. The hotel Bible was lying on the bed next to him. Coleman said he'd be at the scene in less than a half hour and hung up the phone.

"Again?" asked John's wife, Jackie, opening one eye.

John nodded and began putting on his clothes. He quickly brushed his teeth and then opened the bedroom door down the hall to make sure Tonja, his college sophomore daughter, had made it home after he fell asleep. Seeing that she had, he was out the door and on his way to the Stoneleigh.

Lt. Coleman had long ago moved from the small house in Oak Cliff and had migrated again, this time to Cedar Hill, Texas, a suburb of Dallas popular with many of the area's successful and upwardly mobile African American families. As he navigated the residential streets near his home, Coleman thought of the victim, his name in particular: Matthew Michaels. Someone had committed a string of murders, and each of the victim's bore the name of Matthew, Mark, Luke, or John, prompting the Dallas Morning News to label the murderer the "Gospel Killer." Had the Gospel Killer struck again?

In fact, the Gospel Killer was the reason Coleman was still a lieutenant and not a captain. The first victim had been found nearly four years earlier. Eighteen months after that, the twelfth victim named Matthew, Mark, Luke, or John was found much like each of the others, nude, having recently ejaculated, with multiple stab wounds and lying dead near a King James Bible.

Coleman had been the lead investigator throughout and had come up empty. A lack of progress had forced the chief to bring in FBI profilers. The mayor's office was in an uproar and called for an even larger investigation, and each day brought new calls of public outrage. No matter how many trained detectives looked at the case, the pieces would not fit. All the king's horses and all the king's men seemed to be unable to solve the case. Not that any amount of extra manpower mattered, because as lead investigator, the spotlight of failure shown squarely, and seemingly solely, upon Lt. John Coleman.

He was never able to prove a connection between

any of the victims, and there was never any physical evidence. None. It was like a ghost had decided to become a serial killer. Then, as quickly as they had started, the killings stopped. Not another victim for over two years until a man had been recently found dead in a similar fashion—and now this one. Had the Gospel Killer returned? Coleman pulled his Chevy Malibu onto I-20; in less than twenty minutes, he would be at the Stoneleigh to find the answer.

Chapter 3

When Lt. Coleman reached the fourth floor of the Stone-leigh, he found a mass of people. Guests in hotel robes were awakening and coming into the halls to see what had happened. As he was making his way to the crime scene, Room number 421, Coleman ordered the officers in the hallway to question everyone and to take down all the personal information from each guest.

Arriving at Room 421, he found an altogether different situation. There were only two people inside: Dallas' best forensic experts, Mary Trevino and her partner, William Belcher. The head of hotel security and retired Dallas Police Detective David Vaughn had made the call to the dispatcher. Coleman knew Vaughn from their days on the force together and would make it a point later to thank him for keeping everyone away from the scene until the forensics team arrived.

When Coleman walked past the patrolman guarding the door and into the hotel suite, his first thought was how large and extravagant the room was. With a separate living area featuring original artwork on the walls and a stocked bar that could rival that of a mid-scale nightclub, Coleman knew the victim was either well-to-do or had a healthy expense account.

His second thought was the carpet, which he sunk

into as he walked. The carpet was a beige Berber, so thick and with such a high quality pad it felt like a giant marshmallow. If he had this carpet in his house, Coleman knew Jackie would make him take his shoes off before walking on it. As he was still making mental notes of the room, Belcher stuck his head out of the bedroom where the victim was killed.

"Yo boss, come check this fucker out," he said. "He's got more holes in him than my underwear."

Coleman had never cared much for Belcher or his sense of humor, but he tolerated him because Mary liked him. And make no mistake; Lt. Mary Trevino was the highest trained and most competent forensics investigator Dallas had ever been fortunate enough to hire. So if it meant biting his tongue over another of Belcher's stupid comments, then Coleman would just have to have a bloody tongue in order to keep Mary happy.

As he stepped into the suite's bedroom, Coleman saw a sight that would slow even a homicide veteran. The nude Mr. Michaels was lying with his head at the foot of the bed. It was obvious he had suffered multiple stab wounds, and there was a closed Bible lying on the bed next to him. There was blood under the Bible but none on its cover; the Bible had been placed there after the murder. Another staged scene.

"Got anything yet, Mary?" Coleman asked Trevino.

"Little bit. Gold wedding band in his pants pocket, a lot of blood samples, some semen from the bed sheets, and we did pull some black fibers and two sequins from the carpet, but no prints yet."

"Sequins?" Lt. Coleman repeated to make sure he had heard correctly.

"Yeah, found two of 'em over in the corner. They kinda stood out; didn't exactly go with the rest of the décor."

A photographer joined the group and began snapping photos of the scene as John carefully looked around. Coleman knew the ferocity and amount of the victim's wounds normally would indicate someone who closely knew the person had committed them. The blood splatter was huge. Rage was on display here; this was not a mere killing. That had been the case in each of the Gospel Killer's earlier works and the investigation had found no evidence that any of the victims knew one another or traveled in any of the same circles.

When Lt. Coleman told Mary to check the bathroom closely, she responded that they already had. "It's clean. The whole place looks like room service just finished with it."

Coleman knew that whoever committed this murder would have been covered in blood, and no one could have just walked out the front door of the Stoneleigh Hotel with that amount of blood on them without anyone noticing. The killer would have had to clean up before leaving, but what about the noise that was reported? The killer would have known the noise could cause a call to the front desk and a following room check; would he still have taken the time to shower and thoroughly clean up? Had the Gospel Killer returned or was this a copycat killer? Coleman had a lot more questions than answers.

"Come over here, John. I did find something else kinda strange." Mary pointed out a nickel standing upright on the nightstand next to the hotel phone. Whether it was a clue or not, it clearly didn't land that way on the wooden table. Either it was Michael's or the killer had carefully placed it in that position.

"A nickel, huh?" asked Coleman. "Better bag it."

She was already ahead of him; her tongs were out and the nickel was well on its way to the bottom of a plastic bag.

"Hell, I think she killed this guy when she got a look at his cock," Belcher blurted out as he continued taking blood samples from the bed. "I mean, shit, that little thing looks more like an innie than an outtie."

Coleman closed his eyes in silent disgust at the unneeded and idiotic comment, when it dawned on him. She? "Did you say, she?" he asked aloud.

"Yeah, John," Trevino answered before Belcher could say something else inappropriate. "Security's got film of Mr. Michaels and a woman leaving the hotel bar last night and coming up here to the room."

"What?" exclaimed Coleman.

"I thought Smithson would have told you. He saw the tape and then took a copy back to the station."

Eager to see the tape, John said his good-byes and headed off. Even though each of the prior victims had been murdered after they had ejaculated, Coleman had never been able to prove if a man or a woman had committed the murders. One FBI profiler was certain the killer had to be male because the depth many of the knife wounds penetrated into the victims would have required great physical strength. Some sort of maniacal, gay serial killer.

The remaining spouses and surviving families all vehemently opposed this theory, but Coleman had been forced to consider all possibilities. Now he drove as fast as the Malibu would go back to the station, knowing this could be his first real break in any of the cases. Perhaps he could finally put a face to the killer.

Chapter 4

The caretaker at the Oak Hills Cemetery was on his knees next to the crematorium continuing to wage his seemingly unending battle against weeds when he saw the white Dodge Charger pull through the front gates. He smiled to himself and didn't even bother glancing at his watch. No need; this was clockwork. Every Sunday for the past nine years since Rebecca Witt had committed suicide, her son Mark had come to her graveside. It was always before morning church service, and he was always alone.

Mark had already been to the Tom Thumb supermarket and purchased the normal bouquet of lilies he would place at his mother's grave. Lilies were his mom's favorite. It was the reason he and Yo-Yo had named their daughter Lily. Mark gave his mom lilies for a birthday long ago, and it was the last time he could remember seeing her smile—the last time he remembered seeing her feel any happiness.

Of all the old memories that haunted Mark, there was at least that single good one, remembering and treasuring his mother's smile. Mark held onto that memory, for once not seeing her in tears, thinking of her being happy instead of her despair.

The lilies helped Mark remember her sheer radiance,

so seldom seen, but nonetheless real. This was a much better image than torturing himself with thoughts of the anger and depression that led his mother nine years ago to wrap her mouth around his father's .357.

Mark parked his Charger on the asphalt path near his mother's grave. He carefully set his constant companion, his coffee, in the car's cup holder and got out with the lilies. It was still too early for the cemetery to have other visitors, so he walked straight to her grave and gently laid the lilies at her head. "Here you go, Mom. Got the lady at the store to cut them fresh just for you," Mark said softly.

He wiped away grass clippings that had been spread onto the grave marker from the previous day's mowing. With the grass cleared, he could easily read the writing he and Yo-Yo had gotten inscribed on her marker: "A better life awaits."

"I love you, Mom," he said as he patted the marker, and then turned and sat down on the bench a few feet away. He thought of how Yo-Yo had surprised him by buying the bench for his mom last year on Mother's Day.

As he rubbed his hands along the bench's wrought iron finish, Mark thought of how much he loved his mother, and Yo-Yo. God, he loved her. The most extreme pressure he felt in the whole world was to be a really good husband to Yo-Yo—the kind his mother had deserved. She had deserved and wanted that for so long. He was equally as determined to be the type of father Lily and Daniel, his son from his first wife, deserved.

"Saw Cubbie the other day," Mark said to his mother from the bench, crouched over with his elbows resting on his knees. "He's doing good—real good. Told him to stop by and see you." Yes, he had told him that, but he doubted that he would.

Mark had a stuttering problem when he was small, and no matter how hard he tried he could not say Jacob, the name of his brother who was three years younger than him. After many attempts, the best he could do was say, "Cub." After a few years, Cub morphed into Cubbie. Mark overcame the stuttering problems, but he remembered them—and his father's incessant taunts of his speech impediment. Yeah, his father was a real beauty, all right. He had been even harder on Cubbie for wetting his bed and any other perceived weakness. But not their mother; she never treated either of her sons with anything other than love. She was an angel.

"And Yo-Yo and the kids, they're doing good, too. You know, last weekend Daniel told me he remembered you and that he missed you. He was so little, but I hope he does. Said he missed not having two grandmothers like the other kids in his class. I told him that he really missed out on not having you in his life for longer." His eyes welled and a tear trickled down Mark's cheek. "Told him we all did."

The tears came with each visit. Mark Witt couldn't get away from them. He was done even trying. By now the tears created twisting streams down his face and were collecting into small pools on the ground underneath the bench. He got up and wiped his face and eyes as best he could. "Better be going now, Mom. Gotta get home and get everybody ready for church. See you next Sunday. I love you."

Before walking to his car, he paused and looked up to the sun, which was just beginning to peep from behind a huge wall of clouds. The warmth felt comforting, and heaven knew Mark needed some sunshine. As he gazed upwards, he wondered if his mother was up there looking down on him at that same moment. He liked to imagine she was and that she was proud of him. That idea and hope made the tears stop and even put a smile on his face. Because he knew she deserved to be there. After all she had been through, Mark knew she deserved, as much as anyone, the promise of the better life that awaits.

Chapter 5

John Coleman was practically a caged bull inside the elevator. How long was it gonna take to make it to Homicide on the third freakin' floor? How long until he could get a look at the security film and a possible first look at the killer? Was this thing even moving?

He would have taken the stairs, but Humberto had the painting crew out early this morning for some weekend overtime pay. So John was forced to ride on this relic, this elevator that he imagined was the spawn of a clubbed foot snail and some overweight, hourly wage union turtle. When the two doors mercifully began their ever-so-deliberate opening, every other cop on the elevator had the good sense to step aside and let Lt. Coleman off first.

Less than five quickening strides later, John was inside the darkened film room. Detective Smithson had already viewed the footage dozens of times and was rewinding it yet again as Coleman sat down to watch it for himself. Smithson, who had the look of a man familiar with disappointment, said to John, "Hope you weren't expecting too much." And with that less-than-inspiring introduction, Coleman watched the tape for the first of what would become hundreds of times. In time, he would be able to close his eyes and visually replay the tape in his mind.

What Coleman saw was Matthew Michaels leaving the hotel bar at 1:33 a.m. alongside a dark-haired woman carrying an oversized, zebra print shoulder bag, and wearing high boots, aged jeans and a black belly shirt. The shirt—a popular type—had a sequined cross on the front of it. Coleman knew instantly that it was the source of the black fibers and sequins Mary and Belcher had found in the room.

The shirt also provided two other clues. It had a sleeveless design that displayed a barbed wire tattoo around the woman's lean and muscular left arm. The back didn't cover all the way down to her low-hung jeans. At one point, the woman dropped her bag; as she bent down to pick it up, her lower back tattoo, known as tramp stamps around the police station, was on full display to the camera. Coleman's jaw dropped and both hands fell to his knees when he saw the tattoo of an angel with wings outstretched, holding a Bible in its hands.

For all it revealed, the tape was astounding for what it didn't show. At no point was the woman's face seen. Throughout the walk from the hotel bar to the lobby elevator, the woman either had her head down or turned away from the cameras; and her hair, appearing to be dark brown or black, was strewn across her face whenever she stopped to kiss Matthews. Coleman knew this couldn't have been only a matter of luck for the woman; no, this killer wanted the police to see the tattoos but not her face. Why? Was she getting cocky?

"Hold on, we got her leaving, too," Detective Smithson said as he fast-forwarded the tape.

Hold on? John thought to himself. Geez, did Smithson

think he was bored or something? Maybe he thought there was some other case the lieutenant would rather be working on? Not likely. Not by a long shot. Coleman was a notorious workaholic, even by cop standards, but this case was different. He was determined to do whatever it required to find this killer. Whatever was needed, however long was needed.

Smithson hit play and Coleman saw the hotel elevators open. The timeline on the bottom of the screen showed 4:03 a.m. as the dark-haired woman exited the elevators alone. She was dressed the same, still carrying the zebra shoulder bag, and there wasn't any blood visible. How was that possible? The blood splatter would have been enormous.

Coleman watched the tape closely, and the only immediate difference he could see was this time the woman wore her hair back with the pony tail poked through the back of a black ball cap — a ball cap that also featured a sequined cross on the front. And it had to be the same woman. The barbed wire tat was still wrapped around her chiseled left arm, and angel wingtips still shown from under the back of her shirt. Unfortunately, one other thing was also still the same — no shots of the woman's face. This bitch walked right out the front door of the Stoneleigh Hotel after murdering a man upstairs, and every time she knew just when to tilt or turn her head to avoid the camera. The two detectives were watching the tape once again when Detective Ramos stepped into the room and turned on the lights.

"Here's the information we got on the victim," he said as he set a folder on the table.

Coleman opened the folder and scanned the victim's bio: software salesman for Tridesic Technologies of

Columbus, Ohio, in town trying to land an account with American Airlines . . . married for eleven years to Elaine Samuels Michaels . . . father of two boys . . . no criminal record. Beautiful. He was just some ordinary guy in from out of town who was trying to get lucky at the hotel bar.

And Coleman remembered what his own father had often told him about luck: it's not always good. Maybe this salesman should have just stayed in, maybe bought a movie off the hotel's pay-per-view package or maybe he should have just called home and talked with his wife.

About his wife... Goodness knows Coleman wasn't looking forward to having to call her with the news. It was always the worst part of the job. John would have to call a woman he'd never met, who maybe lived half-way across the country, and tell her that her husband was dead. This time he'd also be telling the woman that her husband almost surely had been murdered by a woman he'd just finished having sex with. And, oh by the way, that all means your two sons will now grow up without a father. Coleman thought he'd probably skip the good morning and how's the weather part of the conversation. Helluva way to make a living.

"Ohio is central time, isn't it?" the lieutenant asked as he got up from his chair with the folder in his hands. He of course already knew the answer as the two detectives nodded. He nodded in return and told Smithson he'd be back in a bit.

Coleman left the room and walked slowly to his office. Yeah, this was a helluva way to make a living.

Chapter 6

The choir was already on the second chorus of "How Great Thou Art" when Mark, Yo-Yo and Lily slid into the crowded pew. Due to Yo-Yo, the Witts were late again. This was not exactly a big surprise. Yo-Yo was eight days overdue when she was born and had managed to keep the streak intact her whole life. She was never on time for anything. Mark had long ago stopped complaining to his wife about how long it took her to get ready to go anywhere. What was the point? She wasn't going to change, and besides, each time he saw her, he knew it had been worth the wait.

Today was no different. Her gleaming black hair was pulled up, and she proudly wore the diamond heart Mark had given her for Valentine's Day years ago. This seemed to elongate her neck and make her look more elegant than ever. To Mark she looked regal, like an imaginary princess from some long ago fairy tale. Thankfully, she was real, sitting right next to him. Stunning, she sat with her arm around their equally beautiful daughter, Lily. Mark perhaps sometimes lost sight of it, but moments and images like these always made him realize what a lucky man he was.

As he was thumbing the pages of the hymnal trying to locate "How Great Thou Art," a smiling Yo-Yo softly

elbowed Mark and pointed ahead to one of the front
pews. Mark glanced forward to see his beaming son,
Daniel, waving back to him. Mark smiled and waved
to him, and then nodded and gave a polite smile to
Kellie, his ex and Daniel's mother. The smile to Kellie
was the type you might offer a sales clerk who thanks
you for shopping at Target, not the kind associated
with any affection. Not even a distant affection. It was
the way Mark felt towards Kellie; their relationship
ended long before the divorce and Mark couldn't seem
to attach any emotion to it.

For a guy so consumed with his past and in many
ways held prisoner by it, Mark had certainly managed to put away memories of his prior marriage.
He couldn't even explain why they had ever gotten
married. Hell, it seemed to have happened almost by
accident. Faced with such turmoil and pain in his home
life, Mark turned to God and entered the seminary
when he was twenty-one. Kellie worked at the campus
bookstore, and the two struck up a friendship.

Within a couple of years though, Mark realized
that he didn't feel a true calling to become a minister
and that he had entered the seminary only to try and
prove he was nothing like his old man. By this time the
friendship with Kellie had sparked a college romance,
and the two had been married for six months. A year
later, Mark was a rookie patrolman, and had a pregnant
wife he didn't love. Maybe he wasn't so different from
his father after all.

Three years into their marriage, a disillusioned Mark
found himself thinking of other women. He never
acted upon those thoughts, but he knew in time he
would. He wasn't going to repeat his father's actions,

so he filed for divorce. Like all divorces, it was ugly and hurtful. However, at least he wouldn't create the harm and damage of a ruined life spent together; he wouldn't make Kellie waste her entire life with him. Not the way his mother had sacrificed her life with his own dad. He was different and better than his father. He would never, could never, hurt anyone who loved him like his dad had hurt his mother.

To her credit, Kellie had rebounded, remarried and seemed to be doing well in her job as a claims adjuster with State Farm Insurance. Two years after the divorce, Mark met Yo-Yo while moonlighting on a security job, and she instantly swept away any thoughts of other women.

With the music portion of the service ending, Kellie's husband of the last six years, Youth Minister Thomas Colwell, rose and went to the podium. He spoke of the work the youth group had done in the area's recent food drive. He discussed the planned spring break mission-ary trip to Ecuador for eighteen of the church's young members. The Reverend Colwell then prayed and asked that God open the hearts of the church's membership to raise a special offering to help pay for the trip and for the needed work in Ecuador. Evidently God opened Yo-Yo's heart first, as the look she sent Mark said, "Get out your checkbook, big boy." Mark obliged, as he always did, and laid a two hundred dollar check in the offering plate as it passed by.

After the offering, the senior pastor, Reverend James Middleton, delivered a sermon on forgiveness. Forgive-ness was not exactly one of Mark's strong points. He listened closely as the preacher quoted First Corinthians 13:5, where the Bible says that love keeps no records of wrongs. Mark nodded his head and wished he could throw out his ledgers. He kept extensive and meticulous "records"—practically an Excel spreadsheet—of the wrongs he had endured. There was a part of Mark that always thought of forgiveness as a double-sided coin. Were you being strong to let go and forgive or just too weak to keep hate and anger alive? He was not proud of himself in this regard, but Mark could definitely keep hate and anger alive. He could compartmentalize; home with Yo-Yo and the kids he was a teddy bear, but outside his home and away from his family he was a grizzly bear.

As Reverend Middleton continued, Mark looked around the auditorium. The rows were filled with people just like him, but were they really like him? Did they have the same thoughts and feelings he did? Had they endured the same type of past? Had they been treated with hatred? Had they themselves felt real hatred?

Mark listened, heard the "Amens" coming from the pews and wondered to what extent any of these people had been wronged in their lives and needed to forgive others? But at the end of the day, he knew they all needed God's forgiveness; it was the common denominator and the woven thread that linked everyone together. So, he found himself nodding again in agreement. The different backgrounds didn't matter, nor did it matter that Mark's lifestyle and experiences often made him feel uncomfortable in church. All that mattered today was that he was among the flock seeking God's approval. Despite his certainty that he had done nothing to earn or deserve God's forgiveness and approval, and despite often feeling he had turned his back on God by leaving the seminary, Mark was glad he had come to church this day.

After the service, Reverend Middleton reminded Mark of the men's breakfast to be held at the church the following Friday. Mark shook his hand and told the reverend he liked his eggs sunny side up. There were smiles all around, and he even managed to offer a genuine one to Kellie as he went over and picked up Daniel for their weekly Sunday afternoon together. The time-honored ritual of a lunchtime trip to McDonald's followed, and then it was home for some backyard football with the family. All in all, not too bad a day.

Chapter 7

John Coleman had been at his desk for nearly two hours Wednesday morning when, at 7:00 a.m., he finally got a copy of the lab report from the Michaels murder. Coleman hadn't slept much in the days since the most recent murder, and the evidence provided by the report wouldn't have him counting sheep anytime soon either.

The victim had died from thirty-two puncture wounds of varying depths inflicted on his torso. A single serrated blade made all the wounds. It was consistent with the type of wounds suffered by the many other victims who each also had been killed with a serrated-edged weapon. Similar to the others, there were no cuts or wounds to the hands, which would signal some form of defensive action. Matthew Michaels had apparently died like the others, quickly and with the first stab wound catching him either asleep or by surprise.

Coleman learned from the report that all recovered hair and DNA samples belonged to the victim. There were no fingerprints found in the room. Zero, none. Before her departure, the killer had professionally wiped them clean with disinfectants. A trace amount of blood found in the shower drain could not be matched to the victim. However, the amount was so small that any defense lawyer worth his salt would get it laughed out of court faster than Usain Bolt's 100-meter-dash time, if it was even attempted to be entered into evidence.

The trace of blood did fit Coleman's theory that the killer must have showered before leaving the room. How else could the woman have walked out of the hotel without being covered in blood? He even thought that perhaps she showered, cleaned the room thoroughly, and then intentionally made the noise needed to wake the nearby guests. All set up so she could dictate that the body would be found at a certain time. But why? Obviously there was no way to prove any of this, but currently, with as many as fourteen unsolved murders, theories were still pretty much the most concrete things Coleman had to go on.

One thing was certain though; the killer was calm and confident. She carefully picked out her prey, appropriately named men, then seduced and killed them. Afterwards, she masterfully covered her tracks.

After reading the report over again, Coleman determined the only tangible evidence police recovered that there had, in fact, been another person in the room with Matthew Michaels, was the sequin found on the floor along with the black fibers came from the killer's tank top. The killer had been so meticulous in cleaning the room; how could she have missed a shiny sequin or the black fibers that were easily seen on the contrasting beige carpet? Were they left there on purpose as clues for the police?

And what about the nickel found standing upright on the nightstand? It didn't fall out of a pocket and just happen to land and stay that way. No, it meant something, but what? And how was it she was able to find all these men who were named Matthew, Mark, Luke and John in the first place? He didn't know the answers to any of these questions, and not knowing sickened Coleman. Was 7:30 a.m. too early to hit the Maalox?

After a call to Mary Trevino at Forensics asking that she return to the Stoneleigh and conduct a second check for any latent materials, John knew it was time to be heading upstairs. He straightened his tie, put on his navy blue JC Penney sport coat, and then, none too happily, set out for Chief Harrington's office on the fifth floor of the Dallas Police Department.

Dan Harrington had been appointed Dallas police chief three years ago after spending his entire previous career with the Tucson police force, where he had climbed the ranks from patrolman to deputy chief. Despite the fact that Harrington had brought changes to the force that helped lower violent crime statistics, the Gospel Killer hung over his head and that of the entire department. With his four-year contract about to come up for renewal, Harrington was obsessed with solving these crimes.

Coleman knocked on Harrington's door and walked into the chief's office. Decorated in mahogany wood paneling, the office had the feel of success and testosterone. After sitting down, it didn't take Coleman long to find out where the testosterone rush was coming from. Already in Harrington's office was Ron Ellis, FBI lead investigator. Known for his penchant for expensive suits and redheaded women, Ellis was full of himself and about the last person in the world Coleman wanted to see this morning.

Dressed in a gray Brooks Brothers pinstripe, Ellis looked like a Wall Street banker but acted like a street thug and swore like a wounded sailor. Maybe 5'4" and topping out at all of 130 pounds soaking wet, Ellis was the poster boy for "Short Man's Syndrome." He had recently helped solve a series of Denver murders where four young boys had been sodomized and decapitated. It was a high-profile case because of the age of the victims and because of the brutal nature of the crimes. Ellis had come in and located the killer when local authorities had been unable to for over a year.

He was currently the flavor of the day for the Bureau and had been dispatched to Dallas. Beautiful. That was the only thought that came to Coleman's mind. Not that Coleman minded the added help, and goodness knows he could care less who got the credit; John just wanted the killer caught before another murder was committed. He thought the best way to do that would be without any distractions from grandstanding FBI boys.

"What do you got?" Harrington asked Coleman, eschewing any normal or polite greeting.

"He ain't got shit," Ellis interceded before John could answer. "Not jack fuckin' shit."

"Is that right?" Harrington asked.

"Are you asking me or the Oompa Loompa there," Coleman responded, glaring at Ellis. The statement was a rare crack in Coleman's normal, stoic demeanor and one Harrington had not before seen.

"That's enough," Harrington said as Ellis quickly stood and appeared ready to go MMA. "Now sit down. That's enough from you, too, John."

Coleman nodded that he understood the chief's

instructions, and then could only lower his head and smile when the chief turned back to the still standing Ellis and said, "I believe I told you to sit your little ass down."

With an angry Ellis once again seated, Harrington proceeded, "Where are we?"

"The report on the latest victim found very little. No prints, no blood we can match, and no DNA," Coleman answered and then paused. "With the tape, we're still working it, but it's not much. She never shows her face, so we can't use the facial recognition software."

"So I was right. You got shit," Ellis cracked.

"Why the break though, John?" Harrington asked, ignoring Ellis. "Why stop for a year and a half and now have the killings resume again?"

"Don't know," Coleman said, shaking his head. "We're checking everyone who has been in prison the last two years and recently paroled, everyone who has been out of the country on military duty and is now back in Dallas, anyone with a record who got transferred and is now back in town, and anyone who's been in the hospital long term. Basically, we're checking everybody we can think of. Just nothing is coming back a match."

Ellis snickered at Coleman's statement.

"Is there something you want to add?" asked a less-than-thrilled Harrington.

Little Ron took this moment and ran with it. "Well, for starters, I never thought it was a bitch doing these killings, but after seeing the tape, all right, I'm convinced. Ain't no guy got an ass like that. But anyway, your guy here has missed the point. He ain't even said anything about the biblical symbolism. That's what this case revolves around and the way it's gonna get solved."

Harrington told him to continue, and Ron Ellis never needed to be told twice. "There were six killings in the first round, with a body found every twenty-seven days. Then a six-month wait with no bodies. Afterwards six more killings, one every twenty-seven days. Six, six, six."

"So what are you saying, the Devil or the Antichrist did this?" asked the chief, trying to wrap his mind around this.

Ellis did not suffer fools well. "Exactly, the Devil did this. Her name is Lucy Fer. Goddamn, no wonder you guys can't find this whore. Listen, what I'm saying is Jesus had twelve apostles. All the victims were named Matthew, Mark, Luke and John—all apostle names."

The chief looked at Coleman, who awkwardly offered, "I didn't mention it because we all already knew that. And we've been checking the churches, too, and the theology schools, for problem members or students, or anything out of the ordinary."

Geez, John felt like an idiot for blurting out something so stupid. This little Ernie Keebler sucker was schooling him in his own backyard.

"Great, can I continue?" asked an unimpressed Ellis, and Harrington and John both nodded. "Did you know the thirteenth victim, a Mr. Luke Jacobsen, was found exactly twenty-seven months to the day after the twelfth victim was killed, and that the last victim, Matthew Michaels, was killed exactly twenty-seven days after Jacobsen?"

"We knew there were twenty-seven days between these latest two murders, but not the twenty-seven month lapse," Coleman said, trying to regain his confidence.

"So what's the significance of twenty-seven?" the chief asked Ellis.

"Matthew, Mark, Luke and John are in the New Testament, and there are twenty-seven books in the New Testament."

Harrington began to walk around his desk and think carefully about what Ellis had just said. "The last FBI guy in here didn't say anything about this six, six, six shit, but he said the killings stopped at twelve because Jesus had twelve apostles. Now you come here saying there are twenty-seven books in the New Testament; are you saying there are gonna be twenty-seven victims?"

"The last FBI guy they sent down here drinks out of a sippy cup and draws with crayons," Ellis sighed. "He's so fucking stupid, I'm surprised you guys didn't try and hire him."

Ahh, little Ron was indeed an expert at how to win friends and influence people. He was only too glad to push the pointy stick a little further into John and the chief's face.

"Listen, for the record," Ellis continued after a dramatic pause to fully appreciate their obvious and growing anger, "I've only been on this case for three days, but what I'm saying is Jesus may have only had twelve apostles, but he had a lot of disciples. A lot of disciples. The bitch doing this ain't stopping until you stop her. "

"So you think it's definitely the same killer?" Harrington asked, putting aside his temper. "It's not two or a copycat?"

"It could be two. But if it is, they're working together. It ain't no fuckin' copycat. A copycat wouldn't have known about the patterns of twenty-seven days and twenty-seven months. Hell, you guys didn't know it, so it sure as hell wasn't in the papers. And a copycat wouldn't have known about the serrated-edge knife either because that wasn't reported. This is a well-thought-out plan, and it is connected to the Bible. There is too much symbolism for it not to be."

Now it was Coleman's turn to stand, walk around the office and try not to look too impressed. He hated to give the little bastard any credit, but what he said made more sense than anything the DPD had been able to come up with. And he did it in three days? Geez.

Finally, John stopped and nodded at the chief. "It's definitely biblical. But, I think it's more than just symbolism; it's stronger than that. I just haven't quite figured out how yet."

Always the man who got the last word, Ellis responded by pointing to the chief's desk calendar. "You might want to start getting things figured out. Because May 4 will be the twenty-seventh day since Matthew Michaels was murdered."

Chapter 8

Though they had been up late the night before with friends, and although Mark usually had no trouble sleeping, he had trouble this night. If he wasn't able to sleep, there was generally a reason for it, like worrying about money or some family problem. But not this time; he just couldn't sleep. He tossed and turned throughout the night, and finally, at 5:15, he gave up and got out of bed.

His head was still fuzzy from the previous night's relationship with Crown Royale, but he started feeling clearer after his treadmill run and morning shower. Dressed by 6:45, Mark decided to go into the office and finish a couple of invoices he had been putting off.

He was very good at being a private investigator—checking records, finding people, following spouses as they strayed. But he wasn't always good at taking the time afterwards to bill his clients so he could get paid for his work. He sort of figured that as long as people owed him money, he'd never be broke. But this morning would be a good chance to get caught up.

Besides, if he hurried he could still be home by 10:30 or so and catch Yo-Yo's Saturday morning waffle extravaganza. Her waffles were practically an international sensation—well, maybe not international, but at least in their home they were a sensation. Lily and Mark both loved them.

As Mark pulled his Charger into his office's parking lot, he saw only one other car. The single-story office complex that housed Witt Investigations looked deserted and seemed serene, almost peaceful. Much older than the buildings that surrounded it, the complex probably could use some updating, but Mark didn't mind.

It was located in an area that was undergoing major neighborhood revitalization, and Mark enjoyed the differences created by this evolving eclectic mix. He loved seeing the looks on the faces of the yuppies trying to pull into their high-rise condos, of seeing facial contortions as BMWs were forced to idle and wait for tamale vendors to push carts past their entrances. True, he was a simple man, but you have to admit, yuppies and street vendors equal good times.

Punching his code into the complex's keypad was required for entrance on weekends, but it barely slowed Mark down. A few moments later, he was in his office, the first pot of coffee was brewing and Mark was waist deep in daily journals, on a quest to document his work hours. He was making progress when the front door to his office opened. In walked little brother Cubbie and his boyfriend Will, each carrying a box of Krispy Kremes.

"Saw your car out front, bro. Hope you don't mind us droppin' in," said Cubbie.

"He doesn't mind," Will piped in, opening the box of donuts and waving them in front of Mark's nose.

"But, he should. Remember the old saying, 'Beware of fags bearing gifts.'"

Mark grinned and knew that work would have to wait. Ahhh, yet another man brought down by the magical wonder of Krispy Kreme. After clearing his desk, Mark was practically attacked by a donut Will was holding.

"Here you go, big boy. Brought you a nice glazed donut. A big, nice cream-filled donut," Will purred.

"Easy, take it easy," Mark said, pulling his head back.

"Lookie there, Pa. Don't he got a perty mouth?" said Will, quickly turning on his country boy act.

"Damn," Mark said, shaking with laughter. "I thought you gays were all, like, supposed to be witty and sophisticated? Like Oscar Wilde or something. Not, 'I gotta big cream-filled donut for your perty mouth."

"Yeah, I got lucky and got me the last redneck queen in town," Cubbie laughed, coming to his man's rescue. "And what exactly do you know about Oscar Wilde?"

"I know he was British, right?" Mark answered, taking a bite of the donut and then licking the glaze off his fingers. "And those guys are all a bunch of queers, aren't they?" Suffice it to say, the donuts were gone before the laughter stopped.

It wasn't so much that Mark loved Cubbie being gay, but he loved Cubbie. He had known from the beginning that Cubbie was different. He couldn't say for sure if every gay person was born that way, or turned gay because of their environment, or because of some happening in their life, or some happening in the cosmos, for that matter. But he knew that Cubbie had always been different.

Their father had known, also, and had been brutal to Cubbie because of it. Each perceived weakness, each bed-wetting, each dropped pass brought beatings—many of which Mark took on behalf of Cubbie. He would sense it coming and step in between his father and Cubbie, or say something to distract his dad so that the old man would hit him instead.

Just like Mark knew Cubbie was different, Cubbie knew Mark was different. And he loved and idolized his big brother for it. Other than sexual preference, about the only other difference between the brothers were their feelings for their father. Mark could never understand it or even comprehend it, but for some reason, Cubbie still tried to keep in contact with the old man. Every time he knocked on the door, Cubbie knew that insults and slurs were sure to flow, but for some unexplainable reason, he still needed to see and try to be close to his father.

"Saw Dad the other day," Cubbie said, as the empty donut boxes were being thrown into the trash. "He's not doing very good."

"Don't start that shit with me," Mark responded, his blood pressure immediately spiking.

"I think it would be good if you went and saw him," Cubbie said. "He would like that."

"You think it would be good? I think it would be good if someone threw his body off the Empire State Building. And then I think it would be really good if a roving band of crackheads came by and ass-raped his lifeless body."

The remark took both Cubbie and Will aback. "Hey, I like a good ass rapin' as much as the next guy, but I don't know about the lifeless thing," Will finally responded.

"No offense, but about that — there's a lot you don't know about," answered Mark. His tone was stern, and the good feelings brought about by the box of Krispy Kremes were quickly dissipating when the door swung open again. In through the door walked Kim Jacobsen, the kind of woman people notice. They watched her as she walked towards them.

"Excuse me, I'm looking for Mark Witt."

"That would be him," Cubbie said, pointing to Mark.

"Am I interrupting?" the woman asked, reaching out to shake Mark's hand.

"I think we were about done," Mark said after looking at the other two and shrugging his shoulders.

"Good. I want to hire you. You come very highly recommended."

Mark was left a little flat-footed, and finally said, "All right. If you could give us just a minute, I'll be right with you."

"Damn," Will exclaimed, after she stepped back into the outer office. "If I ever went straight, it would be for something like that."

"Let me get him out of here before I lose another one to the power of the vajayjay," Cubbie said, taking him by the arm. Mark was smiling again when Will went on, "I'm sorry, but did you see her calves? Or her purse? Oh, my gosh!"

~~~

Across town, Matthew Owens was just passing the one-mile mark in the Fort Worth Zoo's Annual 10K Run. An avid runner, Matthew's body was getting loose, and he felt great on this bright spring morning. With a personal best time of 39:13 in the 10K, Matthew could have easily surged past the group ahead of him. But instead, he settled in comfortably behind one runner. He was happy to remain a few steps behind her, despite the relatively slow pace.

Matthew accepted the fact that a new PB would have to wait for another day, because today he was staying right where he was, shadowing the lady in front of him—the lady whose sports bra top showed off a shapely, bare midriff—and an angel tattoo on her back. He noted with interest that the angel with outstretched wings was holding a Bible.

Chapter 9

Once Mark got Cubbie and Will out of his office, he called home and told Yo-Yo he was going to be a little longer than he thought. He assured her he would hurry, and she promised to save some waffles for him. Krispy Kremes and waffles in the same morning? Resistance would, of course, prove futile. Mark promised himself he would get out the P90X tapes and start another round come Monday. But Saturday — this Saturday — by God, Mark would relish being a man and eat both Krispy Kremes and Yo-Yo's heavenly waffles.

When Mark motioned for Mrs. Kim Jacobsen to come into his office, she got up and obliged. He noticed she didn't really walk into his office so much as she oozed into it, like the way lava oozes across the rocks it comes into contact with. Apparently coming or going from her own workout, Kim wore a tight white tee and gray Yoga pants — snug-fitting Yoga pants.

Mark noticed these types of things because he was a trained private investigator — not because he was attracted to the woman in his office. He always made mental notes of a person's attire and mannerisms. If he needed information, it was useful to understand these things, in order to figure out the best way to communicate.

As she approached him, Mark knew he was looking at a woman who was a fantasy trophy wife to every Dallas area, rich, middle-aged guy. She was in early forties and fully augmented. Mark guessed she might have lost a couple of miles per hour off the fastball she had as a twenty-year-old but figured she made up for it by knowing how to pitch, how to change speeds, how to work the corners. Yeah, Mark could tell this woman knew what men wanted.

She shook Mark's hand again, introduced herself and sat down in the chair across from his desk, setting her Coach purse on the floor next to her. Before Mark could open his mouth, Kim told him she was the widow of Lucas Jacobsen, a wealthy business owner who had been killed almost six weeks ago by the so-called Gospel Killer.

Mark expressed his sorrow, and Kim let him know that Lucas' estate had been worth tens of millions of dollars and that she wanted to use this wealth to find the killer.

"Why do you think I could find the Gospel Killer, when the police and FBI haven't been able to?" Mark asked.

"I told you earlier that you came very highly recommended. I'm sure you remember Carolina Ramirez?" Her words stunned Mark instantly.

"Who are you?" he demanded, looking the woman squarely in her eyes. "And how do you know about Carolina Ramirez?"

"Calm down," Kim answered. "Carolina's mother, Katherine, is my best friend. I've known her for years. She and Marcus both agreed that you might be able to get certain things done that the police haven't. You remember Marcus, don't you?"

Of course he knew Marcus, and he wasn't likely to ever forget him. Marcus Ramirez was Dallas' largest cocaine dealer. Four years earlier, his daughter Carolina had been kidnapped. The ransom demand was three million dollars, and it stipulated that someone other than Marcus had to deliver the money. If he were seen at the drop, Carolina would be killed.

While Kim was telling Mark how highly the Ramirezes spoke of him and how well Carolina was doing, he was remembering the case. Marcus and his wife Katherine were frantic to have their daughter returned safely, but the demand for someone else to hand over the ransom presented a problem for Mr. Ramirez—he couldn't very well go to the police or to the FBI. Too many questions would come up about how he came to have that much cash lying around. And since he also feared it might be an inside job, Marcus didn't trust any of his men to handle the ransom and negotiations either. A phone call to Dallas' one true power broker—a power broker who had helped Marcus's business get off the ground—and Marcus was told that Mark Witt was the man he should hire.

Mark Witt agreed to handle the drop for Mr. and Mrs. Ramirez. They would pay him well for his work, and the couple only asked two things: bring their daughter home safely and to do whatever was necessary to keep the entire matter away from the press and the authorities. "Whatever was necessary" was a phrase repeated several times by Marcus.

At the exchange, Mark saw Carolina and paid the ransom, but something went wrong. The kidnappers began shooting. Mark was hit three times, and Carolina was shot in the leg as she tried to run away. When the shooting finally stopped, Mark managed to load four dead bodies into the trunk of his car. He got them, along with Carolina and the three million dollars, back to Marcus and Katherine Ramirez.

During Mark's stay in the hospital, nothing about the kidnapping or killings ever appeared in the paper or on the news. The police only came to question him concerning how he got shot. His made up a story convinced the none too curious cops. The story he told Yo-Yo conveniently left out the parts about cocaine dealing and the four dead bodies. It remained the only lie he had ever told her.

He never knew how Marcus got rid of the bodies, but when Mark left the hospital he paid off his mortgage and never told a soul what really had happened. He acted in self defense and was never involved before or after with any of Ramirez' dealings, but Mark still felt dirty about it—for taking two hundred and fifty thousand dollars, which had come from selling drugs, and for lying about it to Yo-Yo. It was Mark's secret, and this woman across the desk from him knew about it.

"So can you find the person who killed my husband?" asked Mrs. Jacobsen, interrupting his thoughts. The detective looked at her for quite some time before responding.

"All I know about this Gospel Killer is what I've read in the newspapers, and believe me, chances are what's in the papers doesn't have too much truth to it. I'd be starting completely from scratch. I really think you'd be better off working with the police."

"The police have been looking for this killer for

almost four years," Kim replied. "I'm not willing to just sit and wait, Mr. Witt." Mark was still trying to think of a way to tell her no when she added, "Marcus said you were a man who would do whatever is necessary to get the job done. I know you were shot, and you still finished the job. That's the kind of man I'm looking for. You do whatever is necessary to find this killer, and I'll pay whatever you ask."

Mark couldn't explain it, but this woman made him uncomfortable. Repeating the phrase "whatever was necessary" just like Marcus had used was almost eerie to him. But he finally relented. "If you could leave me your number and address and give me a couple of days, I'll check around and see what I can find out and then decide if I can help you."

She thanked him and rose from her chair. Then Kim slowly bent over to pick up her purse from the floor and to pull a card from it with her information. As she bent over, Kim artfully made sure her ass was in full view, with its ample and glorious splendor practically shining through the snug Yoga pants. Mark was sure she purposefully stayed in that position longer than was needed. Mrs. Jacobsen clearly enjoyed men watching her, but Mark wouldn't play the game. He turned away to check his smart phone until she stood back up.

He saw her to the door and then watched her drive away in a white Range Rover. As he sat back down to finish his paperwork, he was still uneasy with anyone else knowing about the Ramirez case. Before even deciding if it was a good idea, Mark pulled out his phone and dialed Marcus Ramirez. When Marcus answered and heard it was Mark, he began to laugh.

"There's a lot of ass on that old girl, ain't there?" Some small talk ensued, and Marcus assured Mark that Kim was a close friend, and that he and his wife had indeed recommended him to her. According to Marcus, she was clean.

She and her husband had been married for fifteen years. He was a bit older than Kim, and he had owned a nut and bolt company. They liked to party some, but they were not connected to his business at all. Marcus knew that was really what Mark wanted to know. After asking about her and learning that Carolina was doing fine, Mark hung up the phone.

Twenty minutes later, he too was out the door, and in hot pursuit of a waffle extravaganza.

~~~

Back across town, the 10K run was now completed. Many of the runners stayed behind to socialize and to enjoy a good story or two. Matthew Owens made his way to the front of the pelican exhibit, where he again could focus his interest on the woman with the angel tattoo.

Knowing he was behind her, the woman turned and saw Matthew staring at her. A shy smile enticed him to approach her just as she was finishing her sports drink.

"Ahhh, Gatorade, nectar of the gods," he said to break the ice.

"It's not bad," she nodded. "But I kinda wish it was a cold beer."

"That does sound better," he said with a grin, then stuck out his hand. "Hi, I'm Matt."

"Well, hello, Matt," she said as she smiled and shook his hand. "I'm Angel."

They talked for a few minutes about the completed

10K run as well as their individual training schedules. Since they seemed to be hitting it off, Matt asked if she would like to meet after work the next Tuesday evening at the Arlington Nature Center for an eight-mile run. He was thrilled when she agreed.

Chapter 10

5:00 a.m. Monday morning made itself known to the Witt household with the alarm. Mark always swore that freaking buzzer went off about two minutes after he had fallen asleep. That alarm—sounding like the Aflac duck, except without the personality and with its webbed feet caught in a jagged vise grip—went off twice before Mark hit the clock and mercifully silenced it.

As he got out of bed, Yo-Yo, dead to the world, softly groaned and rolled over to get comfortable in what had just been his spot. Before he could think of sliding back into bed next to her, Mark had his jock strap and shorts on and was lacing his shoes. P90X waits for no man.

By 5:10, Mark was in his living room hitting the play button on the DVD player. By 5:30, the trainer on the tape, Tony Horton, was officially kicking Mark's butt and making him rethink the wisdom of doubling down that past weekend on waffles and Krispy Kremes. A couple of minutes after 6:00, Mark's shirt was so soaked with perspiration that it squished with each movement he made.

Mark couldn't say he ever looked forward to P90X, but he was always glad later that he had done it. Now all he wanted was to get into the shower. As he toweled off minutes later, he sighed; he didn't look forward to what he needed to do next this day.

Walking through the front doors of Dallas' central police station, Mark could feel the stares. Each time he returned one, the person quickly looked away. Police officers he had worked with or who he had known for years were all surprised to see him — and not in a good way. There were arched eyebrows but not a single greeting.

They didn't trust Mark, for one, because he had left the force after only a few years, but mainly, because of his father. Those who thought of him at all thought of dear old dad as a piece of shit. Those who had worked with Richard Witt mostly tried to forget him — and by extension, any of his deeds or offspring. Not that Mark blamed any of the cops for the way they felt; he'd like to forget his dad ever existed too. And, as for reunions, well fuck, he wasn't there for that either.

The stares persisted and the scowls grew longer until he knocked on the office door of the one person in the entire building who would be happy to see him. John Coleman looked up, and seeing it was Mark at the door, practically leaped forward to open it.

John had seen firsthand the life Mark had experienced growing up — not every part of it, but enough to know the difficulties and extremes. Because of that, he had always taken a special interest in Mark and had felt a certain way towards him. Not a sympathetic way, because John knew that was the last thing Mark would ever want from anyone, but more like a feeling of empathy.

It was not Richard, but John who took an interest in Mark and went to his little league and high school baseball games. In fact, as Mark's talent grew and his pitching prowess developed, it was John who had given him the nickname of "No Hit Witt." When an elbow injury sidetracked his baseball career, Mark switched to boxing. And it was John who changed his nickname to "One Hit Witt." "One Hit," as in one good hit from Mark's powerful right hand, and his Golden Glove opponent would surely be knocked out. Both names fit and helped cement the affection each felt for the other.

Before the door was fully open, John was up and hugging Mark. Each was in need of a friendly face.

"Been too long, Mark," Detective Coleman said after some good-natured kidding around and catching up. "Good to see you down here again."

"From the looks I got walking in, I don't think too many of your buddies would agree with that," Mark replied.

"Oh, fuck 'em if they can't take a joke. Now come on and tell me; what brings you down here?"

Mark explained how he was checking on the Jacobsen murder for the widow. He hadn't decided to even take the case yet, but if he did, he didn't plan on stepping on anybody's toes. He stressed that all he knew about the Gospel Killer was what had been in the newspapers—well that, and the fact that if the killings had happened in Dallas, then John Coleman would be the lead investigator.

"So, since you been on this from the start, is there any reason I should get involved with it?"

"Well, I can think of one good reason—a fat payday," Coleman answered. "The wife inherited thirty-five million dollars. You can charge her whatever you want." This news arched even Mark's eyebrows.

"Any chance it was her that killed him? For the money?"

"As an ex-cop, you know we naturally look at the spouse first, especially when there's a thirty-five million dollar estate. But this looks too much like the rest of the killings."

Mark was almost disappointed to hear this. He was still trying to talk himself out of taking this case, and besides, there was something about Kim Jacobsen that didn't feel quite right to him. "So you found nothing on her?"

"Didn't say that," John responded, still smiling. "We found a lot. Word is she got around a bit—quite a bit. But evidently, the husband did too. Friends say they had an understanding. Not exactly Ward and June Cleaver, but nothing to suggest she murdered him. Besides, like I said, the crime scene and the murder itself were just too similar to all the others."

Mark was digesting this and thinking of Mrs. Jacobsen as Coleman began to go over the killings. "It was your dad and I that worked the first of the Gospel Killings. We took the call. In fact, we handled the first two of the murders together before he retired."

His dad had worked the first two murders? Mark hadn't even taken the case yet, but with this news, along with Kim Jacobsen, his head was already swimming. "What was my dad's involvement?"

"I shouldn't even have said that," John quickly said. "Forget it; I'm sorry. It's not important."

"That's not much of an answer." John looked into his eyes and relented.

"Look, I know what kind of father he was to you and Cubbie and what kind of husband he was to your mom. Not many cops up here are angels, but watching what he did to your family, I hated him for it."

Hearing this instantly swept Mark away to dark memories. His eyes began to moisten as the old feelings rushed back. Mark battled back by focusing his attention on a diploma Coleman had framed on his office wall. It was for a bachelor's degree in criminal justice and had been awarded to Jonathon Lewis Coleman from Dallas Baptist University.

"So you finally finished, huh?" Mark managed to say after a moment. " That's good. I'm proud of you, John."

Coleman closed the shades in his office before putting his arm around Mark. "Thank you, Mark. Listen, your father put in for detective a few years before he retired, to up his pension. He got it; don't ask me how. Anyways, I guess I must've pissed somebody off because they paired him and me up again. We worked the first two of the murders together, before the papers gave them the Gospel Killer name. It was pretty preliminary at that time. Then he retired, and I've stayed on it."

Mark nodded, regaining his composure.

"How about you takin' a look at the Jacobsen file?" John asked. "See what you think? Hell, take a look at everything we got and just give me your opinion."

Mark knew this was not exactly normal procedure. "I don't want you getting into any trouble on my account."

"How am I gonna get into any trouble if you solve the case? Nobody's gotta even know, and besides, the only person who would have a big problem with it is this little FBI dwarf—and you know what, fuck dwarfs! Those bastards got those short little baby-like arms and legs; they give me the creeps."

"Really?" Mark said, smiling. "I always thought dwarfs were cool. Figured if I ever got to be a rock star or something, I'd hire a bunch of dwarfs to follow me around and be my posse. Maybe get some who know kung fu and shit and let 'em handle security. You know, my own personal tiny little swat team."

"I swear, I'll never figure you white boys out—wantin' a bunch of midget bodyguards," John said smiling, as he handed the Jacobsen case file to his friend.

John settled in at his computer and began to pull up the video surveillance tape of the killer as Mark studied the file.

"Come see who we're looking for," he said when the video was ready to be viewed. "We got this tape from the last murder at the Stoneleigh."

Mark didn't know of a tape and hurried around the desk. Like the others, he was instantly struck by the tattoos—and the walk. As he watched it over and over, he was amazed at the woman's skill to be so visible to the cameras and yet still be able to completely hide her identity.

"She's very intelligent and very sick. To be so in control in front of these cameras and at that same time filled with rage, boy she's gotta be tough," Mark told John.

"A very sick and very intelligent woman? In Dallas, huh? You ain't exactly narrowing it down for me there Sherlock."

"All right. You say she met this last guy at the hotel bar. How'd she meet Luke Jacobsen?" Mark asked.

"Jacobsen kept a hideaway. Evidently the apartment where he was murdered was where he did his extracurricular entertaining. He had a PC and a laptop there, and both of them were missing the hard drives. We think maybe he met her online, and she covered her tracks."

"What about any other computers?" Mark asked. "At his home or work?"

"They all checked out clean," John answered, shaking his head. "Mainly all business and with a few family pictures."

Sitting back down, Mark began to go through the crime scene photos of Luke Jacobsen as well as the earlier victims. As he compared the photos, he noticed that two of the victims had been mutilated. The third victim, a Mr. John Demus, was missing both hands. Apparently they had both been severed at the wrist. The ninth victim, a very overweight man named Luke Clifford, was missing both of his nipples. According to forensics, both had been cut out postmortem.

Mark made special note of this, wondering why the killer had mutilated these two but not the others. There were now fourteen victims, but oddly, only two had been desecrated. The others were killed in similar fashion, with a serrated-edged knife blade assumed to be six to eight inches in length, but their bodies displayed only the wounds of murder and not the marks of torture.

The morning was quickly turning to afternoon as Mark studied the files. He eventually put them down on the desk.

"Guess you're about ready for lunch?" he asked Coleman.

"Look at me. I can afford to miss a lunch or two," the detective answered. "So what did you see?"

"It's really more what I didn't see. No pentagrams,

no upside-down crosses, no visible signs of satanic symbols. I know the papers have been calling this the Gospel Killer the whole time, but I sort of figured someone really upset with God was doing it. Maybe somebody involved with the occult. But I don't see that from these pictures."

"That's why it's good that you're here," Coleman exclaimed. "We're convinced the killer is using some type of Biblical relevance or message. With your theology training and all, maybe you could be the one to help piece it all together."

Mark felt a long way from the seminary, and the words hung heavy around him. He absolutely believed in Jesus' goodness, but he knew of his own weaknesses. He went to church, but it was for Yo-Yo and Lily; his heart wasn't in it. He didn't read the Bible and pray like he had at an earlier time in his life. The ways of the world had diverted him and seen to that. The time he used to spend praying was now, more often than not, wasted on television or the Internet.

And, if Mark were honest, he'd admit he didn't feel God's love in his heart. How could he feel it and still feel loathing for many of God's creations? Mark felt anger towards many men—men the Bible said were made in God's own image. Hell, he had killed men—he had killed men! He had fallen so far. He drank. He cussed. He gambled. All this, and here Coleman was looking at him like he could be some sort of prodigal crime fighter.

Mark finally offered, "I don't know how much I could help you. That sort of thing isn't really in me now."

Coleman stood and walked around the desk. "I know

what's in you, Mark. And I really hope you take the case."

That did it. As Mark hugged Detective Coleman and said good-bye, he knew how much he owed him. He knew he had to take the case.

Chapter 11

The next morning, Mark searched through the refrigerator before deciding to settle on Eggos for Lily's breakfast. They were, of course, a poor substitute for Yo-Yo's waffles, but with Yo-Yo still sleeping, they were the best option for a cooking-challenged dad. Besides, later he could tell Yo-Yo how she had missed it—how he slaved over a spectacular three-egg omelet creation that would surely have put the greatest offerings from Emeril or Bobby Flay to shame. Not a chance she would believe it, but it would still be good for a laugh.

After breakfast, Mark got Lily ready for school. Getting Daniel ready to go had always been so much easier. Mark could grab a pair of shorts, a t-shirt, Reeboks, and then brush his teeth and finger comb his hair, and Daniel would be good to go. But things didn't work so easily with Lily. She was definitely a little girl on the fast track to becoming a fashionista. Her clothes had to be perfect. Mark could barely get things to match, while Lily demanded that her attire not only work well together, but also that it be properly accessorized.

The morning was not going smoothly for Mark, and Yo-Yo was still comfy in bed. Oh well, he managed like he always did, and they got out of the house ten minutes before the school bell rang.

After kissing Lily good-bye and saying the usual awkward greetings to the teacher and other parents, Mark headed back home. Thoughts of finding and then surprising Yo-Yo while she was still lying in bed were all that was on his mind when he turned the corner to his street and could see his home. Those thoughts, like most amorous thoughts of husbands, suddenly became dashed.

Kellie's car was parked in front of his house. Yeah, not much could get sexual thoughts out of a man's mind faster than seeing or being reminded of his ex. Mark had forgotten that this was Tuesday and that Yo-Yo and Kellie had personal training sessions together every Tuesday and Thursday morning.

When Mark entered the house, Yo-Yo was, as he had expected, running late and still in the bedroom getting ready. He found Kellie at the kitchen table having a cup of coffee.

"Want me to get you one?" she smiled, raising her cup.

"No thanks. You know you should just tell her you're coming over about a half hour earlier than you really are, and then maybe she'll be ready by the time you get here," Mark mused to Kellie.

"Oh it's all right. Besides the caffeine helps me make it through my workout."

Mark smiled back politely, but he knew better. She didn't need any extra help to work out. After the divorce, looking for comfort and a sense of self-worth, Kellie had thrown herself into fitness like a Tasmanian devil throws itself onto a snake. She was obsessed with it. Weightlifting, plyometrics, kickboxing, you name it, Kellie was active with it and devoted to it. And her devotion showed. Her abs were shredded and her shoulders chiseled. Mark could see the veins in her forearms pop each time she raised the coffee cup to her mouth.

As they made small talk while waiting for Yo-Yo, he found he was almost intimidated by Kellie. He had always been an athlete and still tried to exercise, but she blew him away. He decided that as soon as they left he'd go hit play and get in another session with Tony Horton. Yeah, he could count on P90X to help him validate his masculine worth and keep up with his ex.

They were talking about Daniel's fourth grade teacher when Yo-Yo finally made her appearance. He had rarely been so glad to see her, as the conversation was getting more and more forced. But not with her and Kellie; they got along like two sorority sisters, laughing, giggling, and finishing each other's sentences. Mark liked that they got along, and he was glad that Kellie babysat Lily for them every other week on date night. But to see his wife and ex acting like best friends was, well, really weird.

The women prepared to leave, and he kissed Yo-Yo good-bye. As soon as they left, he reintroduced himself to Tony Horton and the good folks at P90X.

After the workout and a quick shower, Mark was out the door and on his way to Kim Jacobsen's house. And what a house it was. In far North Dallas and backing up to the sixteenth green of the famed Preston Trail Country Club, the home more than qualified as a Texas-sized mansion.

As Mark parked his Charger on the tiled, circular driveway and walked to the ornate, wrought iron front

door of the twelve-thousand-square-foot Mediterranean showplace, he looked at the estate and wondered,
just how much money is there in selling nuts and bolts?
After a moment, Kim answered the door and Mark got
the answer to his question. The old fella must have
made a shitload of money to afford that home and
that woman.

After a warm greeting, Mark followed Kim through
the entryway and across the foyer into the formal
living room. No photograph in Town & Country could
have ever been more finely appointed and detailed.
The home was majestic, distinguished, refined and
elegant—but not Kim. Hot as hell—hell yeah!—but
not in a refined or elegant way.

Before sinking into a floral-print, wing-back chair,
she called his attention to the skintight t-shirt she was
wearing, bearing the words High Maintenance…High
Performance.

"Like my shirt?" she grinned. "Hope so, because I
believe in truth in advertising."

"I better not touch that line," Mark grinned awkwardly while shaking his head.

"Well, you're no fun," she said, pretending to pout.

So much for the grieving widow, Mark thought. She
was doing it again —making him uncomfortable and
taking him off his game. He tried to right the ship and
was determined to do what he came for – talk business.
He proceeded to tell her his findings from his visit to
the police station, and then said he would need to ask
her some questions—personal questions. She seemed
to perk up at this.

"Ask me anything you like," she offered with a
wicked smile. "Trust me. I'm game."

"Why do you want me to find this killer? Even if I'm able to, your husband will still be just as gone."

"Well Mark—it's all right if I call you Mark, isn't it?" she said, smiling seductively. When he nodded, she continued. "Good. Mark, I won't insult you and say it's so no other woman has to go through this or so that no other family suffers this type of loss. I could care less about the others. Fuck them. Fuck all of 'em! They can sit around and wait on the police and hope some dumb ass cop finds the bitch that did this hiding in the bottom of some donut box."

As she paused briefly, proud of her clever donut reference, he wondered why she would know the killer was female. "But I'm not waiting, because I have enough money that I don't have to wait. And I got the money from Luke, and I know Luke would want his killer found."

"All right then," said Mark, pulling out his notepad. "So tell me about your husband. Who was he?"

Before answering, Kim called for her Hispanic maid, Ana, and asked in Spanish to be brought a glass of Pinot Grigio. After Mark politely refused a drink, she slinked back down into the chair and pondered his question aloud. "Who was my husband? He was a man. A man's man. Complex, opinionated, silly, coarse, you know, a heart of gold but feet of clay sort."

Mark made special note of the feet of clay response and its biblical reference. "How do you mean feet of clay? Was Mr. Jacobsen a religious man?"

At the question, Kim let out such a laugh that it frightened poor Ana, who was setting the wine down onto a coaster. As the laughter filled the room to the top of its eighteen-foot ceilings, the maid pulled a

Willie Mays style catch of the wine glass to prevent the Pinot from tumbling to the floor and onto the Persian rug. The maid's athletic move wowed Mark, but Kim, taken in by his question, barely noticed. "My husband, religious? Hardly. I think he was probably forty-years-old before he realized God's last name wasn't damn."

As Ana was making her way out of the room, Mark nodded appreciation for her quick save and then explained to Kim the reasoning behind his question. He told her of the biblical significance that was attached to the murders, and that he believed the key to solving the crimes might well be found in the Bible. She let his words sink in for a moment.

"I really don't know what to say," she finally offered. "I know they call the person the Gospel Killer, but I don't know how that could involve Luke. Believe me, we didn't spend a lot of time in church."

"How did you two spend your time?" Mark asked, flipping to a new page in his notebook.

"Fucking mainly," she answered matter-of-factly. "Each other some, but mostly others."

It was Mark's turn to try and pull off a Willie Mays style play and not appear shocked by the answer, but alas, he was no "Say Hey Kid." Kim enjoyed his unease, and continued with her fun. "Come now, don't tell me you get nervous just talking about fucking? Why, look at you. Don't you ever even say the word? Fucking? Come on, will you say fucking for me, Mark?"

"Perhaps it would be better if you hired another investigator," Mark said, getting up from his chair and flipping shut the notebook. "I'm not interested in playing these games; I'm a professional."

"I was a professional when I met Luke," was Kim's counter.

"I wish you the best, Mrs. Jacobsen," Mark said as he walked towards the front door. "There will be no charge."

"Luke saved me from that life," she called to him. "That's why I want to find his killer."

He slowed in the hallway but didn't turn around to face her.

"Or don't you think people like us deserve justice?" she asked him.

He turned and began walking back to her. "I'll help you find justice, but I won't be your therapist or your toy."

She nodded in agreement, and they sat back down.

"Okay then, can we start over again?" Mark asked as he got out his notebook.

"Of course," she smiled.

"Do you think one of the women your husband slept with could be his killer?"

"Possibly," Kim said, sipping the wine. "Or maybe it was one of the women I was sleeping with?" Though his head was down, she could sense his eyebrows arch with her answer. "What can I say? It was one of the things we had in common. We both love—or in Luke's case—loved beautiful women. Their shapes, their mouths, the softness of their hair, how their bodies move when they're aroused. So much more rhythmically than men. And no, my husband didn't like other men. That was my area. All mine."

Mark kept his head down for much of the next two hours. When he left, his notebook was filled front and back. He had enough names to run down, business and personal, that he would be busy for days. As he drove away, he redlined the Dodge Charger. He couldn't get away from that house and North Dallas fast enough.

Nearing home, Mark stopped and bought Yo-Yo a dozen roses. He hoped the roses would not only show Yo-Yo he loved her, but also, perhaps, cast aside what he had heard that morning. He hoped it would help him escape the ugliness he felt listening to Kim as she casually spoke about her life and that of her husband. But it wouldn't. It couldn't. He knew that.

And he also knew that this was going to be the case of his lifetime.

Chapter 12

Tuesday afternoon couldn't arrive soon enough for Matthew Owens. He hadn't been able to get Angel off his mind since the weekend's race. Her strong body and sexy-as-hell tattoos were all he was thinking of when he was having sex Sunday morning with his wife. Sex he had been forced to plead for and bargain for beforehand, for what seemed like hours.

It wasn't like he even really wanted sex from his wife. He just wanted sex. He needed sex. A hungry dog has to eat out of some bowl—even a soft, mushy, cellulite-covered bowl. Oh well, at least he was able to close his eyes and imagine it was the hot-ass Angel. Shit, why couldn't his wife have a body like that? Why couldn't she work out some, at least a little, instead of planting her ass on the couch and watching TiVo'd Oprah every evening?

Earlier in their marriage, Matt had amused himself by thinking his wife's favorite form of exercise was bitching. Bitching about the kids she taught at school, bitching about her sister and mom, and bitching about him for just about any freakin' reason. Hell, if fitness came from bitching, then Matt knew his wife could win the Ironman.

But enough wasted energy thinking of her. Today is

about Angel. So much so that Matt could hardly hear his wife's bitching as he walked past her, through the kitchen to the garage. In twenty minutes, he would be at the Arlington Nature Center, but mentally he was already there.

On the way there, a horrible thought crossed his mind. What if Angel didn't show up? Damn. How stupid and foolish he would feel. A woman like that probably gets hit on so much, why would she agree to meet him? Him? Hell, his own wife was no prize, and she was sick of him. Why would a woman like Angel want anything to do with him?

The doubts grew stronger. After all, she had practically just met him, even if they were just going to run or train together. Then it hit him. What if that morning at the zoo she had agreed to meet him just to get rid of him? Shit! Was he that creepy? Well, maybe, he had tracked her pretty closely throughout the race; some women might have called it stalking. Why bother even driving all the way over there?

But what if he was wrong? Of course, he had to continue on to the Nature Center. Excitement began taking over the feelings of foolishness, even more so when he turned into the parking lot and saw Angel stretching in the warm-up area.

He hurriedly pulled his truck up to one of the telephone poles lying on the ground, which marked the boundaries of the gravel parking lot. He parked his pickup, took a quick swig of water, and exited the truck. He couldn't believe it. He was here, stretching alongside his Angel.

With knees straight, her chest on her thighs and palms on the ground, Angel said to Matt, "I was starting to think you were gonna stand me up."

Still loosening his core, Matt was relieved to hear she had worried he might not show. "Oh, no. I hit some traffic over on 360, and they were just crawling over there. But I got here as quickly as I could."

He watched as she straightened up and began doing neck rolls to loosen her neck and shoulders.

"Good," she laughed. "I was afraid your wife might not have let you out of the house." Matt was grimacing through a hamstring stretch but couldn't hide his surprise, at what Angel had just said. "Don't worry, it's okay," she said to help him out after an awkward pause. "You didn't say it, but I knew you were married. It's cool. And believe me, I know how women are. Half the time I think I'm married to one because, my husband can bitch and moan with any woman."

Lust was quickly giving way to love now for Matt. How freaking cool was this girl? Normally, even running with friends, Matt kept pretty quiet during the run. Speaking only made it harder on his lungs and interfered with his breathing patterns, but today he and Angel talked nearly non-stop throughout their eight-mile, fifty-six minute run. Seven minutes per mile wasn't bad; Matt could run faster, but never happier.

He was beaming at the end of the run. He had learned so much about Angel. They had laughed, really laughed at each other's jokes — especially the ones about their spouses. At one point, sex was brought up in their conversation, and Angel called her husband "The Minute Man," to which Matt was quick to point out that he had run several marathons.

"Marathon Man, huh?" she said to him as they ran alongside each other. "You better not just be getting my hopes up." At the instant she said that, Matt would have sworn the look in her eyes was even sexier than the sweat that clung to her abs.

Toweling down afterwards in the parking lot, Matt was trying to think of a way to keep this from ending when Angel said, "Next time, how about we pick a day that's not so hot?"

"Yeah, sorry about that. Next time, I'll get to work on that heat for you."

"Well, looks like you're the man for the job," she said, smiling and patting the side of his pickup.

Matt's pickup had a vehicle wrap advertisement on it promoting his heating and air conditioning company, Air Express. Now it was his turn to smile. "We usually do smaller jobs, you know, like homes and businesses—not the whole outdoors and all."

"Good thing," she laughed. "Global warming would put you out of business. Goodness knows, it never could've possibly been ninety-two degrees on May 2 in Texas before all of us sorry pieces-of-shit humans started burning fossil fuels. Those people that fall for that global-oney warming bullshit kill me."

Oh, goddamn…Tats, a rockin' body, and a conservative? Matt thought. Are you kidding me? Who was this? Sarah freakin' Palin? Matt was so hooked now that he was just about to call his wife and tell her to keep the house and kids because he was never coming home.

"Listen I need to get going, but can I see you again?" Angel asked.

In his mind Matt was thinking, hell, fucking yes, you can see me again, but he tried to play it cool. "Sure, how about back here tomorrow?"

Angel moved closer to him, took her towel and began drying off his stomach. "Actually I wasn't thinking of running."

Her intent was clear, and Matt instantly was afraid he was about to become a forty-yard dash man instead of a marathoner if she moved that towel or her hand any lower.

"Great," was all he could manage to say, and she moved around behind him and started drying his shoulders and back.

"Matt, my husband is a city councilman," she said softly. "I have to be really careful where I'm seen and with whom." She then leaned in towards him and said, "But he's gonna be tied up Thursday until late. Can you can get away?"

Matt nodded and was racking his brain for a place to meet when Angel made a suggestion. "How about we meet up at your work and then we can figure out where to go?" Again, all he could do was nod like an idiot. "Great. How about I pick up some beer and meet you there around 8:00?"

"All right, let me give you the address," he said, turning to face her.

"Already got it," she said, leaning against his pickup and patting the advertisement on the side of it. A quick peck on the cheek later and she was walking across the parking lot to leave in her maroon Acura TL.

Matt stood mesmerized, watching her ass and that tattoo walk further away. "Then it's a date," he finally blurted out.

"Yes, sir. Mark it down," she said without turning.

Mark it down? How could he forget? Evidently, Angel didn't know she was all he had been able to think about since they first met. Still, when he got in his pickup, he drew a picture of a stick of dynamite on his calendar for Thursday, May 4.

Chapter 13

Mark woke early the next morning. Even though it was a school day, Lily had stayed over at Yo-Yo's parents the night before, so grandma would be taking her to school. That meant he didn't have to worry about picking out the right hair bands or bracelets or managing any of a possible hundred other fashion emergencies for Lily.

But, what it did mean was he missed his little girl. Without her at home, things always felt different—something was definitely missing. Oh well, he knew she was safe and getting spoiled even further at the in-laws. The master of the house could rest easy.

With that in mind, he rolled over and looked at Yo-Yo. Just as he suspected, she was as beautiful as ever. Sleeping beside him with tousled hair and no makeup, she looked peaceful and flawless. That was not the case with Mark. He was no sleeping beauty. When he awoke, there was no telling how big a pool of drool he had to pick his head up from or what type of crop circles the overnight aliens had printed into his hair. And here Yo-Yo was asleep and looking like she just stepped off a Hollywood set. Life was not fair, but he wasn't complaining.

After a couple more minutes spent watching her

sleep, Mark got up, put on his headphones and headed for the treadmill in the garage. A little over an hour later his head was hanging under the shower. The hot water felt so good to his body, soothing his muscles and washing away the sweat from his morning run.

He closed his eyes to fully appreciate the shower and relaxed, knowing few things could feel as good as a hot shower after a good workout. With the water crashing onto his back and his eyes still closed, Mark felt one of those few things that did feel better than a hot shower — Yo-Yo's hand on his side.

Surprised, he turned and faced the beautiful woman who had quietly slipped into the shower with him. Wearing only a braid to keep her hair up and away from the water, Yo-Yo had never looked better. Maybe no woman ever had. She leaned in to kiss Mark, but he pulled back slightly.

"I haven't brushed my teeth," he mildly protested.

"Neither have I," she responded. The kiss ensued. Really, it was unfair to call it simply a kiss; it was more two mouths melding together. Yo-Yo had large, full lips, and they seemed to follow Mark's mouth like a perfect dance partner. Even after years of marriage, Mark loved kissing this woman. With their mouths still seamlessly entwined, Yo-Yo reached around Mark and shut off the water, surprising him again.

"We'll need to shower again later anyway," she playfully said.

After a quick towel off, she took his hand and led him to the bedroom. Yo-Yo was usually not so amorous in the morning. Her actions prompted Mark to ask, "You trying to make up for something I don't even know you've done yet?"

"I'll leave you alone if you want?" she teased.

He squeezed her hand and looked down at his own state of arousal. "No, too late. You've done gone and let the genie out of the bottle now."

"Really?" she smiled, seeing what he meant, and patted his dick. "So is this big genie gonna grant me three wishes?" As they fell into bed together, it quickly became apparent that the genie was going to get his wishes granted as well.

Without children's ears in the home, Yo-Yo was totally open with her feelings and desires and so responsive. The couple had made love thousands of times, but it was still intimate and emotional. The passion felt fresh. Brad and Angelina eat your hearts out; this was damn good sex. Incredible married sex.

As the genie was bringing Yo-Yo to her third climax, Mark tried his best to hold back but couldn't. As she panted and screamed, "Yes, yes," Mark surrendered to his own orgasm—a volcanic, shuddering eruption. Afterwards, almost convulsing, he slumped beside her completely spent. Their bodies were both soaked with sweat—not perspiration, but sweat.

"Fuck, you're gonna kill me one of these days," Mark finally offered, after afterglow was fully ablaze for several minutes.

Lying on her back and trying to regain herself, Yo-Yo managed to reach over and touch his arm. "Hope not. I'd never find another genie like that one of yours."

One thing was for certain. Yo-Yo was right; they were both going to need another shower. After the second shower, watching Yo-Yo dry off, Mark thought of manning up and going for round two. But he looked at the clock, and dammit, he knew he had to be getting on his way. Truth be told, after that bout he needed a break anyway. He decided that maybe if he was good, Yo-Yo would rub the bottle again later, and Mr. Genie could bust loose and stretch out again. That thought comforted his male pride, and with that he dressed, kissed Yo-Yo good-bye and headed out.

Within minutes, his Charger was unwinding east on State Highway 114 until he took the O'Connor exit north to Las Colinas Boulevard, ending up at the Venetian Apartments. The Venetian was a year-and-half-old high-rise apartment complex in Irving's popular Las Colinas district. As he entered through the main lobby, Mark could quickly tell that these apartments catered to the wealthy and discriminating. Chocolate brown stained concrete floors set the entrance tone and were accompanied by smooth jazz being played on the audio system. That hip, sophisticated feel was only enhanced by the multiple pieces of modern art adorning the walls.

Looking unimpressed and acting as if he owned the place, Mark strolled past the gawking and nubile-faced leasing agents and headed straight to the elevators. Waiting there, he watched part of a spinning class through the state-of-the-art, glass-enclosed work out area featured by the Venetian. Seeing a couple of the girls pump their bikes while revealing more than they covered, once again Mark was convinced that Dallas was a place where a guy could get into a lot of trouble. And while that was good for the private investigation business, for Mark it was good that he had Yo-Yo at home. Mercifully, the elevator doors opened and he punched floor sixteen.

Getting off the elevator, Mark walked to apartment

1618, the location where Luke Jacobsen had been murdered. He put on a pair of rubber gloves and opened the door with the key Kim had given him. He walked into Luke's "love shack" getaway. Ostensibly, a corporate apartment for out-of-town customers of Luke's nut and bolt company, the $3,000 a month apartment was certainly no shack. With authentic wood floors, a twelve-foot high floor-to-ceiling rock fire place, two LG high-definition flat screens and a patio that provided a see-and-be-seen perch to view the entire length of Las Colinas Boulevard, Mark could just hear those nubile-faced leasing agents pitching this bad boy. To entertain your clients or your freelance side action, there was simply no place like the Venetian.

Even though the Venetian was located in Irving and not Dallas, because of the profile of the Gospel killings the Irving Police Department was more than happy to let their brothers in blue from the DPD handle this case. Nothing like a serial killer investigation to eat up man-hours and the budget. Consequently, Irving's mayor had practically done a double back flip when Dallas Police Chief Harrington called and offered their assistance. John Coleman had been on the scene within an hour of that first call, and since that first day he had not spoken with anyone from Irving. When he told this to Mark, it was clear that John was not exactly upset by Irving's deferring in this matter.

Taking the police report Coleman had given him, Mark began to painstakingly go through the apartment. The most obvious point of interest was the actual murder location itself, the bed. Even though it had been stripped to the mattress, the bloodstain was massive. Forensics found only one type of blood on the mattress and the streaks down the headboard. It belonged exclusively to Luke Jacobsen.

As he looked through the drawers of the chest and nightstands, Mark wondered how the killer could have exited through the elevator and the lobby covered in blood. She would have had to clean up afterwards. This was a huge bloodletting. Was there another exit? He'd have to check that.

Mark got down on the floor beside the bed and imagined the killing. Lying flat on his back like Luke had been, Mark knew the killer had to have been directly on top or over him. The force of the knife blow was too deep. It had to have come straight down in a violent manner and not some outward slashing style.

No blood or skin was found under Luke's fingernails, which proved to Mark that the victim had been caught by surprise and not been given a chance to fight back. Since there was semen found on the sheets, Mark surmised that Luke Jacobsen had been relaxing after sex when the attack occurred. And because Kim said that Luke didn't go for guys and that guys were her specialty alone, Mark believed that the killer in all likelihood was the same woman he had seen on the Stoneleigh Hotel tapes.

But Coleman hadn't found a connection between any of the victims, so how was this woman selecting the men? Even if it were just the biblical names, how would she locate these men and then how was she meeting and seducing them? Regarding the Bible, one had been left on the bed beside Luke's dead body.

Mark knew from Mr. Jacobsen's lifestyle that the Bible wouldn't have been there at the bedside previously, so the killer would have brought it. Perhaps they could check where it was purchased as a way to find the killer? So many thoughts were now running through Mark's brain. Being at the scene and actually immersing himself into a crime always opened Mark's eyes to the possibilities of how the crime was committed and how the killer could be caught.

The police theorized that Luke had met the mystery woman over the Internet, since the computer hard drives had been taken from the laptop and the PC. It was possible, but Mark didn't believe the killer was finding her victims online. This murderer was obviously skilled, and the Internet left too many digital fingerprints. There were too many ways for deleted materials to resurface and directly point out the killer. No, he believed this killer was too smart for that.

Yes, the Internet provided anonymity, to a point, but this woman wasn't being anonymous. Using a knife after sex demonstrated she was killing in a very personal way. She wasn't looking to be caught, but she wasn't worried about anonymity. Killers who want to be anonymous shoot their victims from a distance away. Killers who are bold and wish to not only kill but also leave a message use a knife from close range.

Finally, Mark took one last look around. He was confident he had a good feel for the physical layout and for the crime itself. He finished writing one last page in his old school style notebook and was out the door. While locking the door from the outside, he ran into a neighbor across the hall who was returning home. Phil Wright looked nervously at Mark and then tried to hurry into his apartment.

"Excuse me, can I talk to you for a moment?" Mark asked.

"Actually, I'm kinda in a rush," Phil answered as he finished opening his door.

"It'll only take a minute."

"Man, I've already talked to you guys."

"I'm not a cop," Mark said, pulling out his PI license.

Mark knew that people often feel less intimidated talking with private investigators than with cops. After hearing that Luke's widow had hired the investigator to find the murderer, Mr. Wright sighed and invited Mark inside his apartment. Once inside, Mark realized this was no cookie cutter set of apartments. The layout was completely different than Luke's apartment. Dark tile floors, light wood paneling, and stainless steel appliances gave this apartment a very modern feel. No two ways about it, the Venetians were a high-class, high-rise set of freakin' apartments.

Mark began by jotting down Phil's basic information, full name and workplace, etc., before pulling Phil's statement from the file given to him by John Coleman. Mark quickly read over the statement and then laid it down on the coffee table. The statement was shit. Phil claimed he barely even knew Luke and didn't see or hear anything the night of the murder. The statement combined with Phil's still nervous actions made Mark think there was more to the story than what he was hearing..

"So tell me, how well did you know Luke Jacobsen?"

"Like I told the police, I'd see him in the hall sometimes but not much. He didn't come by that often. I think he just used it for business."

"Listen, I know what kind of business he used the apartment for. I'm just trying to find Luke's killer, and unless I think you were involved in this somehow, the police will never hear anything you tell me."

Phil began relenting. "We were friends. We'd go out... Geez, come on, man, I'm friends with Kim. I don't want this getting out."

"Kim knows what went on in the apartment," Mark said to reassure him.

"She doesn't know he gave me copies of all the tapes!"

"What tapes," Mark quickly asked.

"He had a Flip. You know, a little Flip recorder that he'd tape everything on, and then he'd take the memory stick and burn me some DVDs of all the girls and the sex. Kim was on some of the tapes, so that's why I don't think she knew he gave them to me—especially the ones with her and women together."

Mark quickly grabbed the police report and went through it again at warp speed. There was no mention of a Flip or of any digital recorder of any type being found at the scene. Mark put it back in the folder. "There was no Flip listed in the police report."

"Well she must've taken it with her then," Phil answered matter-of-factly.

Of course, that's it, thought Mark. That's why the computer hard drives were missing; the killer may have been afraid somehow they were wired together and the tape could show up on them. Wait a minute. Phil said *she*. Did he mean she in a way that it had to have been a woman since Luke didn't swing both ways, or did he know something? He had sort of said it in a funny way.

"Why'd you say she must've taken it?" Mark asked.

Phil looked dumbfounded. "Luke recorded all his women. Kept those tapes like fucking trophies. Fucking trophies...I guess they were, you know. Fucking trophies. Get it?"

"Yeah, I got it," Mark nodded. " Now what about the tapes?"

"All I know is that if there was no Flip found, then the bitch took it with her when she left."

Now it was Mark who looked dumbfounded and unsure.

"The bitch. You know the bitch with the tattoos," Phil said.

"Shit. You saw the woman?"

"Just from the back. Whenever Luke was bringing one over, he'd make noise out in the hall so I'd know he was about to score. And me, too, you know, with another tape and all."

"Tell me what you saw."

"Like I said, not much. I looked out my keyhole and saw them kissing while he was opening the door. Her back was to me, and all I could see was she had a tattoo on her back and her arm. Had dark hair, you know, and a good ass. Helluva ass. Luke was definitely an ass man."

"What was the tattoo of? The one on the back?"

"Couldn't really see; his hand was on it. Part on it anyway, and part trying to get down the back of her pants. Fucker knew I was watching so he gave me a thumbs-up sign. That's the last I saw of him."

"Think the tattoo could have been an angel holding a Bible?"

Phil paused and then looked up at the ceiling in thought. "Mighta been. Yeah, it could'a been like angel wings—you know, the tips of the wings may be was what I was seeing. I was just thinking then about the tape and seeing if she had a snatch patch, too."

"A snatch patch?"

"Yeah. A snatch patch, you know, a tattoo right down there on her pussy. Man, when those pussies are waxed right, those tats show up great on tape."

Mark could see that Phil had pretty well gotten over his nervousness and wasn't holding back. "Had you ever seen the tattoo before? Had he brought her to the apartment before?"

Again, Phil seemed in deep thought. "Don't know. A lot of 'em had tattoos and all, but, you know, like I said, I didn't see it that well. I was just hoping to see it on the tape."

Mark was mentally trying to sort this out. "Do you still have the tapes?"

"Fuck, yeah, I still got the tapes," Phil smiled. "You don't throw shit like that out."

He got up and walked towards his bedroom, motioning for Mark to follow. There, Mark saw the treasure trove of over sixty sex tapes made by Luke Jacobsen for his deeply perverted neighbor Phil.

For the next hour and a half, Phil burned copies of each of the DVDs for Mark. As he did so, he gave an almost running play-by-play on what to expect from the tapes. Mark was getting antsy for the copies to be completed, but at least he got Phil to talk about other things as well.

Phil explained to Mark where he and Luke went out most often, and what kind of women they approached. He shared typical ways that Luke used to close the deals and get the women back to the apartments, etc. Mark felt he could use this information to try and find out where Luke had met the killer, and, of course, where he could perhaps also meet her as well.

"Listen, I may need to give those tapes showing women with tattoos on their backs to the police," Mark said when the conversation began to slow down.

"Thought you said no cops?" Phil countered.

"Your name won't be mentioned," Mark assured him. "I protect my sources. Besides, I know you didn't have any involvement with this murder so I won't drag you through anything. You got my word."

Phil nodded in agreement and the two men shook hands. By the time the DVDs were complete, Mark was feeling like he needed not just a bath, but also a scrubbing. The more he peeled back this onion, the more filth fell out.

Why don't nice, wholesome people ever kill one another? Mark picked up the copied DVDs and told Phil how much he appreciated his help, all the while heading for the door as quickly as he could get there. The last thing he heard was Phil asking, "Say, if you ever want to get together and, you know, maybe hang out or something, just let me know."

Mark was closing the door when he smiled back at Phil and gave him the thumbs-up sign.

Chapter 14

Driving away from the apartments, Mark was glad to be away from Phil Wright, but anxious to go over the information he had gathered and to view the tapes. When he arrived at his office, he went back through the notes he had written and then watched the first sex tape.

The woman du jour for Luke that evening proved quickly to Mark she wasn't either of two things: number one, the killer; and secondly, sober. Shortly into the tape, she vomited on Luke while appearing to attempt some type of rhythmless strip tease dance. Mark felt like vomiting himself before he could switch off this clearly not-ready-for-center-stage dance queen.

The second DVD featured Luke with a tall black woman. While any man would have appreciated her beauty, not to mention flexibility, Mark knew that barring a skin pigmentation transplant, she obviously wasn't the killer either. He fast-forwarded through the tape to make sure no others were brought into the action later before popping out the DVD.

This was the part of the job that Mark hated the most: peering into people's secret lives. The woman he had just watched may have been a prostitute playing a role, or she may have been a grade school teacher or emergency room nurse in need of some excitement; Mark had no way of knowing. But he had just watched her in a most intimate situation that she may very well not have known was even being recorded. Mark knew it was a violation of this woman, and he always felt sleazy about it.

Those feelings morphed into something different when Mark pushed play on the third DVD. On it, he watched Kim Jacobsen having sex with a young couple. The young woman was blonde, looked to be in her early twenties and had several tattoos, but there was nothing angelic about her. The man was thin and also probably in his early to mid-twenties, covered in tats, and incredibly well hung. But not more than Kim could handle. Kim dominated the three-way action, albeit with an eye on the camera the entire time. She loved the camera and the attention it offered her.

Even when the man was inside her, Kim seemed infatuated only with the fact that she was being filmed and made sure she was facing the camera throughout. When the young woman went down on her, Kim rested on her elbows and seductively shook out her hair so that it dropped down and covered one eye, leaving her other eye to watch the camera as it worshipped her.

And worship her it did. Kim may have been in her early forties, but her nude body remained glorious. Fit, slender, augmented by the finest surgeons and Brazilian waxed, most men would have forbid her to ever even wear clothes.

Luke on the other hand, clearly had not forbid Kim from anything. Hell, he was taping his wife having sex with a scrungy couple of kids she probably barely knew, and then giving a copy to his friend across the hall. What the fuck was wrong with people? How can you get off watching your wife getting pile-driven by some greasy- haired fuck with a twelve-inch schlong? It was beyond Mark, who turned off the DVD in disgust.

He got up from his desk and paced around his office. This whole mess sickened him. How could a woman behave in such a fashion—much less a beautiful and wealthy one?

Mark poured three fingers of Crown Royale over ice and sat back down to ponder this question. As he sipped the Canadian whiskey, the one truth he had learned since becoming a private investigator filled his mind and gripped him with fear: if you dance with the Devil, it's always the Devil that winds up leading.

Mark couldn't let this happen and understood he would have to be very careful dealing with this Kim devil. But could he? The threat was getting so close to this type person that their behavior seemed normal, that it was no big deal. Hell, everybody did it, right? Well, no they didn't. Right?

By the time the second glass of Crown was dry, Mark wasn't so sure. He had watched several more tapes: a couple with women who fit the general look of the killer, at least without the angel tattoo, and two more featuring Kim. The DVDs were sexual, but certainly not intimate. This was debauchery that rivaled Rome's Caligula, and no one appeared to be having a better time than Kim.

In one, she worked a Spanish man in her mouth all the while keeping eye contact with the camera. It was as if she wanted every man who watched the DVD to feel it was them she really desired, and this time it was

Mark who was watching.

He turned the tape off, and then a few moments later, back on again. He knew what kind of woman Kim was; growing up with his father, he had seen many like her. Okay, they didn't look like her, but they were the same. But Kim was so alluring, her eyes so inviting.

Mark wondered if this is what had happened to his dad? One particular woman proved so seductive that it led downward to a life with so many other women and so much hurt to his family? Mark wouldn't take the chance. He turned the laptop off and headed home.

At that moment he needed home; he needed to be with his beautiful wife and his equally beautiful daughter. On the way home, he phoned Yo-Yo and told her he loved her and not to worry about dinner. A quick stop by Eatzi's and he was off again with two pounds of Mediterranean beef tips; a large gemelli, mozzarella and tomato salad; and three of Yo-Yo's favorites, Normandy pear and blueberry tarts. Mark needed home, and he needed a good meal. He needed his family.

The following morning, he awoke with a clearer, though still unsettled mind. As he drove to the police station, he thought of the night before. Yo-Yo had been surprised by the dinner and in her gratitude had told him very suggestively what to expect as soon as Lily went to bed. Then with their daughter safely asleep, Mark had pretended to be too tired and had asked for a rain check.

Yo-Yo had hidden her hurt feelings, but it was Mark who was really hurting. He had refused to make love to his wife because he was afraid he would have had some thought of Kim, some thought of one of her positions or moves he had seen on the DVDs, and he was afraid he would have suggested that Yo-Yo do this. His wife was beautiful and sexy, and he was afraid he might allow thoughts of some tramp to affect their relationship.

That whole thought pissed him off and caused him to push his Charger through traffic and up to almost ninety-five on Stemmons Freeway. He raced past a startled Prius driver and then cut right in front of a yellow Volkswagen to make the Oak Lawn exit. Two minutes later, he was parking at the station and on his way to meet with Detective Coleman.

Police are funny. If anyone ever leaves the force before retirement, that person is viewed with suspicion, even contempt. Mark was no different. As he walked through the station and passed several officers he had known during his time with the force, he felt their eyes. No "good mornings" or "how's the kids," only cold stares.

These officers knew Mark hadn't resigned because he was weak; hell, they each knew Mark could give an ass whipping to any cop on the force, but that didn't change their feelings towards him. He had quit; he wasn't to be trusted, and he was, after all, his father's son. With head down, Mark never broke stride until he was knocking on Coleman's door.

Once inside John's office, Mark realized he was interrupting a meeting between Coleman and the FBI's evil dwarf genius, Ron Ellis. After an apology and proper greetings, Mark sat down and told the men of what he had learned and of the DVDs.

This instantly ignited Ellis. "Do you have the tapes?" he demanded.

"These are the ones with women who come close to the general description," Mark said, laying out several on the desk.

"But you have others?" Ellis countered immediately.

Mark nodded. "Yeah, but I went through them and don't think any of the others have any link to the murders. No reason to invade all these people's privacy."

This response didn't sit well with Ellis. "We got some kind of fucking ACLU shithead lawyer up here worried about people's privacy. How many dead bodies we gotta fuckin' pile up before you stop worrying about people's precious privacy?"

"You better check yourself real quick and tone your little Hobbit ass down," said Mark, quickly standing up. "Nobody talks to me like that."

John Coleman lowered his head and smiled while Mark set the boundaries for Ellis.

"Are we clear on things," Mark asked after an awkward moment of continued silence and Ellis seething. Ellis didn't flinch or answer. "I'm talking to you, you little Ernie Keebler-looking motherfucker."

With this, Coleman jumped between the two men. As ill fated as it would have doubtlessly proven, Ellis was about to go combat on Mark when Coleman grabbed him. "I've known Mark since he was a young boy. He can be trusted. He's a former cop, and if he says there's nothing else on the DVDs, there's nothing else on the DVDs!"

"Are there any redheads on the tapes?" Ellis queried, slowly beginning to unwind.

"What? A redhead? Have you found some hair samples?" Coleman looked surprised as well.

"No I just wondered," Ellis answered. "Don't try and

tell me ya'll don't think redheads are sexy as hell." This took both Mark and John aback.

"Come on, it's like Clinton said, redheads only come two ways, dog ugly or hotter than fuck," Ellis went on. "But when you get a hot one, oh shit, you gotta watch out."

John nodded. "Yeah, I think I remember him saying that at one of the State of the Union addresses."

This helped to lighten the mood in the room where the three men stayed for the next two hours discussing the case. Though he was terribly bad with first impressions, before the meeting was over Mark could well see the brilliance of Ellis. Ron spoke of evidence in an analytical and authoritative manner and then just as easily spoke of the killer's presumed emotional motivations.

Even though he had been on the case only slightly longer than Mark, Ron had a depth of understanding of the facts and retention of those facts from each of the murders that was amazing. The little man had a big mind. He clearly understood the biblical significance and told of how Quantico was running the information through all their computerized Bible codes looking for possible matches.

Mark learned much more during the meeting than he offered, and he did so by keeping his mouth shut and listening to Ellis. What stuck with Mark the most was the last thing Ron said. "Today is the twenty-seventh day since the last murder. If we don't find the killer in the next few hours, we'll have another Matthew, Mark, Luke or John dead before morning."

~~~

Across town, at about 4:30 p.m., Matthew Owens

started his workout at Lifetime Fitness. He had been up in an attic checking on his men while they changed a condenser earlier and left with his shirt soaked with sweat from the attic heat. Not wanting to deal with the problem of going home to shower and then leaving again, Matt decided to hit the gym and use the shower there to get ready for his big date with Angel.

Besides, it would boost his confidence to get a good pump in and be feeling good about his body before his meeting later with her. After all, Matt had a certain feeling that if he played his cards right, tonight just might be his lucky night. An hour later, after finishing one last set of incline presses to fool himself into thinking he had a chiseled and defined chest, Matt hit the showers.

When he got out and toweled off, Matt found himself grinning like a sixteen-year-old kid. The anticipation of seeing Angel had consumed him for the last two days, and now the meeting was almost here. As he applied Axe body spray over his body, paying close attention to his private area, Matt was struck with how excited he felt.

Though he had met a few tempting housewives in his A/C career, he had never cheated on his wife. He didn't really know if he would be cheating tonight; maybe Angel would just want to talk and hang out, but it felt like cheating to Matt, and it felt good. It felt electric; it felt like living, and Matt was tired of watching life pass him by. He was tired of the regrets he had from missed opportunities. He was ready to live.

As he pulled the tag off and slipped into a new fashionable T-shirt he had bought that afternoon from Macy's, Matt was ready for whatever the evening brought him. A quick splash of Woods cologne, purchased from Abercrombie and Fitch to ensure just the right amount of hipness, and Matt was out of the locker room. He left the gym and walked across the parking lot to his pickup, feeling younger and more alive than he had felt in years.

When Matt arrived at the offices for Air Express around 6:45, he was dismayed to see Phyllis Black's car still parked outside. Phyllis pretty much handled everything for Matt from accounts receivable to dispatching, but damn, enough was enough. She was divorced with grown children and all, but geez, get home to the cats already.

"What are you still doing here?" Matt asked as he strode into the office.

"I'm trying to get the payroll checks ready for in the morning," a surprised Phyllis answered defensively.

"I'll finish 'em up," Matt said. "You just go on and get out of here. There's no reason for you to work ten or eleven hours every day."

A grateful Phyllis got up and retrieved her Tupperware dish from the refrigerator and then looked at Matt. "Don't you look nice; you got plans?"

"Yeah, Mom, I gotta hot date," he playfully answered. "Might not be home till the morning."

She smiled and nodded as she walked past him to leave. "Okay, Romeo, see you in the morning."

"I'll be here," Matthew answered prophetically.

Matt impatiently waited for Phyllis, sitting in her car in the parking lot, to leave. He watched from the window as she chatted on the phone for what seemed like fifteen minutes. When she left at last, he broke into action, cleaning the office, spraying air freshener, taking the cheap girlie calendars off the warehouse walls. He wanted things to look as impressive as possible for Angel. Finally, around 7:30, she called and said she was on her way.

"Great," Matt said, feeling like he was about to greet his prom date. "Just hurry." He was ready to pop when a little before eight, Angel's maroon Acura pulled into the Air Express lot and parked.

Through his office window, Matt watched her slowly get out of her car. When Angel finally straightened up, he saw that she was wearing a white, button-front top along with tight and oh-so-low slung jeans, revealing an uncovered naval on the topside and high boots on the bottom. Taking in this view made Matt feel like his body had suddenly been plugged into an electrical outlet — like when he was in the eighth grade and sneaked into the high school gym to watch the cheerleaders practice.

As Matt stood there, Angel glided across the parking lot towards him. He noted the large zebra print bag hung over one shoulder and the two six packs of Corona Lights she carried. She beamed as Matt held the front door open for her. When she leaned in and gave him a quick peck on the cheek, her gold cross necklace tangled in Matt's t-shirt. After some close, intricate movements, Angel got the necklace untangled.

"Darn, I was hoping you'd have to stay that close all night," a disappointed Matt joked.

"After a couple of beers, who knows, maybe I will."

Matt could only smile at her for what seemed like an awkwardly long amount of time until she bailed him out, asking, "Aren't you gonna show me around?"

After the obligatory tour of the business, Matt

showed her into his office. Angel looked around the office, taking in the certificates hanging on his wall and his golf outing photos, before settling into a large leather chair across from Matt's desk.

"Let me guess; I bet right here is where all the high level A/C decisions get made, right in this chair," she asked.

"That, and some afternoon naps." They shared another smile, and he asked, "Have you thought where you might want to go tonight?"

"Yeah, I have. Tell me, do you like Emmy Lou Harris?"

"Sure," said Matt, who had always loved the unusual and iconic sound of Emmy Lou's voice. Before he could say another word, Angel pulled a portable stereo out from the zebra print bag and popped in Emmy Lou's 1977 released classic CD, Luxury Liner. She twisted off two Corona lids and handed one of the beers to Matt.

"Mind if we stay here? Don't know how long I'll be able to stay out tonight."

With Emmy Lou softly singing Chuck Berry's "You can never tell, C'est La Vie", in the background, Matt didn't mind at all. The first six pack of Coronas seemed to empty themselves. The two talked, laughed and drank freely. As Angel pulled out the first bottle from the second six pack, she asked him a question. "You know when we first met at the race? Were you running behind me just to so you could watch my ass?"

"What?" Matt feigned ignorance. "I don't know what you're talking about."

"So I ran three miles clinching my ass cheeks together for you, and you didn't even notice?" Angel said, feigning hurt feelings.

"Never said I didn't notice. Believe me, I noticed."

Standing with the new bottle in her hand, Angel decided not to sit back down in the leather chair. Instead, she smiled and walked around behind the desk to where Matt was sitting. Emmy Lou was soulfully singing the timeless Kitty Wells country classic "Making Believe," when Angel stepped over Matt's legs and straddled him between his chair and desk. "Maybe you'd like to do more than just notice it," she purred.

Setting her beer down on the desk, Angel took both Matt's hands and pulled them around her, placing them on her ass. As he closed his eyes and began to make love to her ass with his hands, Angel bent lower and kissed him. One kiss led to twenty more, until she slid her hand down on the outside of his pants and began to grind on his dick. A moment later, when she began to lick and bite his earlobe, Matt knew something had to give.

He stood and started pulling his t-shirt over his head. With it off, Angel nestled her face between his pecs. She kissed his chest, while he struggled to get his pants off. "Just sit back, baby."

"No, come on, I want inside you," he whispered in her ear.

"I can't. You're gonna hate me, but it's that time of the month. Next time, I promise."

She pushed him back down in his chair, roughly pulled off his boxers and kneeled to take him in her mouth. For the next several minutes, Matt ran his fingers through her hair and watched her mouth. He couldn't decide which he loved better, the way he felt or the way she looked. Before he erupted, Matt's eyes felt like slot machines spinning in his head, as he was about to hit the jackpot. When it was done, his whole body slumped back into his chair. With his eyes closed, he felt indescribable. He smiled to himself knowing Angel had just given him the orgasm of a lifetime.

After regaining control a few seconds later, Matt relaxed another moment and tried to think of something wonderful or at least witty to say. When it came to him, he opened his eyes just in time to see Angel slash a huge knife across his throat. Terror-stricken, he instinctively reached for his throat to try and contain the spurting blood, but Angel finished the job by burying the knife into his upper chest.

With Matt now dead, Angel went to work. From her zebra bag she pulled out a pair of rubber gloves and a plastic trash bag. In the bag went each of the beers and the cartons. Next out was the Dustbuster mini vacuum, and Angel gave the entire place a military style cleaning.

She looked out the office window to make sure no one was close by, and then she pulled out a bottle of bleach to clean away any possible prints. Not wanting to leave any possible DNA containing saliva to be found, Angel next carefully cleaned off Matt's dick, ear and mouth with a box of handy wipes.

When she was satisfied that everything was spotless, Angel placed all the cleaning products in the trash bag alongside the beer bottles. Setting the bag by the office door, Angel put the Dustbuster back inside her bag and pulled out three other items she had brought especially for the evening. The first was a jacket to go over her now bloodstained top, the second a Bible that she placed on Matt's desk, and the third was a ruler. Now ready to proceed, Angel withdrew the knife from

Matt's chest and used both the knife and ruler to complete her work on him.

When she was done, she couldn't help but stand back with pride and look at what she had accomplished. Yes, it's true that men were dying, but men are pigs, and at least these pigs are getting the reward of dying for a purpose, she thought. A purpose and a message that all men needed to hear, and Angel was proud to be the messenger.

Pulling off the rubber gloves, she walked out the front door and placed the plastic bag and the zebra bag in her car's trunk. She drove slowly away from Air Express and straight to the Hampton Inn on Highway 360 in Grand Prairie. Angel had rented a room there earlier in the day, and she went back to change before going home.

In room 312 she showered and washed away the fake tattoos that adorned her lower back and arm. Out of the shower, she leaned close to the mirror while cleaning off the eyeliner that she would never wear around her husband. Once her normal clothes were on, Angel picked up each piece of the clothing she had worn that evening and placed them all in another plastic trash bag.

As Angel headed home, she made two stops in different apartment complexes. She tossed a trash bag of evidence into each apartment's dumpster. Then only blocks away from her house, she wrapped the murder weapon in a dishrag and threw it off a bridge and into Lake Arlington.

As she pulled into her garage, Angel was proud that no hair, fiber, or weapon would be found. Nothing would point to her. This, along with what she had done that evening, made her happy. That happiness showed as she went inside to be welcomed home by her husband and child.

Chapter 15

The next morning, at 7:20 a.m., Phyllis Black pulled into the Air Express parking lot and parked her Camry next to Matt's pickup. As usual, they were the first two to make it in to the office.

Inside, Phyllis thought it odd that Matt had his office door closed. After a short while spent putting away her things and checking email, she decided to ask Matt if he wanted her to get the coffeemaker started. She knocked on his door as she pushed it open. Phyllis let out a horrified scream and dropped the blueberry muffin she was holding when she saw Matt's nude and dead body still sitting in his desk chair.

~~~

Neither Detective Coleman nor Special Agent Ellis was surprised to get the call. In less than a half hour, Air Express was a crime scene and the police and forensic teams converged on it. When Coleman and Ellis reached the location, John was happy to find that only Mary Trevino and her assistant Belcher were inside with the body.

As Coleman ducked under the police tape, he was proud this investigation, at least in the beginning, looked like it was being done by the book. A boundary had been established, two uniformed cops were already questioning the mechanics who worked at the garage next door, and others were canvassing the nearby neighborhood. So far so good.

Ellis entered Matt's office ahead of Coleman and went straight to the body. Practically pushing aside Belcher, he took one look and yelled for Coleman, who had stopped to speak with one of the uniforms.

John rushed inside the office and saw what Ellis wanted him to see. Next to the gaping chest wound on Matt's body was a large cross that the killer had carved into his torso. "The bitch is playin' us. Look at that cross. It's perfect."

Coleman stepped closer to get a better look when Belcher unfortunately decided to offer his insight. "Most likely the cross was made after he was already dead."

Ellis was never one to suffer fools. "Really?" he shot back angrily. "You think so? You don't think this dumb shit didn't just lie down and let her cut a cross right in the middle of his goddamn chest before she killed him? Goddammit, if I ever want to be a fuckin' serial killer, I'm sure as hell moving to Dallas. You'd have to be retarded to ever get caught in this town."

After an awkward moment, Ellis repeated his earlier statement, "Look at the cross. It's perfect."

Coleman had seen the cross up close and nodded in agreement; the lines on the cross did appear to be perfectly straight.

"No way she just freehanded the cross that straight and centered right in the middle of his chest," Ellis continued.

Belcher was still licking his wounds and not about to open his mouth again, but Trevino stepped in, saying,

"Before you started insulting my man, he found something else out about that cross."

Coleman and Ellis were all ears.

"What?" asked John.

"It's nineteen by nine inches," Mary continued. "Exactly. The vertical line of the cross is nineteen inches long and the horizontal line is nine inches across. And I mean right to the inch."

At this news, Ellis began to pace the room. The handiwork provided by the killer's ruler meant something, but what? Little Ron began to think out loud as he walked around the office. "She's getting bored. She thinks we'll never find her unless she helps us out. And, why does this whole thing look so different from all the other scenes? Hell, did the guy even get his nuts off before she killed him? Did he?"

Before Mary could answer, patrolman Nick Lowery stuck his head in and said to Detective Coleman, "There's something you gotta know."

This shut up Ron, and Coleman said to the officer, "What is it?"

"The woman who found the body, the one that works here, she says she moved the guy and put his pants back on," Lowery answered.

Coleman closed his eyes in disbelief and Ellis let out a string of expletives. Lowery went on, "She said she didn't want pictures taken of him like that or for his wife to see what had happened."

Knowing that moving the body would almost certainly have compromised any forensic evidence, John Coleman let out a dejected sigh. Ellis, on the other hand, appeared angry enough to run and knock a hole, albeit a small hole, through the side of the building.

Sensing a lost cause, Coleman put his arm around Ellis and they started to make their way out.

"Just do what you can, and let me know if you find anything else," John said to Mary as he was leaving.

Heading for the front door, the fire from Ellis' eyes practically burnt a hole through the distraught Phyllis. Between her sobs, the weeping Ms. Black was crying to no one in particular how she had found her boss. The mere sight of this further incensed Ellis. Phyllis wailed how she had moved the body in order to get Mr. Owens' pants back on, and how her own blouse had become so covered in poor Matt's blood she returned home and changed clothes before calling police. She continued and said how it was all going to be such a shame for Matthew's family, how they were fine people, and she didn't know what she was going to tell them or their customers, and as she babbled on and on it was apparent she had no idea the impact her words were having on Ron Ellis. Mercifully, John got the FBI agent out of the office shortly before Ellis lost control and choked the living shit out of her.

~~~

Angel was watching a local channel when news broke in about the latest apparent Gospel killing. When she heard the ring of her cell phone, she glanced at the incoming number and let out a sigh before answering.

"Looks like somebody was busy last night," said the voice on the other end.

"Idle hands are the devil's workshop," Angel answered.

A booming laugh followed and then the man said, "I need to see you."

It was a call Angel dreaded because she knew what

"I need to see you" really meant. It meant meeting the man she called "Short Timer"—the one with the elderly, flabby ass—and letting him wallow on top of her, and, worse still, penetrate her. The wallowing might only last a few minutes—hence one of the reasons for his nickname—but the feeling and nausea lingered so much longer.

She agreed to meet but said, "Give me a couple of days." Angel agreed to meet because she still needed Short Timer. He had taught her so much. It was Short Timer who had taught her to never use the computer to contact any of the men. He had made up the original lists of things for Angel to take with her, things to properly clean a crime scene with. And it was Short Timer who had told her to use a serrated-edged knife for the killings like the actual Gospel Killer; and to always dispose of everything quickly afterwards, all clothes, shoes, supplies—everything, and all at different sites.

Short Timer had also taught her to dress in a certain way and helped her to come up with the idea to use the tattoos as a way to draw people's attention away from her face. Any possible attention from a witness would be focused on her tattoos or attire and not her face. Short Timer had helped her learn how most killers are caught and the amateurish ways most are tripped up. The entire plan and message was Angel's, but she still had more to learn from Short Timer. And, when she had learned all he knew, she knew just what she was going to do with him.

But until then, she would have to pretend to enjoy his crude advances, pretend his wrinkled hands on her skin didn't sicken her. Angel had read a book long ago by the famed motivational speaker Zig Ziglar and learned, "To get what you want, give others what they want." She took this advice to heart and would allow him once more to force her to her knees and enter her from behind, a position which really worked best for her anyway because it meant she wouldn't have to look at him.

But beyond that, it was all right because he was getting what he wanted, which in turn meant that Angel would get what she wanted. One day soon, however, Short Timer would have nothing left to teach Angel and then he would be Out of Timer.

Chapter 16

It was close to 10:30 a.m., and Mark was livid. Trying to get to Kim Jacobsen's house for a meeting about the case, he found himself stuck in a colossal goat fuck of a traffic jam along Highway 635. Locally, the highway was known as LBJ after former president Lyndon Baines Johnson and routinely had by far the area's heaviest traffic, but this morning was different. The cars weren't moving at all.

Finally, Mark saw the flashing lights of Dallas' fire and police rescue units several exits ahead of his Charger. He later learned that two ambitious young women were trying to catch a nice morning buzz on their way to work when the driver dropped a doobie on her mini skirt, causing her to sharply veer out of the HOV lane to keep from burning her leg. Unfortunately, her new BMW skidded into a twelve-passenger van, causing a chain-reaction pile-up of eight cars.

The skirt and leg survived, but the driver got a DUI and a possession charge out of the morning commute. The passenger in the ill-fated BMW fared better. She pleaded out no contest, got deferred adjudication and merely had to get a little repair work done on her recent rhinoplasty.

By the time Mark was finally able to get to Kim's

house, he had spoken with Detective Coleman and had learned of the latest murder. John had filled him in with the preliminary information and told him how the secretary had moved the body and in all likelihood contaminated any possible evidence. Coleman also told Mark of the cross cut into the victim's chest.

As the two men spoke of possible meanings of the cross and how it marked a difference with the other murders, Mark was struck with how strange Coleman sounded. He had never heard John so deflated, so out of answers. Mark knew his friend was under tremendous pressure because of these unsolved murders and feared John was headed to a bad and dark place.

Not really one to offer "Let's win one for the Gipper" pep talks, Mark nonetheless tried to raise John's spirits. He asked if the cross left in Matt Owens' chest was carved right side up or upside down? When John answered it was right side up, Mark responded that was good. An upside down cross signaled satanic symbols, but if the cross was still right side up, then the killer was still in the same frame of mind as during the other killings. Even if the cross were new, the meaning would be similar. The closer to the same mental approach, the closer they would come to finding the murderer. The clues were there; they were going to find the killer.

As he kept talking, Mark didn't know if he really believed what he was saying himself or even if it made much sense, but it did seem to hearten Coleman. Determination came back into John's voice. This strengthened Mark, who kept thinking out loud to John. Mark was soon pumped about finding the killer bitch. Hell, before they hung up, the two of them seemed to be convinced they would have the Gospel Killer in custody before the evening news. Oh well, the best laid plans...

From her entryway, Kim watched Mark as he sat in her driveway and finished the conversation with Coleman. When Mark got out and started walking towards the door, Kim checked her lipstick in the mirror and unbuttoned the third button on her blouse.

She looked out the entryway at Mark as he walked toward her. There was something about his walk—shoulders out, head high, athletic movement. This was a proud walk, a walk of a confident man who could handle himself—and nothing was more sensual to Kim than a confident man.

Although she was watching from behind the front door, she didn't open it and greet him. Instead, Kim made Mark ring the ornate bell. The bell's deep baritone ringing sounded as if it could have come from St. Patrick's in downtown Manhattan or perhaps some European cathedral. She watched through the keyhole as Mark looked upward to appreciate the grand doorbell.

She found him alluring, but it was important to Kim that he always knew his place, and for now his place was to be the hired hand—albeit a very pretty hired hand for a very pretty and wealthy and active widow. In her mind, the possibilities were endless and oh so delicious. After a moment more and with one last fluff of her hair, she opened the door.

Mark entered as Kim apologized for taking so long to reach the front door, saying something about giving Ana the day off. He followed her into the living area and couldn't help but notice her hips sliding side to side as she walked; he thought of melted butter oozing off a biscuit, before you pick it up and turn it just a little so that the butter changes direction before trying to escape off the other side. And this was some biscuit. Instantly Mark began feeling nervous. He hated the way Kim distracted him, and he hated that Ana wasn't working today.

Trying to keep it strictly business, Mark declined Kim's offer of something to drink and started telling her what he had found out. He let her know that actual evidence gathered from the murder scenes was almost nonexistent and that most of what he and the police thought they knew was really no more than guesswork. Mark told her that police had found no connection between any of the victims, other than the similar manner in which each man was killed and the fact that a Bible was placed near each of their dead bodies.

Upon hearing of the Bible's, Kim surprised Mark by asking, "Are you religious?"

He glanced up from his notes at this question and found Kim staring at him deeply, straight into his eyes like she seemed to do while performing on the sex DVD's he had gathered from the apartment. Was she still playing him?

"I mean I'm sure you are," she added, before he could answer. "Marcus said you went to seminary school."

Mark didn't like the reference, veiled or not, of Marcus, and he certainly did not like her knowing his and Marcus' secret. After another awkward pause, Mark answered, "I'm not sure if I'm religious, not now anyway… But yeah, I believe in God."

Now it was his turn to look closely at her. Kim was pouring herself a sparkling water when he answered.

She finished the drink by cutting a thin lemon slice and dropping it into the water. Knowing full well he was watching, she took the remaining lemon and placed it in her mouth. Raising her head and making direct eye contact with Mark, she started to suck the lemon. Without so much as the slightest sour face, she kept slowly sucking until juice began to drip downward and glaze her chin. Smiling, she pulled the spent lemon slice from her mouth and wiped the juice away with the back of her hand. Watching closely for a response from Mark, she offered, "Yeah. I think I believe in God, too."

At that moment, Mark tried to mentally digest what she had just done. What she was trying to get him to do. He couldn't deny he was both aroused and disgusted. Sensing his weakness, Kim walked over and sat beside Mark. "They say God forgives. Jesus even forgave Mary Magdalene."

"I'm not Jesus," Mark said, looking deeply into her smiling eyes. Standing up, he matter-of-factly added, "Listen, I'm not gonna be your fuck buddy. Not now or ever."

She slinked back into the sofa, and Mark now had the upper hand. "You hired me to try and catch your husband's killer. That is the extent of our relationship."

Not used to being rejected, Kim took a moment and finally said, "I guess your wife really must be something then, huh?"

At her mention of Yo-Yo, Mark's blood pressure went way north. "Yeah she is," he managed to say. "And you don't need to ever mention her again."

Feeling Mark's tension rise, Kim relented. "Sorry, I'm sorry. Okay, all work and no play then. So about the case then, if there's no evidence, how do you find the killer?"

"Somebody knows something," Mark answered. "Cases like this can get moving with a reward."

"A reward? You mean like the Old West Wanted Dead or Alive kind?"

"Pretty much, without the Dead or Alive part anyway," he replied. "Serial killers usually aren't trusting or social people; they don't share their actions or dreams with too many others, but if enough money is offered, someone will think of something. A brother or sister, a co-worker, a neighbor, someone will remember something and believe they know who it is. Sooner or later one of them will be right."

"How much do you need?" Kim asked, standing up and thinking over what Mark had just said.

"It will need to be big. I'd say a hundred thousand will get things rolling."

"Stop thinking small," she smiled and said almost demurely. "Make it $500,000."

Mark assured her he would make the arrangements for the reward and the public announcement. As he was leaving, she was already planning a new outfit she could wear. True to herself though, she was not so deep in thought to not peer out the window and appreciate how Mark's jeans hugged his ass as he was bending down to get into his Charger. Ahh, such a waste.

Chapter 17

Mark rented a well-appointed conference room in Dallas' historic Adolphus Hotel for the afternoon press conference announcing the reward. The hotel was located in downtown Dallas near the three local television news stations as well as the headquarters for the venerable Dallas Morning News. Mark selected a 2:30 starting time to allow the TV stations plenty of time to make the 5:00 p.m. news. He needn't have worried as the whole thing went viral by 3:15.

Shortly before the start of the press conference, Mark and Detective Coleman were drinking coffee in the back of the room and chatting with newspaper reporter Daryl Blackman when an audible gasp erupted from the male-dominated press corps. Kim Jacobsen had arrived. She entered the room wearing a wine-colored, woven, taffeta shirt over a silk paisley skirt accented with a trench buckle belt and calfskin equestrian boots. Kim immediately sent the cameras into overdrive. She walked confidently through the gathering and sat down at one of the three chairs next to the podium. When she smiled and pulled off her black cat eye sunglasses, Mark and Coleman shrugged at each other and decided it must be time to get things started.

Mark began by telling everyone the purpose of the news conference. He introduced both Detective Coleman and Kim Jacobsen and then turned the podium over to John. Coleman had checked with Chief Harrison and DPD media coordinator Jocelyn Cox on how best to describe the police department's stance on the reward being offered for the Gospel Killer. He spoke of the huge amount of man-hours being devoted to the case and then, for the sake of public relations, fibbed and said the police had also garnered significant amounts of forensic evidence. In closing his short remarks, John spoke of the danger posed by these crimes and asked for assistance from the public in apprehending the killer.

Next up was Mark again. He alternated from reading his prepared statement to speaking off the cuff to the reporters. He read that a $500,000 reward was being offered for information leading to the arrest and conviction of the so-called Gospel Killer. He continued with the details concerning how both he and Detective Coleman could be contacted and how anonymity could be insured, if so desired.

Setting the statement down, Mark told the reporters that while gains had been made, the reward was being offered to hopefully bring a faster resolution to the situation. He asked for understanding from the media regarding the fact that certain details from the killings had been kept from them. Mark continued by saying that it was those details that could possibly be provided by that particular someone with direct knowledge of the killer.

As Mark spoke of the biblical significance and symbolism involved in the killings, he felt he was beginning to lose the audience. Just as he was about to implore the public for assistance, Kim changed positions in her seat and, much to the appreciation of the cameramen, re-crossed her legs. Mark knew his moment was gone and asked that the widow Jacobsen please step forward. Kim didn't need any extra urging.

She started by speaking about her husband, Luke Jacobsen, and the life the two of them shared together, how they had met and how Luke had been such a wonderful husband to her. She spoke of his success and of his generosity; his personal warmth and caring; his love for animals, the outdoors and of children. Strangely, she did not talk of his love for other women.

Mark was seated in a chair next to her on the podium, and he couldn't help but be amazed at how Kim handled the situation. While she spoke, the cameras clicked on her at NASCAR speed, and she seemingly offered a demure smile for each one. She never bobbled over a single word, and Mark knew the breathless press corps would be having wet dreams of her for weeks. As she continued and spoke further about Luke, one could only assume that word of possible sainthood would be soon forthcoming. She worked the room like Wayne Newton works the Hilton; the press wasn't just hearing hers and Luke's story – they were feeling it.

Before beginning about why she had decided to offer the reward, Kim stopped to take a drink of water. After setting the glass down on the table and seeing the cameras were following her every move, she turned and took Mark's hand in hers. Kim closed her eyes and gently squeezed his hand, as if to draw strength from him and perhaps even from Luke above. The cameras loved it, just as she had planned. Mark knew he had been used as a prop in her play, and he knew he would no doubt hear about it later from Yo-Yo when he got home. But, there was no stopping Kim; the lady was on a serious roll.

As if Mark's hands strengthened her, Kim looked out at the press corps and continued. She said she was offering the reward for the conviction of the killer because of loss—because of the loss she and so many of Luke's family and friends were now feeling. And, though the loss she felt was at times unbearable, she knew it would be much worse if she sat back and did nothing to try and prevent others from suffering a similar loss.

With perfect timing, tears appeared and started to slowly trek their way down her cheeks. Kim paused to dab away the tears, and the press was glued to her. As they inched closer to her, Mark sat there trying hard to suppress his amazement at Kim's performance. What she was selling the press had been much different than what she had told him privately about her reasons for wanting the killer apprehended. It made him feel a little sleazy sitting there and being a part of such a charade, but sleazy went with the job description for a private investigator. Besides, Mark did realize that this performance would play so much better publicly.

With the tears now wiped away and seeming magically to not have affected her makeup, Kim finished by saying that in addition to the $500,000 reward, she would also be making a similar half-million-dollar donation in Luke's name to the renowned Children's Medical Center of Dallas. She began to cry, softly at first, when she said her biggest regret had been not being able to give Luke a child of his own, and that she hoped the gift to the Children's Hospital would be his legacy.

The crying began to accelerate when Kim said she hoped the donation would help area children and their parents in difficult times. "And if it does, I know that would make Luke so happy," she managed to get out. "Knowing that will get me through this."

Now sobbing, Kim turned and buried her head in Mark's shoulder. He hesitated and then put his arm around her shoulders as the cameras zoomed in. While he was thinking how he could explain this picture to Yo-Yo, Kim looked up and asked him to get her out of there. Mark obliged and played like a fullback, leading Kim through the hole as he plowed through the press corps line of defense.

In the hotel's hallway and with the press in quick pursuit, Kim told him to take the elevators. Mark caught an open elevator door and the two of them hopped in just as some idiot photographer lunged forward and snapped a picture of the two of them together. Mark pushed the camera and hand back out into the hallway so the doors could close, and then closed his eyes, thinking about what he had just witnessed and once again, how he could possibly explain it to Yo-Yo. When he opened his eyes, the elevator was rising and Kim handed him a room key.

"I got us a room. Thought you might need to unwind," was all she said as she was staring at herself in the elevator mirror and checking her mascara.

Taken aback, Mark asked, "So what was that performance in the press conference all about?"

"Come on, you're a big boy," Kim turned to him and said. "You know the easiest lie to tell someone is to tell them what they want to hear. So I played the grieving widow. So what? That was for them; this can be for us."

Mark hit the button for the fourth floor. "Listen, there will never be an us. You can call or email me to check on the case, but I don't ever want to see you again," he said as the doors opened and he got out of the elevator.

When the doors closed, with Mark in the hall and Kim standing in the elevator, it would have been a coin flip as to which one was the most pissed.

Chapter 18

The Charger and Mark barreled out of the Adolphus' underground parking garage like Marines storming a beach, with neither being in the mood to take any prisoners. Mark's head was spinning from the press conference and the elevator scene when a Dallas Area Rapid Transit bus stopped almost right in front of him to let off all two of its passengers.

Tires squealed and Mark gave the overweight Hispanic driver a "screw you" look when he swerved around the bus to avoid it. He didn't let it keep him down for long though as he punched the Hemi and zoomed through a yellow light at Commerce and Elm streets. A moment later, he was eastbound on I-35, and by the time he passed the Oak Lawn exit, he was pushing well past eighty.

Passing cars like proverbial fence posts, Mark's mind was on Kim and what she had pulled on him. Did she really think all she had to do to get him in bed was to dangle a room key? Maybe back in his single days it would have been Mark throwing down the room key for an attractive widow worth tens of millions of dollars, but not now. No woman could ever make Mark feel complete like Yo-Yo did, and he couldn't fathom how she and Kim Jacobsen could even be of the same species.

Concerning women, Mark felt that they always looked different to him after getting to know them, either better or worse. Yo-Yo was like a Reese's peanut butter cup for Mark, great on the outside and even tastier inside. Kim was so different, seductive on the outside but tainted and spoiled inside. The inside was all Mark could see now, and it pissed him off that he had taken this job in the first place and had to have any contact with her at all.

Around 183 and Loop 12, near where the old and now torn-down Texas Stadium (home of the Dallas Cowboys) used to sit, traffic slowed and Mark was forced to downshift and pull his Charger in a notch. While the traffic and thoughts of Kim Jacobsen did nothing to help Mark's blood pressure, a phone call from his ex-wife did. Kellie called to ask if he could be a sweetie that evening and take care of their son Daniel. She said something about a church function her and current husband Thomas needed to attend, but none of it mattered to Mark. His blood pressure instantly fell back into the normal range. Mark was happy to do it, happy to see Daniel whenever he could.

Mark already had a family dinner planned with Cubbie and Will that evening and having Daniel over would only make it better. He told Kellie he would love to and that he could pick Daniel up in about forty-five minutes.

Mark hung up suddenly wondering about his theory about women—the one about always looking different after getting to know them and all. To him, Kellie might be the exception; she was pretty much the same. To Mark, Kellie was…well, she was just Kellie, a woman he had been married to, but not a woman who had really made much of an impression on him. Still, they did have a beautiful son together, and that was something. Add to that, their son would be dining that evening at Mark's Casa de Witt, and to Mark that was more than something.

Staying on 183 West before cutting south on 360 to Kellie's house, Mark began to relax and think back about the afternoon and the press conference in a different light. After all, aside from the situation with Kim, he was hopeful that the reward being offered would help create some momentum with the investigation.

It would be so nice to stop pretending to be a profiler, to stop coming up with presumed characteristics and motives of the killer and to begin focusing on a few actual suspects, running and checking some actual leads, which might direct him to finding and ultimately putting an end to this entire Gospel Killer saga.

Those were his thoughts as he was pulling up in front of Kellie's modest but well-kept South Arlington home. After a knock on the door, his thoughts became quite different. A quick exchange with the ex and then seeing his son made Mark content to let the case wait till tomorrow.

On their way home, Mark and Daniel chatted about the Texas Rangers and how they had gotten off to a quick start this season, and that maybe, just maybe, the Rangers were going to be for real and turn into perennial contenders. They had made the World Series now not once, but twice, and who knows, maybe now they were ready to actually win one.

Daniel, like his dad, loved baseball, and also, like his father, had some talent for it. His little league team was undefeated, and Daniel was their top pitcher. That fact actually led to the one pebble in the shoe of this father and son relationship. For despite Daniel's constant pleading, Mark wouldn't allow Daniel to throw a curveball. With Daniel still young, Dad insisted that his son get the hitters out with a hard fastball and an overhand change up.

He did this because, from his own experience, Mark knew there would be time later on to screw up his son's shoulder and elbow throwing breaking pitches. So once more while driving home, and in spite of Daniel's eloquent depiction of his almost life and death need to learn how to unleash Uncle Charlie on unsuspecting nine-year-old hitters, Mark stood his ground and wouldn't budge. No curves or sliders until at least high school.

As Daniel unhappily settled back into the front seat of the Charger, and with the knowledge of another futile attempt at changing his father's mind written on his face, Mark looked over and couldn't help but grin. Giving in just a little, he told Daniel that if there was time after dinner maybe they could go play catch and that he'd show him the art of throwing the knuckleball—the knee-buckling, forget-about-hitting-it knuckleball. Daniel's face lit up, banishing any thoughts of curveballs. These were their fights—a little give and a little take. Much different than the father-son fights Mark endured growing up.

Arriving home, the two entered through the garage and came into the kitchen where Yo-Yo and Lily were busy preparing for dinner. Lily immediately whisked Daniel away, and while the kids played, Mark sidled up behind Yo-Yo and said, "Something smells good."

"We're having lasagna," she replied without turning.

He spun her around in his arms and kissed her maroon lips. "I wasn't talking about the food."

"I just saw you on TV with your client," she answered, holding back just a little. "That poor, lonely widow."

Going down onto her neck, between kisses Mark explained, "I'm sorry. That wasn't my doing."

She let the kisses go on just a little bit longer before pulling away. "Well, if you want to be doing anything, at least around here, you better watch yourself."

Leaning back in and beginning to nibble up and down her dark neck, Mark offered, "You know who I want to be doin'?"

Her act was up. Dammit. She could withstand many things, but neck nibbling was certainly not one of them. Between moaning from the continued nibbles, all Yo-Yo could manage to get out was, "Just make sure that bitch knows you're married."

A moment later, the kids ran back into the kitchen, interrupting Mark and Yo-Yo. Mark was disappointed, but the interruption almost surely prevented the lasagna from winding up burnt.

A short time later, Cubbie and Will arrived, bearing gifts, as always. The offerings tonight were a Selena Gomez CD for Lily and a bottle of Pinot for dinner. Not expecting Daniel to be there, Cubbie brought no gift for his nephew. He apologized, promising to make up for it, while Will was busy telling Lily to be sure and listen to track eight on the Selena CD because it was "fabulous" and was no doubt going to be her next single.

A curious eyebrow raise from Mark caused Will to exclaim, "What? Don't tell me you didn't know gay men and young girls both like the exact same music?" Mark could only shake his head and start opening the wine.

When both the wine and lasagna were gone, the family remained at the table enjoying each other's company. Between jokes from Yo-Yo about his television debut that afternoon, Will and Cubbie telling of their upcoming planned "gaycation" to British Vancouver, and Daniel tickling Lily under the table, Mark couldn't have wiped the smile off his face with Ajax. It was one of life's moments he wanted somehow to freeze, to be able to pull out at a later time, plug in the memory bank and remember. It provided a mental snapshot for Mark to replay and remember — a happy, smiling family enjoying one another and wanting nothing more than to remain together. Between the talk and laughter, no one in the group heard the knock on the front door.

After a second, louder and more forceful knock, Yo-Yo asked, "Are you expecting anyone?"

Mark shook his head no as he got up to answer the door. "Maybe it's a Hollywood talent scout wanting to sign me after my smash television debut today?"

Not to be out done, Yo-Yo shot back, "Long as it's not that slut co-star you had."

Mark was laughing along with the others as he opened the door, but then his laughter stopped. Instantly, Mark appeared frozen in the doorway, unable to move or to speak. Although the family was eating dinner at the large table in the dining room only feet away from the door, none of them could see out onto the porch and see who was at the door.

An awkward pause followed until Yo-Yo asked, "Who is it?"

Mark still didn't move or say a word, but a raspy, Marlboro-strained voice from outside said, "Well, aren't you gonna invite me in?"

Mark hesitated, but finally stepped back from the door, and in walked Richard Witt. As Richard was looking over the place from top to bottom, including and especially Yo-Yo, Cubbie got up and walked over to meet him.

"See you got Tinker Bell with you," Richard said, looking past Cubbie and focusing on Will.

Will rose, walked over and hugged Cubbie while smiling at Richard. "It's so good to see you again, Richard. Or is that Dick?"

Richard glared into Will's eyes. "Can't you queers ever think of anything except dick?"

Mark stepped between Will and Richard while simultaneously waving for Yo-Yo to get the kids into another room. Never before having met Richard Witt, and unsure of what was happening, Yo-Yo began hustling Daniel and Lily into a back bedroom.

Between questions from the kids about what was going on and why they had to leave the table so suddenly, from down the hallway Yo-Yo heard Richard ask, "Now what's up with that? Aren't you even gonna let me meet my own grandkids or that pretty daughter-in-law of mine?"

Instantly, she felt her stomach tighten and a sickening feeling of fear and dread flood over her. Even before knowing who he was, Yo-Yo had not liked how the stranger in the doorway had looked at her while she sat at the table, in a leering, skin-crawling way. Now finally seeing her father-in-law for herself, she knew the stories she had heard of him from both Mark and Cubbie were true.

He was ominous, like a tree rustling on a dark and windless night. Calming the children, Yo-Yo did her best to strain against the wall and attempt to hear what was being said between Mark, Cubbie and their father. She didn't like what she heard.

Back in the dining room, the family reunion wasn't going smoothly, and it quickly became loud enough that Yo-Yo didn't have to strain to hear. With his back to the others and staring at a family portrait on the wall, Richard casually said, "Boy, I heard you went Tex-Mex and all, but I just couldn't believe it."

Knowing the rage that could erupt from Mark at this slight, Cubbie immediately put both hands in the middle of Mark's chest and pleaded with his eyes for his brother to remain calm.

"What do you want?" Mark relented and asked.

Turning back towards his sons, Richard wasn't ready to show his hand. "Not that I blame you for wanting a taste and all, but back in my day we would just fuck 'em and then…"

With his blood rapidly heating to the boiling point, Mark quickly cut his father off. "Be real careful before you say another word."

Richard was ominous, but not careful. Instead, he offered his old "fuck you" smile, the one the boys had seen and feared so many times before. "As I was sayin', before I was so rudely interrupted, back in my day, sure we'd fuck 'em, but then we had sense enough to have 'em put their uniforms back on and finish cleaning the goddamn house."

Cubbie didn't stand a chance; Mark slung him aside as he reached to throw a straight right hand at his father. The punch landed flush into that fuck you smile, sending Richard stumbling backwards and crashing over a coffee table. In the bedroom, the kids began to cry at the noise and were fearful of what was happening with their dad. As Yo-Yo tried to calm them, she secretly hoped her husband would continue his rage-filled beat down.

He would and he did. A framed photo of Mark and the family from their Hawaiian vacation had been knocked off the table onto the floor, next to Richard's now bleeding head. Not that he would let a little of his father's blood stop this furious assault, but the picture did serve as a contrast of how different Mark's youth was from his adult life. Different in so many ways, but also it provided a glimpse of the thread that tied his life together.

Cubbie and Will were finally able to pull Mark off his father. As he regained his senses, Mark heard crying and screaming coming from a back bedroom. Instantly, his mind flashbacked and he relived the pain of remembering times spent listening to his mother and Cubbie cry uncontrollably as he suffered one brutal beating from his old man after another, and now here he was listening to his own children cry in terror at what was happening. Although it was out of their sight and out of their understanding, it was still for the same reason – his father.

As Mark struggled with his breath and his emotions, Will bear-hugged him to prevent another attack, and Cubbie went to help his father to his feet. Richard managed to stand upright and grimaced as he touched his obviously broken nose. He slowly tried to move his jaw back and forth while wiping away the blood from his nose; after a moment, a smile again appeared on Richard's face.

"Guess I did something right after all," Richard said, shaking loose from Cubbie, as he smiled and stared at Mark. "Finally made a man outta you."

Mark wanted to tell his dad what he had really made him into, about all the torment he had caused, about the pain everyone around him had been forced to endure, but instead only said, "Why are you here? What do you want?"

"How 'bout I tell you after the fruits are gone?" Richard said, tucking his shirt back into his pants as he looked at Cubbie and Will.

"Fuck you. Get out of my house," was Mark's immediate reply. Richard stood rigidly, staring at his son.

"I said get the fuck outta my house!" Mark said, violently grabbing the doorknob and flinging open the front door.

Running his hand through his thinning hair, Richard, still smiling, kept his eyes trained on Mark. "I know who's doing it. I know who the Gospel Killer is."

Mark stared at his old man is disbelief. Age had been cruel to Richard Witt. The youthful and handsome face that had captured the attention of so many women was now creased with deep-set lines running across his weathered and aged skin, but this old man was still full of surprises. Before Mark could gather his thoughts of what he had just heard, Richard said, "I saw you on TV this afternoon with that piece of ass. That's why I'm here."

Snapped back into the moment, Mark answered, "You here for the reward or for the piece of ass?" Another familiar smile, a craggy-toothed and lecherous one, formed on Richard's mouth. "Could be both."

Mark glanced at Cubbie and Will, who were both speechless from what they had seen and now heard. "I still want you out of my house," Mark spit out, looking back at his father. "If you really do know something, you can talk to me at my office tomorrow. It's at 5831..."

Richard cut him off as he headed for the door. "I know where your goddamned office is. I was a fucking detective too, you know."

Richard left and closed the door behind him without looking back. Mark hugged Cubbie as Will gently patted both of them on their backs. None spoke, but both Cubbie and Mark felt emotionally drained from just that short return of their father.

Meanwhile, Yo-Yo had heard Richard leave, and she and Lily and Daniel made their way back into the living room. Ignoring the broken items scattered on the floor from the fight, they gathered around Mark, who consumed each in a huge embrace.

During the embrace, Cubbie held the kids and began to cry. Will and Yo-Yo's tears quickly followed, and soon only Mark was left dry-eyed. That night proved to Mark that his father could still create hatred in him, fury and rage in him, and perhaps even fear, but he could not create the feelings needed to force Mark to break down and cry. He had been there, done that and was not going back.

Chapter 19

Mark was in his office early the next morning — not so much anxious to see if his father would show, but anxious to be by himself. Last night after everyone had left, Mark's right hand began to swell and ache in an all-too-familiar way. A trip to the emergency room confirmed what he already knew; for the sixth time he had broken the fifth metacarpal bone in his right hand.

This break occurred as the all others had with Mark punching someone in their face. The first three breaks had happened in the ring and, collectively, had ended Mark's promising boxing career. The last three had occurred outside the gym and perhaps outside the strict boundaries of the law, but each was necessary.

Though Yo-Yo playfully scolded him for not leading more often with his left, Mark knew she was worried — about the possible influence his father could have on him and their family. He calmed her and she trusted him; she trusted his strength and his commitment, but she still worried nonetheless.

After returning from the emergency room, Mark knew there wouldn't be much sleep on his menu that night. He lay in bed with his right hand throbbing, his restless wife tossing and turning, and his own mind racing over thoughts of the day, of the case and of his father. So a few hours after Yo-Yo finally fell asleep in Mark's arms, he decided to head to the office. He knew Yo-Yo and Lily would be safe. Mark was confident his dad wouldn't be coming back around, at least not any time soon.

Twenty minutes after he arrived at the office, he was on his second cup of Community morning blend coffee. The rich aroma and stark taste would normally have provided a safe haven for Mark to get a better grip on his problems of the moment, but this day was different. As he sipped his hot coffee, he intently listened to the flood of voice mails of possible leads that had come in on the reward hotline, in hopes that one or more of them might actually offer some real hope.

He was listening and jotting down notes when he finally had to stop and laugh at one of the callers. An obviously intoxicated man had called not once, not twice, but three times, and on each occasion was completely sure he had specific knowledge of who the killer was. On the third call, after repeating that he was taping this conversation himself for proof that he should be entitled to the reward, the caller even said the name of the suspect.

It seems the caller was convinced that the Gospel Killer was in fact the Boogeyman. The evidence to support the caller's belief that only the Boogeyman could possibly be responsible for the killings, was the caller's personal statement that when he himself had been a young boy the Boogeyman would often come into his bedroom late at night with the sole purpose of frightening him, and yet, would always manage to disappear whenever his parents rushed into the room and turned on the lights. The man repeatedly said that only someone so cunning could be able to pull off these crimes undetected.

Mark was grinning as he conceded the point that the Boogeyman was indeed quite the evil and clever bastard when the front door to his office opened and in walked another evil and clever bastard, his father. One look at Richard showed that his whole body felt like Mark's right hand. With his left eye closed shut from the swelling inflicted by Mark's fist the previous night and a homemade tape job on his busted nose, Richard slowly trudged into the office and gingerly sat down in a chair across from Mark's desk.

Not a word was said between the two as Richard looked closely around the office with his one open eye, paying special attention to the framed awards and pictures. Meanwhile, Mark watched his father just as closely and studied Richard's reactions until their eyes met.

"I guess chasin' down runaways and spying on cheatin' husbands must pay pretty good, huh?" Richard said without the slightest bit of pride in his son's success.

For a moment, Mark considered the irony of his father talking about cheating husbands, but he didn't want to go down that path again. "You said you knew who the killer was?"

"Now you gonna remember where you got this from, right?" Richard asked, still staring into Mark's eyes. "I mean when the reward time comes around and all?"

"You think I'd fuck over my dear old dad?" answered Mark, without taking his eyes off his father.

The smile returned to Richard's worn face. "The bitch's name is Diablo."

Mark shut his eyes and thought Diablo? Really? Freaking Diablo? Suddenly, the Boogeyman wasn't sounding so bad after all.

Sensing his son's disgust, Richard continued, "It's her stage name. She's a dancer. Some nights she's Diablo, some nights she Raven, and sometimes she's Destiny. All depends on which set of tattoos she's wearing."

Instantly Mark's eyes shot wide open. "Tattoos?"

His dad nodded. "They're fake. She changes them out. They even say sometimes she's known as Sin, with a big green snake coming up her leg and waist and holding an apple on one of her tits."

Richard now had his son's full interest. "How do you know this?"

"She dances some and she's also an escort. Her name was on both the first two dead guy's cell phone contacts. Her real name is Bethany Adams. She was the only connection I could find between the two victims."

Mark's mind was churning. "Did you question her? What happened?"

"I tried, but couldn't locate her," Richard said, lighting a fresh Marlboro. "Roommate said she moved out in a big hurry."

"What do you mean you couldn't find her? They just quit looking for her?"

Richard shifted from one side of his chair to the other. "That's about the time I retired. And since nobody up there thought I gave a shit or knew what the fuck was going on, I figure they probably never even bothered to read my notes. Probably didn't even kept 'em."

The words were sinking into Mark's mind. His father generally didn't give much of a shit, and it was true that the other cops certainly believed he didn't have a clue about what the fuck was going on, but then again, none of them had ever found any connection between the victims.

"But I didn't throw my notes out," Richard said while Mark was still thinking of these possibilities. "I kept copies, and I kept checking up on the bitch."

This catapulted Mark's thoughts back to the here and now. "So you've been checking up on things and haven't said a word to anyone else while all these other men have gotten killed?"

"Who would listen to me?" Richard said, flicking ashes onto the carpeted floor. "And besides, no one else offered a reward. Half a million, I believe it is, right?"

The words flowed over Mark's mind and they were a perfect summation of his father. He didn't much care what people thought of him and definitely wouldn't do anything unless there was something in it for himself.

Richard was not such a deep thinker, and he went on, "Yeah, a half million would sure be nice, but I bet no nicer than that honey offering it. Tell me, she offering you anything, son?"

Mark was forced to try to keep his emotions in check, try to keep focused on the case and not be drawn down into his father's labyrinth of perversions. And while Mark didn't say a word, Richard was relentless. "Come on, you can tell your dad. She as good as her hot little ass looks? Now come on, I know you gotta be hittin' it."

Mark could feel his face redden and blood pressure surge as he glared at his father. "No, I'm not hittin' it. Sorry, Dad, but I'm married, and my wife and children wouldn't approve."

Richard knew Mark's meaning and felt the sting of the words. He responded by putting out his Marlboro on the cushion of the chair he was sitting in. It dropped to the floor as he lit another one. "Beautiful. One son's a fag and the other one might as well be." Ahh, the moments that cement the bond of a father-son relationship.

Mark was seething and wanted to break his left hand on his father's face, but somehow refrained. "If you got anything else about the girl, then tell me now; otherwise, your fuckin' time's up."

Richard grinned and took a drag from the cigarette. "Touchy, touchy. Looks like somebody got up on the wrong side of the bed. Tell me, did Mr. Grumpy Bear take a shit on your face this morning?"

"You need to leave while you still can," Mark said, getting up from his desk.

"Sit down," Richard commanded, blowing smoke towards Mark. "I've got more. A lot more."

Mark didn't like it but sat back into his chair as Richard went on. "She goes by Bethany Adams, but that's not her real name. She was orphaned and took the name of a foster family she lived with—a foster family who happened to make their living by being God-fearing missionaries to Africa."

Hearing the word missionaries, Mark was again hooked and listened closely as Richard continued. "Yeah, according to the roommate, Bethany knew the Bible like the back of her hand but didn't believe a bit of it. Seems like she quit believin' about the time that evangelical foster father of hers started coming into her room at night and "laying hands" on her, if you know what I mean?" Mark was furiously writing notes when his dad continued. "Roommate would laugh and say Beth could quote scripture all day and fuck all night."

"Where is she? Did you ever find her?" Mark asked, setting down his pen.

Richard shook his head no. "After she ran out, she became a lot lizard." Mark was familiar with the term lot lizard. It means a cheap prostitute who specializes in working truck stops, offering the truckers a little fun in the sleeper in exchange for a small monetary donation. And if the driver is running low on cash, a lot of the lizards will pull a trick just for a ride down the road. Cops call it a 'blow and go.' They all know it's a great way for a girl to get lost. By the time they get the taste out of their mouths, the girls can be three states away and pulling the same thing in another truck stop to get even further down the line. It's not exactly like flying first class, but it's a way a girl can see the country in a hurry, albeit with a little effort.

"Kinda thin, but it's a start," Mark opined, rocking back in his chair. "The connection with the first two and the religious tie-in and all, that's something to look at."

"Might not be so thin after all," responded Richard. "She cut out on her roommate about three years ago, but she resurfaced in town about six months ago."

"How do you know that?"

Richard gave his son an exasperated "Do you really have to ask that question?" look, before finally saying, "How do I know everything? Bubba told me."

Bubba Furh, pronounced Fur—since, as he was fond of saying, that was his favorite part of a woman—was a man Mark had long known and despised. It was rumored that New Orleans Mafia kingpin Carlos Marchello had selected him in the early sixties to run the rackets for the mob in the Dallas–Ft. Worth area. Bubba was now in his eighties but still a man to reckon with.

Years ago, he had abdicated his drug empire to Mark's friend, Marcus Ramirez, but Bubba still got a tax on each shipment. The cutback allowed him to better concentrate his time on his two personal passions, gambling and pussy. If there was an escort service, a backroom craps game, a massage parlor, a bookmaking outfit, a strip club, an underground poker room, or an Internet porn site doing business in Dallas, Bubba either owned it, controlled it, or took the biggest cut of the profits.

Mark knew that Bubba had long kept DAs, police chiefs and judges on the payroll, and he was a man who got what he paid for. All legal problems seemed to routinely go away, and come to think of it, his other problems usually went away also—permanently.

As he grew up and learned more about the world, Mark came to view Bubba and his father as the same man. He held each in the same contempt. God only knew how many paychecks over the years Richard had signed over to Bubba to cover gambling losses. Mark knew that even more than the money, his father had signed away his soul to the old bastard. He had long provided information to Bubba, had forever been a hanger-on at one or the other establishments owned by Mr. Furh, and had also, doubtlessly, done a lot of the dirtiest work for him, all so he could get another bet down or bed down another whore. It was an ugly picture being repainted in Mark's mind, and this canvas would remain stained. He couldn't get the images out of his mind, and he also knew he couldn't get out of taking his dad to visit Bubba.

~~~

As Mark and his father drove across town to Bubba's, an interested Marcel Durand peered over his horn-rimmed glasses at a customer in his art and frame store. The thin Frenchman had seen the woman in his shop at least twice before this week, and rarely were customers ever that much in need of his shop or his services; even more rarely were customers as attractive as the shapely, young, dark-haired woman who was smiling at him.

Marcel politely smiled back, perhaps slowly and a bit awkwardly, but it had been a long time since a pretty girl had smiled at him. He had left his wife in France to run away to America with what he thought was the love of his life, Brigitte. But soon enough, Brigitte left him after finding the love of her life. After that, Marcel, too ashamed to return home, stayed in America and opened a small art shop. He had tried to forget women, as much as a Frenchman can forget women, by selling prints of the types of paintings that as a young man he dreamed of being able to paint. The prints, though, like his own paintings had been, were garbage. Yet this striking woman appeared so inter-ested in them; either that or perhaps, and he knew he was probably out of his mind, could it possibly be him she was interested in?

Just as Marcel was coming out from behind the shop's counter to assist the young woman, she knelt down in an aisle to get a closer look at an absolutely hideous print of an absolutely hideous Jules Page painting. With the woman kneeling, Marcel approached and found himself playing peek-a-boo with the tips of an angel-winged tattoo poking out from between the top of her pants and the bottom of her shirt. Marcel loved tattoos and had already admired the barbed wire one that highlighted her shapely right bicep. As the woman was standing back up, Marcel offered his hand. "Is there something I can help you with?"

"Thank you, and yes I think there is," smiled Angel, shaking his hand.

Chapter 20

Naturally, I-35 was bumper to bumper, yet Mark couldn't figure out which was irritating him the most, the mass of brake lights in front of him or the fact his father was making a habit of dropping ashes on his leather seats. Richard made no attempt to even open the ashtray, smoking one cigarette after another and letting the ashes fall where they may. Truth was he knew what he was doing and enjoyed pissing off his son.

Mark was also aware of what his dad was doing, so he tried not to let it show how much it bothered him; but if ejector seats had come as optional equipment on the Charger, Richard Witt would have been shot into orbit. To keep from committing homicide right there on the freeway, Mark called Detective Coleman to see how things were going and to fill him in on the possible connection with Bethany Adams.

When Coleman learned that Mark had gotten this tip from his father, John was beyond incredulous. When he learned that in addition to this new tip, Mark also had a freshly broken right hand, John smiled to himself knowing that Papa Witt no doubt suffered far worse injuries during their "family reunion." Mark finally got off the line, after relaying all the new information and promising to get back with John.

A half hour later, Mark was at last able to inch to the Walnut Hill Lane exit and take a right. A block later, he turned right again on Composite Drive and headed for Bubba's hideaway, Club Fuxx. Arriving well before opening hours, Mark pulled his Dodge in under the front door canopy and parked next to Bubba's black Bentley Mulsanne. Waiting for the Budweiser man to roll his two-wheeler hand truck into the doorway, Mark casually turned his head and blew a perfect snot rocket directly onto the hood of the Bentley. Proud of the well-positioned handiwork of his nose, Mark smiled to himself and followed the beer man and his dad into the club. It would be the last time Mark smiled that day.

Upon entering Club Fuxx, Mark was left wishing he hadn't cleared out his nasal passages so completely with the deadly accurate snot rocket. Smells from the previous night's business provided an assault to his senses. From vomit, to cheap cologne, to semen, to a certain odor that either came from poor feminine hygiene or a Saigon back alley during a heat wave, Club Fuxx had something to offer every degenerate.

The nausea Mark felt from these smells was made worse by listening to his father, who had made a bee-line to the bar and was now attempting to flirt with a particularly homely bartender. Hearing his dad tell the young woman how the fishnet hose showed off her great legs, Mark could only wince, since he had seen better legs on a couch. After wasting another moment listening to his father and looking at the club's black velvet walls, its mirrored-tile center stage floor and a sign promoting hot tub lap dances in the VIP section, Mark finally and sternly asked, "Where's Bubba?"

The bartender had not been enamored with Richard's attention, but Mark's tone seemed to be even less welcome. She put down a beer mug that she had half-assed been trying to clean and glared at Mark for several seconds before finally putting her hand out and half ass motioning down a hall towards Bubba's office. Feeling the love, Mark walked past her and smiled, while saying, "Thanks, Legs."

Heading down the hallway to Bubba's office, Mark and Richard first passed the open door of the adjoining office, which belonged to Bubba's constant companion and bodyguard, Lou Frazier. Lou, nicknamed "The Magician" because of his talent for making people disappear, looked up from the sports page he was reading when the men walked by and with a grin said, "Hey, too bad last night about those Phillies, huh?"

Richard shook his head. "Fuck Roy Halladay."

The Magician offered a not-too-convincing nod of understanding and then motioned that it was all right to proceed. A quick knock, an opening of the door, and then Mark followed his dad into the belly of the beast.

Upon seeing his unannounced guests, a seated Bubba pushed away the head of a young Asian girl, which had been buried in his lap. "You go on now, Honey," he told her. "Looks like I got company." Then looking down at his rather flaccid groin area, he went on, "Besides, those goddamn pills ain't working yet anyway."

As the girl struggled with her tube top and attempted to balance herself on her platform heels while she walked past Mark and Richard, Bubba laughed and called out one further piece of instruction for her. "And come on back in about twenty minutes or so; I still want to get me some of that good pooh-pooh platter."

As the girl closed the door behind her, Mark closed his eyes and was left to take in what he had just witnessed. An old man, wearing a colostomy bag and hooked up to an oxygen tank, was telling a girl who might be all of fifteen-years-old at the most to hurry back for sex as soon as his Viagra kicked in. Just how fucking bad was it that he wanted to find this killer?

While zipping up his pants, Bubba leered at the two men. "It sure is good to see you two havin' a little father and son bonding time."

"Yeah, it feels great, too," Mark quickly interjected. "But listen, I'm here about Bethany Adams."

Not through with his fun yet, Bubba continued, "Hell, maybe next you two'll be on a camping trip somewhere together, makin' up for lost time and all. Like I always say, family first. Right?"

While Richard shrugged his shoulders, Mark said, "I need to know about Bethany Adams."

Bubba leaned over in his chair and began pouring, first himself and then Richard, three fingers of Glen Levitt Scotch, before answering. "I know why you're here. Hell, your daddy's been down here chasin' all my girls around every day about Beth and who knows what all else, and then I saw you yesterday on TV with that reward."

"Then you don't mind answering a few questions?" Mark asked, looking him dead in the eyes.

Bubba smiled. "Of course not. As a citizen and small business owner, I feel it's my civic duty to help uphold the law." Richard gave a smirking laugh as he took a long drink of the aged scotch, and Bubba added, "Seeing Kim on TV with you yesterday brought back a lot of memories. Did she tell you she used to dance for me over at the Cabaret?"

Mark didn't want to waste any more time thinking of Kim Jacobsen and didn't want Bubba to get inside his mind either, so he plowed forward. "Do you have an address for Beth or a telephone number where we could reach her?"

Bubba finished the last of his drink, sat the glass down and began to run his finger around the outside of the coaster.

"Tell you what, I used to think there was only two kinds of pussies in the world, big ole good ones and good ole big ones, but that was before I met Kim," he smiled. "That bitch was in a whole different category all by herself. It's like she was sent from the future to teach people how to really fuck, but I guess I ain't got to be tellin' you that, do I?"

Mark looked down at the floor and wondered why he had even bothered coming to see this old man. His father held out his glass to Bubba for more Scotch and said, "The boy claims he ain't getting' any of it. It's a cryin', fuckin' shame if you ask me."

"Must be saving it for that pretty little senorita of his," Bubba laughed.

"Fuck you," Mark said, looking up from the floor.

With Mark's eyes shooting daggers into Bubba, it was time for Mr. Furh to set the boundaries. "Watch your mouth, boy. You need to remember that the Magician is right outside that door."

"Yeah, well fuck him, too," Mark said without missing a beat.

Though Bubba cared little for Mark's morals, he had always admired his toughness and competence, so after a pause, he poured another drink and smiled. "You know you ought to be a little more mannerly to your elders, especially since it was this old man who got your house paid off."

Mark's expression showed he didn't understand, so Bubba enlightened him. "Come on, why do you think it was you that Marcus Ramirez called? Think he just picked your fuckin' name out of a phone book?"

Caught flat-footed, Mark stood there remembering how Marcus had said, "You come highly recommended." How could he have not known Bubba was involved? How could he have been so stupid to give Bubba this type of leverage over him?

"And before you leave here and insult the Magician on your way out, you should know it was him that made those four dead bodies you killed disappear," Bubba said to further drive home his position of power. "Wouldn't it be a real shame for both you and Marcus if someone called the police and told them where they could find those bodies? If something like that were to happen, why even dumb shit cops would start asking an awful lot of rather difficult questions."

Mark suddenly felt numb. He knew he should be feeling something, but he couldn't seem to process it all. Bubba had evidence implicating him in four deaths, and Mark knew that judgment day would surely come. At some point Bubba would call in the marker, and Mark would be forced to do what the old man asked. Then, the numb feeling and dumbfounded look on Mark's face went away. He began to feel again, a hot and sinking feeling in his gut and his head. The bit of news from Bubba felt to Mark like being in an examination room and the doctor saying the cancer was terminal. Can't operate, chemo's no use, just a lot of pain until you die.

"You working for Marcus Ramirez now?" his father asked, neatly putting out his cigarette in Bubba's desktop ashtray.

"It was personal, and it's none of your business," Mark shot back, trying to keep from exploding.

"Must be hard finding out this way about your son not being the pristine snowflake he pretends to be," smirked Bubba, going in for the kill.

"I always told him he was just like me and that he would wind up doing the same things I did," Richard shrugged.

With these words, the cancer went to code blue in Mark. Imminent danger. His father's words caused an eruption in Mark. Hatred and rage instantly filled every pore of his body. He wanted to pull out his Glock and add to the body count the two old men seated before him, and then put down the Magician as well when he barreled through the door. The clip was in; the safety was off; Mark could end things right here in a matter of seconds.

It's a play that Richard himself might have made thirty years earlier, but no matter what he said, Mark wasn't his dad. He had killed to save a young girl's life, but he wasn't a cold-blooded murderer, and so his gun remained in its holster.

Instead, he looked intently at Bubba. "Will you help me find Bethany Adams?" he asked, almost meekly.

Bubba sat back down, satisfied Mark had understood his message. "That's much better. Now what do you need?"

While the angst still clutched tightly in his shoulders,

Mark began to force himself to breathe. "Whatever you have—address, phone number, Social Security number, anything to identify her."

Bubba sipped the scotch and shook his head. "Ain't got no Social Security number. No need. We don't pay our dancers; they pay us $100 each shift we let them work here and then they keep all their own tips. Sort of an independent contractor arrangement. Less paperwork that way. But Trisha might know how to get a hold of her."

After Bubba yelled for the Magician to send in Trisha, Mark asked, "When was the last time you saw Beth?"

The old man paused. "Probably four, maybe five months ago. She stopped by and asked about coming back to work here."

"Why didn't she?" Mark asked as he wrote down information in his notepad. "I mean why didn't she start working here again?"

"Guess she didn't want to go through the interview process again," Bubba smiled, perching his eyebrows up like a church steeple. Knowing the interview process consisted of a young woman allowing Bubba to explore the inside of her mouth with his dick, Richard got a good laugh from this comment.

"These murders have all been clean," Mark said, gritting his teeth. "No missteps. You tell me, is Bethany Adams smart enough to pull all that off?"

"We don't exactly make our girls take IQ tests around here," said Bubba, shrugging his shoulders. "So I couldn't really say how smart she is, but I know that she's mean enough to do it."

"Why do you say that?" asked Mark, looking up from his notes.

"The reason we got rid of her in the first place was one night she was in the back room with a guy and pulled a razor on him," Bubba answered, without the slightest expression. "Cut one of his balls smooth off."

Mark went back to work on his notes. "What happened? Why did she say she did it?"

"Didn't ask," Bubba responded incredulously. "There was blood spurting everywhere and this fucker was running through the club holding his nut sac. That sort of thing is bad for business, so we didn't exactly do a whole fuckin' CSI investigation into why it all happened. We just sent the whore packing."

This story interested Richard. "What about the guy? What happened to him?"

"Let's just say, we convinced him it would be best to just take his ball and go home," answered Bubba, with a smile the Devil himself would've been proud of. Richard was in full knee-slapping mode when Bubba added, "He still stops by for a drink now and then. The girls call him Uno."

As Mark was flipping the page on his pad and continuing with his notes about this case of the man with the mysterious missing ball, the door opened and the Magician led Miss Trisha into the office. Whoever it was that said hope springs eternal had never met Trisha. One look into her eyes and Mark could easily see that her spring filled with hope had long ago been drained dry, or probably more accurately from the looks of her, had been pumped dry. The needle marks on her arms were as dark as the roots of her dyed blonde hair. Mark could only imagine what kind of man would pay this woman to get undressed.

Wearing a bikini top emblazoned with an American

flag and a sequined mini skirt, Trisha continued in and stopped just short of Bubba's desk. After a quick introduction and a very limited amount of small talk, Bubba told Trisha to answer any questions Mark had.

Mark began by telling her why he was there and asking when she had last seen or spoken to Bethany Adams. Trisha paused; after looking again at Bubba, who nodded for her to answer, she said, "Beth called a couple of weeks ago. She called to see if I wanted to make a few bucks."

"What was the job?"

Trisha again hesitated. "To come pull a three-way with this Filipino chick she was staying with."

"Who's the girl?" asked Mark, quickly looking up. "Where does she live?"

Trisha sighed and looked at the ceiling. "I didn't go. I don't even like chicks. I only do 'em when I'm runnin' low, you know, and really need some cash."

"Gay for pay, baby," Richard chimed in. "Now tell me this ain't a great country."

Mark took charge, telling his dad to shut up and then turned back to Trisha. "We need to talk with Beth. Can you tell me everything you know about her and this Filipino woman?"

Trisha sat down. "I like Beth; I don't want to get her into any trouble."

"Just answer the fucking questions," Bubba demanded.

Loosening up, Trisha told Mark that the Filipino was a woman named Cat. "I don't know her last name but she said she was some kind of nurse or therapist at like this nursing home in South Dallas. I was at her apartment once with Beth, but I was drunk, so I can't remember exactly where it was. Somewhere off of I-20 near Duncanville, I think."

She went on to say after that meeting, when she left the next morning, she could barely walk because Cat had been way too rough with the vibrator. Another thing she also remembered was that Beth had told her she got all her fake tattoos from Cat and that Cat bought them online from someplace in the Philippines.

After writing down her answers, Mark asked if Trisha had been at the club the night Beth attacked the man with the razor. When she nodded yes, Mark asked, "Why did she do it?"

Trisha again hesitated. "Well she told me that he was, like, leaned back and she was, uh, you know, like, doing him, and he told her to hurry up. He said his wife and kids were at church that night, and he needed to be home before they got back."

As Mark quickly wrote down what she was saying, it was obvious even to Trisha that he was intrigued by her answer. "Beth always seemed to get really mad whenever anyone said anything about church or the Bible or anything like that. It was kinda weird."

Mark didn't think he would get much else from her, but he had one final question for Trisha. "How smart would you say Beth is?"

"She's real smart," Trisha shot back. "Really smart. I mean, she used to like to watch those cake decorating shows on TV and she said she could do some of those things, like make the roses and get the icing real smooth and all. Said she had learned to do it all from watching a YouTube video."

After Trisha's definitive assessment of intelligence, Mark thanked her for her cooperation and the Magician escorted her from the room. Mark turned his attention back to Bubba, telling him that he would need a photo of Bethany, preferably a face shot, that he could show around to possible witnesses for identification.

"Got lots of pictures of her, but most of 'em ain't of her face," Bubba smirked. "I'll see if we can find one with clothes on."

~~~

Marcel's body may have been sitting in a Starbucks, but his mind felt as if it was racing down the Alps. This seductive woman, whom he knew only as Angel, was drinking lattes with him and hanging on his every word. She had a wonderful habit of reaching over and touching his hand each time she laughed at one of his silly jokes. Her smile was constant and seemed to be trained only on him. She asked questions about art and about him and then, almost unbelievably, actually listened to his answers and responded to them. When she dabbed the foam of the latte from her mouth with her hand and then licked the remainder off from her finger, Marcel was ready for lift off.

Well after the lattes were gone, Angel said she really should be leaving but hated to go. She paused, sadness engulfing her, and then asked Marcel if she could tell him something personal.

He said of course, and Angel told him that she was trapped in a loveless marriage and was planning a divorce, but her husband was insanely jealous and wouldn't let her go. "I hate to get you involved in my life, it's so difficult and complex," she said. "And I don't know, maybe I'm only behaving like a schoolgirl with a teenage crush, but I haven't been able to think of anything other than you for the past week."

Marcel quickly took her hand. "Don't worry. I've developed feelings for you as well." He looked deeply into her eyes, and with his most exotic French accent, told Angel that her difficult and complex life could be changed, could be transformed into a new and wonderfully fulfilling life.

"I would do anything you asked." he said, kissing her gently on the forehead. "Whatever door you opened, I would walk through."

Perhaps it was his longing for her, or perhaps his foolish male pride, but the look in her eyes made Marcel believe Angel wanted this, too, wanted all the possible barriers to their relationship to be overcome. Part of him could hardly believe it; he knew it was true that outwardly they appeared a mismatched couple, but Angel made him feel that she wanted him as badly as he desired her.

"We will have to be careful," she cautioned. "But I will find a way to get free."

He couldn't believe that this beautiful woman was saying that even if it were only for an evening, she was determined to be alone with him. She would bring over a bottle of wine, and they could talk of their long set-aside dreams. Hearing these words, and the way they were said, made Marcel believe when the wine was gone, they would surely give in to the passion that threatened to consume them.

Marcel wrote down the address to his apartment and after Angel slid it into her pocket, she touched his face and kissed his lips, softly, fully and completely. It may have been only a single, small kiss, but to Marcel it signaled a long-awaited change from a life of desperation to one filled with hopeful anticipation. A moment in time he could look back on as the event that triggered his personal turnaround from a reader of life to a writer of it, from dreaming of making love to the beautiful women he could only see in magazines to actually holding an angel in his arms.

As she was unlocking her car door, she looked back over her shoulder. "It's really gonna happen," she answered to his unasked question.

Chapter 21

When Mark left Bubba's office his mind was spilling over the banks. He was thinking of Trisha's answers and how to best locate Bethany Adams. He was also tormented that he had walked into a trap and given such leverage to Bubba over himself. Why hadn't he insisted on notifying the police at the time of the Ramirez kidnapping? By not doing so, he instead allowed Bubba and the Magician to now know literally where the bodies were buried. His mind was still jumbled when he followed his father out the door of Club Fuxx. The sunlight caused his eyes to recoil after coming from the darkness inside the club.

Mark took a moment to put on his sunglasses, and then looked around to get his bearings. Trying only to clear his eyes and his mind, he glanced through the parking lot of the club and suddenly felt a tinge of pride when he noticed the dried snot rocket still clutching the hood of Bubba's prized Bentley. Sometimes it seemed the world only existed to pile drive a man further down life's confidence meter, but every so often when the stars aligned just right and a guy occasionally did actually do something spectacular, he owed it to himself to feel pretty good about it.

And Mark knew this snot rocket was pretty

spectacular. Deftly delivered like a sniper's bullet from a silencer-equipped rifle, this rocket hit its precise target and undoubtedly would inflict a huge amount of mental damage to poor Bubba. In fact, if Mark hadn't been so giddy about his accomplishment, he might even have felt sorry at the thought of Bubba anguishing over the cruel vandalism that had violated his $200,000 car; but on the other hand, fuck the old prick.

As Mark roared his $35,000 Charger to life, his thoughts quickly turned to fuck this old prick next to me. His father immediately began his chain-smoking ritual, and Mark stepped on the gas; he couldn't wait to get back to his office and to Richard's car. He didn't wish to talk with his father, didn't want to discuss the case or anything they might have learned at Bubba's with him, and certainly didn't want to discuss the events of the Ramirez kidnapping with his dad. To spare each of them any uncomfortably awkward car silence, Mark pulled out his cell and called Detective Coleman again.

When John got on the line, Mark said hello and then didn't get to say another word for what seemed like an awfully long time. Mark was forced to drive and grit his teeth as he held the phone to his ear. John must have been working on his stand-up routine, as he hit Mark with one daddy joke after another in a full frontal assault on how terrific it was to at last see father and son putting their differences aside. In a different time and place, Mark would have even had to admit some of the jokes were pretty funny, but right now most of them made him want to punch his already broken right hand through the windshield of his car.

Mercifully, when John finally paused to take a breath,

Mark filled him in about what he had learned from Bubba and also bragged of his beautifully executed, high arching and deadly accurate snot rocket. When he asked John to see if he could locate a Filipino lesbian named Cat who reportedly worked at some local nursing home presumably as either a therapist or a nurse and who lived somewhere off I-20 near Duncanville, Coleman made no attempt to suppress his laughter.

"One day around your old man and this is what kind of private investigator you turn into," he roared into the phone. "Calling about snot rockets and wanting me to try and find some Filipino lesbian chick named Cat."

"That's a Filipino lesbian therapist chick named Cat," Mark interjected.

"Oh shit, well in that case no problem. Lotta solid police evidence there. And you're sure you don't want me to pull a bag of magic beans out of my ass while I'm at it?"

Mark swerved onto the shoulder of the highway to avoid a stalled Toyota pickup while deadpanning into the phone, "No, not a big bag of ass beans. Especially not coming out of your big ass."

"Hey, easy; I'm sensitive," John protested. "You know I retain water."

Mark couldn't miss the opportunity to razz his overweight friend. "Did you say water or water parks?"

After another round of good-natured rips, Mark told Coleman to see what he could find and that he would come see him as soon as he dropped his father off. Ten minutes later, he pulled into his office parking lot, stopped behind the only car parked there, hit the unlock door button on the side console and silently dismissed his father.

Chapter 22

By the time he arrived at police headquarters, Mark had on his game face. Quickly moving past the usual glares from his former colleagues, he found Detective Coleman at the coffee pot, and they, along with the diminutive FBI agent Ellis, headed to John's office.

On the way to his office, John explained that he had gotten the phone company's report concerning calls to and from Matthew Owens' cell phone the night of his murder. The records indicated the air conditioning company owner had received just one call after 6:00 p.m. The incoming call was received at 7:26 and had been placed from one of Dallas' few remaining pay phones. The phone was located in front of a popular liquor store named Goody Goody on Northwest Highway near Loop 12.

Store security camera's showed the backside of a woman at that precise time using the phone. The partial, lower back tattoo and the barbed wired tat on the woman's arm convinced John that the caller was the same woman from the earlier murder committed at the Stoneleigh Hotel.

Coleman marveled at how the woman once more avoided her face being captured on film, despite the camera showing her walking through and out of the store's parking lot. She had even parked her car off the property to avoid detection. Mark arched his eyebrows, and all three men grudgingly recognized the need to give the killer props for being so competent.

Inside John's office, for Ellis' benefit Mark again went over what he had learned from his father, Bubba, and the dancer. John had already heard of the possible suspect, Bethany Adams, and had his men trying to locate her, so he spent his time carefully watching little Ron as Ellis listened to Mark. Clearly, Ellis found this interesting, particularly Bethany's childhood and early experience with the church and her evangelical foster father.

Just as he was demanding to know why no one except Richard Witt had ever discovered Bethany's link to the first two victims, John's office door swung open.

"Hey boss, I think we may have found her—the Filipino chick," Detective Smithson breathlessly exclaimed as he rushed in.

Smithson explained to the men that a Filipino woman named Catherine "Cat" Binaohan had been placed into custody three days earlier on a domestic abuse charge. A woman named Cinnamon Moore had filed the charge. The arrest report showed that Cat lived in the Linwood Apartments on Camp Wisdom Road in far south Dallas and listed her occupation as a physical therapy assistant working at the Williamstown Nursing Home and Rehab Center in the suburb of Duncanville.

When Coleman learned that Cat was unable to make bail and was sitting in Dallas' Lew Sterrett county jail, he immediately instructed Smithson to have her transported to headquarters. "Already on her way,"

Smithson smiled.

As John was saying that this had to be the same girl Trisha had told Mark about, Ellis grabbed the arrest report and opened up his laptop; in a matter of seconds he would have access to everything known about Ms. Catherine Binaohan. Coleman was speaking to Mark about questions he should ask Cat when Ron interrupted. "I'll handle the questioning."

Knowing the slight wouldn't sit well with Detective Coleman, Mark remained quiet.

Before John could voice his displeasure, Ellis with his head still buried in the laptop said, "Says here that her last name, Binaohan, means 'Hit by coconut', hmm."

~~~

His first sight of Catherine Binaohan convinced Mark that she may well have never seen a pair of coconuts much less been hit by one, at least not in an up close and personal way. Seated behind a two-way mirror, he watched as two deputies escorted Ms. Binaohan into an interrogation room. The right arm sleeve of her orange county issued jumpsuit was rolled up and over a pack of cigarettes. She had a military-style buzz cut hairdo and a neck tattoo featuring some lengthy Sanskrit. Mark was pretty sure this Cat was the butch in any relationship.

The scowl on her face only intensified when the two deputies left and were replaced by Coleman and Agent Ellis. Mark smiled, leaned back in his chair, and turned up the volume from the room's speaker; he didn't want to miss a word of what was to follow.

Ellis didn't bother asking Ms. Binaohan if she needed a drink or a smoke or a public defender; he immediately got down to business. Setting down his coffee on the table in front of Cat, Ron started by pointing towards John, who was standing behind him. "This is Detective John Coleman of the Dallas Police Department and I'm Special Agent Ron Ellis of the Federal Bureau of Investigations."

Cat framed her eyes in an odd way and shot back, "Federal Bureau...The FBI's after me? For what? For slapping the shit outta my own bitch when I caught her in bed with a whore?"

Little Ron had his head down checking the arrest report and never bothered looking up. Instead, he vocalized a hugely annoying end-of-the-game buzzer type sound. "Come on, get with the program. In here, I ask the questions and you answer them; got it? It's a system. You only answer questions; you don't ask them."

Cat didn't seem to appreciate Ellis' rather off-putting tone. As inevitably happens when two bulls are placed in the same pen, they locked horns as she tried to assert her male dominance. "I'll ask any fuckin' thing I want to, and if you don't like that, fuck you, and fuck the Shetland pony you rode in on."

Cat was snickering from her joke and Coleman was biting the inside of his mouth to keep from doing the same when little Ron calmly set the arrest report on the table. "I get it. That's funny because I'm such a small guy that probably the only kind of horse I could ride into town on would be a little Shetland pony?"

"That's right," she said, her snicker turning into a full grin. "A Shetland would work, at least if somebody helped you up on it. Like say, maybe your leprechaun daddy, the Lucky Charms guy." Her grin gave way to laughter.

"I see here that you're in America on a work visa," Ellis answered, with the bone-chilling emotion of a Nazi death camp doctor.

Ms. Binaohan got the implication and her laughing stopped. "I'm applying for citizenship."

Ellis smiled and Coleman would have sworn he could see Ron's pearly canines becoming fangs when he answered, "Yes, you are. I see where you listed sexual discrimination in your homeland as a reason for your desire to live here in the good ole USA. Let me guess; the Muslims back home must make things rough on a poor little rug muncher like you, huh?"

Through the two-way glass, Mark could see Cat's cocky attitude giving way to something closely akin to fear. At the very least, she was now quickly beginning to understand that the little guy across from her played to win.

Ron didn't let up. "Now brother, since we both piss standing up, I'm gonna lay it out to you straight. Either you're going to tell me everything I want to know, or I'm going to have your dyke ass on the next plane to whatever fucked up jungle town they got over there that has an air strip." She was clearly cracking but remained silent. "So talk to me now or the last piece of American pussy you'll ever get a whiff of will be what's leftover on my dick from last night."

Crack. This Cat was through trying to act like a big dog. "All right. I'm sorry I hit her. I mean I am. Really. But can't we work this out?"

"Forget that. I could give a shit about who you hit. What I want is for you to tell me everything you know about Bethany Adams, starting with where I can find her."

"That's what I'm trying to do," Cat said, looking perplexed. "She's been staying with me, and I'm sorry I hit her."

Mark was listening closely to every word, but like Ellis, he didn't understand Cat's answer. "What are you saying?" asked Ron, reopening the arrest report. "It says you hit a woman named Cinnamon Moore."

"Cinnamon Moore?" laughed Cat, leaning back in her chair. "That's Beth. That's one of her dance names. 'Hi, I'm Cinnamon; my friends call me Cyn.' Get it? Cyn Moore."

Ahhh. Sin More. Ellis, Mark and John got it. Ellis turned to signal Coleman, but was too late. John was already running out of the room to dispatch an arrest team to the apartment address to bring Bethany Adams into custody. John returned within minutes, but instead of re-entering the interrogation room, he decided to sit down in the adjoining room alongside Mark and watch Ellis continue dissecting this poor kitty.

As Ellis questioned Cat, he paced around her, forcing her head to turn to follow him as he circled her. It was something out of a National Geographic wildlife film where a Cape buffalo has wandered away from the herd and now finds itself alone and encircled by a pack of hungry lions. The buffalo is a formidable opponent, but the lions were undefeated and would again emerge victorious. In this case, there was only one lion, and though he may have been closer in size to a jackal, it was clear Ron intended to eat all the meat from this carcass.

"Police report here says Cinnamon Moore showed a valid photo ID, a Texas driver's license, at the time of your arrest. You wouldn't be fucking with me now, would you?"

"It's her. A driver's license, big fuckin' deal. How hard you think it is to get a fake one? She's got ten or fifteen of 'em."

"This one fooled a Dallas policeman."

"That dickhead cop couldn't keep his eyes off her tits. Beth could have showed him a cartoon picture and he wouldn't have caught it. You know, if I could've gotten loose, that fuckin' pig was getting his ass whipped, too."

Ron slowed and was making mental notes. "So why do you think Beth needs all the different ID's? And where does she get them?"

Cat was puzzled why all the questions were of Beth and not of the incident that had happened between them, "Would you just tell me what's going on here? Why is everything you've asked me been about Beth?"

Ron relaxed his no-questions rule this once and answered Cat. "What this is about is finding the Gospel Killer."

Both John and Mark zeroed in on Cat's face when she heard this, and neither was disappointed. It was as if her face was a huge movie screen and in a split second, they saw an epic featuring disbelief, shock, fear, and acceptance.

"You think Beth is the Gospel Killer?" she asked, taking shallow breaths.

"Right now we just want to speak to her," Ron said as he approached her. "But do you think she could be the killer?"

Cat's eyes now began to redden and she hung her head. "Do I need a lawyer?"

Ron sensed the moment and eased off on the throttle;

he seemed to become sympathetic to Cat. "We'll get you one if you like, but unless you had anything to do with the killings or helped Beth conceal the crimes, we're not after you."

"I've never killed anyone," she said, raising her head. "And I don't know if Beth has, but if I help you, will you get me out of here?" Ron nodded and Cat continued. "The charges will go away and you won't deport me?"

Ellis bent down and spoke into the microphone on the interrogation table. "In return for information provided on Bethany Adams, all charges will be dropped against Catherine Binaohan."

"All right; what do you want to know?" Cat asked as she slowly rubbed her face in her hands and raised her head.

"Let's start with your reaction. Why do you think she's the killer?"

"I didn't say I think that…I don't know what I think. It's just something I've wondered about, you know? I mean, I read where the murders are related to the Bible or something, and maybe a tattooed woman did them."

"Why would the Bible make you suspicious?"

"Beth goes crazy when people start talking about the Bible or religion; says everyone's a hypocrite."

"Does she know much about the Bible?"

"That's what weird. She knows it forwards and backwards. Can quote verse after verse and then'll just start ranting about it. Off-the-wall shit. Goes crazy talking about it; says it's all fairy tales and that preachers just use it to take money away from stupid people."

After hearing those words, Mark was in the middle of a silent prayer asking forgiveness for anyone who believed that and for the wisdom to always know better, when the door flew open and Detective Smithson, clutching a handheld radio, rushed in.

"The team's there, but there's no answer at the door," Smithson told Coleman before even catching his breath. "They say they can't hear any movement from inside."

"Hang on and stay here with Mark," Coleman ordered as he got up from his chair and took the handheld from Smithson. John hurried from the room and entered the interrogation room where he interrupted the questioning. "Excuse me. Listen, Cat, we didn't have time to get a search warrant for your apartment, but will you give us your permission to enter and search your residence?"

Cat hesitated before answering. "I don't know; what if your guys find some pot there?"

"Then it must've belonged to Beth," said John without missing a beat.

"Well, go for it then," Cat said, smiling.

Getting the go ahead, John took the radio and directed the officers to go inside and proceed with the search.

While waiting to hear back from the on-site officers, Ron continued with the questioning. Cat told him Beth got some of her fake ID's from an escort customer of hers who supposedly owned a print shop, but she got most of them by paying drug addicts down at the mission a hundred dollars or so for their personal information.

She would then take their Social Security numbers, birth dates, and last addresses to the Department of Public Safety. She would pretend to be the addict, claim she had moved and apply for a new license. The DPS worker would hit a few computer keys and snap a new photo. A few weeks later a state-issued license would arrive in the mail at her new address. That address just so happened to be Cat's apartment.

By now, the officers reported back that the apartment was empty and that according to neighbors and the leasing manager, Beth hadn't been seen for at least a couple of days. John radioed to bring back all photos and albums they could find in the apartment along with computer hard drives and anything else they deemed appropriate.

"If she's not at your place, where would she be?" Ron asked Cat.

"I dunno," Cat shrugged. "Maybe she's got somebody else taking care of her. That or if she thinks you're after her, she'll be runnin'."

"Where would she run to?" Ron immediately asked.

"I don't know which one, but check the truck stops. Anytime before when she would be in trouble, like if she owed somebody money or something, she'd be gone for a few weeks and then come back telling me where all she had been. She'd have money in her pocket and talkin' about how nice some of those big trucks are."

By the time Bethany Adams' face was plastered on all three local evening newscasts, the police had learned quite a bit more about her. She did not own a car, had recently lost her cell phone, had no bank account or credit cards, dealt only in cash, and had no brothers or sisters to turn to. Through address records provided from Austin by the head of the Department of Public Safety, they learned of six different licenses she had obtained. At least six different aliases were now known, along with the fact she had been arrested twice before – once on a charge of solicitation and once for petty theft. On the petty theft charge, she was given deferred adjudication, and the solicitation charge was thrown out of court when the arresting officer admitted under oath that on a prior occasion he had asked for and received oral sex from Ms. Adams.

For Mark, John and Ron alike, the lack of a violent criminal record was troubling but lessened by the incident at Club Fuxx, where she had performed delicate, testicle removal surgery by the nontraditional, non-anesthetized razor swipe method on the poor patron destined to become affectionately known as Uno. In total, the information concerning Beth that they learned both from Cat and from their own investigation made each detective sure that Bethany, at the very least, should be considered a person of interest and someone they needed to locate. With only four days remaining before day twenty-seven since the last killing, all three men also knew they needed to locate her quickly.

Chapter 23

As Yo-Yo was putting Lily to bed, Mark dropped a couple of ice cubes into the glass and poured himself three fingers of Crown Royale. Afterwards, he filled a wine glass with a cabernet from Landers Jenkins, well past the midpoint, for Yo-Yo and set it on the coffee table next to the lit, apple spice scented candle. With this accomplished, he parked himself in his recliner, swallowed about one and a half of those fingers of the whiskey and began to mentally go back over his day. It had now been two full days since the search for Bethany Adams began and they were no closer to finding her than when they had begun.

While police had spent the last two days in Dallas area truck stops speaking to truckers, they had gotten nowhere. Mark had found, as a general rule, truckers were second only to bikers with regards to being suspicious of the police. Add to the fact that cops started asking about a prostitute, then it was little wonder that every trucker with a wedding ring on swore they had never, ever, honest to gosh ever, seen a single lot lizard in their entire careers. The unmarried drivers didn't exactly prove to be gushers of helpful information either.

Mark himself had fared no better. Between calls

continually coming in from the reward hotline, as well as calls of the possible whereabouts of Bethany Adams prompted from the seemingly round-the-clock coverage by the local TV stations, Mark had spent most of the last forty-eight hours chasing down one worthless lead after another.

He had drained the glass and was sucking on the ice cubes while wondering if he had the strength to get back up and pour another drink when Yo-Yo came back from Lily's room.

"Sorry about that, but we had to pick out her wardrobe for tomorrow," she said, exasperated. "She couldn't decide between the Uggs boots or the silver sparkly Tom's shoes."

"Ahh, the eternal struggle. So who won?"

"She went with the Tom's; looks like the bling wins again," Yo-Yo answered, smiling. When she spotted the glass of wine he had poured for her, the smile grew bigger. "How do you always know just what I need?"

"Cheers," he said, smiling, with a mock clink of his glass with hers.

Yo-Yo took her glass and gave a delicious moaning endorsement of the wine as she drank it. "Damn, that's good," was all she could say as she set the wine back down on the table. Seeing Mark's empty glass, she asked, "Looks like you're empty there cowboy; how 'bout another round?"

Without saying a word, he gave his best, tired-as-hell smile and held out his glass. A moment later, Yo-Yo returned with his drink and brought along the rest of the bottle as well. "In case you run out again," she said, setting them both down on the end table next to Mark.

He took the drink and watched her walk away to the

couch. Even feeling like a zombie, Mark always loved watching Yo-Yo's ass. Seeing her take just the few steps to the couch for Mark seemed like being on a boat and feeling the waves rocking it side to side. Yo-Yo's hips gently rolled east and west as her ass worked north and south in a seamless and effortless act of seduction. Sometimes it was good to be Mark Witt; sometimes it was very good.

They both enjoyed another drink and talked about the case for a half hour or so. Then, Yo-Yo got up from the couch and walked over to him with her hand open. "I think someone needs to get his mind off things."

"Honey, I'm pretty beat," Mark said, mildly protesting.

"Leave everything to me," she answered softly as she took his hand.

Not wanting to appear ungrateful, Mark let her take his hand, and he followed her obediently into the bedroom where she quietly locked the door.

"What if that dead tired bit of mine was just all an act to get you in the sack?" Mark asked as he watched her unbutton his shirt.

"Well then, it worked," she answered, kissing his chest and then pushing him backwards onto the bed.

Mark put up no defense as she unzipped his pants and tossed them into the corner along with his Cole Haans. With her nude husband closely watching her every move, Yo-Yo began to remove her own clothes, slowly, piece by piece. When she reached around her back to undo her bra, Yo-Yo could see that Mr. Genie didn't seem so tired after all. Pulling her hi-rise briefs off, she climbed onto Mark and his magical Genie.

Not letting him inside at first, Yo-Yo shook her head and let her black hair cascade down onto Mark. Rolling her head side to side caused the hair to feel like strands of silk gently blowing across Mark's face and chest. Lowering her head and feeling for his mouth in the dark, Yo-Yo began to kiss him. As his hands traveled the length and breadth of her body, Yo-Yo continued to kiss Mark. Deep, hungering, complete kisses. Moments later, she reached between his legs and brought him inside her. Yes, sometimes it was very, very good to be Mark Witt.

~~~

The following morning, at the same time Mark and Yo-Yo were spooning and awakening, still in the after-glow from the previous night, Bethany Adams was bent over in the doggie style position inside a cramped sleeper. The location was a hundred miles to the north, in Ardmore, Oklahoma. The trucker who was screwing her was named Dane Corbin.

The long-haul driver was headed west with a load of produce when he picked up Beth two days earlier in Memphis. Several hours later, he blew an axle in Ardmore, and since he was an independent operator with a maxed-out credit card, his load was lost and he was stuck like Chuck. A few calls to some friends got him no money, no sympathy, and no closer to getting a new axle for his trailer, so Dane started hitting what was left of the eight ball of meth he had hidden under his seat.

Sharing it with Beth, the drugs were soon gone and then the sex began. She had been with more than her share of meth heads in the past, and she knew that it surely increased a man's sexual libido and endurance, but Dane was something else. Off the freakin' chart. While you could say he certainly left a lot to be desired in the looks department, put a couple of grams of hill-billy crank in him and ole Dane would go porn star on you in a hurry.

Several hours later, when Dane finally and mercifully fell asleep, it was with much gratitude and a certain well-earned respect that Beth climbed over him and left his big rig for the first time in two days. She so appreciated Dane's stamina and prowess that she almost felt bad about stealing the last thirty-seven dollars out of his wallet. Almost.

Chafed and raw from the roughrider who seemingly had been mauling her non-stop for the last ten hours, Beth folded the money into her purse and slowly walked across the parking lot while adjusting her eyes to the early afternoon sunlight. Entering the Flying J truck stop and restaurant, Beth glanced over to the newspaper rack while waiting to be seated. What she saw stopped her in her tracks.

Her face was on the front page of both the Dallas Morning News and the Daily Oklahoman with head-lines screaming of the Gospel Killer. Frozen in disbelief, Beth did a double take to make sure it was indeed her image in the papers. Seeing that it was, she put her head down, and from the corners of her eyes, looked each direction to see if anyone had noticed her. Not detecting anything, but with the hair-netted hostess walking towards her, Beth turned and quickly left the Flying J.

Panic-stricken, she moved through the gravel park-ing lot cutting between the tractor-trailers, not knowing what to do. A couple of the more amorous truckers called for her and tried to catch her attention, but Beth wasn't looking for a date right then. She was looking for a way out. With less than a hundred dollars in her purse, no phone, and not knowing the area, Beth desperately weighed her options. She could hook up with one of the truckers in hopes of getting to a more distant locale, but what if he had seen the papers? And if it was in the headlines, was it on TV, too? She had no way of knowing, but she was too afraid to take the chance. Finally and surely, Beth came to the conclusion that her only choice was to call Boy.

While she and Cat Binaohan maintained a rather tumultuous, on-and-off- again relationship, Boy Russell had for years been Beth's one true friend. Half Choctaw Indian and half African American, Boy, like Beth, knew how it felt to be considered an outcast, to be thought of as expendable by society. Named Charlie by his Indian mother, he grew to answer only to "Boy" out of convenience.

After all, it was what the entire Caucasian population in his hometown of Jasper, Texas, called him, so he figured he might as well accept it. Fact was, Boy grew to accept many things and always actively sought out convenience. For instance, he conveniently left Jasper shortly after a local task force was named to begin investigating a string of recent car thefts. On another occasion, Boy conveniently decided to take a job as a bar back and dishwasher at Club Fuxx shortly after his partner in crime was gunned down by a rival drug dealer.

It was at the club that the two met and had become friends. Perhaps it was their commonality, their similar disdain for accepted morals, or the fact that both simply liked to get laid, but Beth and Boy developed a close relationship. The only thing surprising about their friendship was the fact they were able to keep it secret from their co-workers.

Having made up her mind to phone Boy, Beth checked her purse for change to place the call. When she found only a dime and two pennies in her wallet, her stomach began to churn. The sun was beating down, but she was sweating much more than a person should. She was alone in a crowded parking lot with truckers all around who could possibly identify her, and she was without a phone to call the only person in the world who would come and save her.

She suddenly remembered seeing a calling card in Dane's billfold earlier when she had been robbing him of his last thirty-seven dollars. So with her head held low, Beth set out across the parking lot back towards Dane's Peterbilt. She knew that the meth head would be dangerous if he had awakened and discovered that his money was gone. But she didn't want to risk asking someone for change to make the phone call.

Beth crossed the parking lot with one hand inside her purse clutching her only weapon, a large, serrated -edged knife. No one approached her in the parking lot, and her luck continued when she found the truck's passenger side door unlocked, just as she had left it. Slowly and deliberately, she opened the door and looked inside. Dane was still very much asleep, so the knife stayed in her purse. Quietly, she went through his pants pocket and withdrew his wallet. She quickly found the calling card, and made her escape.

Moving more quickly now, she left the parking lot and walked to the closest business she could see, a greasy spoon hamburger joint named The Shack. Inside she was glad to see that it was darkly lit and had few customers. As she made her way to a booth in the back, she noticed a pay phone on the wall between the men and women's bathrooms.

A short, round waitress wearing too much makeup walked towards Beth carrying a glass of ice water and a menu. Setting them on the table, the waitress smiled and asked Beth what she would like to drink. All she wanted was to get to the pay phone as fast as possible, but she didn't want to draw any undue attention, so Beth ordered a coke and a cheeseburger without even looking at the menu.

The waitress, whose name tag read Cookie, had one more question to ask: Did she want the cheeseburger basket with onion rings? If so, they were running a special where she could get an extra patty and bacon added to her burger for only ninety-nine cents more. Still strung out on meth, not to mention an overload of adrenaline, food was pretty much the last thing on Beth's mind.

"That's sounds great," she said, desperately wanting to get rid of Cookie. With the waitress gone, Beth took out the calling card and headed for the payphone. Boy answered on the second ring.

"What the fuck's goin' on?" he shouted when he heard Beth's voice. "You're all over the news."

Sliding over towards the women's restroom to ease the path for a rather large overall-wearing Okie entering the men's room, Beth hesitated and then answered Boy with the words that were written all across her face. "Oh, fuck."

By the time the corn-fed Okie was done wiping his ass, Beth was back at her table. She had told Boy where she was and he had promised to get there as quickly as possible. As she sipped her ice water, Beth thought of Boy and smiled to herself. For after all, there was at least one person in the world who cared about her, at least one person she could count on, and that made her feel better. Those feelings proved to be short-lived, however, as the Okie from the bathroom shuffled past her and smiled towards her while sexily clearing his sinuses.

The Dr Pepper clock on the wall read 2:30 when the cheeseburger basket arrived. It was too greasy for Beth's taste, and she picked at the onion rings while listening to the regulars engage in small talk. The Shack was the kind of place where the customers knew each other by name and spent most of their time either telling one another how much money they had recently lost on the slots at the Indian casino in Durant or discussing the power train packages on the new three-quarter-ton Chevy Silverado.

Keeping an eye on the door just in case ole Dane woke from his sleep, Beth couldn't help but get enthralled with the locals. Each one was out living in the middle of Podunkville, getting their news from the Cornpone Gazette, fat as toads, and seemingly as happy as could be. To look at them and listen to them, it was as if they had not a care in the world. And here was Beth, with more troubles and worries than she could possibly escape. Each time the smiling Cookie would fill up her ice tea and then waddle away, Beth felt more and more jealous of these damn, fat, happy ass Okies.

Shadows would soon be appearing in the parking lot when the front door opened at 6:15 and in walked a gentleman. Beth was disappointed that it wasn't Boy, but at least Beth had a new regular to watch and dissect. But it was soon apparent this man was no regular. Wearing pressed clothes with shined shoes and walking confidently with an erect posture, the man canvassed the room. He clearly was looking for something…or someone.

Beth's eyes were glued to him as he stopped for a moment to speak with the affable Cookie. She could have easily been attracted to him, but there was no time. Was he the police? Trying to hold back a panic attack, Beth closed her eyes and worked to control her breathing. Gaining a semblance of control while wondering if she could beat the man to the back exit next to the kitchen, Beth opened her eyes just as the man sat down in the booth opposite her.

"Something wrong with the burger?" he asked, smiling, and then reached across the table and picked up an onion ring from her basket.

Beth didn't say a word. Instead, she watched the man closely as he ate the onion ring and then neatly used a napkin to wipe his mouth. He sure didn't eat like a cop. There was something about him. He wasn't big or muscular, but he had a presence.

And those eyes. Beth had never seen a man with eyes like this. They were light turquoise—a shade so pale she wondered if they could even be real. The contrast of his eyes with his tanned skin was mesmerizing. While she sat there trying to forget his eyes and focus on what she should do next, the man reached back across the table.

"Do you mind?" Before she could shake her head no, he pulled the whole basket towards him and cut the burger with a knife. Wrapping half the burger with the napkin, he picked it up and started eating. "I'm just so hungry, and it doesn't look like you are."

"Who are you?" Beth finally managed to say.

"Geez, I'm sorry," he said, wiping his hands off on his pants before reaching across the table to shake Beth's hand. "I'm Nick. Boy's friend." Seeing the puzzlement still on her face, he added, "Hadn't he told you about me?"

"Yeah, but let me see your license," she demanded suspiciously.

He shrugged his shoulders and laughed as he pulled his wallet out and handed it to Beth.

"So you're the mysterious Nick, huh?" she said, inspecting the photo and then tossing the wallet back to him. "Mr. Nicholas D. Claxton…So what does the D stand for?"

"Delicious," Nick answered, giving his best evil grin.

"So where's Boy," Beth asked as she began to relax. "Why didn't he come with you?"

"They called him into work right after he hung up with you," Nicholas answered, being careful to swallow the bite in his mouth before speaking. "I guess somebody got sick."

"That sucks," was all Beth could come up with as she began to get lost in those pale turquoise blue pools.

While he was quickly finishing the burger and what was left of the rings, Beth was busy sizing him up. She could see why Boy had wanted to keep this one all to himself. Smooth skin, hairless face, the body of a dancer or perhaps a gymnast, and, oh my gosh, those eyes. Beth's mind was shifting gears when Nicholas wiped his mouth again.

"We better get going."

As he paid the bill and they left The Shack, Beth made sure to walk a couple steps behind Nicholas. Just for the view. And what a view it was. Pure eye candy. How good a friend was Boy again? While knowing she couldn't afford to lose her only true friend, it was still a long way back to Dallas and a little flirting and perhaps even some dirty talking wouldn't hurt anything, would it?

"So, Mr. Delicious, are you like Boy?" she asked after they had arrived at his car in the parking lot.

"How do you mean?" he grinned, pretending not to know what she meant, as he opened the passenger door for her.

"You know. Do you swing both ways?" she said, pressing closer to him.

"Me? No, not me. I'm gay all the way. Strictly dickly," he lied and answered, holding his hands up in mock defense.

Shaking her head in disbelief, Beth immersed herself in his eyes. "I don't know if I believe you."

"I suppose if I wanted to change sides, you'd be just the one to teach me?" teased Nicholas, who was clearly enjoying the game.

Never taking her eyes off his, she slid one hand onto his belt buckle and began to playfully tug upon it. "You tell me. Know what winks and fucks like a tiger?"

"I give up," Nicholas answered after a short pause, piercing through her with his eyes.

Beth then gave him the slowest and sexiest wink any man, straight or gay, ever received. Seeing that Nicolas tilted his head upward and bit his lip in mock pain, and Beth smiled broadly before finishing with a slow blown air kiss to him. Afterwards she slid into Nicolas' car feeling pretty pleased with things for the first time all day. Not that she was all that excited to be heading back to Dallas, but thinking that during the ride to Big D she just might have herself some fun. Unfortunately, she had no idea what type fun Nicolas had in mind.

Chapter 24

It was day twenty-seven since the last Gospel Killer murder and dawn was rising on the fourth day since the search for Bethany Adams had begun. Mark lay curled up next to Yo-Yo, while across town, Marcel Durand was already awake from the excitement of his planned evening. A day earlier, Angel had phoned him at his store with the news that her husband was going to his brother's bachelor party that Saturday evening, and she would be free. Free to see Marcel, free to be held in his arms, and free to dream of their future.

Marcel was trying his best to maintain some semblance of sanity concerning Angel. After all, he barely knew her. But her visits to the store were almost daily now, and the words she said and the way she said them made Marcel believe the impossible could be true. Perhaps the man in the corner, the man invisible to most of society, could have his dream come true. Perhaps the heart of the heroine in his favorite literature could actually be swept away, not by the prince, and not with his handsomeness and bravery, but by the intellect and charm of the town's soft-spoken cobbler.

Either way, there was much work to be done. The store opened at 10:00 in the morning, and before that, Marcel still had to clean his apartment and go to the market. He had decided to prepare filet mignon for dinner. Why not live a little? Money was always tight for Marcel, but that worry could wait until tomorrow. This night would not be hindered by worry or by hesitation; it would be special because he would have it no other way.

And besides, Marcel had long enjoyed cooking, but like so much of his life now, what was the point? Cooking and fine food should be shared and enjoyed with friends, and being without too many friends, Marcel generally fixed something simple each night and ate alone. But those were the nights of his old life, not the nights of his possible life with Angel. He would share his love for food and fine wine with someone special this evening, someone who thrilled and excited him.

It was this excitement and anticipation that had Marcel wide awake and cleaning his hall baseboards at 7:15 a.m. At 8:20, his small apartment was spotless. By 8:55, he had showered and was leaving his apartment with just enough time to complete his shopping, return home with the food, and still open his art and frame shop by 10:00.

As Mark walked through the station to Coleman's office for his 11:00 a.m. meeting with John and Ron Ellis, he glanced around and thought to himself how much a police station reminded him of a casino. If you didn't look outside through a window, you had no idea what time it was. The place was just as bustling and busy and crowded at two in the afternoon as it was at two in the morning.

Monday morning or Friday night was just the same. The cops were at their desks just as the dealers were at their tables – and both were looking to take you down. The citizens or customers were always there, also, some drunk, others bemoaning their bad luck, and many trying to run a scam and cheat justice. As Mark knocked on John's door, he thought all that was missing were the cocktail girls, a roulette wheel, and the always present and, oh so lovely, patterned and brightly colored wall-to-wall carpet.

Upon entering Coleman's office and greeting both John and Agent Ellis, Mark was introduced to the third person already in the room, Chief Harrington. During the introduction, Detective Coleman gave Mark a glowing recommendation to the chief and told of his work on the case and how it was Mark who had first uncovered the possible link concerning Bethany Adams and the murders.

Despite the praise, Harrington gave Mark a rather suspicious hello and handshake, one which caused Mark to feel safe in assuming the chief surely must have already heard about dear old dad from others on the force. After sitting down and being brought up to speed concerning the fact that the whereabouts of Ms. Adams remained unknown, and that all other leads were hitting similar roadblocks, the conversation took a more dramatic turn.

"Chief, the real reason we asked you down here was to make a decision for us," John said.

Mark sensed right away that Harrington was some-one who took pride in being the man to decide things, as the chief instantly displayed a heightened sense of alertness. "Go on."

"Today is day twenty-seven since the last murder. We all believe that if the killer isn't caught today, she will kill again, today or tonight. I believe we need to get the word out through the media about this, and maybe we can stop a murder before it happens."

The chief listened but didn't offer a response, instead turning to Ellis. "Guessing you think different?"

"Damn sure do," Ron answered, standing up from his chair. "The whole twenty-seven day pattern has been kept out of the media. If we give it up now, we're throwing away our one ace. We let her know that we know this, and maybe she changes her pattern; then we gotta start back over from fuckin' square one."

"Chief, we have to do the right thing here," Coleman added as the chief hesitated. "We knew about it last time and kept quiet, and now the air conditioning guy is dead. We gotta get the word out and let the people know."

"Today, tomorrow, next week, this bitch is gonna keep killing until we stop her," Ron said, not to be outdone.

"Tell me what you know," the chief interrupted. "I mean, what do you really know about this killer?"

"What we got are mostly theories and guess work," Ellis responded. "What we really know about her, well, you could write all of it in capital letters down the side of my dick – limp, not hard."

While Mark had to admit that little Ron certainly used very interesting language choices, the chief appeared taken aback at this answer.

"Listen, what I know about this bitch is we need to keep her thinking we're a bunch of fuckin' ingrates who can't find our own asses with a GPS tracking system," Ellis clarified. "That way, sooner or later, maybe she gets sloppy and makes a mistake."

Chief Harrington rubbed his palm across his mouth

and began to nod his head in agreement.

"Chief, we are talking about someone's life here," Coleman spoke up.

"Yeah, some fucker is gonna die," Ellis added, trying to put a positive spin on things, "but at least he gets to bust a nut one more time before he cashes out."

"We need to get the word out right now — TV, radio, the Internet, newspapers, everything," John countered, not giving up.

The chief had heard enough. He stood up and held out his hand for quiet. "No media. They're already turning this into a circus, and I'm tired of being the organ grinder. Just get out there and find the bitch."

As he was picking up his hat and heading towards the door, Coleman tried once more. "If the reporters ever find out…"

The chief had made his decision and did not wish to be second-guessed. "Next time I see you talking with a goddamned reporter, it better be at a press conference announcing we caught this cunt."

As the chief left, Mark's eyes turned to Coleman. He knew the chief's words had wounded his friend. He had put down his views like a grown-up puts down the silly thoughts of a child. It was so obvious that even Ellis recognized this and refused to pile on. Instead, he patted John on the back. "Come on, guys. Lunch is on me."

~~~

Nearing dusk, Angel parked her car slightly down from Marcel's building, and with the large zebra print bag over her shoulder, began walking briskly. She was halfway up the stairs to his second floor apartment when the front door under the stairs opened and out walked an elderly woman. Angel kept up her stride and had almost made it to Marcel's door when the woman spoke to her. "You must be Angel," she called out.

Angel stopped and stepped part of the way back down the stairs. "Yes, Ma'am, I am."

"Oh, he's so right about you!" the woman exclaimed, beaming at Angel and clasping her hands together. "You are a beauty."

"Well, thank you. That's so wonderful of you to say," Angel answered as she took off her sunglasses and walked the rest of the way back down the stairs. At the bottom of the stairs, Angel attempted to shake hands with the woman, but instead, she found herself wrapped in a huge embrace.

"My dear, I was watching for you. I just had to meet you. Why, Marcel has been walking on clouds since meeting you," she said as she hugged the smiling Angel.

"Thank you. That's so great to hear, Miss, or is it Mrs?. . . ."

"Pardon me!" she answered, stepping back and releasing Angel. "I know all about you, and you don't even know who I am. I'm Joyce Seeber; and yes, it's Miss, because I never married. But that doesn't mean I don't believe in love. I do, and I know Marcel does, too."

"He's such a sweet man, really kind and so thoughtful. I tell you, Miss Seeber, I've been looking so forward to finally getting a chance to spend some time with him."

Upon hearing Angel say such nice things about her dear neighbor Marcel, Joyce swooped Angel back into her arms. "I know you are just what he needs. Marcel has waited for you his entire life. Now get upstairs and have a beautiful evening together," she said, before beginning to softly cry.

Angel was touched. "I've been waiting for this evening, too," she said, before going back up the stairs.

Inside Marcel's apartment, the two hugged and Angel told him about meeting his downstairs neighbor. Marcel apologized and explained how he and Joyce had become close friends over the years.

"She comes on a little strong sometimes, almost like a one-woman neighborhood watch committee, but she means well. She doesn't have anyone, and...well, I guess we're just a couple of lonely hearts looking out for one another. But she really is sweet."

As Angel listened to Marcel describe Miss Seeber, she saw a sweetness in him, as well as a true tenderness, prompting her to kiss him. His pleased reaction to the surprise kiss made her almost wish that she had picked out another appropriately named man for this night. It was such a real response—the response of a man who believed a life raft was floating his way to save him from the deepness and solitude of an unhappy life.

Eyes closed, mouth wavering, wishing to savor the kiss, Marcel stood before her until she had to reach in and give him another kiss—longer and more forceful. With this kiss, Angel took her hand and pulled Marcel's head to her, running her fingers through his thinning hair with one hand while reaching down and clutching one of his hands with her other. The evening was just starting; they were still only a couple of feet inside his apartment, and Marcel already sensed it was going to be everything he had dreamt.

Despite his repeated offers of assistance, Angel put away her shoulder bag in the hall closet herself and then followed Marcel into the kitchen. There, a glass of chardonnay welcomed her, along with the opportunity to watch Marcel prepare dinner. Though the kitchen was cramped, Marcel moved nimbly and even offered a commentary of his cooking. He had decided to serve the filet with mushrooms sautéed in wine sauce, along with roasted asparagus and mashed potatoes.

He thought it was a relatively simple and direct meal. Angel was extremely impressed as he cleaned and stemmed the shiitake mushrooms and then sautéed them in butter with a half cup of red wine for the sauce. The filets were done just before the sauce was finished. Marcel prepared two plates, and then he and Angel sat down at his small wooden table for their candlelight dinner.

The meal tasted even more wonderful than it looked. Delicious, satisfying, the filets were spot on, pink and easily flaked apart. The asparagus was crisp and had a dash of lemon splashed on them. The mashed potatoes had a thick, earthy, almost smoke-like flavor. For the wine, he had carefully chosen a somewhat extravagant, prized Mondus La Tyra 2005 Madiran.

Angel was dumbstruck by the meal and the conversation. Over dinner, the two talked of so many things. Most of what Angel had to say were lies, but she knew each word from Marcel was the heartfelt truth. What he lacked in strength, he made up for in emotion and conviction. He could do many things, perhaps, but he could not lie. Not to her.

When she asked about the two small porcelain pieces that sat on a table close by, Marcel went and got the two Limoges. Handing them to Angel, he explained they were pieces from his homeland. He told her about visiting the plants where the pieces had been made in the town of Limoges, France. Marcel carefully pointed out the delicate intricacies of each piece, showing her the raised enameling added to the tiny roses on the vase. He described to her and showed her the deep color of the violets on the small punch bowl piece. He explained to her in such detail the work that added artistic dimension to each piece.

It was interesting and illuminating to Angel. She marveled at him. Marcel was certainly a man who paid attention to detail, who appreciated beauty, and who understood the importance of a man taking his time and being proud of his work.

Even before that dinner, Angel had learned that Marcel was indeed different than most of the men in her life. Not overly strong, not overly decisive, yet not afraid to show these weaknesses. Marcel was vulnerable, almost fragile in many ways, and for the first time since she had started this whole thing, Angel was developing feelings for the victim.

This was a gentle man, a man she felt certain wanted to have sex with her this evening, but a man who she knew would never broach the subject in a profane or vulgar way. He would never take her head and push it downward, not even in a supposedly playful manner. Marcel was a dignified and romantic man. She could sense he was not a man who would just discard her, not one who would put her aside when he simply tired of her— like he had done to his wife when he was a younger man. As she listened to and watched him, Angel almost felt she would always have been enough for Marcel. Very different indeed.

After dinner, the two sat together on Marcel's thrift

store couch. There, the conversation continued easily but it soon gave way to caressing. The caressing led to kissing, and Angel knew the kissing would quickly lead to lovemaking. With Marcel kissing her softly, she looked into his face, trying to see into his closed eyes, trying to see him in a different and harsher light.

After all, how different was he really? He, too, had left his wife—left her and ran off to another country with some other woman who, at least, fortunately, had the good sense to leave him before he grew tired of her as well. As she was trying to convince herself, Angel didn't know if she believed Marcel was like all the others. It's just that she was forced to believe it. She had come to complete a job, and she had to look past his sympathetic eyes and stop listening to the pain in his words when he talked of his ex-wife in France. This was part of her bigger plan, and besides, things weren't always easy. Her father had taught her that when making a choice in life, usually the most diffi-cult choice was the right one. Going through with the killing of Marcel would be difficult.

~~~

Afterwards, when Angel had cleaned up everything with bleach and had put her clothes back on, she closed Marcel's front door and headed downstairs. The bag on her shoulder now seemed heavier, perhaps from the wet rags and towels she had cleaned with, and the humidity of the night seemed to invade her. The streetlight in the parking lot seemed terribly bright and seemed to be shining directly on her. So many thoughts were going through Angel's mind. She was a planner—probably well past the borderline to OCD. She hated responding to things without first thinking everything through first, but there was no time.

With the second knock on the door, Joyce's front porch light came on and she opened the door a tiny bit. The chain from the door lock was still latched across the doorway, and Miss Seeber peered out from behind it. Putting her glasses on to see, she was happy to find that it was Angel at her door.

"Hello, Miss Seeber. Hate to bother you this late, but can I come in for a moment?" she frantically said.

"Oh, of course, dear. Is everything all right?" answered Miss Seeber.

"Oh no, I cut myself, and I'm bleeding," Angel said, holding up her left hand, which was wrapped in a bloody rag. "Marcel thought you might have a bandage."

Seeing Angel's hand, Miss Seeber rushed to unlatch the door lock and open the door. "Let me see your hand," she said sympathetically.

Once inside the door, Angel quickly straightened up. Before the elderly woman could say another word, she shoved the covered hand into her mouth. With her other hand, she shoved the same knife she had used to kill Marcel into Miss Seeber's stomach. The shocked woman tried to scream, but the wrapped hand went further into her mouth and muffled all the sounds.

Angel felt Miss Seeber's teeth trying to bite into her hand as she was ripping the knife upward. She watched the veins in her forearm pop outward from stress before the old woman finally succumbed and died there next to the wall. Before opening the door and leaving, Angel looked around Miss Seeber's small apartment. She had only brought one Bible and had left it with Marcel's body, but, yes, there was one right there on the end table. Angel placed the Bible on the floor next to Joyce's body, checked out the peephole, and then quickly left.

Driving west along Highway 114, Angel was a troubled woman. As she pulled into the Ramada Courtyard, she was very concerned about the possible loose ends she had left. There had been no need for other victims any of the other times, and killing Miss Seeber was needed, but it took away from the message.

Inside her hotel room, Angel undressed and then placed her clothes and shoes in the plastic bags she had brought from home. Thoughts were still rampant in her mind when she stepped into the shower to clean herself and wash away the fake tattoos. Once there and alone, she had to face the reality of what had occurred that evening.

First, she had to admit and deal with the fact that earlier, when she and Marcel had been having sex, she had come. It had never happened during any of the other times with any of the other men. She knew why she had experienced the orgasm. The thought made her begin to cry as the hot water poured across her body.

For try as Marcel might have, it wasn't he who had made her come this evening. It had been the thought of Angel's first and one true love, a man so much different from Marcel, but one who shared certain meaningful qualities. Marcel's bicep was probably smaller than her man's wrist, and he lacked any real manly presence, but in her mind, they shared the same kindness, the same thoughtfulness.

Angel had seen the same tender look in Marcel's eyes during sex, and it had triggered thoughts of her old love. Trying to prevent the orgasm, she had attempted to concentrate and open her eyes and really look at Marcel and his soft body. Once even, God forbid, she forced herself to think of her husband, but even thoughts of hubby could not keep thoughts of the other man from creeping in.

Creep in they did, until she could almost feel *him* thrusting inside her. She could feel *him* pulling her upward to his chest, with his powerful arms underneath her body until they climaxed together. She felt *him* in that bed, but he wasn't there. He hadn't been in her bed in such a long time. He was her first and only true love, and he had left her. He hadn't touched her in years, and he was still the only man who could quench her. He was the reason she was doing this. He was the reason this message had to be delivered.

While still in the shower, she gave in to the thoughts of him once again. With the tears now slowing, Angel took a washcloth in her hand. Slowly and rhythmically, she began touching herself. She knew it was dirty, but she couldn't help herself. Her husband hadn't liked it when she had waxed her hair off from down there; now, without the pubic hair to cover herself, she used a wash cloth to keep from having to look at her own vagina while it was being pleasured.

This was dirty, but by now she could feel it swelling, could feel his hands exploring it, could feel the hot water raining down onto her. Thinking of past times when he would overwhelm her proved to be too much. She could taste him; she could feel him on her body. Angel lay down on the shower floor and imagined the water was him, covering her entire being. As her fingers went inside herself, she imagined it was his dick once again. With back arched and feet extending over the side of the tub, she exploded in an orgasm that left her body shaking for minutes.

Once clean and dressed in her normal clothes, Angel drove home in silence. The radio was on, but she didn't hear it. Her thoughts remained on him. He had left her, and that was wrong. God knew it was wrong. He had said so. And so, she would keep delivering this message.

She drove on to different locations, disposing of the plastic bags containing all her clothes and materials. As she did, she never once managed to get her mind off him. As she pulled into her garage, she began to get angry. It was the first time she had killed and returned home without a feeling of accomplishment—without feeling she was doing something important, something people needed to know about. Why did he have to ruin everything?

Chapter 25

On one side of the city, Mark was singing along with the hymns in the morning service at the same time that across town maintenance men were entering Marcel's apartment, after the building's water valve had burst. Inside they were shocked to discover his dead body on the bed.

On yet another side of Dallas, Kim Jacobsen was fretting about being late for a nail appointment. Kim had planned brunch at the club at noon with friends. By then, it was essential that her French manicure be perfect. Even if that married private detective wasn't ready to admit he wanted her, there were plenty of others who did, and Kim wasn't about to disappoint them. She herself would be perfect that afternoon as she walked from the buffet lines at the Preston Trails banquet room to her table, and everyone would want her.

With her heels clicking across the tile driveway, she hurriedly threw her bag in the back seat of her Range Rover, put the keys in the ignition and backed away from her home. She was a few blocks from her home, turning south on Coit Road to Miss Sue Chi's Nail salon, when her phone rang. As she drove, she fumbled through her purse, and at last pulled out her phone, only to find that the screen was dark and it wasn't ringing. That was odd. If her phone wasn't ringing, whose phone was, and where was it?

The ringing continued as Kim neared a stoplight. Glancing at the passenger seat, where her purse lay, she spotted a cell phone she didn't recognize. "Hello," she said impatiently, as she answered it.

"I was wondering how long it would take before you finally picked up," she heard a male voice say. When she didn't respond, Nicholas D. Claxton coaxed her. "Come on, Kim, talk to me."

"This isn't my phone. How do you know my name?"

"Now, who doesn't know the lovely widow, Kim Jacobsen?" he toyed with her.

The traffic light turned green, but Kim didn't notice until cars began to honk. As she took off from the inter-section, she spoke into the phone. "Do I know you? How did your phone get in my car?"

"No, you don't know me," Nicholas said, chuckling. "And my phone is in your car because I put it there."

Now more concerned than confused, Kim quickly turned and checked the backseat.

"I'm not in the freaking car with you," Nicholas said, laughing.

He wasn't in the car, but he had to be watching her, Kim thought, and this quickly made her frightened. Instinctively, she slowed to look at each car on the road near her.

"Geez, you better pull over before you cause a wreck," Nicholas cajoled.

"Who is this? Who are you?" she demanded.

"My real name isn't important, but the newspapers call me the Gospel Killer," Nicholas calmly responded.

A combination of terror and anger instantly seared through Kim. "Where are you? No, fuck that and fuck you. You motherfucker, you killed my husband!"

"I'm the Gospel Killer, but I didn't kill your husband," Nicholas sternly said, regaining control. "And, if you do exactly what I say, I won't kill you either."

"No, fuck you, I'm going to the police," Kim cried out, beginning to speed. "There's a station right ahead."

"You'll never make it," Nicholas calmly said. "I promise you that. And, by the way, you really should do something about your language. It's so unbecoming of a woman of your wealth."

Terror had taken the upper hand for Kim, and she slowed the Range Rover.

"That's much better," Nicholas soothed. "Besides, think about it; if I wanted you dead, I would have already killed you. However, if you want to continue to live, you need to do exactly what I am about to tell you."

"What do you want me to do?" Kim finally asked, sounding like a six-year-old trapped in a nightmare.

~~~

The service and sermon were almost complete when Mark felt the cell phone in his pocket vibrate. Knowing the timing, he thought it could well be Coleman telling him of finding a new body. After checking his phone, Mark saw it was Kim Jacobsen's number, and he scrolled the screen down to stop the call.

Why was she calling him? He had made things pretty clear with her, and now she was calling him during church? The phone vibrated again almost immediately and it was Kim again, this time with a 9-1-1 attached to the end of her number. What the…?

Mark again didn't answer, but without looking, he could feel Yo-Yo seated beside him leaning over and checking his phone. The third time the phone vibrated with Kim's number and again with the 9-1-1, Mark got up, walked outside the auditorium and answered her call.

"Didn't you understand you weren't to call me?" he said sharply.

"You need to come to Bubba's now," Kim answered.

"Bubba's? Why in the hell would I go to Bubba's?" Mark yelled into his phone, shocking the ladies at a nearby table who were preparing to hand out church pamphlets at the end of the service.

He was apologizing to the women in the foyer for his outburst when he heard Kim's phone being handed off.

"We got a problem," he heard his father say. "You need to get down here now."

With no more information than his dad's insistence that this was important, Mark was left standing there dumbfounded as the service ended. He found himself explaining that he was being called away because of work, first to Yo-Yo and then to his son Daniel and ex-wife Kellie.

When dropping off Yo-Yo and Lily at home, he gave both of them a kiss and told them he would be back as soon as possible. Smiling, he did his best to put the minds of both of the women in his life at ease as he drove away. Once out of the neighborhood, the smile disappeared as Mark wondered just what he was heading into.

Chapter 26

Pulling into the Club Fuxx parking lot, Mark saw Bubba's Bentley, Kim's Range Rover, a black Mercedes he didn't recognize, and an out of place Oldsmobile Aero. The Olds, with the back bumper on the driver's side hanging halfway to the ground, belonged to his dad.

As he entered the office, Mark figured out who owned the Mercedes. Joining his dad, Kim, Bubba, and Lew the Magician was drug kingpin Marcus Ramirez. Mark nodded to the others and shook Marcus' hand, all the while thinking, just how fucked up is this shit that Bubba, the Magician, and Marcus are all involved?

Mark was taking his place on the red leather couch that ran the length of one entire office wall when he noticed a cell phone sitting on Bubba's large wooden desk. Normally cluttered, it was now clean, and the phone seemed to have been placed almost perfectly in the center of it, standing out in its solitude.

Mark noticed something else; all the people in the room seemed nervous, their faces etched with fear and worry. These were faces that Mark thought should have been comfortable sitting alongside Hitler and Bin Laden in the seventh ring of Hell. If these people were nervous, it was not a good sign.

"Okay, what's the problem, and why am I here?" he

asked after a second's hesitation.

"You're here for the same reason we all are," Bubba spoke up, with just the appropriate amount of gruffness. "Because of that phone."

That didn't exactly clear things up. Mark was still trying to understand what the old man meant when Kim got up from her chair, came and sat down beside him. "That phone was placed in my truck by the Gospel Killer. He called me on it and told me to get each of you together."

"The Gospel Killer called you?" he exclaimed, thinking that whatever he had expected, that was not it. "The woman who called, she said she was the Gospel Killer?"

"It wasn't a woman," the still frightened Kim said, placing her hand on Mark's knee. "It was a man's voice. And, yes he said he was the Gospel Killer, and he knew each of you by name. Said all of you would want to hear what he had to say, and that if I didn't do just what he said, he would kill me."

She lowered her head and waited for Mark to sympathetically put his arm around her, but he refused.

"The killer's not a man," he said as he leaned forward. "I've seen the video. This is horseshit."

While the others remained silent, Kim raised her head. "All I know is that he said to get you all together and that he would call back at 1:00."

Mark checked his watch and saw it would be one o'clock in just a few minutes.

"He's supposed to call on that phone?" he asked, pointing to Bubba's desk.

"He said to tell you not to try and trace it," she said, nodding. "Said you wouldn't want what he was going to say to be recorded."

Mark was unsure what to make of things as he looked around the room. He happened to be staring at his father when the cell rang, and he saw the dread in his dad's eyes.

"This is Bubba Furh," Bubba said, after grabbing the phone. "Who the fuck is this?"

"I'm the Gospel Killer," Nicholas answered point blank.

"Good for you," Bubba fired back. "Now what the fuck does that got to do with me?"

"Well, before I get going, Mr. Bubba, could you hit the speaker button on the bottom of the phone so everyone can hear me?" Nicholas wryly said.

With everyone watching anxiously, Bubba fumbled with the phone before getting it on speaker and setting it back down on his desk. "All right, the fucking speaker's on."

"Very good. Suppose now I should start with calling the roll to make sure the gang's all there. Know that Mr. Bubba is there, so how about the beautiful Kim Jacobsen?"

"We're all here!" Bubba roared.

"We'll do things my way," Nicholas shot back. "Kim, are you there?"

"Yes, I'm here," she said, glancing at Mark before answering.

"What about Lew the Magician? What a great name by the way, fucking great. You there, Lew?"

"I'm here," Lew responded, void of emotion.

"Super, and how about Dallas' one man drug wave, Mr. Marcus Ramirez?"

"I'm here, you fuckin' cocksucker," Marcus fired

back.

"Well, you do have me there, Marcus," Nicholas said, appearing for the first time to be taken somewhat aback. "I do love sucking a nice fat cock. Perhaps we could meet for some Cervezas later, and I could show you?"

"Fuck you, you faggot. When I see you, I'll run your goddamn ass through a fuckin' tree grinder."

"What is it with you Mexicans and lawn equipment?" laughed Nicholas. "Want to run my ass through a tree grinder? Damn, Marcus, you are one hot-blooded Latino, aren't you?"

Bubba put up his hand for Marcus to stand down. After a pause, Nicholas said, "All right. Well, moving on; is one of Dallas' former finest there, a Mr. Richard Witt?"

"I'm here," Richard growled.

"Not that this really pertains to you per say, Mr. Witt. I just wanted you to be here to learn of your son's secrets and to perhaps lend some fatherly advice."

Richard was eyeing a nervous Mark when, with a laugh, Nicholas added, "And now, last but not least, that son of yours, the man of the hour, drum roll please. Is Mr. Mark Witt in attendance?"

Mark sat on the edge of the couch with his hands on his knees and appeared ready to either strangle someone or to launch himself onto the phone, until finally and with everyone in the room looking at him, he answered Nicholas.

"I'm here. Now who the fuck are you? Cause I know you're not the Gospel Killer," was Mark's rather harsh greeting to Nicholas.

Laughter came through the phone before Nicholas

answered. "And we're going to be working so closely together. You know, I was really hoping we could start out by being friends."

Mark had never really learned the art of tact and responded, "Listen, dumb shit, I may be a lot of things, but I ain't your friend." More laughter followed.

"Oh, I know what all kinds of things you are Mark Witt. In fact, you'll see that I know just about everything about you."

Mark usually met threats, even veiled ones, with hostile and alpha male aggression, but this one gave him pause. There was something chilling in the way he had said the word everything.

Bubba, the Magician, and Marcus all looked at him and waited for his response as Mark sat there thinking of everything, which to him meant the safety of Yo-Yo and Lily.

"Come on, I said I wanted to be friends," Nicholas spoke up, sensing Mark's thoughts from the silence. "I have no reason to hurt your family. Really, how big a monster would I have to be to do something to Lily or Yo-Yo?"

Hearing his wife and daughter's names was like someone pushing the plunger down on the dynamite. Mark leaped from the couch and ran towards the phone screaming, "Goddamn, you motherfucker, I'm gonna find your…"

Marcus and the Magician grabbed Mark from behind and tried to control him.

"It's a bad idea to threaten this man's family," Bubba said to Nicholas. "I've known him since he was a boy, and I'm tellin' you, if you hurt either of his girls, God himself won't be able to save you."

Hearing these words from Bubba proved sobering. "All right, how about both of us stop with the threats and get down to business?" Nicholas said after a short pause.

Mark took a deep breath to gather his thoughts. "The Gospel Killer is a woman," he said, after Marcus and the Magician had released him.

"That's why I'm calling you, Mark. You see, I killed the first twelve, that was act one of my play. Then this bitch came along, and now she's ruining my plan, so naturally, I need to find her. Finding people is more your line of work than mine, so I want you to find her for me."

The answer bit Mark. He knew of the possibility of a copycat killer, and he knew the police were puzzled by the lapse in the timing between the first twelve killings and this second set of murders. These thoughts made Mark ask, "How do I know you killed the first twelve?"

"Due to your friendship with Detective Coleman, I'm going to assume that you've seen the case files. If so, you will then know that two of the first twelve victim's bodies suffered varying degrees of mutilation."

Mark knew the hands of the third victim, John Demus, had been severed and never found, and that the nipples of the ninth victim, Luke Clifford, had been cut off. "All right, which of the twelve and what did you do to them?"

"The third man, John Demus, scratched me during sex, and I was afraid he might have my DNA under his nails, so I cut both his hands off. The other time, I believe it was with the ninth man, a fellow named Luke Clifford. He was very, very fat but had wonderful dark maroon nipples. They were like sucking soft mushy eggplants. I just had to cut them off and take them with me. But then they started smelling, and I had to put them down the disposal."

Everyone's face in the room was glued to Mark. For the most part, these were hardened criminals and killers themselves, and their faces showed shock and disgust. As Mark slowly nodded to the group that this was indeed the Gospel Killer, he saw Kim bury her head in her hands and begin shaking in fear.

Mark paced around the room as he tried to gather his thoughts. "All right, say I believe you're the Gospel Killer; now tell me why I would help you find someone?"

"For the greatest reason of all! For self-preservation," Nicholas shouted with glee.

"I thought you were through with the threats?" Mark shot back.

"Oh, my dear Mark, it's not me you have to worry about. For you see, if you don't find this woman who is attempting to steal my rightful glory, I'm quite sure the men in the room with you right now will be the ones threatening you."

Standing still at the front of the desk, Mark felt like a train had just hit him. What the fuck did this guy mean? Mark knew he wasn't exactly among friends, but why would these men want to help the killer? Evidently, Bubba was wondering the same thing.

"Quit fuckin' talking in riddles and tell us what you mean," he angrily asked.

"I realize you're an old man, but does everything have to be in such a hurry for you?" Nicholas gasped in exasperation. "Can't you enjoy the slow and defined development of my story?"

"I don't give a fucking, rat shit about your mother-fuckin' story," said Bubba, who wasn't used to being talked back to in this manner. "Tell us what it has got to do with us or go fuck yourself."

"I'm sensing a great deal of pent-up hostility in that room," replied Nicholas, almost giggling. "But, all right, hold on and let me get a drink; this may take a while. And please, let me finish, and afterwards there will be time for a short Q and A."

Kim and all the men anxiously listened as they heard the killer pick up a glass and take a drink. Finally, after setting the glass down, Nicholas cleared his throat and continued. "Okay then, if everyone is ready, please follow along. Several years ago, Mr. Marcus Ramirez' sweet daughter, Carolina, was kidnapped and held for ransom."

"How the fuck do you know that?" exploded Marcus.

"Would someone please deal with Mr. Machismo?" Nicholas asked. "This will only take longer if I keep having disruptions."

Each of the men in the room was more than apprehensive, but Mark put his arms around Marcus' shoulder. "Try and take it easy. Let's hear what all he's got to say."

The people in the room heard clapping as Nicholas applauded. "Thank you, Mark. You know when I saw you on TV the other day, I just knew you would be a take charge, he-man kind of guy."

"Just go ahead," Mark said, motioning everyone to keep quiet and play along.

"Very well. After the kidnapping, Marcus enlisted the services of Mark Witt to handle the matter and bring his daughter home safely. The brave Mr. Mark performed his duties handsomely and returned with the beautiful Carolina relatively unharmed. However, the same could not be said for Mark or the four bodies he had killed and dumped in the trunk. Afterwards, as fate would have it and as Mark recuperated in the hospital, Marcus turned to Mr. Bubba for assistance in ridding himself of the four unfortunate men in the car's trunk."

Bubba, Marcus, and the Magician were clearly on pins and needles as Nicholas went on. "For this matter, Bubba turned to his trusted aide, Lew the Magician. Once again, I love the name. But anyway, the Magician disposed of the bodies on a piece of property outside of Stephenville, Texas. I understand it was property used for deer hunting and owned by a Mr. Darrell Nottingham. Mr. Nottingham would remain nameless, but unfortunately he was a degenerate gambler and frequent customer of Mr. Bubba's. Last fall, after a particularly bad weekend of college football, he was forced to sign over the property to Bubba to cover gambling losses. So now you see, Mark killed four men; Marcus no doubt paid him handsomely to do so, and then the Magician disposed of the four bodies on property then used by and now owned by Mr. Bubba Furh."

This was getting uglier by the minute. The killer's remark about self-preservation could well prove correct, for Mark could sense the men in the room becoming nervous, and he knew they were as stable as nitro when nervous. Bubba, in particular, looked ready to twist off.

"And, exactly how is it you know all this?" he said into the phone.

"Oh well, I suppose it won't hurt to tell you now. I learned it from an employee of yours, Boy Russell," Nicholas replied after a short pause.

Bubba began hurling expletives and the Magician checked the gun in his shoulder holster.

"But don't worry, he won't tell it to anyone else," Nicholas said. "You see, I had to kill poor Boy, but not before he told me exactly where it was the Magician had him dig the holes for the aforementioned four unfortunate souls. Found it rather easily and right where he said, ten yards due west of the stock tank that backed up to the tree line. Not far from the back end of the property, I believe."

The Magician hung his head and slowly nodded affirmation of the location to Bubba, who slammed his hands into the desk. Marcus looked at the ceiling in anguish, and Mark glanced at Kim, who seemed to have lost all her appeal and confidence.

"We think the woman you are looking for is named Bethany Adams," Mark said to the killer. "The police should find her anytime now."

"Yes, I know they will," Nicholas said without hesitation. "Because after I hang up with you, I'm going to call and tell them where they can find her body —or at least most of it. For you see, I'm afraid she has lost her head. After I killed her last night, I removed it and then drove about an hour and a half to bury her poor head in Stephenville right alongside the four bodies that you killed, Mr. Witt. So my dear Mark, if you allow me to be caught, I will lead the police to the location where they can find Ms. Adams' head along with the four other bodies. And since I do not like taking credit for other's handiwork, I will also be forced to tell them how you gentlemen were involved in the deaths of the other bodies they find."

"Who the fuck would believe you?" growled Marcus. "You're just some sick psycho motherfucker."

"Do you want to bet your life and livelihood on that, Mr. Ramirez?" Nicholas answered, with perfect time and no emotion. "Look at the faces of the others in the room with you now and see if they think my story would be compelling? For even if the killings were all self defense and done while trying to rescue a poor kidnapped girl, the fact is you denied anything happened for years and buried the four men that were killed. I can't believe that would help your case."

Mark knew that it wouldn't. He was stunned by what he had heard, and he didn't have to look at anyone else's face to know they felt the same way.

"How do you know that it wasn't Beth Adams who did the other killings?" Mark finally asked after stumbling for words.

"Mark, please, the poor girl was almost feral," Nicholas said, sounding deflated. "She didn't have the ability to perform these crimes. I must say, I'm disappointed you could even ask that. Perhaps, I've overestimated you. Either way, a word of caution going forward; it would be most unwise to doubt me, just as it would be unwise to go to Stephenville and attempt to move the bodies. For I have placed outdoor cameras at several locations close by, and if I notice any activity or if any of the cameras suddenly stop working, then I will be forced to notify the police post haste."

Silence fell over the room. Feeling defeated, Mark stared at the phone on the desk instead of looking up and having to see the faces of the others.

"Come now, Mark, I know this must come as a shock to you, but I need you to focus," Nicholas said after a lingering pause. "You have to find this bitch for me. She can't be taking my credit."

"Why do you need my help?" Mark managed to say. "Seems like you're doing pretty good on your own."

"Flattery is always appreciated, but the fact is I got lucky. If I hadn't known Boy so well, I never would have learned of Beth or you gentlemen. And while I terribly hated killing poor Boy, now that he is gone I will need your detective skills to find the woman who has taken it upon herself to continue my work. Also not to place any undue pressure on you, but it is very important that you find her before the police do. I simply can't allow anyone else to receive the fame my own efforts deserve. So, that is your assignment; find this woman who is trying to piggyback off my endeavors. And remember, if the police find her first, I'm afraid that will be most problematic for you and your friends. But if you find her first and then end her life, well, then you can get on with the fun of trying to catch me."

With his head still down and staring at the phone, Mark closed his eyes. This call had caught him out of left field, and he wasn't prepared, but he couldn't show that to the others in the room or the killer. To gain focus, Mark tried to control his breathing. Though he was standing still in an office, he had been breathing erratically from the stress of the call, so getting a hold of his body was job one.

Job two was getting control of the situation. He knew it was imperative for him to try to remember each word that came from the killer's mouth. Anything could be a clue — not just what he said, but how he said it. As Mark was going over the conversation in his head, looking for things which stood out, Nicholas grew tired of the pause in their talk. "Well, I guess that's enough for right now, ole Mark. You have your assignment, so ciao."

After Nicholas hung up, Mark stood there motionless, still concentrating on the conversation. He was still searching through the killer's words when Bubba spoke up and broke the silence. Sounding like a Hollywood sound engineer's version of the Grim Reaper, Bubba said, "This can't go any farther."

Mark was vaguely considering all the implications of this statement when Bubba added, "Find that motherfucker before the police do and put him in the ground."

Mark hated to agree with the old man. But the truth was, he already knew that would be the best option.

Chapter 27

As Mark was leaving the meeting and heading home, thoughts were exploding in his mind about the phone call. There were too many to count and too depressing to work through, but not more than were running through Detective Coleman's mind across town.

His brain felt like it had been scattershot by a twenty-gauge shotgun. First, the call he had been expecting Sunday interrupted morning breakfast. Another man found dead from knife wounds. Maintenance workers trying to stop a water line break had discovered Marcel Durand. Ron Ellis was waiting for John when Coleman arrived at the scene and informed him that all indications were this was yet another victim of the Gospel Killer.

Before Detective Coleman could even inquire and display his lack of language expertise, Ellis told him that Marcel was French for the name Mark. The names, once again, matched. Inside, Mary Trevino nodded when he asked if the murder weapon had again been a serrated-edged knife.

The apartment had been sealed and forensics was once again going through the location and cataloguing all possible evidence. Not that they expected to find anything. Even the new Bible left beside the body would prove untraceable. All the Bibles had been King James versions and were new, but the police had been unable to locate any retailer who could identify any suspect as the one buying the Bibles.

Certainly, the Bibles had been bought separately and not in a large or single purchase or in any manner that could prove memorable. As Coleman looked at Durand's nude body, he almost felt beaten before the game had even begun. This bitch would again prove better than him. He knew the day she would kill; he knew a small number of appropriately named, possible male victims; and he still could do nothing to stop it.

He was thinking, if only the chief had let him make public what they knew, maybe this man lying before him would still be alive. He was thinking this as he looked down on the multiple knife wounds in Marcel's chest and thinking about how a bitch could do something like this and execute it flawlessly each time. He also caught himself thinking about what the heck the little porcelain pieces on the shelf were called when Patrolman Dan Blackburn stuck his head inside the taped-off room and yelled, "Hey Coleman, we got another one downstairs." Another what?

Not bothering to ask the question, much less wait for the response, Coleman and Ellis rushed out of the apartment and headed downstairs. There they found the dead Miss Joyce Seeber. Officer Blackburn and his partner, Officer Walker, explained they had been going door to door seeking possible information or witnesses to the Durand killing when through the side window, they saw Miss Seeber's body lying on the floor. Entering the apartment, they found it to be very neat and organized, other than of course for the dead woman being on the floor. Nothing had been touched, and Officer Walker had begun taping off the entire location as Blackburn raced upstairs to notify Coleman.

Once inside the small apartment, Ron Ellis kneeled down and began looking closely at the body as Coleman instructed Blackburn to go back upstairs and send down Mary Trevino. Then Ellis stood up and began reenacting how he thought the murder must have occurred by stepping toward and pretending to open the front door and then being immediately attacked and falling down. Seeber was close to Ellis' height, and little Ron fell very close to her body in his reenactment.

"Damn," exclaimed Trevino as she entered the room.

"She never knew what hit her," Ellis added. "Bet the old girl got it as soon as she opened the door."

While Trevino got to work, Ellis continued with his reenactment follow up, trying to determine what the killer must have done after the murder, where she must have stepped or her hand touched. Coleman took out his pad and began to make observations. According to the driver's license in her purse, the victim was Joyce Seeber, and she was seventy-six years of age.

The apartment was a one-bedroom unit, and it was decorated in an aged manner with white doilies on the arms of the couch. A Bible was lying on the floor next to Miss Seeber, but it was definitely different than the one upstairs found next to Marcel. This Bible resembled the décor. It too was aged and appeared well used, with fraying pages.

Coleman knew the Bible must have belonged to the victim but would bag and dust it for prints, as it obviously had been placed next to the body after the murder. He knew this because there was blood on the bottom of the Bible that could only have come by setting it atop blood that was already spilled. Coleman made one other note; the blood itself looked very much like that found upstairs in Marcel's apartment. It appeared congealed, which indicated a time of death of at least eight to ten hours prior.

As Ellis silently tried to morph into the killer in his ongoing individual reenactment, Mary stood up from examining the body.

"Is it the same weapon?" Coleman asked.

"Won't know for sure till I get both the bodies downtown, but the eyeball test says yeah," she answered, sighing tiredly.

"But this body only has one wound!" Coleman remarked.

"Only one fucking wound because that is all it takes for this bitch to kill," Ellis spoke out, breaking his self-imposed silence and resorting to his usual behavior. Pointing at Miss Seeber, he added "She gutted her like a fuckin' catfish."

"It does look like one continuous cut," added Trevino. "Whoever killed her had to have a lot of strength."

"But what about the others?" Coleman asked, writing in his notebook. "If she is some super strong Amazon woman who can kill with one strike, why the multiple wounds?"

"Because she's giving us clues," Ellis answered, as if he knew all along but only now thought of it. "See, she thinks we're a bunch of fuckin' Homer Simpsons. Thinks we're a bunch of losers who couldn't catch a case of the clap in a whorehouse, much less catch a brilliant fuckin' genius killer like her. I'm telling you, this whore is laughing at us. Thinks she has to leave us clues to make it any fun at all."

Though Mary was taken somewhat aback by Ellis' verbal portrait, she paused and then nodded. "Maybe so. The guy upstairs has ten wounds on his chest and stomach and eleven on his back. Only one on his upper chest is deep. It may have killed him or would have in time, and the others are shallow and not much more than surface cuts. By the bloodstains, it looks almost like the murderer killed him and then rolled him over and stabbed or cut on his back eleven more times."

Coleman grabbed this news. "So, one kills the guy and then she cuts him what, another twenty times to leave us a message, to leave us a clue?"

While Ellis and Coleman were mentally racing through possible meanings of the number of cuts and wounds, an additional thought was rampaging through Coleman's brain—what in the hell was he going to tell the chief? John checked his watch and was surprised he hadn't already heard from Chief Harrington. The information went out on the police radio hours earlier, but still no call from the chief.

Coleman figured some Sunday get-together at the country club was perhaps taking precedence over Harrington's police duties, but either way, he knew he had to inform him before he heard about it on the news. Harrington didn't like his face being associated with the failure to capture the Gospel Killer, but the politician in him knew it was important to always be the face of the force, no matter the circumstance. Harrington was a figurehead in some ways, ass kisser in some ways, and taskmaster in many others, but he was determined to always be the face the people of Dallas expected to see leading their police force.

Knowing this, at around 2:30, and although he would
be at the scene for hours to come, Coleman trudged
to his car for some privacy to make the dreaded call
to Chief Harrington. He was trying to work through
the best method to inform the chief of two additional
Gospel Killer murders when, opening the car door,
Coleman caught the last part of a radio message where
a woman's headless body had been found off Balch
Springs Road.

"Did they say a woman's body was found without
her head?" he asked a nearby uniform, to make sure
he had heard this correctly.

"Yeah, my buddy, James Lucky, was first on the
scene," said the uniformed officer, a patrolman named
David Carroll. "Called me and said he found a butter-
head chick. Said everything was there but her head.
Did say it was a waste too. He's a tit man and said this
girl had a helluva rack."

Not responding, Coleman sat down in his car and
closed the door. Listening to the young patrolman, John
knew it was time for him to find something else to do
with his life. He was too disconnected to the new hires
and no longer had the desire to even try and close the
divide. It was at that moment that he decided to retire.
When he was through with the Gospel Killer, he would
be through with being a cop. Of all the thoughts that
had rampaged though his mind this day, that was the
single thought that was clear and certain. The finality
of the thought even made him smile as he dialed the
chief's cell.

~~~

A hundred miles away, Angel was stopping for gas
on I-35 in Hillsboro. After each kill, she followed Short

Timer's instructions and disposed of all her tools: the knife, the clothes, the phones, the wigs. Then the following day, she always traveled a couple hundred miles away or farther and bought the new supplies she would again need.

Short Timer had drilled into her the importance of not being the killer caught on a Home Depot video buying lighter fluid and rope a half hour earlier and two miles away from where an arson and murder were committed. Working her plan, she had purchased a new track phone from a Wal-Mart in Round Rock, a set of cooking knifes from an outlet mall in Temple, and a dark wig from a mall kiosk in Austin, all with cash and all with a purpose. Still, she remained bothered. Not by thoughts of the disgusting Short Timer, but rather, it was the continued thoughts of *him* that haunted her.

She certainly was not bothered by thoughts of her husband. He had completely bought her story about why she needed to skip church that Sunday and drive to Longview to visit her best friend, Anne. No, only he bothered her. She was still upset with herself from the previous night. She had let thoughts of *him* interfere. Thoughts of *him* had made her do bad things. She was getting away from her plan.

Also, she had developed feelings for Marcel and killed a woman who would have been a witness. Killing women was not part of her plan. Is this what happened before people got careless and got caught? She could not let that happen because there was still so much of her plan left to unfold.

Angel knew these mistakes, these slip ups, were only symptoms. The real problem was that he was still in control of her. She hated this – that he had been gone for so long and still could control her thoughts and actions. He had made her have such bad thoughts and act upon them. He had made her touch herself and made her crave his body. He had made her think of *him* whenever her husband insisted on having sex. Made her feel the difference of her husband's soft, almost boyish body and his hardened thick body, made her think and feel the difference between the touch of a weak and almost feminine man and the touch of a man who knew how to deliver pleasure.

As Angel slid her prepaid MasterCard into the gas pump, she knew going to Round Rock earlier had been a mistake. It was too close to Lake Travis, where they had spent their first weekend alone together. During those times, he had tried so hard to make her happy, saving his money and making time for a getaway to a Lake Travis bed and breakfast.

Once there, he was afraid it was going to be a disaster. The room didn't have television, and the air conditioner was broken on that sweltering June weekend. She could have cared less about any of that; she had him and had never experienced such an awakening. They never left the room. He had wanted her then. He had pleasured her time and again and he had helped her experience things unknown to her.

He had been her first, and though she knew it was against God's law to engage in sex before marriage, she felt it would be okay since she was certain they would marry. On the drive home from Lake Travis that weekend, with their hands squeezed tightly together as he drove, Angel remembered thinking, now it was she who had something over all the other girls at school. They used to talk about sex and boys in ways she couldn't understand, and now she knew things they could never understand, for she knew how it felt to be with her man. Her man, just the sound seemed distant and from so long ago, but thoughts and memories of him were still so fresh, still hauntingly fresh, though he was gone and she was married to another.

Leaving the gas station to pull onto the highway, Angel saw a man walking across the parking lot that reminded her of her man. The guy in the parking lot was not as handsome as her man had been, but he did have a similar rugged look and broad shoulders. And he walked with his head high. He glanced at her as she drove by and gave Angel a friendly smile. These thoughts were still fresh when on the radio, Travis Tritt began to sing his soulful country ballad, "Anymore."

She listened intently to the lyrics: "My mind keeps recreating a life with you alone. And I'm tired of pretending I don't love you anymore." The words poured through her car as tears began streaming down her face. She, too, was so tired of pretending. As she drove, she wiped away the tears from her eyes and looked at them in her hand. Feeling the tears with her fingers, Angel knew they weren't as wet as she was getting between her legs. A road sign showed a rest stop a mile ahead; a rest stop where she would pull over, recline the seat, and give in to her desire for him once again.

Chapter 28

When the alarm rang the following morning, announcing it was 6:30 a.m., Mark was already on the road.
As the horrific sound grew louder, Yo-Yo was finally
forced to wake and turn it off. As her hand managed to
grope the alarm before mercifully finding the button to
turn it off, she turned her head and looked for Mark.

Seeing he wasn't there was further proof to her that
something was wrong. Daniel had spent the afternoon
and evening with the family the previous day, and this
was usually all that was needed to ensure a great day
for her husband. But when Mark did get home from
his business meeting, even Daniel being there didn't
seem enough to brighten his mood.

Throughout the evening, Mark had seemed distant. Even as they lay in bed the night before with
her head on his chest and Mark running his hands
through her hair, Yo-Yo could sense he was far away.
As her hand began touching him and drifting lower,
he didn't respond. His body may have responded, but
Yo-Yo knew his mind was in a completely different
place. If there were one thing she could change about
Mark, it would be that he could allow himself to be
open and reveal more. Whenever he refused to, Yo-Yo
worried, and as she got out of bed this morning, even

her flawless face showed concern.

Mark was going up the on ramp to Interstate 20 when he took another drink from his coffee cup. It was home-brewed Community brand coffee, his longtime personal favorite, but still Mark wanted more. Why couldn't they just have caffeine IV's for people like him who needed their fixes and didn't want to wait for the whole digestive process to take effect? Anyway, it would be gone before he was out of Tarrant County, and he would have to stop and purchase another cup at a roadside convenience store.

Leaving the store and getting back on the highway, Mark attempted to once again go over his thoughts and try and form a plan. The previous night had been restless, to say the least. Lying with Yo-Yo and watching her sleep, and getting up periodically and checking on his sleeping daughter — the stakes of this game were clear to Mark. There was a madman out there who knew where he lived, knew his girls by name, and who knew things about him that Mark could never allow to be made public. Mark was a guy who, when push came to shove, would pull a gun and do what was necessary. And what was necessary in this instance was to find and kill the man he had talked with on the phone the previous day. For the only thing Mark was certain of this morning as he drove west on I-20 was that regardless if the woman doing this second round of killings was caught or not, the original Gospel Killer would continue to threaten him and his family until he was put down. Catching and putting him down were the reasons Mark was headed to Stephenville this morning.

Pulling into town, Mark, who had not watched the

evening news the night before, heard on the radio from station WBAP about the two new murders committed by the Gospel Killer. Then, almost as an afterthought at the end of his segment, the newsman squeezed in the unrelated fact that a nude, headless woman's body had also been discovered at a different location Sunday. Of course, Mark knew who the headless woman would prove to be, and while that didn't exactly strengthen his appetite, there wasn't much else to do in Stephenville at 7:15 in the morning. Still too early to call and get directions to the property from Bubba, Mark decided to stop for breakfast at a local diner.

Sitting at the bar, he ordered two eggs sunny side up, hash browns, a double side of bacon and rye toast. He thought the young girl who kept filling his coffee cup might not have been too bad looking if a guy could get past her grill. Problem with her grill was that much of it wasn't there, and the parts that were there weren't exactly pearly white. The girl, who called herself Karla with a K, seemed to take to Mark right away. Not having time for the regulars, she kept Mark's coffee topped off while filling him in on every-thing Stephenville. By the time he got out of there, the only thing that Karla with a K had taught Mark about Stephenville was that if she were any example, their public school system had serious problems.

Mark left the diner's gravel parking lot quickly before Karla with a K could get away and chase after him, then picked up his cell and called Bubba. Not used to early rising, the phone was handed between at least two of what sounded like very young Hispanic girls before the old man finally answered.

"Do you know what fuckin' time it is?" Bubba asked

with a particularly gruff voice, eschewing any charade of politeness.

Mark assured him he did and then said the reason for the call. "I'm down here in Stephenville and remembered you saying I was welcome to go fishing at your place sometime. Got my son with me down here but forgot exactly where it was."

Bubba paused, but understood what Mark was talking about. Always aware of the possibility of police or federal wiretaps, he exhaled, gave Mark directions, and wished him luck with his fishing trip.

Taking the farm and market road off I-20 to Bubba's place, Mark pulled up to the front gate in only minutes. There, he saw the first proof that someone had indeed been there. The chain connecting the gate and post to a combination lock had been cut with a pneumatic cutter. Entering the property, he followed the tire path to an opening and then got out to take a closer look.

While walking, Mark saw some old deer tracks, several fresh cow patties, and not much else, before spotting a stock tank near a heavily treed area. Drawing closer, before he even had to walk ten yards west, Mark saw the signs of fresh digging. Stopping and looking at the tree line, he spotted four outdoor cameras. Knowing he was probably being watched, he waved as he neared the cameras and then took out his notepad and wrote down the makes and models of each camera. Stepping back towards the tank and taking a bigger look, he could not see any other evidence someone had been there recently. After a moment and hearing a bass splash behind him in the tank, Mark wished he had in fact brought his fishing rod but of course knew today was not for relaxing.

Fixing the gate together the best he could, Mark drove away and let the Charger roll back to Dallas. On the way, he called Yo-Yo to apologize for leaving so early and without saying good-bye. He told her he loved her and assured her everything was fine and not to worry.

Knowing he had been unconvincing, Mark told his wife not to worry about cooking, because he wanted to take the two prettiest girls in the world out to dinner that evening. That brightened her mood, but Mark knew she was still concerned when he told her he would see her soon. For a few miles after closing his phone, Mark thought of nothing else but Yo-Yo and Lily being targets for the killer.

A short time later, he glanced down and saw that the Charger was pushing past a hundred and realized his blood pressure was surely racing even faster. He slowed the car, picked his phone back up and called Coleman.

Glad to see Mark's number on his phone, John picked it up and quickly went over the details of the Durand and Seeber killings. Their conversation stretched on with each detail creating a different question and possible reasons or answers.

"If this woman, Beth Adams, is really who we're looking for, with all the news coverage and all, how could she still be in Dallas and getting away with this without anyone noticing?" Coleman asked Mark.

Mark knew that Beth was still in Dallas, though not in any condition to do the killings. But since he couldn't reveal this information, he answered, "Maybe someone did notice. Maybe that's why the woman was killed too."

Coleman reluctantly agreed, and Mark told him he was working on a couple of things and would stay in touch. Mark hated lying to anyone, but lying to Coleman seemed even worse. John had cared so much for him for so long, had done so many things to help him throughout his life, and now Mark was hiding things from this man? There were so many reasons why he had to find this killer, but to Mark the two most important were to protect his family and to stop being dishonest with his friend.

Shifting those thoughts from his mind, Mark knew he had to get to work. His first stop would be the Bass Pro Shop in Grapevine, Texas. Entering the mega sporting goods store north of the airport, he asked for and received directions for the manager's office. Once there, he met the acting store manager, Mr. Glenn Danielson. Mark found Mr. Danielson, a thin man with a sharp nose, to be very friendly, at least until he explained the reason for his visit.

Explaining that he was a private investigator working on the Gospel Killer case, Mark said he had reason to believe the killer had possibly purchased four Bushnell outdoor cameras recently and was wondering if the store could check their sales records for the past few days. The request seemed to perplex Mr. Danielson, who grew suspicious almost immediately and asked why the police weren't investigating this. He also said he was only acting as the store manager, while the actual manager was on vacation, and that he wouldn't be able to help with Mark's request without some form of written authorization.

Mark tried to reason with him by saying he was working with the police on this matter and that, really, all he was hoping for was perhaps a credit card receipt if they, by chance, had sold a number of the cameras within the last few days. Despite being reminded how important the case was, Mr. Danielson said he was very busy and kept repeating he would need some sort of authorization.

Mark was playing a hunch that the killer had no time to plan out the Beth Adams killing and that the situation presented itself and was acted upon. With this thought came the hope that the killer had not been equipped with the cameras and was forced to buy them within the last few days. So when Mr. Danielson doused these hopes, Mark, for just an instant, felt like grabbing the skinny Barney Fife looking motherfucker and beating his sharp nose down to a flattened, bloody, fleshy mess. Thinking better of it, he instead gave Mr. Danielson a "fuck you" look and said, "Thank you so much for your help."

Leaving Bass Pro Shop, Mark headed out Highway 114 to the area's other sports superstore, Cabela's. Mark generally favored Bass Pro Shop because it was closer to his home, but entering Cabela's, he decided he might have to reconsider. The store was even bigger than Bass Pro and had a superior gun and shooting section. When Mark met the manager, Ms. Jessie Kimbrough, he knew he would never set foot in Bass Pro Shop again.

Ms. Kimbrough had a strong resemblance to Dara Torres, the Olympic swimmer, and looked to be in her late thirties or early forties, with a body Mark felt sure was built to last and eyes that could make a man forget he was married. Luckily, Mark had a very good marital memory and explained to Ms. Kimbrough who he was and why he was there. When hearing it could help solve the Gospel Killer case, Ms. Kimbrough, who insisted on being called Jessie, told Mark to follow her.

Entering the manager's office, Jessie introduced Mark to her executive assistant, Mrs. Christy Hallman. Mrs. Hallman was probably north of twenty pounds overweight but it didn't hurt her self-confidence. Jessie told Christy who Mark was, what he was working on, and to give him everything he needed.

Mark couldn't believe the reception he was being given, forget any freakin' authorization; these ladies dropped what they were doing and were helping. As he explained what he was looking for, it quickly became evident that the two women were amateur sleuths themselves.

As Christy checked sales records, Jessie was on her computer going over inventory of Bushnell outdoor cameras. Both peppered him with questions of the case. Since they were helping, Mark gave them all the answers he could. There was genuine sadness on their faces each time Mark shrugged and said, "I really can't answer that. I'm sorry."

"That's okay," Christy responded the second time he gave this answer. "We're only sorry you're married."

Mark again shrugged and held up his wedding ring as both women giggled.

"I'm sorry," blurted Jessie as Mark was still holding up his ring. "And I'm only surprised she didn't ask if you were happily married."

"Come on, have you ever met a happily married man?" Christy shot back as they were all laughing.

"Well, I guess I'm your first then," Mark said as Jessie laughed, shaking her head no.

"I think you're about twenty-five years too late if you were wantin' to be her first," Christy said, laughing even harder.

"It's twenty-two, thank you very much," Jessie went on, not missing a beat. "What can I say; I like men. And he was a cop, and there was just something about that uniform and that gun on his hip."

Continuing on while Mark smiled, Christie followed with, "Sure it was the gun on his hip you were interes… Hey hold on, Jessie, check out Friday evening."

Jessie was right with her. "We sold four Bushnells that night." Excited, Christy went on, "One sale, cash, with teller fourteen at 6:13 pm."

Now it was Mark who was excited. "Any chance you have a security camera on teller fourteen?"

Christy responded with a "duh" look for Mark while Jessie said, "Over here."

He and Christy immediately went to Jessie's desk, where Mark got his first look at Nicholas. He knew instantly that the man on the screen wearing a hooded sweatshirt with large dark sunglasses was the Gospel Killer.

"This is June in Texas; who wears a fuckin' hoodie?" Jessie asked aloud while he studied the video intently.

Without answering, Mark watched as the man on the screen paid the teller, adjusted his hood and glasses, and walked out of the store with his head down. He could make out very little of Nicholas, except that he was probably average height, maybe slightly shorter, had a dark mustache and had a slender build. He asked Jessie if the store also had cameras covering their parking lots, and within seconds, Jessie showed him the man leaving the store at 6:17 p.m. and entering a cab waiting out front. A cab? Mark wasn't expecting that but wrote down the cab company.

"I hate to ask after all that you've done for me here, but is there any chance I could get a copy of that film?" he asked Jessie.

"Any chance you'll come back and let us know what you find out?" Jessie asked.

Smiling, Mark promised he would.

"Any chance when you come back, you might be a little bit less happy?" Christy asked.

"How could a man not be happy around you two girls?" Mark answered as he prepared to leave with a copy of the film.

~~~

Short Timer was nude and sitting upright in bed. And while The Camelot Inn was no great shakes, it was not the room that was making him nervous. Angel had stopped with her oral pleasuring of him and had said she needed to go to the restroom. The sudden stop was what had him nervous and had his hand on his Smithfield .45 hidden under his pillow.

Short Timer was old and certainly a fool, but he was no old fool. He knew he was expendable. He knew this beautiful young woman he had been fucking would sooner or later surely fuck him. So as Angel opened the bathroom door and reentered the room, Short Timer was prepared for whatever was about to happen. He had rented the room in his name; it would be messy, but if only one walked out this day, it would be him.

"Turn around for me, honey," he said as Angel walked the short distance back to the bed.

Angel played along and held her arms out as she slowly turned for him to see her entire body. Seeing she was concealing nothing, Short Timer took his hand from the gun and motioned for her to resume. Stroking her hair as she tasted his dick, Short Timer relaxed and was satisfied that all was still well.

Listening to his pig-like grunts and groans, with her head buried in his lap, Angel didn't know if she could do this again. Only moments before, he had so sickened her that she had been forced to stop and quickly retreat to the bathroom to keep from vomiting all over his sorry excuse of a dick.

And now, he was forcing her to endure this again. As he exploded, she kept her head down to hide the pained look on her face. Even his cum was old, smelling like a nursing home, but she forced herself to swallow it. But she would not swallow it for much longer. Short Timer was indeed a short timer. He knew too much about her. Angel knew she would have to kill him, and as she kneeled there trying to get his taste out of her mouth, she was so looking forward to ending his life.

Chapter 29

As Mark was wheeling the Charger out of the Cabela's parking lot and heading for I-35 South, he glanced down at his watch and saw it was not even two o'clock yet. He had already been to Stephenville, two sporting goods retailers, and his efforts had resulted in catching his first look at the Gospel Killer.

The day was proceeding nicely and was much more productive than most others had been recently, and that brightened Mark's mood. This case had already brought so much concern to him that he was actively seeking things to help him push aside the worry and have some optimism. The video of the man purchasing four outdoor cameras provided the reason for his newfound enthusiasm.

As he exited off southbound I-35S and turned east on the forever-under- construction mass parking lot otherwise known as Highway 820, the traffic was quickly conspiring to devour his brightened mood when suddenly it hit him. The video showed that after leaving Cabela's, the killer had gotten into a cab from Excel Cabs. About freaking time Mark caught a break.

Excel was owned by Bryan Hart, who years before had employed Mark during a messy divorce. Mark had provided surveillance and filmed proof that Bryan's soon-to-be ex-wife didn't exactly believe in keeping herself only for her husband. When these facts were brought up in court, the woman's attorney claimed she suffered from an active and acute sexual addiction, and while Mark didn't know how cute it was, he was pretty sure it was active and also rather loud. Either way, Mark's work had saved Mr. Hart hundreds of thousands of dollars in the divorce proceedings and more importantly helped him get custody of his two sons as well. So, it was like talking with an old friend when Mark scrolled down through his listed phone numbers and called up Bryan Hart.

Bryan was in his office when he took the call. After the usual family inquiries and pleasantries, Mark told him what he needed. While he was going through his company's records to find the fare, Bryan asked, "Hey, you remember my ex? The one you followed around?"

"Yeah," Mark answered, weaving through traffic. "In fact, I remember a lot of things about her."

"Yeah, I bet a bunch of guys do. But anyways, she came over last weekend to pick up the boys and brought her new flame."

"That sucks, man, but what are you gonna do?" Mark responded sympathetically as Bryan started laughing.

"No, I don't care about that; it's just her new love is a gal named Diane. The bitch has done went and switched teams."

"Wow, wouldn't have seen that comin'," Mark said, joining in on the laughter. "She seemed to like the old team so well."

"I don't know what I expected," Bryan said with a sigh. "I remember after we got married, one time she said I was her sixty-second lover. I'm thinking, damn, that's a lot, ain't it; and then she says, no, I mean sixty seconds is all you can last."

"Who the fuck did I call?" Mark was laughing so hard he practically went off the shoulder of the highway. "What are you Shecky, the cab company owner, or somebody?"

"Yeah, that's me. Shecky McDougal doing two shows nightly at the Holiday Inn."

Stuck behind an almost stopped Nissan, Mark continued, "Too bad your shows only last sixty seconds."

"Hey, they always last long enough for me!" Even though he was going about fifteen miles an hour at 2:00 p.m. on the highway, Mark was relaxed and smiling bigger than he had in weeks.

What Bryan said next made the smile disappear. "You're gonna hate me, but I don't have a record of picking up any fare Friday evening from Cabela's."

Mark again relayed what he had seen from the video that had displayed the date and time. "Hey, hang on a minute," Bryan interrupted. "Didn't pick anyone up from there but looks like we took a guy from the airport to Cabela's, waited, and then took him back."

"Took him back to the airport?" queried Mark, perking back up immediately. "What time was that?"

"Yeah, picked him up at twenty after five from American Airlines Terminal B," Bryan said as he continued reading from his computer. "Took him to Cabela's and at 6:15 left there with him and returned to Terminal B."

The whole airport thing made no sense to Mark. After hesitating, he asked, "Could I talk with the driver?"

"Don't see why not. His name is Frank Delgado, but he only works weekends. He's a custodian at a high school during the week, but I can try to get a hold of him and tell him to give you a call."

After a sincere thank you resulted in Bryan deferring any credit, Mark said, "No, I'm serious, if this helps me catch the guy, I'll do something to show you how much I appreciate your help. I'll hook you up with a supermodel or something."

"I got a better chance of beating a twelve-year-old Pakistani kid in a spelling bee than hooking up with a supermodel," Bryan deadpanned. "But what the hell, knock yourself out."

"I don't know. I just met a girl out at Cabela's; next time I go out there, I'll take you with me and introduce you. Can't promise you anything, but trust me you'd go for her."

"Yeah, but what's the chance she'd go for me?" Bryan asked in his self-deprecating style.

"Good point, considering how you look and all. Better bring along a copy of your financial statement there, Shecky boy."

Hanging up the phone and still laughing from the conversation with Bryan, Mark shifted gears and began thinking about the whole airport situation and the killer. It just made no sense. As he slowly made his way eastward, he began to understand. It was all bullshit. The airport was a smoke screen to get Mark distracted. No way the killer was flying in from somewhere and doing the murders.

With airport security these days, there was simply no way the Gospel Killer was using the airlines or airport as part of his pattern. Too many checkpoints and ID clearances for that. This guy used the airport because he knew Mark wouldn't be able to get video shots of him there without going to the police and through all the proper channels—channels Mark wouldn't be willing to go through with the four bodies he killed still buried in Stephenville.

"Motherfucker, this piece of shit is slick, isn't he?" Mark yelled to himself, slamming his hands down on the steering wheel. "But then again, maybe he ain't the only one."

Sick of the traffic and feeling now more energized than he had in weeks, Mark hopped off 820 at Precinct Line Road and headed to Southlake Town Square. Southlake, Texas, is an upscale suburb in the Dallas-Ft. Worth metroplex—the kind of place J.R. Ewing would have lived if he weren't a fictional character and well-known dick wad. Southlake is a shining example of the area's robust economy; in fact, while driving through the city one notices there appears to be at least one banking location for each of its 27,000 citizens. Southlake Town Square is its social and shopping hub. A crown jewel of retailing, Southlake Town Square features Brooks Brothers, Coach, Eddie Bauer, Ann Taylor, Michael Kors, Williams-Sonoma, and a host of many other overpriced, overhyped stores to shop in, and more importantly, for the self-conscious locals, to be seen in.

Pulling into the parking lot, Mark passed by the Victoria's Secret store, with its huge posters of beckoning, young, buxom models, but even Marissa Miller couldn't give him pause because he knew what he was after. Lucking into a parking space directly in front of the James Avery store, Mark went in and found exactly what he was seeking. Then working within their "who the fuck thought of this" system,

Mark was forced to take a small pencil and write down the number of the two pieces he wanted on a tiny piece of yellow paper. As the older woman was on her way to the back of the store to retrieve the two pieces, Mark was already daydreaming how the black leather cord choker with the soft, square, black onyx pendant would look against Yo-Yo's caramel skin. It was a simple and inexpensive gift, but one Mark knew he would benefit from.

Arriving back at his office, Mark went right to work transferring his notes from mental ones to ones on paper. It always helped Mark to write things down; it helped him make sense of things and occasionally helped him notice patterns that otherwise would have eluded him. Usually his notes wound up with lines running across them connecting one idea to another, and perhaps frequently, the pages resembled cave drawings, but to Mark they made sense.

He was busy writing down the words and phrases the killer had used on the phone from the day before, his thoughts of what they could signify, his findings from the Cabela's video tape, his beliefs about the cab and airport. He drew question marks on his notes as he looked for differences between the murders committed by Nicholas and the more recent ones by Angel. Within an hour, Mark was totally immersed in the crimes, looking at photos, rereading reports, and using the Internet to speed up his search of Bible verses with any possible connection, when he heard a knock at his office door.

Before he could get up to open the door, in walked Yo-Yo, bearing gifts. Greeting him with a warm smile and kiss, Yo-Yo set down a huge cup of Sonic Drive

Inn Diet Coke. Smiling devilishly, she knew the way to his heart. The Diet Coke was fine, but to Mark the real treasure was the Sonic ice. Loosely defined in his mind as the fourth wonder of the modern world, for the record trailing only push-up bras, Las Vegas and bacon-wrapped shrimp, Sonic's magical, flaky, melt-in-your-mouth ice cubes were a taste of heaven to Mark. So much so, that he closed his eyes and sucked on a mouthful before even thanking Yo-Yo for his unexpected treat.

After experiencing a near mouth orgasm, Mark sat down at his desk and listened as Yo-Yo told him that her mother had taken Lily to the water park for the afternoon and that she had been shopping.

"Oh, another Neiman's expedition?" Mark asked at the mention of shopping.

"You'll just have to wait for the MasterCard bill," Yo-Yo answered, laughing.

As they relaxed and the conversation easily flowed between the two, Mark let go of the case and concentrated only on his beautiful Yo-Yo. He knew she was worried about him, worried about what this case might do to him, worried about what seeing his father again might do to him; but she never expressed those worries directly, never added to his stress with question after question. Instead, she showed her concern by drawing even closer to him. How had he ever found a woman like this?

When his Diet Coke was probably halfway gone, Yo-Yo, who had been sitting in a high-backed leather seat across from the desk, got up and walked to the credenza behind Mark.

"Out of Crown," she said with disappointment as

she slid open the bottom compartment. "Guess Jack'll have to do."

Pulling out a half-empty bottle of Jack Daniel's, she added a small splash of the whiskey to her Diet Coke and then added a more healthy and manly portion to Mark's drink. Without a spoon nearby, she used her finger to help swirl and mix the liquor into his drink. Mark was fine with this. When Yo-Yo pulled her finger out and placed it in her mouth to lick the whiskey from it and perhaps to clean it as well—well, Mark was more than fine with that, too. Something about seeing her finger in her mouth with her cheeks sucked in. Mark set back and again wondered how in the hell did he ever find a woman like this?

After Yo-Yo sat back down in the leather chair across from him, Mark wondered another thought. While listening to her talk about where they could have dinner that evening and what time they needed to pick up Lily from her mom's, Mark was looking at Yo-Yo and wondering how many other men thought their wives were this beautiful after so many years of marriage. She was radiant. The white, sleeveless sundress she was wearing so very well illuminated her beauty.

Mark had planned on waiting until at least dinner and perhaps even later to give the choker to Yo-Yo, but he wasn't very good at holding out. Adding another manly pour of Jack into his dwindling, ice-filled Diet Coke, Mark walked over to an office wall and peered into the large mirror hanging there.

"Sit down, gorgeous; you're still as handsome as ever," Yo-Yo razzed him, after adding a not-so-feminine Jack splash of her own.

"No, it's not that," Mark said, continuing to stare.

"There's something here on the mirror. Come look."

With a pretend exasperated sigh followed by a healthy gulp of her drink, Yo-Yo walked over to inspect the mirror. Stepping aside to offer Yo-Yo a better look, Mark reached into his pocket and withdrew the James Avery black onyx choker. For a moment, Yo-Yo looked intently into the mirror.

"What are you talking about?" she finally said. "I don't see anything."

Seizing the opportunity, Mark stepped up close behind her and with one hand pointed to the mirror. "See? Right there."

She leaned in even closer to the mirror while Mark put his hand on her shoulder and showed her the gift box.

Shrieking like a schoolgirl, Yo-Yo turned back to face Mark, grabbing the box and kissing him at the same time. Opening the box, the shrieking stopped but the look in her eyes intensified. Telling him it was beautiful, she turned again back to face the mirror while Mark waved aside her cascading hair and placed the choker around her neck.

Seeing her beaming smile, Mark knew the simple choker on her elegant neck was like cheesecake after a Porterhouse steak—the perfect finishing touch. Standing behind her and being taken in by her happiness, Mark leaned in and began to softly kiss Yo-Yo's wonderful bronze neck.

"You better stop," she said halfheartedly, closing her eyes for a moment to fully enjoy Mark's kisses.

He didn't stop. Instead, Mark kissed her neck deeper, along with adding an occasional nibble and teasing lick.

"Really, you better stop," Yo-Yo softly said.

He wouldn't. Leaning hard into her and still kissing her neck broadly and hungrily, Mark began to run his hands through Yo-Yo's gleaming hair. There were huge gobs of hair streaming between each finger as he pressed his hand up from her neck to the top of her head. It was like Mark was searching for treasure and was sure it lay there hidden somewhere within the mounds of her glistening black hair. This wasn't fair. Having his hands on her scalp and running his fingers through her hair over and over, having her neck alternately kissed, licked, and bitten, left Yo-Yo with only one thing to say. "You better lock the door."

Mark turned and went to lock the door while unbuttoning his shirt. Feeling giddy inside, he knew he was a lucky man. He wondered how many other married women in the world at that exact moment were in their husband's office about to do the same thing. With the door safely locked, Mark turned and saw Yo-Yo wearing only a bra and thong. The sundress had been slipped off and lay harmless on the floor. Walking towards Mark, who began to remove his shirt much more quickly, Yo-Yo reached out and grabbed his belt buckle. Undoing the buckle while kissing him, she slid downward and removed Mark's now unwanted pants. Kneeling before him, she took Mark in her mouth. With eyes closed, he reached down and continued to stroke his hands through her hair as she sucked and kissed his dick.

After withstanding more pleasure than most men could endure, Mark bent down and pulled Yo-Yo up to him. As he wrapped his arms around her and kissed her deeply, Yo-Yo managed to pull her head back.

"Why did you stop me," she protested. "I wanted to finish."

"Shh," was Mark's only answer.

Not that she really minded. With Mark's large and warm hands covering her body, gently squeezing her breast, rubbing deeply into the small of her back, and softly feathering his fingernails up her sides, Yo-Yo knew she was being loved. Mark had now pressed her against a wall and continued kissing her neck while his hands explored her body. After slipping out of her thong, Yo-Yo turned around with her back to his chest and asked Mark to undo her bra.

He obliged with surprising deftness, and with Yo-Yo now facing the wall, went to work on her back. Yo-Yo's workouts and exercise classes really showed on her back. Long, lean striations of muscle were visible and so beautiful. Mark was lost and wrapped in his woman, kissing her back, rubbing it, biting it, and kneading her ass like bread.

"Come on, Mark," he heard Yo-Yo say. "Come on, baby."

Feeling her push her bottom back and into him, Mark bent his knees and heard Yo-Yo gasp as he entered her from behind. As he slowly pushed deeply inside her, Mark took one hand and again ran it through Yo-Yo's lush hair while reaching around to touch her breast with his other. Yo-Yo's face was pressed into the wall when she pushed one leg out and wrapped it around the back of Mark's right knee. It was as if their two bodies could not have been more entwined, could not have been more rhythmically synchronized, and could not have been more in love.

Yo-Yo's breathing became more shallow, her moans

deeper, her rhythms and movements quicker. Mark was doing his level best to hold off and let her orgasm first when there was a knock on the door. Turning his head while maintaining full motion, Mark looked back at the door as he heard a second knock. He never stopped but let out an audible, "Dammit."

"Come on, baby," Yo-Yo cried out. "Fuck the door!"

She rarely cursed, perhaps an occasional shit or damn, but during sex it was a different story and it drove Mark wild. There was just something about someone so pure talking naughty, talking dirty at exactly the most perfect time. Turning back to concentrate on his wife, Mark pushed faster and harder into Yo-Yo until he could feel her body tighten and begin to shudder until it exploded. The aftershocks of Yo-Yo's orgasm, her body squeezing and convulsing, led to Mark's own explosion just as a package of a different sort was being pushed inside his office through the mail slot on his front door.

He collapsed onto the floor, pulling Yo-Yo's sweat-glistening body with him. Using his body as a pillow, she lay on his chest in full afterglow. Lost in a love-drunken stupor, they were unaware of the package lying only feet from them until it began to ring.

Chapter 30

Ring? At first the ringing did not register with Mark, but the second ring sounded and brought him back to the here and now. Quickly easing Yo-Yo aside, he rolled over and saw the package—really a large envelope, lying on the floor vibrating and ringing once more. Scrambling his nude body towards it, Mark grabbed and ripped open the envelope in one motion. Inside was only a ringing cell phone. With Yo-Yo watching, he hesitated before flipping the phone open and answering, hello. While looking into Yo-Yo's eyes, Mark held the phone to his ear.

"I was beginning to think you weren't going to pick up," he heard Nicholas say. Upon hearing this voice, the ecstasy from the full body, mind-blowing sex Mark had just enjoyed immediately vanished. "Hello, hello, anyone home?" teased Nicholas into the phone.

"I'm here," Mark answered. Seeing his facial expression and hearing a tone in his voice that she had never heard before, something akin to a mixture of fear and dread caused Yo-Yo to stop putting her clothes back on and again sit down in the leather chair. She watched Mark closely and listened to this phone conversation.

"You may be in your office now, but you were somewhere else this morning," said Nicholas. With no answer from Mark, he continued. "Saw you out at the place in Stephenville. Didn't I tell you what a bad idea that would be?"

Seeing the concern on Yo-Yo's face, Mark had enough of just listening. "Maybe I don't much give a shit what you say? And for the record, I saw you today, too, at Cabela's buying the cameras."

Now it was the Gospel Killer's turn to be silent. Normally Mark would not have said this to a suspect, would not have given away this information, but what the hell, doing things the normal way hadn't worked too well on this case so far. After the hesitation, Nicholas began to laugh uneasily.

"And the whole deal with the cabs and airport, I know that's all bullshit," Mark added. "There's no way you're flying in and out of here every time you kill one of these fuckers. But, don't worry, I'm going to find out how you left the airport and where you went." After another pause, the unease disappeared.

"You're feeling pretty good about yourself, aren't you?" answered Nicholas. Well, he certainly had been a few minutes ago, but now Mark was a long way from feeling good as Nicholas continued. "For the record, I left the airport at 8:15 in a Community Cab, which took me to 1710 Robinson Road in Garland. It's a vacant house and a friend picked me up there later. And, unfortunately for you, I'm pretty sure there was no security camera out there to get my friend's license plate."

Mark hated that Yo-Yo was hearing this, but he went on as he wanted to try and get under the killer's skin. "Maybe that's so, but it's still more than we've had on you before. That tells me you're off your game plan, and that's when guys like you fuck up."

"Firstly, there aren't other guys like me, and secondly, if I fuck up, you should remember that would be very bad for you," Nicholas said, growing annoyed. "Yes that would be so, so bad for you, bad for your very pretty Hispanic wife, bad for your adorable daughter, and bad also for your son from your first wife. I believe Daniel is his name, correct?"

Mark sat there in a raging mixture of anger and fear, but with Yo-Yo's pleading eyes staring at him, he did not respond.

"I really wish you wouldn't make me say such awful things, Mark," Nicholas added, after keeping silent for a moment to let things sink in. "I hate doing it, but it's just that I need you to focus. Now, I get that you want to find and kill me, but you must understand that right now I am only a distraction for you. Your job now is to find and kill the person trying to claim my glory. After that, we can have our day."

Mark wanted that day, wanted it badly, but with the pressures of Bubba and the gang and now Yo-Yo's worry and fear added to it, he knew it would need to wait. He knew the killer was right; he did have to focus. So, he attempted to put himself into the mind of this mass murderer.

"You know, you talk about your glory, and I presume you mean having your fame and being renowned, but don't you know serial killers only become famous after they're caught?"

"That's not true, Mark. They never found out who Jack the Ripper was and yet they're still writing books and making movies about him over a hundred years after his crimes."

Mark had to concede the good point, but said nothing

as Yo-Yo resumed putting her clothes on, all the while watching him closely. The pause allowed Nicholas to continue.

"And not that he rose to the level of being a murderer, but for a more recent example, you can look at the infamous D.B. Cooper case. His identity is still a mystery forty years after the hijacking, but he's a legendary figure nonetheless."

"So you think a person has to rise to a certain level to become a murderer?"

"To do anything well requires a certain commitment, a certain discipline, that forces one to push their self to a higher level of performance. Killing, and doing so in a way that is very difficult to detect, is no different."

"Interesting…Ever wonder if maybe the real reason you want me to find this copycat is that you're afraid they might be better at killing than you are?"

"That question makes me wonder if perhaps I haven't overestimated you," Nicholas laughed. "Do you really think you are going to get to me by issuing a third-grade dare that so and so might be a better killer than me?"

Mark could tell the question had pissed off the killer and bruised his vanity when Nicholas continued. "Think I'm going to have to motivate you a little more. When I hang up, I'm going to call the police and tell them the poor headless girl they found yesterday is none other than their lead suspect in the horrific Gospel Killer slayings. And, if they check, they will find her time of death is probably close to at least twenty-four hours before the last murders were committed; therefore, it couldn't have been the unfortunate Ms. Adams."

Mark decided to take the stick and poke him one

more time. "Be careful; that'll be your second call to the police. Those 911 calls are taped and with voice analysis and all, it can come back to bite you." Nicholas on the other hand, was not one to poke someone with a stick; he preferred to take the stick and drive it through someone's heart.

"And, for another piece of motivation, if you haven't found and killed this other murderer before they kill again in twenty-five days, then I'll place my third and final call to the police and inform them of your Stephenville cemetery. And, lastly, you can throw the Track phone you are holding away; I will provide you another when I need to speak with you again."

There was much more Mark wanted to ask. "Hold on, I..." he hurriedly said, but to no avail. Nicholas was done communicating and hung up the phone.

Throwing the phone down, Mark rushed to put on his clothes. After getting his pants on, he ran for the door.

"Wait here," he said to Yo-Yo. "I'll be right back."

Outside his office, he looked for any signs of who may have been the one to deliver the package into his office. Seeing no one, Mark went to the curb; while looking for unfamiliar cars, he saw his friend Jim. Clutching his usual brown-paper-bag-covered bottle of gin, homeless Jim was a fixture in the neighborhood. Mark had for years looked after the battered old man. Pulling a pair of twenties out of his pocket, he approached Jim and asked if he had seen anyone around the office ten or fifteen minutes before.

"You got an office?" Jim asked, taking another swig from the bottle and gazing at Mark.

Jim frequently slept on the office's front porch, but

the gin had long since robbed him of his memory. Mark smiled and patted him on the back while stuffing the twenties in his coat pocket. Saying good-bye to Jim and walking back to his office, Mark had no idea what to tell Yo-Yo. He saw the worry and fear in her eyes, and he didn't know if he could look in those eyes and lie to her. He knew it was best that she didn't know the truth, best that she still believe the lie he had told her for so many years, but still lying to her again right now would not be easy.

The lie, of course, was that every time Yo-Yo had asked about the gunshot wounds he had received while rescuing Carolina Ramirez, Mark had told her that after making the exchange and getting Carolina, the kidnappers had started shooting, and he simply got away with the girl as best as he could. When she asked if he had shot any of the kidnappers during the getaway, Mark had always said he didn't know.

Now, he couldn't tell her that he had gotten away with the girl, the money, and with four dead bodies stuffed in the trunk. And he sure couldn't tell her that secret now endangered their lives and their daughter's as well—danger which came not only immediately from the Gospel Killer but also soon enough from Dallas' most ruthless and notorious criminals, Bubba, the Magician, and Marcus. His shoulders were thick, but this burden was so heavy. God, what was he going to tell Yo-Yo? He opened his office door and saw her sitting in the leather chair, looking none too comfortable.

Part fearful, part angry, largely confused and thoroughly apprehensive, Yo-Yo asked, "What's going on? Who was that on the phone?"

Resisting the nervous urge to crack a joke and ask

if she was ready to get back to their marital fuck fest, Mark said only, "It was the Gospel Killer." This confirmed Yo-Yo's fears.

"You talked to her?" she asked. "How does she know who you are? Why is she calling you?"

"The Gospel Killer is a man," Mark answered somberly. "He killed the first twelve and now a woman has come along and is carrying on with the killings. He's not happy about that and wants me to find the woman." None of this did anything to calm Yo-Yo.

"How do you know this?" she pleaded. "And why is he calling you?"

Seeing her so frightened was tearing Mark's heart out. "He called me yesterday," he managed to answer. "He told me enough things, unreported things about the killings, that I know he's who he says he is."

Yo-Yo's crying weakened Mark. "As for why me, I guess it's because he saw me on TV. But he knows things about me, so I've got to go along with him until I can find out who he is."

"What do you mean he knows things about you? What kinds of things?"

He swallowed hard, weakening but still too strong to tell her the whole truth. Mark finally answered, "He knows about you and the kids."

Yo-Yo's crying went up several octaves and then asked, "He knows about Lily? Oh my god; what is he gonna do?"

"Look at me," Mark said, wrapping his arm around her. "Nothing is going to happen to Lily or to you or to Daniel. Nobody is going to hurt my family. You know that. You know I would never let that happen."

This strengthened and quieted Yo-Yo, who held

tightly to Mark. She knew how wonderful and gentle Mark was to her and his children, but she was no fool. She knew full well what her man was capable of doing when pushed. Though he had tried to hide her from such things, Yo-Yo had seen how men, how bad men, thugs, convicts, and bikers treated Mark. Part respect, part fear, part just keep the fuck out of his way. She knew when he came home with a broken right hand that someone else would be staying overnight in the hospital.

"What are we going to do?" she asked.

And that was it. No more questions, no blame, no hysterics, no more apprehension. Yo-Yo just needed a plan from the man she loved and trusted so much. Mark squeezed her tightly, happy he would not need to lie further, and thrilled she was his wife.

Chapter 31

After following Yo-Yo to her parent's house to pick up Lily, Mark returned home with both of them. They ate dinner at P.F. Chang's, and then Mark told Lily that she and Yo-Yo would be taking a surprise getaway the next day. In fact, it was such a surprise he would not even tell her where the getaway was.

Later, after finally getting Lily to sleep, he confided to Yo-Yo that he would need to find a secure place for them to stay, at least for a while. He didn't know where yet, but wherever it was, they would be safe and should keep their whereabouts secret. His next step was to call Kellie and tell her that work troubles made him feel it would be best if Daniel stayed with him and Yo-Yo for a short time.

"It's summer and he wouldn't have to miss school," he told his ex. "Just tell him it will be for an extended visit."

Kellie didn't like the sound of things, but she agreed with the plan because she wanted Daniel to be safe. Mark promised to let her know the hideaway site as soon as he knew himself and hung up.

Dog-tired from a dizzying day, Mark found he couldn't sleep. Yo-Yo had drifted off after Letterman, but for Mark, the events of the day kept whirling through his mind. Getting out of bed about 12:30 a.m., he went into the den and did something he should have done earlier: he picked up a Bible and began to read. Concern with the case prompted this, but he knew he also needed a spiritual checkup. He had backslid, had fallen so many times, he seemed farther from God's grace than ever before.

As he read the words, he wondered if he killed this mystery copycat woman to keep secret other killings he had committed, if he did so at the instruction of the actual Gospel Killer, would God wash his hands of him? Would he finally exhaust even God's patience? Someone who knew God's love, but yet had turned away to the ways of the world so easily and frequently, would he even have the nerve to beg again for God's forgiveness?

Concentrating on the Gospels, Mark read the books and made notes of any references to murder and punishment. He had felt from day one that this case would be solved because of the Bible. He had gotten away from that thinking because of other factors such as his father's reemergence, Bubba's knowledge of what he had done in the Ramirez kidnapping case years before, and now the calls from the real Gospel Killer; but reading the books, he began to wonder if the calls weren't a distraction themselves.

The killer kept telling him to focus on finding the woman and to avoid any other distractions, but what if the killer feared he was getting close and actually wanted to confuse Mark? If that were the goal, then the Bible was a good place to send someone for clues.

As Mark read, his mind wandered. He set out trying to search for signals or clues to solve the case—clues contained in the Gospels that a serial killer might use as an excuse or reason to kill—but instead he found many verses more applicable to his own life. Mark read and reread John 15:6: "If anyone does not remain in me, he is like a branch that is thrown away and withers; such branches are picked up, thrown into the fire and burned."

He knew he had not remained with God. He had seen firsthand God's forgiveness and love and had turned away. Would he now be thrown into the fire and burnt as an old branch? This troubled Mark, and he wanted to pray, but he knew that God knew his heart and that God knew what he planned to do, so he decided against it.

He closed the Bible and poured a drink of Crown. As he swished the whiskey in his mouth, Mark wondered about life, about his role in the world, and wondered if God would give him another chance. Finishing the second drink, he decided to give sleep another chance, since he knew the next day would be a busy one.

He was up before the alarm sounded. Truth be told, unless tossing and turning counted as sleep, Mark had slept very little, but he got up anyway and showered. This time Yo-Yo had not surprised him with a visit in the shower; his companions were just hot water and a troubled mind. Dressed now, he hated to wake Yo-Yo. Watching her alone in the bed, curled up right next to where he had been, was a reminder to him of what was at stake.

The Bible reading from the night before had in many ways frightened him, but seeing Yo-Yo there with that tousled black hair framing her face, if someone was going to try and take that away, well then, goddamn, he wasn't about to turn the other cheek. After all, God helps those who help themselves, right?

Nudging her awake, Mark told Yo-Yo to pack and that he would call back as soon as he made arrangements. She kissed him good-bye, and he left knowing he would need to call her back in a couple of hours to repeat the message, since Yo-Yo was almost completely incoherent whenever she was first awakened. After a quick check to make sure Lily was asleep and fine, Mark filled his cup from the coffee maker and was out the door. Checking his watch and seeing it was still only 7:10, he pulled out his phone and took a chance.

Dialing up the Excel Cab company, he was surprised to hear his friend Bryan Hart answer the phone.

"What the hell? They got the boss in this early?" said a joking Mark.

"I gotta do it myself 'cause I can't afford to pay anyone else to come in and open up."

"Yeah, right. Well anyways, since I got ahold of you and all, I was wondering if you still had that lake house down near Possum Kingdom?"

"Thanks to you, I do. Otherwise, my oh-so-lovely ex would be there now with her not so lovely girlfriend," cracked Bryan. "Why, what's up?"

"You remember that fare I called you about yesterday? Well, he's becoming a problem, and I'd like to get my family away from the house and somewhere that can't be found too easily, if you know what I mean."

"Mi casa es su casa. And, hey, speaking about that, the driver that took the fare, Frank Delgado, is here in my office right now if you still want to talk to him. With school out for the summer, he decided to get a little extra time in."

Mark excitedly thanked Bryan and promised to repay the favor before asking to speak with the driver. Once on the phone with Delgado, Mark explained why he was calling and why it was important.

"Yeah, Bryan asked me about it, and I remember the little guy," Frank said. "Little prissy fuck, if you ask me."

"Little fuck, huh? How big would you say he was?"

"Hmm, well I weigh over three bills so pretty much everybody is a little fuck to me, but the guy was pretty thin. Guess I'd say probably 5'7 or 8 and maybe 140."

Mark was making mental notes as he drove. The size of the Gospel Killer fit with a possible theory that the man perhaps found his victims while pretending to be a woman.

"What did he look like? Anything stand out?" Mark could then hear Frank slurp a swig of coffee.

"You know, geez, not that I'm queer or anything, but I'd say he was a pretty boy. You know, the kind of guy who'd be real popular in prison. Like maybe he coulda been a model or something."

"What about his hair? Mark asked. "What color was it?"

"Well, you know that's what I remember about the little guy," Frank laughed. "I take him from the airport to Cabela's, and then he gets out and starts waving his finger in my face, telling me I can't leave before he goes inside and does his shopping. You know, I'd sat there with the meter runnin' all night, but there was just something 'bout him saying I must not leave without him. Fuck him, I was about to up and leave his little ass, but I seen he was wearing a wig."

"A wig?" asked Mark, immediately perking up.

"Yeah, I swear. He was outside my window tellin' me this and that, and I see his wig start to move. And, the wig was brown, but his eyebrows and lashes were a lot lighter. Me, I always figure the curtains match the drapes. I swear I couldn't hear what all he was telling me 'cause I got fixated on that fuckin' wig."

Mark didn't find a disguise to be unexpected. "So you think he has light brown hair or maybe blonde?"

"Well, not that I been laying awake thinkin' about it, but I'd say probably more blonde than brown. I didn't really see it though, because he had a hoodie on and pulled it down tight when he saw me looking at his wig. He wore a fake moustache, too, if you ask me. So say, you really think that little fucker is the one killing all those guys?"

"Yeah, that little fucker is a serial killer. No doubt about it." Mark thanked Frank for his help and spoke again with Bryan, telling him to leave lunch open.

Getting to the office, Mark called and spoke with Detective Coleman, ostensibly to talk about the case and the latest killings of Durand and Seeber, but really to see if the Gospel Killer had actually called the police and informed them that the headless corpse found Sunday was none other than Bethany Adams. Mark didn't have to pry to uncover this.

"Well, it ain't your girl," was the first thing John told him. "Don't know if you heard or not, but the same day as the Durand killings we found a woman's nude body off Balch Springs Road whose head had been cut off."

"Good gosh, and her head was off?" Mark interjecting, feigning ignorance.

"Yeah, and then yesterday we get an anonymous phone call saying the woman was really Bethany

Adams. We ran the prints against her conviction, and sure enough, it's her. And, with time of death and all, well, it wasn't her."

Mark was sitting at his desk talking with his friend and trying to be helpful and insightful, all the while knowing the clock had indeed been reset. He felt like the Gospel Killer had just stuck about six more voodoo needles in the Mark Witt doll. Nicholas had followed through with his threat, and now without Beth Adams to slow the investigation, Mark knew the time he had to locate the second killer had just been shortened.

But listening to John talk about the investigation, Mark suddenly had a thought, and the thought was, fuck the voodoo doll. Pressure either busts pipes or makes diamonds, and Mark knew it was time for him to stop feeling like he was busting at the seams. It been difficult for Mark to get a grasp on this whole case from the very beginning. First, Kim Jacobsen had disarmed him with her advances. Then, Bubba had shown his knowledge and involvement of getting rid of the bodies Mark had killed during the kidnapping rescue, greatly unnerving him. Next, Nicholas called with his demand to find the copycat or he would spill all the secret beans. Each of these things had put Mark on his heels. And if there was one thing Mark learned from his days as a boxer, it was that it's a whole lot easier to fight going forward as opposed to back peddling. So now, he decided it was time to get to work and put the Gospel Killer on his heels.

Mark took a drink from his cup. He didn't just taste the coffee; he smelled the grounds, inhaled the aroma, and also felt a new level of concentration. As he listened to Coleman talk about the progress, or lack thereof, he

was immediately taken with one fact. Coleman told
him they had found a used condom at the Durand
killing, and there were two sets of prints on the package. One belonged to Marcel Durand and the other,
presumably, to the killer.

The second set of prints had been run through their
database and was clean. Whoever it belonged to had
never been arrested. Coleman theorized that the
woman had helped Marcel get the condom on before
sex and then afterward had either forgotten or missed
it as she cleaned her tracks.

"She's been so careful up to now," Mark said. "Why
would she have missed it?"

"I don't know, maybe she got spooked by something,"
John opined. "You know, with the second killing and
all, something must have happened to throw her off
her game. I mean, it was a Trojan package, right on top
of the comforter on the floor, as plain as day. So, either
she made a mistake, or we finally caught a break."

"Yeah, 'cept the last break I got was my right hand,"
Mark answered, looking at the cast on his hand.

"Right, your hand," John laughed. "So how is ole
Daddy doin' these days? Guess he's gonna be pissed
that it wasn't Beth Adams, and he won't be picking
up that reward."

Mark thought to himself that his father already knew
it wasn't Beth, but he laughed it off. Afterwards, John
explained that Ron Ellis had been called back to headquarters to report about the progress of the case.

"Those FBI boys always spit out the same horseshit,"
John said. "According to them, every serial killer is a
single, white male, early thirties to mid-forties, loner,
mama's boys, antisocial, trouble maintaining erections

with women, blah, blah. The fact that this is a woman has really thrown them for a loop."

"A lot of loops have gotten thrown on this one," Mark said. Looking at his watch, he added, "Say, John, the real reason I'm calling is I've been reading the Bible, and I really believe the answers to this whole thing are there. I know I said that earlier and all, but I might have some ideas. I was wondering, is there any way you could get me the files of the last three or so murders, say, beginning with the Luke Kimbrough killing and then moving forward?"

"No problem. I've got copies at the house if you want to run by and pick 'em up. Might be easier than someone up here seeing you walk out with them and all. Besides, Jackie would love to see you. And Mark, I'm glad you're back reading the Bible."

Mark thanked him and promised to get back soon with any ideas or suspects since the reward hotline was proving to be a waste. Mark told him next time he would cap the reward at a hundred thousand, since the half million was getting every crazy in the country to call. These calls claimed everyone from the pope to Pee Wee Herman was the Gospel Killer, and since both had airtight alibis, the search continued.

Both Mark and John enjoyed talking with one another. At the end of the conversation, Mark thanked him again, and John promised he would call his wife Jackie to tell her Mark was on his way.

Chapter 32

Before leaving his office, Mark wrote out a couple of checks for the rent and utilities and then opened his gun safe. He withdrew two Glocks and a Remington 870 pump, twelve-gauge shotgun, along with an armful of ammunition. He loaded it all into the trunk of the Charger and then returned to the safe to take out all of his own outdoor camera and security equipment. He had never been to Bryan's lake house, but he was determined it would be as secure as possible for his family.

Mark pulled out of the parking lot and rolled his window down to say good morning to his homeless friend Jim, who was already well on his way to complete inebriation. Jim managed to tell Mark he had been keeping his eyes open and looking for his office. That nugget could perhaps provide a laugh, but Jim had practically stuck his entire body through the car's window while he told him. The smell that reeked from him could only have come from a combination of urine and malt liquor.

Sticking a twenty in Jim's pocket just to get rid of him, Mark was forced to drive to his bank with the windows still down, trying to rid the car of the smell. No such luck. Entering the bank, Mark walked through the lobby, where he couldn't help but pick up a fresh chocolate chip cookie from a tray next to where he was writing out a withdrawal slip. Handing the slip to his favorite teller, Miss Amy Blount, Mark could see that she wasn't her normal self that morning.

"Do I smell bad?" Mark asked her, after she counted out the two thousand dollars in twenties for him.

"Well, maybe a little musty," Miss Amy said, smiling but stepping back farther.

Mark apologized and was out the door. On the road, he checked his watch and saw it approaching eleven. A couple of expletives later and Mark called Yo-Yo and asked if she remembered what he had told her that morning. She hadn't, so he repeated it and told her he would be there to pick them up that afternoon.

Hanging up the phone, Mark muttered that a nuclear war could break out and if Yo-Yo was asleep or had just woken up, he would have to call back a few hours later and give her the news. Thinking of that, of Yo-Yo sleeping through a nuclear attack, caused a big smile to break out across his face as he pulled into an Albertson's Supermarket in Cedar Hill. He was there to buy some flowers for John's wife, Jackie, who he was on his way to meet.

He decided on a bouquet of spring flowers for Jackie, who had meant so much to him growing up. As happens, he hadn't kept in as close of contact with her as he grew older, but there was no denying how good she had been to him. After his mother had died, it was Jackie who had helped with so many details and had looked after both him and Cubbie. They had both been grown by that time, but having a mother figure worry over them and always being there with either advice or a home-cooked meal had meant a great deal.

She helped with some of the loneliness and hurt and pushed those feelings a little farther away. Jackie had been there and answered some of their "why" questions: Why did this have to happen? Why did our father not love her? Why didn't she just leave? Why did she use a gun? Why didn't she use it on him instead of herself? She had answered them the only way they could have been answered: with a hug and a sad shaking of her head while saying, "I don't know, dear. I'm just so sorry."

Driving to Jackie's brought back so many of those thoughts for Mark, most of which included Cubbie. Then he got angry with himself for not thinking to call Cubby earlier. He knew he would need his brother's help; getting him on the phone, Mark asked Cubbie if he and Will were busy for a few days. Cubbie said he could get free, but that Will was flying and his trip wouldn't be over till the weekend.

Mark explained to him that he was having a difficult time with the Gospel Killer case and thought it would be a good idea to get Yo-Yo and the kids out of town. He said he needed to keep working and would really appreciate it if Cubbie could go with them and look after things. Cubbie had never been asked to do such a thing before, and because of that he knew it must be pretty serious for his big brother to ask.

"When do I need to be ready?" was his only question.

As he was pulling up in front of John and Jackie's house, Mark told Cubbie to get packed and be ready in a couple of hours. Walking inside the home and being greeted with a big kiss from Jackie, Mark had the feeling of opening a hall closet and seeing his old letter jacket for the first time in years. It hadn't been nearly that long since he had seen Jackie, but the feelings and memories of a happier, prouder time were the same. She had shared so much sadness with him, but had been there during the better times also.

As they talked, Mark chose to remember more of the good times. After ball games, with his father nowhere in sight, it was with John and Jackie, either here or in their earlier home in Oak Cliff, where Mark, his mother and Cubbie would celebrate. After he won the Texas Golden Gloves Heavyweight boxing championship, John and Mark came back here, so they could share the victory with Jackie and his mother, who never attended any of his fights because of her nervousness. And when he had graduated the academy, it was here that John had hosted a party to celebrate and mark the occasion.

Jackie loved the flowers and enjoyed seeing Mark again. The conversation flowed easily and both promised to not let it be so long next time before seeing one another. When she gave Mark the files, she also told him that John had decided to retire when the case was solved.

"So, I expect you to take these files and catch this girl in a day or two," she joked. "John's done his time, and I'm ready for him to be home now."

Mark smiled and assured her he would do his best. "You know how he's always talking about going to Alaska and fishing for salmon someday? When he retires, I'm going to take him. That'll be my retirement gift to him, a camping trip to Alaska with just me and him and maybe a couple thousand hungry grizzly bears."

Hugging him with tears in her eyes, Jackie said

good-bye and told Mark how much that trip would mean to John. Back on the road, Mark called Bryan at the cab company and asked if he could meet at 1:00 for lunch at JR's.

"JR's? Damn, kinda swanky for lunch, ain't it?"

"Well, if a guy lets you borrow his lake house, the least you can do is buy him a good lunch."

Bryan finally agreed and said he'd be there, which set up the rest of Mark's plan. Hanging up with Bryan and zipping through traffic, he called Cabela's and got the store manager, Jessie Kimbrough, on the phone. "Hi, this is Mark Witt. I talked with you yesterday about the Gospel Killer case."

"Geez, like I wouldn't remember you? How's it going?"

"Not bad, but listen, I was callin' to see if you were free for lunch today?"

"Lunch? You not so happily married now?"

"No, I'm still happy," Mark laughed. "I was thinking of fixing you up with a friend of mine."

'I don't understand," she said, with just the right amount of overt flirting in her voice. "If I'm not good enough for you, why would you try and pawn me off on a friend?"

"You can sure twist a man's words around, can't you?" laughed Mark. "Besides, who knows, if I weren't so happily married and all, you might just be in a whole lot of trouble."

"Yeah, yeah, big talk. But you are pretty good at letting a girl down; gotta give you that."

"So what do you say, you want to hear about my friend?"

"Oh, hell, why not?"

"Well, his name is Bryan Hart. I met him a few years ago when I worked his divorce case for him. He owns a cab company. He's pretty funny. He's a, geez I don't know, he's a mature, secure, stable guy."

"Wow, mature, secure and stable. He sounds like a Toyota. Does he come with an air bag?"

"Okay, you want to bust my chops, all right. So what do you want to know?"

"Can I put you on speaker?" Jessie asked, laughing. "My gorgeous assistant, Christi, is in here now trying to butt into our business and just has to know everything."

"Sure. And, hey Christi."

"Hey Mark, we want to know how big the guy's hands are," she responded.

"Don't pay any attention to what Christi says," a giggling Jessie said before he could answer. "Ever. But, tell me, what does the guy look like?"

"Geez, you can't ask a guy what another guy looks like. I don't know, he's tall, probably 190 or so, I don't know."

"What about compared to you? Let's say if you're a rib-eye, what kinda cut would old Bryan be?"

"Well, I don't think I'm a rib-eye for starters, more like hamburger."

"If you're hamburger, then I've been shopping at the wrong market," Jessie shot back.

"If you're hamburger, then I've been eating dog food," Christi added.

"How does Cabela's stay open?" Mark asked. "I mean, are you two ever serious?" After some school girl laughter, he added, "He's a decent looking guy. You can trust me."

"Last time a guy told me I could trust him, I wound

up gettin' pregnant," Christi couldn't help adding.

"Never mind her. So why do you think your friend would even like me?" Jessie asked.

"Is someone fishing for compliments?"

"I do run a sporting goods store. And flattery is always appreciated."

"Well, let's see; what's not to like? You're hotter than hell, have a sassy little attitude and know how to bait a hook."

"Oh, I know how to bait that hook."

"How about JR's at 1:00?"

"I'll be there."

"Bryan will never know what hit him."

Mark hung up his phone, smiling, while Jessie and Christi jumped up and down like they had just made the cheerleader squad. He normally didn't play match-maker and couldn't explain why he chose to this time. But it seemed right to him. Both Jessie and Bryan were fun people, and maybe they provided a way for him to temporarily decompress.

Arriving at JR's Steakhouse in Colleyville a few minutes after one o'clock, Mark found Bryan already there, waiting for him in the bar. JR'S was a restaurant and jazz bar that offered fine dining at its high dollar best. The kind of place where expense accounts went to die, JR's was owned by a rather infamous Dallas area figure, Johnny Ragsdale, who in his youth had spent years in prison for a number of jewelry heists. After parole, he became a local legend in the restaurant and bar business.

Mark and Bryan were soon seated at a table for lunch, and, as is the custom, Johnny Ragsdale himself came over to welcome them. A "regular" and now a personal friend of Johnny's, Mark was glad to see his old friend and introduce him to Bryan. To show his appreciation for their business, Johnny sent over a bottle of Chardonnay on the house for the table before leaving to welcome yet another table's occupants.

Mark and Bryan were then able to speak privately with one another. Mark explained he had spoken on the phone with the actual Gospel Killer and the veiled threats from the killer were the reason he needed a place for Yo-Yo and the kids.

"Stay as long as you need," Bryan said, handing over the keys. "Is there anything else I can do?"

Just as Mark was about to answer, he saw the maître de leading Jessie to their table. He waved to her and said to Bryan, "No, but I thought there was something I could do for you."

Arriving at the table, Jessie looked terrific. She had ditched the work uniform and instead wore a pair of jeans that looked like they had been made for her alone, a pair of high heels that tilted her ass ever so upward and a pale yellow blouse. Mark introduced the two, and Jessie saw the surprised look on Bryan's face.

"Let me guess, you didn't know anything about this?" she asked.

"No, he didn't, but I bet he'll get over it," Mark answered before Bryan could. Smiling, Bryan nodded his head yes and poured Jessie a glass of the Chardonnay.

"I told her you were divorced," Mark said, patting him on the shoulder. Then to encourage his friend Mark offered, "And that's okay, everybody gets bucked off, but ain't it time you get back up on the horse?"

"Back up on the horse?" Bryan grinned, and in his

country boy act, said, "Hell, I ain't even been to the barn in three years."

"Three years?" Jessie said, reaching over and placing her hand on his. "Well, you sure ought to be ready to ride." With that, Mark was feeling pretty good about his matchmaking intuition.

"Oh, I like to ride," Bryan answered. "It's just I was figurin' on startin' back over with a girl who came with training wheels."

"No training wheels, just high heels," Jessie said demurely, shrugging her shoulders. "But I will hold on to you tight."

At that point, Mark stood up. "I think my work is done here." With smiles all around, he dropped two hundred dollar bills on the table, saying, "Lunch is on me. You two have a great time." He added to Jessie, "But not too great; he's still got to get back to work this afternoon."

"Thanks, Dad," Bryan shot back, "and you're forgetting, but I'm the boss."

"Not at this table," Mark answered, with Jessie smiling ear to ear.

Chapter 33

Mark had told Yo-Yo he didn't know how long to expect to be away from their home, so she had the Escalade packed like a rented U-Haul. Garment racks lined the backseat, and Cubbie stacked bulging luggage tightly into every available space. Makeup kits and toys lined the back floorboards. The Cadillac SUV resembled a bloated bulldog trying to get the energy to lick the bowl clean one more time. By the time Mark placed Ricky and Lucy, Lily's two pet hamsters, and their cage in the front seat, it was apparent that Lily would have to ride with Uncle Cubbie as there was no more room left in the Escalade.

Mark was rushing the whole time, desperately wanting to get to the lake house before dusk so he could get the security systems installed with the help of the daylight. Rushing with Yo-Yo involved seldom led to positive results, but he noticed a more serious and determined attempt by his wife this time. It was as if, once again, she knew what he needed. Getting the house locked up, she led the group out with Cubbie and Lily behind her and Mark bringing up the rear.

They stopped in Arlington to pick up Daniel on the way, and by four o'clock the convoy was on the road headed west on I-20 towards Possum Kingdom Lake.

Crawling through the afternoon workday traffic didn't help Mark's mood any and made his task of making sure the group hadn't been followed even more difficult. Near Weatherford, he suddenly zoomed ahead of Yo-Yo and Cubbie and pulled off the highway and into a roadside McDonald's. Waiting several minutes to closely watch and see if any trailing car also pulled off or went ahead and then backtracked, Mark finally parked and led his crew into Mickey Dee's.

Getting the kids out of the indoor play area was no easy feat for the antsy Mark, who picked at his food while watching after his children. Looking at his half-eaten hamburger, he thought to himself that instead of naming it a Big Mac, a more truthful description would've been a Big McShit. The moment of good feeling he had experienced at JR's with setting up Bryan and Jessie had now disappeared.

Mark was facing the reality that he was about to hide his wife and family out at a location he had never been to before. Then, in the morning, he would be leaving them to return home and continue his work. He would be alone and away from the only people in the world he cared about, and he would be pursuing a killer who could be pursuing him as well.

Clearly he was uneasy, and Yo-Yo quickly picked up on it. While Uncle Cubbie pulled his niece out of a multicolored, plastic-ball enclosed kingdom and his nephew off a hanging, Playskool-type crawling tube structure of some sort, Mark walked out into the parking lot to take another look around. As was his custom, he had made mental notes of the license plate numbers of the three other cars parked in the lot when they arrived. Each of the cars remained where they had been parked and were joined by two others, one belonging to a single mother who had brought her two children into the play area also, and one to an elderly couple who sat near the window and drank coffee.

Also, while the family ate, Mark had paid close attention to each car that passed through the drive-through and was now in his mind running those descriptions against the cars parked in other nearby and almost adjoining fast food restaurants along the highway. The concentration he was forcing upon his mind felt good to Mark until it was broken by a hug from Yo-Yo. Either he had been completely engrossed in his thoughts or she had used ninja-style techniques in coming up behind him undetected.

"We're gonna be all right," she said, nuzzling her head into his shoulder.

It was simple but soothing. Mark hugged her back as Cubbie got the kids into the cars, and soon they were back on the road.

Arriving at the lake house, Mark could quickly see why not losing it in the divorce had been such a huge deal for Bryan. Before him stood a two-story home with a rock-faced exterior that was built in the custom of the Texas Hill Country. A rustic, iron Lone Star, symbolizing the owner's love of Texas, hung near the front door. Inside, they found an open layout with high ceilings featuring exposed natural timbers.

Two of the three bedrooms were small, but welcoming, and even in his state of mind, Mark could see that the master would sweep a woman off her feet. A huge pine and wrought iron bed sat opposite the back wall, which was comprised entirely with floor-to-ceiling windows overlooking the lake. At night, looking out the windows and seeing the stars dance upon the water, perhaps catching a hawk flying low in search of a meal, or maybe even looking upon lovers stealing away for a midnight swim, could all prove intoxicating.

But it would have to wait. To Mark, this wasn't about a getaway with Yo-Yo or a family vacation; this was about survival. So as the kids ran through the house and then out the back to excitedly inspect the boat and jet skis tied to the dock, Mark hurriedly unpacked the truck and got to work.

While Cubbie stayed close by the children and Yo-Yo put away things from the bags that Mark managed to drag inside, Mark started to quickly install the security equipment he had brought. Getting four cameras positioned on the corners of the house, one on the backside of the mailbox for a full frontal view of the home as well as two battery-operated motion sensors around both the front and back doors, was a job Mark completed well after sundown with the help of a large flashlight. Back inside, he showed both Cubbie and Yo-Yo how to check the laptop and see a full view of the exterior of the home, and he also set off the sensors so both would be aware of the sound.

By this time, the crew was again hungry. Finding the fridge empty except for the remnants of two singles left over from a Shiner Bock twelve pack, Mark herded everyone up, and like the hawk flying low seeking a meal, they, too, set out in search of food. The closest two restaurants were already closed, but they found the Boar's Breath still open. Perched high on a point surrounded by trees, it offered an amazing view of the lake and a pretty good chicken-fried steak.

Thinking only they were on a vacation, the kids were

enjoying themselves. Cubbie relaxed with a cold Bud Light and drifted away to Leona Lewis on the jukebox while Yo-Yo drank white wine and made sure to keep holding hands with Mark. Even he, for a moment, relaxed and was able to appreciate his family and the setting.

Later, after returning to the lake house and getting the kids to bed, Mark went outside and brought in the weapons he had brought. As he lay the shotgun and shells down next to the Glocks and a table full of ammunition, the feeling of relaxation went away.

Cubbie knew how to handle each of the weapons, but he was still uneasy around them. Mark had taught Yo-Yo how to drop in a new clip, hit the safety off and fire, but she viewed the guns with a sense of dread. Was this all really necessary? The look on Mark's face told them it was.

"I need you to count on me," Cubbie said. "I got this. You go and do what you gotta do."

Hearing this, Yo-Yo turned and hugged Cubbie. They shared a look in each other's eyes that would have caused tears any other time, but not tonight. They knew that wasn't what Mark needed.

Before slipping into bed, Mark took the two thousand dollars he had withdrawn from the bank and put it in the top drawer of the nightstand. Doing so, he turned to Yo-Yo, lying in bed wearing only a thong and a blue University of Florida Tim Tebow jersey.

"In the morning, go to Wal-Mart and buy everything you're gonna need," he instructed her. "Food, deodorant, wine, sunscreen, bug repellant, batteries, anything you can think of; go ahead and buy it. And pay with cash. That's what this is for; use cash for everything and not the credit cards."

"You said deodorant and bug repellant," she said, pushing hair from her eyes. "What about bug deodorant? Some of them do get kinda stinky you know."

Seeing his seriousness was being seriously undermined, Mark grinned. "No, the bugs'll be okay. I just didn't know how to say it, but the deodorant is for you."

He began to wave his hand in front of his nose like Yo-Yo had an odor problem. The hand waving stopped at exactly the same time she slammed a large pillow into Mark's face. The pillow was soon replaced with two arms, which grabbed Mark and pulled him to bed.

As the two laughed and giggled and rolled and kissed on the bed, it was like Mark's worries were banished from his mind. No matter the circumstance, Yo-Yo had that effect. The way she made him feel, the feelings she made him have for her, the life she breathed into him, combined and carried more weight than any worry possibly could.

"Did you lock the door?" she purred, kissing him and feeling her body warming.

"Why?" he asked teasingly.

"Get your ass up and lock the door," she said, biting him hard on the shoulder.

While she was pulling Tim Tebow over her head, Mark rolled out of bed. "What if I'm not in the mood?" he asked, pretending to trudge towards the door.

Watching his silhouette walk across the darkened room, Yo-Yo couldn't help but notice that his enlarged and extremely rigid piece of manhood was making his Jockey style boxers fit rather tightly.

"Looks like something is in the mood," she

teased again.

"Oh, you mean this?" Mark asked, stopping and turning towards her while pointing at his dick. "It's just because I was thinkin' of someone else."

Before he was able to turn back to the door, a perfectly thrown Tebow jersey hit Mark in the face.

"Well, does the bitch have an arm like that?" asked Yo-Yo smugly, while Mark wondered if the jersey had left welts.

"I dunno," Mark said over his shoulder as he closed the door. "I hadn't made it to her arms yet."

Walking back to the bed while deftly pushing down his Jockeys, Mark heard, "Oh, you know your ass is in trouble now."

"There's no lock on the door," he whispered, sliding in next to her. "You're gonna have to be quiet."

"I'm not good at being quiet," she answered.

"Baby you're a lot better than good," he said, smiling and reaching for Yo-Yo.

As he entered her, he could feel her warmth. Hearing the soft groan and listening as her breath accelerated, Mark was on a mission. He was out to prove he deserved such a woman. With one hand, he grasped both her wrists and pulled them overhead as he thrust into her. She felt secure in submitting to him.

Covering her entire body with his, Mark reached beneath her with his other hand and brought her even closer to him. Her lower back arched and then relaxed as Mark sent wave after wave crashing into her. She felt small beads of sweat growing on her forehead as he brought one of her legs inside his and he began to rhythmically grind down upon her.

The thrusts felt like they were going all the way

through her and her entire being. And no matter what body movement Mark engaged in, the constant was his mouthwatering kisses. His kisses were complete, deep, and given with a hunger that could only be quenched with a ravenous gorging. Their mouths were one. Melded by lust and desire, their lips were inseparable. Their hands and bodies and mouths defied marriage. Their love was something more.

As her body shuddered and her eyes began to glass over, Mark knew full well he was hitting the spot. When her arms reached around him and her head tilted back while stifling a scream, Mark felt her explosion. With this, he was no longer able to hold back, and Yo-Yo's explosion led directly to his. As he finished, Yo-Yo's eyes were now suddenly opened wide and her mouth even wider, as she battled the physical need to vocalize her passion.

Afterwards, feeling spent, he rolled off beside her, and she nuzzled close and placed her head on his shoulder. The urge to vocalize was now gone, and Yo-Yo simply ran her fingers through Mark's chest hair. At that moment, the lovers did not need words. Each knew how fortunate they were.

Pushing the sheets back to help cool his body, Mark lay next to Yo-Yo as she drifted off to sleep. While most men quickly gave into drowsiness after sex, Mark gave into something altogether different. Though Yo-Yo was sleeping next to him and though they had shared a special brand of lovemaking, Mark was wide awake as his mind played a game of hide and seek.

His thoughts were of the man who would try and take this life from him. Mark thought of the Gospel Killer and thought how he would catch and kill him.

These thoughts led to Mark going over the details contained in the police reports. Over and over each small and perhaps meaningless detail, he searched for a clue. If he needed to catch the copycat first, then so be it. He would play Nicholas' game, but there would come a day when the game would be Mark's. For it was the Gospel Killer who had threatened his family, and it was the Gospel Killer who had brought Bubba and the Magician and their sphere of influence into Mark's life so front and center. So it would surely be the Gospel Killer who would pay for these mistakes with his life.

As he stared at the spinning ceiling fan, Mark contemplated each of these people: the Gospel Killer, the copycat, Bubba, and the Magician, as well as the threat each posed for his family. He hated that he had allowed such people leverage over him. This hatred spurred a fury within Mark. He would see this through and take back his life.

As the sun was about to break the horizon and illuminate the lake and shoreline, Mark finally closed his eyes and fell asleep. Two hours later, he was awake, showered and about to leave for Dallas as he kissed the head of his sleeping Yo-Yo. He did so, thinking that today would be the day that brought him closer to ending this ugly chapter of his life.

~~~

In Dallas, a short time earlier, Nicholas' alarm rang at 6:00 a.m. Turning the lights on, he reached for his laptop and logged on. Within a couple of strokes, he located Mark's Charger, still parked at the mysterious address near Possum Kingdom Lake. The GPS he had paid to have attached to an isolated place inside Mark's wheel well worked exceedingly well and had alerted him the prior evening to Mark's location.

Hoping it was perhaps a lead that had led Mark to such a place, Nicholas was now thinking that since he had spent the night there, it was more likely a retreat, perhaps a secretive, out-of-the-way place to try and hide his family. Nicholas smiled his devilish smirk at such an absurd attempt. Didn't this private investigator realize what type of man he was up against?

He was the type of man who could dress as a woman and pay two undesirables a sum of money to install a freaking GPS system on Mark's car in broad daylight while it was parked at his freaking office. He pulled that off along with more murders than any Dallas police officer even imagined, and this man was going to be outsmarted by moving a family to an out-of-the-way location seventy miles away?

Later Nicholas stood in his bathroom admiring his nude body in front of the full- length mirror. Moments before, while he emptied his bladder, he looked down on his glorious cock and could easily see why so many women and men desired it. He thought of the men who feigned surprise when, alone, they "discovered" he was actually a man.

He smiled when remembering how he would coo to them as they pretended not to know what to do with his beautiful cock. For his cock was beautiful, supreme, and mighty. He was sure it was as glorious as he himself was. After all, he was destined for greatness; it was obvious to anyone who would dare notice. So, would a private investigator deny him this greatness? Deny him his ordained glory? Deny him the opportunity to become infamous for ages, all the while retaining his anonymity?

Still looking into the floor length mirror, these questions clouded his vision until Nicolas was no longer able to appreciate his own beautiful reflection. His patience with Mark was wearing thin. The private investigator would have to pick up his game considerably, or else Nicholas would again have to provide additional motivation.

Chapter 34

The next week and a half for Mark was almost a blur. Sixteen-hour days in the office on the case, checking phone records, going over forensic reports, reading the Bible, wasting time with one weak-ass reward tip after another. Receiving daily phone calls from Bryan, which were part thank you for introducing him to Jessie and part wildly descriptive calls of her sexual appetite and prowess. Then back to interviewing victim's family members and co-workers for any possible clue how the victims may have come into contact with the killer.

Eating Tums like they were candy, digesting them like they weren't, contacting knife manufactures about shipments of serrated-edged knifes to Dallas area retailers, checking with the retailers about any sales to shapely women who perhaps donned tattoos, daily talks with Detective Coleman. All this and he felt like he was no closer to the killer's identity than when he started. It was as if he was either chasing a ghost through a swamp or trying to drown a fish.

He was getting nowhere. What was he missing? It just didn't add up that two separate killers were trolling the same territory and both were avoiding detection. Were there even two killers? Was Nicholas playing him, and the thought of a copycat killer, just part of some sick game? Mark didn't know. He couldn't know that Angel was, indeed, very real and a totally separate animal from Nicholas, a completely different threat with completely different perversions and motivations. All he did know for sure was that if not for the two speeding tickets he had received on I-20 racing back and forth each evening to Lake Possum Kingdom to see Yo-Yo and the kids, there would be no evidence of his efforts over the last ten days at all.

Two things of interest did occur during this time though. Mark thought one could potentially be helpful; the other was downright strange. First and most importantly, Ellis returned from Washington armed with a new plan. He changed directions and sold Harrington on the idea of going public with as much information as possible about the killer. He said that reaching out to the community in this manner would be considered proactive and evidence of both his department's advances in the investigation and personal concern for the citizens.

Chief Harrington was now much more open to changing course since he was coming under intense pressure concerning his department's failure to capture the Gospel Killer. The local NBC affiliate Channel 5, started each evening newscast by tearing a day from a calendar and then forcefully, with both graphics and booming voice-over, proclaiming what the new count was of how many days Dallas had been held hostage by this murderer.

So, being a natural born politician, Harrington quickly agreed with Ellis. His plan offered hope in finding the killer and provided a not-so-veiled means to cover his own ass, while touting all the work his force had done on the crimes and even bragging of the overwhelming amount of useless information they had gathered.

When Coleman and Ellis held their press conferences, in addition to the useless piles of information the chief bragged of, they also got him to highlight actual facts garnered by the investigation. Quickly, the papers and local news were filled with the stills, as well as video, from the Stoneleigh Hotel of Angel walking through the hallways.

Soon, callers to local talk radio were immersed in hearing of the Biblical implications of the killings; the twenty-seven day pattern between each killing; the wild theories of what the exposed tattoos might mean; the danger that any man named Matthew, Mark, Luke or John might face; warnings of how this woman might try and disguise herself now that her identity was as least partially shown; the emptiness of discovering the killer was not the previously named Bethany Adams, and then learning that oddly she herself had become a murder victim also.

It was all more than enough to be a terrific boon for TV ratings and newspaper sales, but failed to provide the desired cover for Chief Harrington's rather ample posterior. Channel 5 now started their evening news with not only the changing calendar, but also an ongoing countdown until the next date in the twenty-seven-day pattern, and the Dallas Morning News ran a scathing editorial about how the chief's refusal to release this information earlier had perhaps led to the deaths of Marcel Durand and Miss Joy Seebers.

As far as Coleman and Ellis—the two men on stage next to Chief Harrington during the press conferences—were concerned, this was a win-win situation.

The newly released information and video might lead to someone coming forward with the big break they were seeking.

If so, thanks to Channel 5, the prick Harrington wouldn't be able to spin things and take all the credit. One afternoon in Coleman's office, Ellis explained to him and Mark what the thought process was behind the new effort and the publicizing of so many of the facts.

"It's about pressure," Ron said as he took a drink of Sprite. Before continuing, Ellis loudly swished the drink around in his mouth in an incredibly annoying fashion prior to finally, and mercifully, swallowing it.

"We gotta turn this shit around on the whore," Ellis said, after a moment and the obligatory Sprite burp. "So far, all the pressure's been on us. Puttin' all this out in the press, well, now it's her turn to start feeling some heat."

Mark of course agreed with the concept of trying to shift the pressure but before he could respond John asked, "So you think she's more likely to make a mistake now? Now like you say, that the heat's been turned up."

Ellis turned to answer, but before doing so, he let out a second and more forceful Sprite burp that Mark and John couldn't help but both smell and taste. "Sorry about that, but, yeah. Fuck, yeah. You know, like they say, the heat'll burn you."

"They also say it ain't the heat, but it's the humidity," Mark said, shaking his head. Then, while wiping the figurative burp stain from his face with the back of his hand, he added, "And I only say that because that last burp of yours felt a little hot and wet. You know, for the record, you gotta be the grossest little motherfucker in the world."

While Coleman shook his head in agreement, a grinning Ron answered Mark, "That's because I ain't wantin' to fuck you. But, if you had a pussy, I'd be actin' a little different, and you'd be swearing I was Cary-fucking-Grant."

After that meeting, Mark decided he needed to put the case on the back burner for an hour or two, and to take some action or else people might start considering him for the grossest motherfucker on the planet award. Not having worked out in almost a week, Mark was feeling lazy and mushy and altogether beyond gross. And for this feeling he knew who to thank. In addition to the stress of the case and of being away from his family, it was at this exact time that he had, unfortunately, made the acquaintance of what would prove to be his next arch enemy – a Blue Bell ice cream flavor, oh so cleverly named Christmas Cookies in July. This was literally taking Blue Bell ice cream, the most addictive substance known to man, and then crunching up sugary Christmas cookies and blending the two together.

What kind of satanic worshipping, FDA bureaucratic pinhead could have ever approved such a thing for human consumption? Jenny Craig and bariatric surgeons worldwide could only have devised this recipe. So, it was against this villain that Mark would battle, and he was determined he would win the battle for his waistline.

With victory all that mattered, he decided to run, or perhaps in his mind now, waddle might be a better and more appropriate description, by his house and get in a boot camp session with fitness general Tony Horton. The battlefield would be his living room, and the weapon of fat destruction would be P90X video number two – Plyometrics. With a week of physical inactivity compounded by the extra junk in the trunk courtesy of Blue Bell Christmas Cookies in July, Mark was already sweating before the tape's warm-up section was complete.

By the time he was halfway through his first set of Heisman "high steps," his shirt was drenched. By the time he completed the second run through the "skier moguls," he was beginning to think General Horton had gone and went insane like Brando's general in Apocalypse Now.

Straining to breathe, much less keep up, Mark was anything but disappointed to hear his phone ring during the middle of the session. From the caller ID, he could tell that it was his son Daniel. Hitting the pause button and attempting to catch his breath, Mark answered the phone.

Daniel told him he had forgotten his baseball glove at home. He was having a great time at the lake and all, and he did understand his regular season was over, but fall league tryouts would be here before you know it. And, it just so happened, a neighbor boy had stopped by to play, but, alas, there was no glove to play with. Could dear old Dad go by his mom's house and pick up the trusted Mizuno 11-inch infielder glove?

Could he? If the truth were told, Mark was glad that his son was talking almost non-stop when asking this question, because at least it afforded him the opportunity to bend over and breathe. So with sweat dropping from his face faster than Kim Kardashian drops to her

knees in an NBA locker room, Mark managed to tell
Daniel that he would go by and pick up the glove and
see him that evening. After that, he hit the pause button
again and continued the onslaught. Damn Blue Bell
ice cream to Hell.

Getting out of the shower after the workout, Mark
did feel like the perceived jiggle he was imagining was
gone but, unfortunately, soreness had replaced it. Not
a full-blown muscle soreness yet, but Mark could tell
from both experience and from bending over to tie
his shoes that the following morning was going to be
no fun at all.

Grabbing an apple and a Diet Coke on his way
through the kitchen and laundry room, he then, thanks
to the soreness, rather gently sat down in the Charger
and set out for Kellie's. On his way through the traffic,
his mind was going over one detail of the case after
another, so much so that he nearly sideswiped a Nissan
Altima getting onto the highway. The close call, and
the ensuing magnified finger display from the driver
of the Altima, caused Mark to realize he needed to
relax and stop thinking of the case.

Turning the radio up, he punched several different stations before finally hitting something he knew
would do the trick. Coming from a small alternative
station out of Dallas' Deep Ellum district, a voice sang
out that Mark recognized well. Part woeful and part
wistful, and all together weird, the venerable Tom
Waits was singing his old standard, the Black Rider:
"Anchors away with the Black Rider. I'll drink your
blood like wine. I'll drop you off in Harlem with the
Black Rider, out where the bullets shine. And when
you're done, you cock your gun; the blood will run,

like ribbons in your hair."

Mark could make no sense at all of the lyrics—no one not currently experiencing a heroin trip possibly could—but there was something about Waits' music. His voice, his sound, his phrasing, collectively Tom Waits was hypnotic to Mark. By the time he reached Kellie's house, his mind was decompressed and on autopilot. Devoid of any thoughts of the case, and for that matter devoid of any recollection of traffic signs or other cars he must have seen on the road, Mark arrived feeling almost refreshed and just in time for the real weirdness.

It was a little after seven when Mark pulled into her driveway. Seeing the garage door up, he decided to knock on the side utility room door instead of going around to the front. Getting out of the Charger, he was still at least partly wrapped in the Tom Waits experience when, while walking up to the door, loud barking from the neighbor's new dog shook him from his "trip."

And if Ellis' return from Washington with different marching orders were the first, then the barking dog "awakened" Mark to the second notable, this one being completely and thoroughly odd, thing which occurred while Yo-Yo and the kids were staying at the lake house.

Mark knocked. He waited a moment, but when there was no answer, he knocked a little more forcefully, He was beginning to think that perhaps he should have called first. He stepped back from the door and reached into his pocket for his cell. While he dialed the phone with his head down, he was startled to hear the door open and see his ex-wife. With makeup streaked down her face and mascara clotted onto her eyes, Kellie obviously had been crying. Mark immediately wished he was someplace else.

"Come in," Kellie said between sobs as she held the door open.

Mark hesitated and then entered the house and walked past the piles of dirty clothes on the floor of the laundry room and into the kitchen. Seeing a half-empty wine bottle on the countertop and hearing Kellie struggle to close both the garage and side door, Mark knew she had been drinking. He also knew how she got whenever she had even a little alcohol.

"Are you okay?" he asked as she finally joined him in the kitchen.

"I'm fine; I'm sorry," she managed to get these words out, but the emotions on her face betrayed her lies. Lowering her head and trying to stifle the tears, she poured another drink and stepped away from Mark and towards the kitchen window. After an agonizingly awkward pause where he couldn't think of a single coherent thing to say, she finally helped him out.

"Is Daniel all right?"

"Yes, he's fine," Mark said, seizing the moment. "I'm sorry."

"You're sorry he's fine?" Kellie asked, tilting the glass upwards and with her back to him.

With the creepiness level of this entire crying ex-wife situation elevating quickly to Code Orange, Mark stumbled before saying, "No, of course not."

"What exactly are you sorry for then?" she shot back immediately, like pouncing on prey.

Looking desperately around for her husband or a giant noose to slip his neck through, Mark again hesitated before answering. "It looks like I caught you at a bad time, and what I'm sorry for is that I didn't call you first to tell you I was stopping by. But Daniel called and asked me to pick up his glove, and he didn't say it, but he'll probably want his bat, too."

Saying this, Mark watched as the muscles on her back tightened instantly, her shoulders went taut, and then just as quickly they went back to normal. Finishing her drink, she composed herself and set another wine glass from the cabinets onto the counter.

"Pour yourself a drink," she said as she turned to Mark. "I'll be right back."

While she was gone, Mark thought of a lot of things. He thought of leaving and buying Daniel a new glove; thought how in the world Tom Wait would handle this situation; thought of a lot of things, but he did not think of pouring himself a glass of wine. When she returned, it was obvious that Kellie had cleaned her face and freshened her makeup.

"You don't have to call," she said, setting the glove and bat on the breakfast table. "You bought this house; you can stop by any time you like."

"It's not like that," said Mark, taken aback. "Is Thomas home?"

"Of course note," Kellie said, emptying the remainder of the bottle into her glass. "He's always gone. Just as well though; the little fag doesn't know what to do when he is here."

Oh geez, Mark was now listening to his ex-wife talk of her current husband as a "little fag." Check please, it was time to find the exit.

While Mark was looking for an escape hatch, Kellie asked, "Can I ask you a question?" Of course, that was a question, and before Mark could even answer, she asked a second one, "Do you ever think of when you lived here? With me? With us?"

"Look, I'm sorry about whatever is wrong with you," Mark said, slumping his own shoulders and trying to decide how to answer the question. "But I don't know what you are wanting from me right now."

Laughing, she went to the sink and stared out the window and into the backyard. "You used to know what I wanted."

"I need to be leaving now," Mark said, knowing this was a losing proposition. Looking at Kellie, he again could see the muscles tighten; he could see the tension rise in her neck.

"Well, go on and go," she said, and he couldn't help noticing that the tension wasn't going away. "Leave. You're good at leaving."

Closing the door behind him, he could hear her begin to cry once again. He had heard it before, back in a hurtful and sad time, but now the tears sounded odd to him. The whole encounter was strange. Nothing like it had happened since the divorce had been fresh, but seeing her that way and hearing her sobs sounded to Mark like a washed-up high school athlete recounting his long ago perceived brilliance on the fields.

It was faded, no one cared any longer, and showing that it affected the person still in such a strong manner only showed that person's weakness. He drove away quickly as he searched the radio dial for one more hit of Tom Waits.

~~~

Luke Colbert came here most every day after class, but he had never seen her here before, and he would have remembered any woman with an ass like that.

For even at the dog park, Luke was the biggest hound of all. So, while he threw the tennis ball for his Lab, Cassie, to fetch time and again, it was the woman's ass that firmly held his attention.

Then damn, she bent down to pet her huge Bullmastiff, and Luke caught a glimpse of a lower back tattoo that seemed to be playing peek-a-boo with him. She would stand and it would disappear, and then she would bend or kneel and it would pop back out for Luke to salivate over. It looked like maybe an angel of some type. He couldn't see for sure from this distance, so the next throw to Cassie sailed closer to the woman and her tattoo, and quite naturally, Luke just happened to follow the ball towards its target.

Pulling the ball from Cassie's mouth, Luke was now no more than fifteen feet from the woman with the ass and tantalizing tattoo. Then the woman did just what he hoped: she bent down and with both her hands part playfully shook and part petted her big dog's face. Doing so revealed an even larger image of the tattoo, which indeed was an angel with outstretched wings. The closer view made Luke want to see even more, and as he walked further towards her, he imagined what treasure lay at the bottom of that oh so inviting tattoo.

He started casually by petting Cassie and looking at the Mastiff. "And I thought my dog here was big."

"You ought to see his poop piles," she quipped, glancing over at him with a smile.

Nice icebreaker, an ass and a sense of humor; this would be fun. She was a good bit older than him, but Luke was fine doing that Cougar thing, so he laughed and stuck out his hand. "Hi, I'm Luke."

"Well, hello there, Luke. I'm Angel," she said

demurely as she straightened back up, wiped her hands on her pants and shook his hand.

Chapter 35

Saturday morning at the lake house came equipped with Yo-Yo's famous waffles along with a side order of humility. For some reason, which at the present he could not possibly explain, Mark had told his lovely wife about the strange experience the evening before with Kellie. Yo-Yo was friends with Kellie and way too secure for any jealousy, but not too mature to have herself a rather good time at her husband's expense.

In bed the night before, there had been comments such as: "Are you doing to me what Kellie wanted you to do to her?" and "You know, maybe if you keep eating that Blue Bell ice cream, maybe she'll stop wanting your big sexy self so much?" Finally, after her second thunderous orgasm, she bit into his shoulder so hard it almost brought blood and said, "Oh goddamn, no wonder she still wants that dick."

While at least some of those words spoken in the midst of some rather heated sex were admittedly food for his ego, what he was hearing before the kids sat down at the table was nothing short of cruel. As fate would have it, along with Yo-Yo and brother Cubbie, he had to endure the taunts of Cubbie's boyfriend Will, who was in town for the weekend. Yo-Yo all too gladly told the boys about the longings of Mark's ex, and they together teamed up to express their understanding of poor Kellie's plight.

"Poor Markie, it's so tough being a sex symbol," Will said, feigning sympathy.

"Sex symbol?" Cubbie chimed in. "I was thinking she must be impaired or going blind or something."

As the laughter grew, Will took his finger and wiped it along the edge of the bowl Yo-Yo was pouring her waffles from and then licked the batter from his finger while coyly saying, "Maybe you could stop by and give her a quick lick around the edges?"

Yo-Yo swatted him away with her wooden spoon. "He better keep his licking to my edges — and he better not be quick about it."

It didn't stop there; the trio pulled out their best material.

Borrowing the voice from the well known Dos Equis commercial, Cubbie grabbed Yo-Yo's wooden spoon and held it as a microphone with one hand while pointing at Mark with the other, proclaiming, "He is the most sexually desired man in the world."

"His sexuality is so magnetic, he cannot carry a compass," Will chimed in again, like an old vaudeville act.

This raised the level of laughter and Yo-Yo quipped, "Women have lost their virginity to photographs of him."

"Strippers dance and then tip him," Cubbie carried on.

"No matter how he orders his salads, they always arrive undressed," added Will.

Finally and mercifully, the three standups seemed to be out of material and said almost in unison, "Mark Witt is the most sexually desired man in the world."

This bringing-down-the-house act was causing Mark's face to look like a ripe cherry, and he was more than glad when the kids hit pause on their cartoons and came into the kitchen to see what was going on. Only then did the kidding slow and he was able to stop blushing and enjoy the pancakes. After breakfast, he kissed Yo-Yo and told her he needed to get to the office.

"Besides, ya'll probably need to get ready for your Comedy Central special anyway," he said.

"Just be sure to get your sexy self back home for dinner," she smiled and answered.

After the kids had finished their plates and returned to the cartoons, Mark was saying his good-byes and walking out through the kitchen when Will playfully slapped him on his butt.

"Um, wish I had a biscuit; I'd sop all that up," he said.

Needless to say, these would-be three stooges all found this quite hysterical, and Mark didn't even bother to turn around and face them. Instead, he pushed the button and waited for the garage door to open, a beaten man ready only to get into his Charger and race away from this assault.

~~~

It was a little past noon and Richard Witt was already well into his fourth beer. His drinking was with a part anger, part depression, part what in the fuck happened to the Yankees and how could they get swept in a doubleheader by the Blue Jays, part what in the fuck am I going to do now, frame of mind that so engulfed his thinking he barely noticed the next-to-nude dancer grinding on the pole in front of him. With the song now over and Richard appearing glassy-eyed to the point no financial award would be forthcoming, the sullen dancer finally trudged away as Lew the Magician settled into the chair next to Richard.

Lew's opening words of "We need to talk" were not what Richard wanted to hear. He prepared for it by leaning back and finishing the remainder of his beer.

"Bubba says we gotta do something about you," the Magician said. "About what you owe."

"What am I supposed to do?" Richard answered as any degenerate gambler would. "Pettitte goes out and gives up seven runs in five in a third to the Blue Jays—to the fucking BLUE JAYS—and after they had already given away the first game?"

Lew listened but he lacked what could be termed a good bedside manner. "It's over thirty now, and we got to get some cash from you."

"You'll get it as soon as I do," Richard said, shrugging his shoulders.

This was not good enough. In matters of money, there was only one acceptable solution; pay up and do it now. Not that everyone understood this, and not that reminders weren't frequently needed. So many different people in his life had told the Magician so many things, but the one constant was how things always turned out. Lew knew the ending even if the others didn't want to accept it.

"That's not good enough," he said sternly, leaning closer to Richard. "If I go tell Bubba that, he'll start thinkin' I've gone soft, and a man in my line of work really can't afford the boss thinking he's soft. So here's the deal; you are gonna go borrow some money from that son of yours, as much as you can and as quick as you can. 'Cause we're not waiting for your pension checks; we're not running a revolving line of credit finance company here. You're late; you owe over thirty large and the juice for being late is two percent a week. So, from now on, you owe six hundred every week on top of the principal until you get squared...And, you do want to get squared, right?"

Richard was thinking he would like to put his fist right square in the middle of Lew's rather large pineapple-looking face, but realizing that doing so inside of Club Fuxx was not conducive to lengthening one's life span, he thought better of it.

"Of course I want to get squared away with Bubba," he answered. "And I'm gonna do my best."

Rising from the table, Lew smiled and patted Richard on the shoulder after hearing that last part. "You're going to need to do better than that."

As he watched Lew walk away, Richard squinted his eyes and it was easy for him to imagine the black-suited Lew morphing into the Grim Reaper right before him. Some people were good at their jobs, some people even really liked their jobs, but Lew the Magician lived for his job. It was like he was going to be disappointed if by some chance in hell Richard was actually able to come up with the money, that he would be deprived from having the opportunity to once again perform his magic and make another poor soul disappear.

These not so comforting thoughts were only pushed from Richard's consciousness by the ringing of his telephone. Not recognizing the number but feeling in the mood to really go off on some unsuspecting legitimate bill collector, Richard answered the cell only to be surprised. At first, he didn't recognize the voice and he had to step outside to avoid the fanatical AC/DC song "Highway to Hell" pounding from the club's speakers before he understood who was calling him.

"Richard can you hear me? It's me, David. David Vaughn."

Richard knew Vaughn, but he was wondering why he would be calling him after all these years? They were both retired Dallas cops but hardly friends; Richard had heard David landed a cush security job at the Stoneleigh Hotel; maybe he needed some contract work.

"Hey, David, sorry about that," he said after a lengthy pause. "I couldn't hear you for a minute. How you been?"

"Not good," David answered much quicker. "I need to talk to you."

Richard could see this coming, so he answered, "Look, if you're calling to borrow money, you're barking up the wrong tree."

Still quick about things, Vaughn shot back with, "I know who the Gospel Killer is. I helped her, for Christ's sake, and now I need your help."

This revelation caught Richard flat-footed. Before he could think of anything to say, David came back with, "From the music, I'm guessin' you're down at Bubba's, so can you meet me in a half hour down in the River Bottoms?"

Richard knew the spot well. Since he was now more than curious, he checked his watch. "I'll be there."

Exiting Irving Boulevard and winding down the narrow asphalt road leading to the baseball and soccer fields that sat next to the Trinity River and occupied the area locals commonly called the "River Bottoms," Richard passed a city work truck leaving the fields and saw only an older model Toyota Camry sitting in the parking lot. Driving slowly past it and seeing the driver nod his head, Richard eased up next to the car and parked after seeing the driver was David Vaughn. Throwing a cigarette out the car window, Vaughn motioned for Richard to come over to his car so they could talk.

Hearing the locks unlock, Richard got in, sat down on the worn cloth seats, turned and looked directly into the eyes of David Vaughn. He looked older than Richard remembered, noticeably heavier, and one other thing also stood out about him: Vaughn was a scared man. It was not something that Richard remembered seeing in Vaughn before and it added to the intrigue of the meeting. After perhaps twenty or thirty seconds of obligatory greetings and catching up with one another, Richard cut to the chase.

"So what's this shit about you knowing who the Gospel Killer is?" he asked bluntly.

David lit another cigarette, handed one to Richard, and stared out the windshield.

"It's no shit. Look, she didn't kill all 'em, but she's done the killings since they started back. She started with that guy Jacobsen."

Richard knew there were two killers responsible, so this answer revved him up. He also knew a man who wanted to talk when he saw one.

"Tell me what it is you know," he prompted.

David was eager but still a little apprehensive in dealing with Richard. He knew the stories that went around about Witt at the station, and he knew most were true.

"Look, this is my life, my family's life," he said before continuing. "You can't fuck me on this."

"You called me for a reason," Richard said, feigning hurt feelings. "The reason must be you think you can trust me."

The reason most surely was not that. He had called him because he knew Richard was morally corrupt and would do just about anything for money, including what it was he needed. But, he had no intention of being overly honest or saying more than was necessary, so Vaughn hesitated and thought a moment before answering.

"After I retired, I got to drinking quite a bit. Got into trouble with it. And I had to do something to keep my security job at the Stoneleigh, so I started going to some meetings that my daughter suggested. Turns out they were run by a friend of hers, a girl she knew from church. Anyways, after a few meetings, her friend and me started talking about other things besides rehab. We got to be friends, at least I thought. She even gave me a nickname, Short Timer—'Cause I'd been sober just a short time. Anyway, then things got out of hand, and you know one thing led to another."

"Yeah, it led to your dick getting up inside her pussy. So what happened then?"

"I mean, you gotta keep this between us. If my wife or daughter ever found out…"

Richard did remember meeting Vaughn's wife years before, and his best guess was she was pushing at least three hundred pounds, so in Richard's mind, that more than made it okay to fuck a serial killer.

"You got my word," he said. "Your family stays out of it."

Finishing off his cigarette, David sighed deeply. "Well, pretty soon she starts asking me about being a cop, and from there it went to did you ever kill anyone? To how did you do it? And then, to how could someone get away with murder? So before long, I wind up telling her everything I know about how police operate and what they look for. I just thought she was fascinated with that sort of thing. I didn't know she was using me the whole time. Then after a while, it sorta snowballed, and by then it was already too late."

"So what all did you tell her?" Richard asked.

"Mainly about how to clean up things, you know, use bleach and all. I told her what kinds of things DNA can be taken from, and how a killer should always take everything with them they even possibly could have touched. Told her to bag it and get it away from the crime scene."

"This bitch is good. She knows more than that. What else did you tell her?"

Vaughn sighed deeply. "I told her about the pattern, too." Staring blankly out the windshield, he shook his head before adding, "Then a while, you know, after she had gotten started and all, she told me she had picked when to kill that Jacobsen guy because that date to the day had been exactly twenty-seven months since the last man had been murdered by the Gospel Killer. Said she got the calendar out and figured it all up. Thought it would be a good way to try and tie it to the original killer."

This extra bit of effort and attention to detail by the killer impressed Richard. "Anything else?" he asked, arching his eyebrows.

"I also told her a killer needed to give a witness something to see besides their face. Told her about the eight guys that Gotti had pull the hit on Paul

Castellano—how they came in pairs from all four directions and how each of the eight wore big white Russian hats and long white fur coats. Killed Big Paulie on Christmas Eve right in the middle of downtown Manhattan in front of hundreds of people, and all anyone could tell the cops they saw were these guys with big coats and hats."

Richard believed what David had said up to this point, but a good cop always throws in questions to confirm things. "So what does this woman use? To divert people?"

"Tats. Said every time she saw someone with tattoos, that was all she seemed to remember. Said she bet that if she dressed like a whore and slapped tattoos on her ass, nobody would even notice if she had a face. So she went online and learned how to make fake ones herself. The tattoos around her arm and on her back are all fake. Guess I wound up telling her too much."

Though Richard believed that David was being truthful, he couldn't help but be a bit of an asshole. "Don't be so hard on yourself, Vaughn, sweet young pussy is hard to come by."

It wasn't like that," David protested. "I mean it turned into that, I guess, but not at first. I just loved being with someone new, somebody who was interested in me. It had been a real long time. Hell, but even that seems like a long time ago now. Anyway, then things turned scary. I don't know; it's just I gotta find a way to stop it now."

"And you know she killed the guy at the Stoneleigh because you recognized her from the tape?"

"Yeah, but there's more to it than just that. See, we were in my office one night real late, and she gets on the computer and starts looking at the guest list. Didn't say anything about it but two days later, Matthew Michaels gets killed there. And yeah, it's her on the video, but I couldn't say shit 'cause I led her right to him."

"Well, if she looked up and found this guy on the fuckin' guest list, how did she find all the others? You know, guys with the right names and all. Did you help her with that, too?"

"No. And I'm not sure 'cause she never told me, but I think it had to do with her job. She was able to check on shit like that."

Despite all the alcohol and mistreatment Richard had put his body through, his mind was still sharp; he knew Vaughn was not telling him the whole truth.

"You know, I want to believe you," he said after pausing and replaying the story in his head. "But one thing doesn't make any sense. She starts killing men. With precision, you know, with real expertise, and then there's you, the little ole ex-cop who knows all this and can see beyond her tattoos and could bring her down. Why would she let you live?"

"She needed me at first," David said, gulping hard. "And, back then, I needed her, too. But after this shit started really happening, everything just changed. I guess she thinks I'm an accomplice and can't turn her in, but I also wouldn't be surprised if she's put me on her list, too."

"And, you're still seeing her? I mean, goddamn, that bitch must be able to suck a golf ball through a garden hose. You know what kinda chances you're taking here, don't you?"

"I keep my eyes open with her now. And I just tell her basic things, like make checklists, things to take with her, things to make sure she has when she leaves the places. Told her where to buy things, how to always use cash, but not to flash too much of it. And I taught her to buy track phones and use phony names and then throw them away as fast as she got 'em so as not to leave any records they could trace."

David's feelings were all over the map. He was frightened. He was still trying to dance around the complete truth, sick of what he had done, not wanting to admit to more than was needed, fearful of how to have the relationship remain undetected, and also perhaps somewhat relieved to be sharing his burden. Then he looked at Richard and felt pissed. He knew he had fucked up, helping a woman kill men, cheating on his wife, fucking a friend of his daughter; but the look on Richard's face still pissed him off. If one man existed who had no right to look down on him, it was Richard Witt, and yet there he was giving him a "what the fuck were you thinking" look. It bothered him to the point he had to respond to this unspoken disdain.

"Look, after it started, I had to keep helping her. She said if I didn't or if I got pinched and talked, she would kill my daughter and grandson. Whatever you think, I believe the bitch would do it. I couldn't take that chance."

"So what's changed? Why did you call me now?"

"The last few days, all the news coverage, it's just a matter of time before she gets caught; and when she does, I know she'll roll over on me. It would kill my girls."

"Okay, that's what has changed. But one more time, why are you calling me?"

This was going to be hard for David to say. No matter

what he had done, no matter what he had become, no matter how complicit in murders he had been, he had never actually ordered or called for the murder of anyone. But, he wanted Angel dead and he didn't have the guts to do it himself.

"You know the reward. I was thinking we could split it," he said, lighting another cigarette. "I give her to you, and you take care of things—where she can't ever talk about me."

The look in David's eyes was unmistakable. His intent was clear. Richard was thinking of it, thinking how he had done things no worse than this for a lot less than two hundred and fifty thousand dollars, thinking how the money could make his Bubba problems go away and even leave a nice little chunk left over, thinking how no one had called lately and offered a job with a similar payday. And thinking, after all, the whore was a psycho killer, so who would be the worse for it. These thoughts were running through his mind, but David misinterpreted the hesitation and thought Richard had a problem with the job.

"Quarter mill, just keep my name out of it," he cajoled. "She's gonna get caught and get the death penalty anyway. I'm just trying…"

"You're just trying to save your own ass. I got the picture."

Vaughn didn't appreciate the shit from Richard, but Richard didn't much give a shit about what Vaughn appreciated. He had heard the story and didn't need a sales job, just a name and an address. "Just tell me who she is and where to I find her."

"She goes by Angel, but this is her real name and that's her address," he said, writing the information on a slip of paper. Richard took the paper and began reading it.

"You know, I can't just go and kill her," he said. "We've got to prove she is the Gospel Killer to collect the reward."

"I got that covered," David said, smiling for the first time throughout the whole meeting. The look on Richard's face showed he didn't understand, so Vaughn went on. "I knew I needed some insurance, so I've followed her the last couple of times. I fished out of dumpsters a garbage bag from each of the last two murders with her fingerprints and DNA all over everything she used. I got both of 'em in the trunk of my car right now."

"No shit?" Richard exclaimed.

David started to get out of the car to show his prize to Richard, but before his second foot hit the gravel parking lot, he turned back to Witt. "Now don't fuck me on this."

Richard smiled as he, too, was getting out of the car and told him not to worry. As David was opening his trunk, he repeated the "don't fuck me" plea. That got Richard to thinking, five hundred thousand dollars was after all better than two fifty. And, he had indeed done worse for far less.

A quick look showed no one around anywhere so Vaughn opened the first plastic trash bag and showed the contents to Richard. Seeing the items it contained, Witt yet again remembered that he had done worse for far less, and then he also remembered that David Vaughn was in fact a cheating murder accomplice. So as Vaughn set the second plastic trash bag on the ground and closed his trunk, Richard pulled an unlicensed and clean .38 from an ankle holster and shot David in the chest. Vaughn fell to the ground, and Richard walked to the back of the car and shot him twice more in the stomach and chest.

Moving quickly now, Richard unlocked his car's trunk and started putting the plastic trash bags into it. With the second one safely inside, he was about to close the trunk and get out of there as fast as possible when he simultaneously heard and felt the bullet rip into his back. As Richard fell to one knee, David fired two other shots. The first bullet ripped into his shoulder and the second into his lower back.

Blood gurgling from his mouth, Richard rolled over and faced the dying David Vaughn, who had managed to pull his own revolver and fired three times. The two were found dead lying feet from each other less than an hour later, but not before the wind had blown the killer's name and address from Richard's hand into the nearby Trinity River, where it became wet and unreadable after floating miles downstream.

~~~

He didn't even like yogurt, but here he was at TCBY waiting on her, waiting and watching the yogurt melt and drip down the sides of the cup. Luke Colbert pulled his cell out and called Angel once more. He got the same recording as before, something about the phone number that was being called was currently out of service. This had to be some type of mistake. He had talked to her that afternoon.

Only two nights previous to this late Saturday afternoon, Luke had taken Angel for a ride on his Kawasaki Ninja 650 ABS. It was a sport bike, and Luke liked to ride fast—too fast for most girls but not Angel. She held on tight and leaned into every turn. When he stopped at the duck ponds, a local area of ponds and walkways and a favorite of the area's romantically impulsive types, he didn't even make it off the bike.

Angel slid around in front of him and while sitting on the gas tank, wrapped her legs around his waist. And he thought he was taking her for a ride. When she was finished dry humping and kissing him, Luke, ready to explode, begged for more.

"Not tonight," she whispered in his ears. "But soon."

As he pulled her closer, she bit and pulled his earlobe, holding it between her teeth until blood almost shot forth. Forget blue balls, for his were then a deep crimson. No matter how he pleaded, she always smiled and answered, "Soon." He knew she was married, but fuck! She was killing him. Whatever her old man wasn't giving her at home, Luke was prepared to supply; and there she was telling him about how anticipation makes everything sweeter.

Luke took a napkin, wiped up the melting yogurt and remembered how she looked that night, how she felt, and more importantly to him, how she made him feel. He had been with plenty of girls, and even some ladies probably close to her age, but Angel seemed so different. It was going to be so good, so fucking good! He could already taste it.

She had called him that morning and asked him to meet her for yogurt. Her husband was playing golf or something, and she could get away for an hour or two and just had to meet him. And now, she was more than an hour late and her phone wasn't working right.

Hearing the shop's door open, he looked up only to see it wasn't her and be disappointed. His gaze drifted to a flat screen TV on the wall of the yogurt shop where a local news crew was reporting live from a crime scene where two seasoned citizens were found dead after apparently killing one another. There was even an unsubstantiated report that the men were former Dallas cops, but it couldn't be commented on pending notification of the next of kin.

Luke wasn't paying too close attention, but the reporter said that in addition to the victim's identities the police were also keeping quiet about the contents of two large trash bags that were found close to the two bodies. Sounded pretty weird to him; two old guys shooting it out with each other Wyatt Earp style, but fuck them, because he had bigger problems to worry about. Where was his Angel?

Chapter 36

He had stopped at the Tom Thumb supermarket for his normal Sunday bouquet of lilies, and now Mark was pulling through the gates of the cemetery, and yet something was different. As usual, he was alone, but the sorrow he normally felt when he was about to visit his mother's grave was today being pushed aside, at least somewhat by the news and happenings of the day before.

Detective Coleman had not drawn the assignment, but requested it because of his close relationship with the family, and he had been the one to call and tell Mark of the death of his father. Hearing of his father's death did not cause the emotional reaction he might have guessed. There was no jumping for joy now that the wicked witch was dead, no glee or wishing it had been at Mark's own hands, as he had imagined many times, no discernible bump either way in his pulse. Just, "All right John, what do I need to have done with the body?"

For all the pain his father caused, for all the rage he had built up inside himself over his father, for how close to the surface these feelings still existed, hearing he was dead was not a cause of happiness or relief for Mark; instead, it just really opened a strange and eerie nothingness. Perhaps an empty and hollow chamber resided within Mark where feelings and good memories of one's father normally lived in ordinary people. But Mark wasn't ordinary and certainly his father wasn't ordinary either—so fuck him. What needed to be done with the body?

While hearing of his father's death created no greater interest or response in him than of hearing a co-worker's pet cat had died over the weekend, hearing the circumstances surrounding his dad's death did create many questions. He pulled up to his mother's grave and got out of the car with the flowers, thinking not of her, but of what his father was doing with David Vaughn and what was inside those plastic bags.

John had told him that it was too early to tell, but it was possible that at least some of the bags' contents had come from recent Gospel Killer crime scenes. Judging from the plates and glasses inside the bags, many appeared to John to match the styles and décor from the Marcel Durand and Joyce Seeber killings.

This revelation, or even the possibility of it, was shocking to Mark. To the best of his knowledge, his father maintained no relationship with David Vaughn, certainly they were not friends, as his father had really zero friends anywhere but definitely none from his days as a Dallas cop. Vaughn had not made any calls to the rewards hotline, at least none identifying himself. When Coleman reminded Mark that Vaughn had been working as head of security for the Stoneleigh Hotel, and of his knowledge of the murder that occurred there, Mark's mind raced about how a possible link to the Gospel Killer could have been created. It led to many questions, and Coleman assured him they would conduct a complete investigation into the recent activities of his father and David Vaughn, as well as determine if the contents of the bags had any connection to the recent murders.

Kneeling and placing the flowers on his mother's grave, Mark found the customary sadness returning. Seeing her headstone, her engraved name and the dates of her birth and death brought Mark back to why he was there. He again quickly found himself consumed with memories of his mother and of Cubbie. He remembered the pain his mom had felt at the hands of his father and of the pain expressed the prior evening by Cubbie when told of his father's death.

It was unexplainable to Mark how Cubbie could cast aside the countless cruelties done to him by this man and, instead of hatred, be filled with longing and dreams of a better relationship with his father. He reacted with such distress when told of his father's death, as if their lives together had been magically altered into some sort of Ward and Beaver Cleaver existence. Mark simply couldn't understand why Cubbie had spent so much of his life, so much of even his adult life, trying to please and develop a relationship with a man who so clearly despised him.

The hope of a better relationship grew from a need inside Cubbie, a need for acceptance from his father that was never going to be forthcoming. As Mark kneeled there at the grave, he thought that maybe even Cubbie was now forced to realize his father's death ended any possibility of ever gaining that acceptance. Perhaps that is what had triggered the response Cubbie exhibited when told of the death. Or, perhaps Cubbie was just much more forgiving than he was, and that in fact it was Mark who was the one who was fucked up.

As Mark placed his palm on the headstone to try and get closer to his mother, to feel her being, to remember her alive with him and Cubbie, the feelings of nothingness ended. Tears welled in his eyes as he tried to remember happier times, but no matter how hard he researched his memory bank, those thoughts quickly evaporated, as memories of his father always stormed back in. Holidays, ballgames, afternoon trips to McDonald's, simple times like enjoying homemade desserts after dinner; they always ended the same – with his father ruining them.

Coming in drunk and smelling of perfume, of being angry from losing a bet, of being generally pissed off because he was one of the world's genuine losers, whatever the excuse; Richard Witt used every one to inflict huge suffering on his family. On his wife whom he drove to suicide; on his youngest son, who he never showed anything other than the most unrestrained contempt for; and for his oldest son Mark, whose primary youthful role seemed to be to serve as Richard's private punching bag. He seemed to ruin every moment that Mark remembered, and he was still doing it. Mark kneeled there unable to be solely with his mother, to think only of her and to try desperately to celebrate her life alone; instead, he was trapped thinking again of his father.

Mark stood up from the grave and simply lowered his head. The tears that had welled in his eyes had now accelerated and were streaming down his face. He didn't even wipe them away. What was the point? He knew there was no way to wipe away the stains that caused the tears, and he stood there lost in the moment, knowing he would never be able to escape these dark memories from his past.

Because of those memories, Mark was determined not to carry on this family tradition. He would be a good father to his children, and he would be a good husband to Yo-Yo. This case preoccupied his mind almost non-stop, but at moments like this at the cemetery thinking of his mother, Mark knew he was still trapped by his past. Trapped and having no way out created such hopelessness that at times the burden seemed just too fucking heavy. The worst thing about these memories was that Mark knew there would be no happy ending to the story, no silver lining to this awful cloud, no rainbow leading to a better place from this past pain. The pain was real, the scars remained fresh, and neither was leaving him. Not ever. Thanks, Dad.

Immersed in these thoughts, Mark had not heard a car door close nearby. He did not hear the footsteps approaching, and was taken aback when he felt a hand on his shoulder. Turning, he saw one of the few people who could have made the moment even worse: his ex-wife Kellie. Wearing large dark sunglasses that dominated her face and contrasted with her pale lip gloss, Kellie could tell she had surprised Mark.

"I'm sorry, I didn't mean to startle you," she said, quickly pulling her hand back.

Mark shrugged it off, and although he was apprehensive about seeing her, he tried not to show it. "Oh, that's okay. I was just thinking of something. What are you doing here?"

"I'm sorry if I shouldn't be here," Kellie answered, gathering from his reaction and tone that perhaps this wasn't her best idea. "I remember you came here to visit your mother every Sunday, and I heard about your father on TV last night, and I just wanted to tell you I was sorry."

Mark knew there was more he would have to hear, and though he was silent, the look on his face made her continue.

"I know you guys had major problems and all, and I didn't know if you would be at church today or not, but I was thinking of you and just wanted to talk to you…to tell you I was sorry."

Mark began wiping his eyes and Kellie took out a Kleenex from her purse and handed it to him.

"That's nice of you to say, but you really didn't have to come out here just for that," he said, looking up towards the sky as if imploring strength from above.

Then the shoe dropped — the one that he both expected and feared. "Well, also I wanted to talk to you alone…to apologize for how I acted the other night… when you came over and all."

Not seeing a trap door close enough to escape through, Mark instead shrugged his shoulders. "No need to apologize. I didn't think anything of it."

"No, it wasn't right. I made you uncomfortable. I'm making you uncomfortable right now. I just…I was just, I had just been drinking and we are having some trouble at home, and I don't know, I guess you got caught in a perfect storm."

Not knowing how to make her stop, Mark finally stepped forward and put his arms around her. "It's okay. We all have our moments."

Feeling his arms around her again was not what she expected, but it did feel good, so she nuzzled into his chest as tears of her own began to fall. Trying to soothe her to get the crying to stop, he petted the top of her head as he again looked upwards and wondered how much more he was expected to withstand.

Misreading his kindness after a moment, she stepped back from him and collected herself. She walked over and sat down on the bench near his mother's grave, on the bench that Yo-Yo had bought as a Mother's Day gift, and motioned for him to come and sit with her. Looking at his watch and hoping for something like an apocalypse to immediately befall mankind, he hesitated. Then, sensing the end of times was not going to save him, Mark slowly walked over and sat down beside her.

"The news said your dad was killed along with another former Dallas cop," she said, dabbing at her tears with a Kleenex. "Did you know him, the other man?"

"Yeah, his name was David Vaughn," Mark answered, staring at the ground. "I never worked with him; he was on homicide. I didn't really know him, but, yeah, I knew who he was."

"Were they friends? Are there any ideas about what happened?"

"Who knows; anything was possible with my dad."

"The news said something about trash bags being near the bodies," she pressed further for information.

"Yeah, that's what John told me. You remember John Coleman, don't you?" Kellie nodded. "Well, he doesn't know for sure yet but thinks maybe some of the stuff in the bags came from a couple of the Gospel Killer crime scenes."

"The reason I ask, is this going to make things worse for Daniel?" asked a shocked Kellie. "Yo-Yo told me this whole getaway thing was because the Gospel Killer had called you, and I mean, I know ya'll are taking care of him and all, and I trust you if you think he still needs to stay with you, but this…this just scares me."

"He's safe, and it's best he stay with us a little longer," Mark said, patting her knee. "It's just this whole thing is taking a lot longer than I hoped, but…but maybe this will help to crack it open."

She placed her hand on his and forced it to stay on her knee longer than he wanted.

"Just take care of him," she said, looking at Mark, who nodded. "Has the killer called you anymore… and threatened you?"

"No, nothing new, and I'll get Daniel home as soon as I can," Mark answered, pulling his hand free and standing up to leave. "I should be going now. I won't be at church today, but give everyone my best. Maybe next Sunday."

He nodded good-bye to her and started to walk off when she cleared her throat. "Mark…Mark, there's one other thing." He stopped and turned back to face her, fearful of what that one other thing might be.

"Did you tell Yo-Yo about the other night?"

"No, of course not," Mark answered, understanding the compassion in a well-placed lie.

Kellie smiled for the first time that entire morning. "Good. I've just been so worried that I might have made things weird between us. She's such a good friend; I just didn't want to upset her. I would have hated myself for that."

"Don't worry about a thing," Mark said as he was unlocking his Charger, to both make her feel better and to make his getaway easier. "It was no big deal, and it's just between us anyway. Yo-Yo loves you and is always talking about how happy she is we can all be friends. So no worries, all right?"

  She smiled, sighed with relief, and waved good-bye to Mark as he drove away.

Chapter 37

Sunday afternoon, Monday, Tuesday, all the days seemed to run together for Mark. He was reading the Bible for clues to the crimes but also finding himself reading it more for strength. He was also rereading and rereading again the case files, and going over each of the new leads brought in on the reward hotline. On top of all that, he was dealing with a difficult personal issue, dealing with Cubbie concerning their father's funeral arrangements.

Mark felt like in some respects he was getting closer to finding the killer, closer to finding a pattern, if one really existed, and then in some ways, he still felt clueless. But either way, he knew the stress created from dealing with Cubbie about this funeral wasn't helping. He needed to be mentally clear and alert, to not have his mind dragged down, and yet, his father's death and the now burgeoning situation involving a possible funeral was doing just that.

Mark's preference was to have his father cremated. He felt pretty comfortable in believing the old man was burning in hell anyways, so why not be consistent about things. But the idea evoked a truly terrible response from Cubbie. Thoughts of his father being placed in the crematorium and being reduced to ashes filling up an urn triggered a reaction of horror from Cubbie. He would simply not hear of it.

Mark didn't want this to come down to a money issue, but the truth was, because of the time constraints this case had created, Witt Investigations wasn't working on any other cases, and therefore, had no other income coming in. While at least a part of him was still hopeful about receiving a big payday from Kim Jacobsen, he couldn't count on it and actually hated the thought of even billing her for his services.

In the meantime, his money was all going out and not coming in, so he had to be aware of that fact. But Cubbie insisted on a regular funeral with a large mahogany casket, a plot and flowers. The bill reached well over twelve thousand dollars. Mark finally agreed to split the cost with Cubbie with the understanding there would be a few stipulations.

First, there would be no visitation the day prior to the funeral and no mention of family or friends to step forward and speak well of the deceased during the service. During the meeting with the funeral home director, the man tried hard to not show these two things were unusual requests, but he had trouble hiding his facial reaction when Mark told him there also would be no photographs shown of his father at the funeral either. Just a closed casket and a hole in the ground.

When the director looked up to make sure he had heard this correctly, Mark met his stare with a steely one, and Cubbie was forced to look to the ground. At the end of the meeting, when he wrote out the check, Mark thought it was actually a small price to pay to finally know he would never have to see his father again. He only wished somehow he could write another check of an equal amount to have his father's memories buried away with him in that mahogany casket. Alas, no such luck.

The service was scheduled for Wednesday at one o'clock, and Mark and family arrived around 12:30. Only Cubbie, Will, and John and Jackie Coleman joined them.

Standing in the lobby before going into the funeral home's auditorium, John gave Mark an update regarding the contents of the plastic trash bags recovered near where his father had died. Fingerprints had come back confirming many of the items belonged to Marcel Durand, Matthew Owens, and a couple from the apartment of Joy Seeber. Also, and most importantly, many of the items also bore an additional set of prints, which came from the same person and were on items from the different locations.

Detective Coleman said they hadn't been able to match the prints of the unknown person to any police or FBI database. DNA testing still had not been completed, but they were sure the prints came from the killer and would prove damning in court. Mark and John were discussing this and considering how these things came into the hands of Vaughn or Richard when the funeral home director opened the doors to the auditorium for the service.

Mark was still thinking only of how this connection between his father and Vaughn could have happened while a paid preacher who had never met Richard Witt read scripture near his casket. The words from the preacher were nicely read, and perhaps comforting under most similar circumstances, but they seemed

so out of place in this situation. There was no goodness in his father, no goodness awaiting his father, and
the eight people in the audience, with the possible
exception of Cubbie, knew this. Mark was fidgeting
from the news that Coleman had confirmed, and here
he was stuck in a suit and tie listening to something
akin to a eulogy being performed by a stranger for a
father whom he detested. Could we please just cut to
the chase and get the casket in the hole in the ground?

On the drive to the cemetery, all eight in attendance
rode in the funeral home's limo. No procession, no long
line of cars driving slowly with their headlights on,
no grief-stricken masses lining the streets, just a single
limo following a hearse. A fitting send off.

During the ride, Mark felt odd talking with John.
Here he was next to the man who was certainly the
closest thing to a real father he ever had, and he wasn't
able to open up and be honest with him. John had
helped him on this case, had brought him in and provided case files and intel that would never have been
offered to most private investigators, and he couldn't
tell him of the phone calls he had received from the
quote unquote real Gospel Killer. They were looking
for two killers, the original and the newer version.
Mark knew why he couldn't tell, and he wouldn't get
weak and let honesty get the best of him, but it still
made him uncomfortable, and he found himself fidgeting again.

Stopped at a red light, and with the family making
small talk, Mark looked out the window at the nearby
cars. The woman driver of a Nissan minivan had her
head buried downward intently studying her smart
phone; while in another car alongside the limo, Mark

saw a young boy, perhaps three or four, riding in the backseat and sitting on his booster. His parents looked like nice enough people; the dad even glanced over and offered a solemn nod of respect toward the limo following the hearse, but the boy captured Mark's attention.

They locked eyes, for really only a few seconds, but for that instant Mark found himself envious of the boy. Innocent, hopeful, so much to look forward to, nothing in his past to regret, nothing to hide, a blank canvas to paint his life on; as the light changed and the cars drove away, Mark watched as the boy's car turned at the intersection. It figured, the boy almost certainly deserved to go down a different road than Mark had traveled, and while he silently wished the boy the best, Mark also wished desperately that his life, too, could have taken some different turns.

The boy was now gone. Yo-Yo held onto his hand as he sat between his two own beautiful children. He was with Cubbie and Will and joined by John and Jackie. He again looked out the window of the limo and wondered why he couldn't be more thankful for the blessings he had and less worried and consumed by the darkness that seemed to follow his life.

This thought had barely seeped away when the limo pulled into the cemetery, and Mark saw that he was about to again come face-to-face with that darkness. Standing at the gravesite were Dallas' two darkest figures, Bubba and Lew the Magician. From the car, John saw the two men first and nudged Mark to alert him. What the hell were they doing here? Paying their respects?

Not likely, but Mark knew he would need to find out and would be forced to do so under the watchful eye of Detective Coleman. This could raise questions for John, and Mark did not want to lie to him again or be forced to hide more facts from him. Could this day get any better?

As the family got out of the car and watched as the funeral home workers pulled the casket out of the hearse and place it next to the grave, Mark kept an eye on the two notorious men making their way toward him. They were quite a sight actually, as the Magician pushed Bubba's portable oxygen tank along behind him over the uneven ground until he finally gave in and picked the whole thing up and carried it behind the old man. Not wanting to have to introduce either one of the men to Yo-Yo, Mark stepped forward and walked over to Bubba before he could get all the way to the family.

Knowing John would be watching and that he needed to make this quick, Mark didn't extend a hand to either Bubba or the Magician. "Why are you two here?" he asked.

Bubba didn't appreciate the shortness of the question but did enjoy games. "Sorry about your dad, but say, this isn't the same cemetery your mother's buried in, is it?"

It wasn't. It was one of the other stipulations Mark had made and Cubbie had agreed. His mother would not be forced to rest eternally in the same piece of ground his father did, but how in the fuck did this old bastard know where his mother was buried? Mark didn't waste the time trying to think it through.

"No, it's not, and like I asked before, why are ya'll here?"

John looked suspiciously at the two men when he

led Yo-Yo and the family past them and to their seats. Yo-Yo looked at them also and then to her husband, as if asking, "Are these friends of your father?"

Mark didn't answer her inquisitive look. Instead, he stayed focused on Bubba, who seemed in turn to have one eye trained on Mark and his other on Yo-Yo. The old man couldn't help but express his observations.

"She's still got quite a figure. You know most Mexican women inflate up like a fuckin' life raft after they have kids."

Why had Mark listened to Yo-Yo and left his Glock at home? Hell, the hole was already there, just feet behind these two. He could drop them both, push their bodies into the grave, have the casket lowered onto them and nobody would ever be the wiser. He would have to kill the four funeral home workers who would be witnesses, but that could probably be considered acceptable collateral damage, and it was a deep hole.

After these hasty thoughts and calculations, Mark took a quick breath and again realized his Glock was locked in the gun case at home.

"Don't ever say another goddamn word about my wife," he quietly said, almost under his breath so as not to draw any more attention from John or Yo-Yo. Then without waiting for a response, Mark angrily walked past the two men and sat down under the canopy next to his wife and friend.

During the short gravesite service, Mark felt like he was in a vise. He didn't hear a single word the preacher said; instead he felt the stares of Bubba and the Magician and the doubtless unasked questions from John. Mark imagined that the tie around his throat was becoming tighter, his air and breathing seemed to be more difficult, more strained. Could they just please get the freakin' box in the ground already?

When the service was completed, and after Cubbie tossed a rose onto his father's casket as it was being lowered, Mark quickly hurried his family and John and Jackie into the limo for the ride back to the funeral home. Before getting in, Mark closed the limo's doors and returned to Bubba and the Magician.

"I know you motherfuckers want something, so what is it?" he once again asked.

This time it was the Magician who didn't appreciate the tone. "Your daddy died owing us thirty thousand; maybe we came to tell you the debt is yours now."

The hole wasn't filled in yet, but Mark still didn't have his Glock. "Whatever debt you had with him died with him. I won't ever pay you a goddamn cent."

Before things escalated any further between these two, and knowing that all eyes from the limo were trained on them, Bubba put his hand into the middle of the Magician's chest.

"We got a package today at the club," he said, turning to Mark. "It's another phone, with a note that the son of a bitch is gonna call tonight at seven o'clock. Says for all of us to be there."

They turned and walked away, Bubba, slowly and almost feebly, with the Magician following close behind towing the oxygen tank, leaving Mark to make his way to the limo. Head down and filled with thoughts of this new phone and later call to be received, Mark opened the car door and quietly sat down in the limo without looking up or saying a word. He felt all eyes in the car on him, but he never raised his head. What was the point? He couldn't answer their questions, not now anyway, and he sat there knowing this was going to be a long ride.

Had Mark raised his head and had he been thinking clearly at the time, he would have had his first opportunity to see Nicholas D. Claxton in person. Dressed as his alter ego Nikki, wearing a blonde, layered wig and a smart grey hounds tooth knit dress along with simple but tasteful black flats, Nicholas had watched the entire service from no more than a hundred yards away. Crouched down and pretending to grieve next to an unknown grave, Nicholas saw Bubba and the Magician speaking with Mark. He felt sure they had told Mark about the track phone he had mailed to Club Fuxx.

He could only guess what else they talked about, but whatever it was, even from a football field away it was clear to Nicholas that it had created hostility between these men. Were these men coming unhinged with one another before the work of finding this second killer had been completed? Some tension in the workforce, after all, was good for productivity, but too much, and before you know it, a disgruntled mailman walks into the post office and turns it into a shooting gallery.

Nicholas thought he should use this evening's phone call to try and gauge the overall stress level these men were facing. He wanted to push and to motivate, but not to overdo it, because the truth of the matter was, he, in fact, needed Mark. He needed for Mark to find this woman and kill her before the bitch got caught and tried to soak up all his fame. That simply was not acceptable. Yes, he would have to push a little, just not too much.

With that, and after the limo drove past, Nikki stood

up and straightened her skirt, thinking that evening she/he would have to very carefully choose just the right words. Yes, just the proper words would be needed to create a sense of urgency among the men; yet still stop short of sending one of them over the proverbial edge.

Chapter 38

As usual, Nicholas' instincts were correct. Leaving the cemetery, Bubba began to boil while thinking of the way Mark had treated and spoken to him. Even though angry, the old man hadn't grew so old and powerful by losing control, he always was obsessed about what he said, to whom he said it, and who might be listening. Because of this Bubba wouldn't verbalize his thoughts even to the Magician, who was driving, so instead, he took out a notepad from his shirt pocket and wrote down a cryptic note and handed it to Lew up front. The note read, "Dim Witt ain't cutting it. Make plans."

After reading the message, the Magician smiled broadly in the rear view mirror as he handed it back to Bubba. "More than happy to," he replied.

Bubba took the note while pushing in the backseat cigarette lighter, and when it popped out signaling it was ready, he lit the note on fire and watched it burn in the ashtray. When the note was completely burned, Bubba placed the mask on his face and began to breathe deeply from the oxygen tank. He did not smile outwardly at the thought of killing Mark, not in the manner the Magician did, but he smiled from within, secure in the knowledge that though his body was weakening, he was still strong enough mentally to see what needed to be done and remained more than able to still dispatch someone to get it accomplished.

Hours later, Mark made his way north on I-35, trying to get to the venerable and appropriately named Club Fuxx in time for the call. Ahead of him and already joining Bubba in his office were the Magician, Marcus, and Kim Jacobsen. Each of the four had a scotch in their hands, while making small talk, when Bubba made a request to the Magician. "Lew, could you take Kim up front and bring back a bottle of Johnnie Walker Black. I need to talk to Marcus alone for a minute."

The Magician did as instructed. Kim followed him, but not before casting an unsure look at Marcus as she was leaving the room. Once alone, the old man got down to business. "Want to give you a heads-up. I'm not gonna let the clock tick down to zero on this."

Marcus looked at his drink while letting those words sink in; he had learned over the years that Bubba spoke frequently in vague terms, almost in code, never saying exactly what he meant for fear of tape recordings, but opting instead to allow for interpretation. Whatever the old man meant, whatever plan he and the Magician had thought up, Marcus understood it to mean that Mark's life would soon be in serious danger.

"I know he helped you out," Bubba, said, watching Marcus as he looked down into his scotch and remained silent, "but that was personal and this is business."

Marcus didn't know why he was even being told this, but he knew that if he objected, there would simply be another set of plans made, and his wife would become a widow and his daughter would be without a father.

"You know I'm with you, Padre," he said, looking up into Bubba's eyes. "Whatever you think." Bubba was smiling as the Magician and Kim returned with the bottle, though Kim could see from Marcus' expression that he clearly was concerned with whatever news he had just received.

So it was into the belly of this beast that Mark was about to enter. Earlier, he had managed, with some difficulty, to get Yo-Yo and the family off and headed back to the lake house, with the assurance he would join them there later that evening. While driving to Club Fuxx, Mark was filled with angst, still angry from the afternoon's confrontation with Bubba and the Magician and still confused about the circumstances of his father's death and how it could somehow be connected with evidence from the recent murders.

Add in the anticipation of the expected call from the Gospel Killer, along with the dread of being in a closed room with Bubba and the Magician, it was fair to say that Mark's mind was redlining when fifteen minutes before 7:00 pm, he pushed open the door and entered the old man's office.

Once inside, he saw the gang waiting for him. He made no sign of acknowledgement to either Bubba or the Magician. Instead, he shook hands with Marcus, while noticing Kim in the corner nursing a drink and relaxing on a couch that had no doubt seen its share of sin. She looked right at home on the well-worn couch, and Mark nodded towards her before turning his attention to the plastic bag sitting on Bubba's desk containing a cell phone.

"How did this get here?" he asked, grabbing the plastic bag along its edge.

"The mailman delivered it," Bubba answered.

"Then where's the package it came in?"

Mark responded.

The Magician pointed to a trashcan behind the desk. Mark immediately went over and pulled out an opened Express Mail delivery box. Setting it on the desk next to the phone, he studied the box and its label. There was no postage meter; instead, the box was covered in what looked to be more than fifteen dollars of stamps. The label was addressed to Mr. Bubba Furh, with the club's address. Under the sender's information, he saw the name GK with a return address listed as 616 Balak Avenue in Dallas. Mark suspected the GK stood for Gospel Killer; he also knew that some theologians thought the number 616 was the real sign of the beast discussed in Revelations instead of the more commonly thought of 666 number.

"Who all touched this box?" Mark asked, looking at each one in the room.

"Me, Lew, a couple of the girls up front, the fucking mailman, who knows who else," Bubba again answered in his affable manner.

Closing his eyes in an attempt to gain control, Mark understood it was a long shot. The killer probably wore gloves, probably used a watered sponge to moisten the stamps, probably dropped it in a mail collection box instead of taking it into a post office. And yes, probably many fucking mailmen had touched it before it was delivered. Still, Mark didn't want to hear any shit from the old man.

Mark knew his secret prevented him from taking the package and sending it to Coleman or Agent Ellis with the FBI, so he carefully took the box and sat it on the floor next to the door. When he left, he would take it with him, along with the block printed note telling the time and instructing everyone to be present. It was possible it contained clues, perhaps clues the killer meant for him to find and perhaps others the killer didn't intend to leave behind.

All eyes were on him as he sat the box on the floor, returned to the desk and opened the bag holding the phone. He was writing down the model and serial numbers when the phone rang, startling everyone. Mark found the speaker button on the phone and pushed it while setting it back on the desk.

"Hello?" he answered the phone.

"Good evening," Nicholas answered in a curious, moribund tone. Mark was wondering just what in the fuck was so good about it when Nicholas continued. "I see that I'm on speaker, so that's great. Now let's get started. Is everyone here? Mr. Bubba, the Magician, Mr. Marcus, Kim and Mark?"

"Everybody's here," answered Bubba with a half-grunt and half-snarled response. "Now what do you want?"

"You, you I don't like," Nicholas said, sighing heavily. "I feel very negative energy from you."

"I don't give a goddamn rat shit what you…" Bubba began, leaning down to the phone, before Mark covered the phone and placed a hand on the old man's chest, signaling him to ease up. After a moment, Mark uncovered the phone again.

"What a pitiful old bastard he is," Nicholas said. "Kim. Kim Jacobsen, are you there?"

Surprised, she looked at the men and then answered, "Yes."

"Good," Nicholas responded with a laugh. "No real need for you tonight, but just love the thought of such a beauty right there in the middle of all that raging, hostile testosterone."

Mark had brought his tape recorder and was placing it on the desk next to the phone when Nicholas turned more serious. "Before getting to the real reason of my call, I do want to tell you, Mark, how sorry I am to hear about the death of your father."

"Thank you," Mark answered without emotion. "Now can we get down to business?"

Nicholas could see the son was not exactly grieving, so he agreed. "Actually, that goes right along with the purpose of my call. You see, according to reports I see on the newscasts, your father died with certain evidence from the last few murder scenes."

"That's what it looks like," Mark answered, and Bubba and the Magician were all ears.

"That's very troubling," Nicholas said after a moment's hesitation. "I have attempted in the past to express to you, Mark, how important it is that you find this woman before the police do and then I hear this unfortunate news." The group was on edge but remained silent as Nicholas went on. "The twenty-seven day cycle will be up in three days, and now the police have these bags of perhaps all sorts of evidence. I hope you can understand how this concerns me."

"I don't know what all was in the trash bags," Mark said, breathing deeply, "but I can tell you the blood all belonged to the victims and the print and DNA evidence doesn't match anything the FBI has on file."

This information was churning through Nicholas' mind. Was it true? Was Mark trying to buy time? What was he holding back? Finally, he asked, "So if that's true, then you're telling me a rookie is doing this? Somebody with no record at all?"

"Isn't that possible?" Mark asked, smiling for the first time in what seemed like days. "What kinda record did you have before you started killing?"

"This isn't about me and you, Mark, not yet anyway," Nicholas answered after counting to ten, realizing he may have let out more information than he wanted. "You need to concentrate on finding this woman, and then we'll have our play date later."

Mark was smiling even more broadly, knowing he had hit on something, when Nicholas in turn hit one out of the park. "Before you start dreaming about that play date, Mark, you better find this woman, because my guess is the men standing next to you are growing impatient. Volatile, impatient, violent natures, it all adds up to a very toxic mix for you, Mark. I would suggest you watch your back."

"Well, since you're so concerned with my well being and all, why don't you help me out?"

"I'm already helping by trying to motivate you. What more can I do?"

"Your killings are biblically related, and these new killings try and copy that theme but yet seem different."

"The Bible is a wonderful book," Nicholas said. "Love, lust, deception, treachery, sex, sodomy, whales swallowing people, talking donkeys, heaven and hell, fire and brimstone, just amazing. Pretty much everything a best seller needs, but as for me, my special interest can be found in the New Testament. Perhaps this copycat has a different inspiration?"

"Are you saying the Old Testament?" Mark asked.

"Maybe, maybe not. I don't really know. But there's

a pattern; there always is, intentional or not. But, yes, I would look closely at the Old Testament. And numbers, something tells me numbers will prove to be important."

Numbers? Thoughts were rushing through Mark's mind as he attempted to determine what Nicholas meant. He said numbers twice and seemed to emphasize it. Did he mean regular numbers, numbers like numerology, or was he saying the killer could be found through clues in the Book of Numbers? Were these murders an attempt at some sort of twisted, eye-for-an-eye Old Testament revenge scenario that existed in this killer's mind? Or, was Nicholas just full of shit? Weeks into this investigation and Mark still felt as if the sands were shifting under his feet.

"Can you think of anything else?" he finally said.

"Well, Mark, I think I've been quite helpful," Nicholas answered, after a pause. "And now I think it's time you earn your money as a private dick, because at the end of the day, that's all you are. Right? Just a rock hard, throbbing, ready to explode for the highest bidder, big ole, swinging side to side private dick of a man, huh, Mark?"

It was true, Mark's head was throbbing, and he did feel like exploding, but instead, he bit hard into the sides of his mouth. Before he could answer, Nicholas continued, "Must be a real charge being the paid private dick for a woman like the lovely Miss Kim Jacobsen isn't it, Mark? Come on, you can tell me."

Mark loosened his teeth's grip on the insides of his mouth and while exhaling, said, "How 'bout I tell you in person?"

"Soon enough. Soon enough," Nicholas said,

laughing, and with that, hung up his phone and was gone.

Inside the office, Mark clicked off his recorder and picked up the Express delivery postal box.

"You just gonna up and leave now?" Bubba asked as Mark was preparing to do just that.

"I've got work to do," Mark answered.

"What was that shit about numbers?" Bubba asked, not appreciating the shortness of the answer. "And the Old Testament?"

Mark sat the delivery box down on the desk and looked at the old man. "The Book of Numbers in the Old Testament basically tells the story of when Israel was forced to wander through the desert for forty years after disobeying God. I'm leaving here to go read and study it verse by verse tonight. But I don't know if that's even what the guy meant. Maybe it's some other type of numbers, or maybe the fuckhead doesn't even know what he's talking about, or maybe the fuckhead is playing some type of game, and maybe he's not really interested in helping us at all."

"Or, maybe you're just not good enough for the job," the Magician said, as Bubba's steely glare fixed on Mark.

"Maybe that's right," Mark exclaimed, turning towards the Magician. "Then again, maybe something else that's right is the guy on the phone probably knows a lot more of your secrets. Like maybe during pillow talk with your dearly departed former employee, Mr. Boy told him of some other holes you had him dig for your fat, stupid, lazy ass?"

The combination of rage and worry on the Magician's face showed Mark that there were other holes, other secrets.

"Just how fucking stupid can one motherfucker be?" Mark said, leaning over to the Magician and driving his sword through Lew's midsection.

The Magician threw open his coat and went for the .45 in his shoulder holster, but Mark countered with a left hook to the ribs, then used his still broken right hand like a sledgehammer on Lew's face. Three rapid blows blasted through the Magician's septum and tore apart his nose. The two men went to the ground. On top, Mark threw left and right-handed bombs, while the Magician struggled to withdraw his gun.

With Kim screaming, Marcus looked to Bubba, who nodded and gave him the okay to stop the fight. As Marcus pulled off Mark and wrapped him with a bear hug to stop the punches, the Magician finally succeeded in getting a hold of his gun.

"Not in here!" Bubba yelled. "Goddamitt, not in here!"

Regaining control just before firing, the Magician wiped away the blood that was flowing into his mouth from his destroyed nose and then re-holstered his gun.

"Get him outta here," Bubba said, turning to Marcus.

With Bubba and the Magician behind them in the office, Kim and Marcus pushed Mark through the club and out the front door. Making their way through the parking lot to the Charger, Kim got the keys from Mark and opened the door. Marcus forcibly sat him down in the driver's seat.

"Amigo, you need to end this," he said point-blank to Mark. "Cause even if this guy on the phone knows more secrets about 'em, that ain't gonna be enough to save you. You gotta find that bitch killer."

The almost frantic seriousness of Marcus' tone clung

to Mark. He started the car to drive away when Marcus pounded the message home one last time. "Look, I don't know any of the details, but trust me, you need to keep both your eyes open, comprende?"

As he was pulling away from the club, Mark looked in his rear view mirror and saw Kim with her head on Marcus' shoulder. This sight triggered two thoughts in his mind: one, what were the two of them so worried about, it was his life expectancy that was rapidly dwindling and not theirs; and two, even if he did find this bitch killer, he and his family would never be free of this threat as long as Bubba and the Magician remained alive.

So it was at that precise moment, turning out of Club Fuxx and onto Composite Avenue, that Mark decided he would be forced to kill both Bubba and the Magician.

~~~

Across town, Angel sat nervously on her patio smoking a cigarette—not a regular tobacco cigarette but a brand of clove cigarettes that she purchased from a specialty shop in the mall. She hadn't smoked in years, not since she first started when seeking help dealing with the stress from her breakup—her breakup from *him*. But she started back, because here again, she found herself dealing with unneeded stress.

The cloves didn't provide the same relief as nicotine did, but it was something, and it did offer the added bonus of a little comedy. The laughs came when her husband would finally arrive home, he who would react almost in horror at the mere smell of tobacco, would now walk over, kiss her forehead and wrinkle his nose while saying, "Hmm, dinner smells nice."

That really was his one endearing quality: he was a complete fucking idiot.

But enough about him; Angel had other worries on her mind. Before this past weekend, she had planned to fuck and then kill Luke Colbert on Friday. It would be the twenty-seventh day since her last killing and would lead her one step closer to the final piece of her plan. And, really, in fact, she had looked quite forward to ending the life of Luke.

The egotistical prick was so cocky, so sure of himself, and so stupid that she couldn't help but want to kill him. But then he made some comments about how his friends had warned him and joked with him about his name matching one of the names of the victims of the Gospel Killer, and how they had told him he should be careful meeting any new women. Because of that, and because she was afraid one of Luke's friends may have seen them together unbeknownst to her, she had blown him off at the yogurt shop Saturday. She now couldn't decide whether or not to call Luke back and carry through with her original plan or forget him and move to the final stage.

The real reason for this uncertainty and battle of self-doubt was of course the death of David "Short Timer" Vaughn. Hearing of his death was not of great concern; she was preparing to end his life very soon anyway. But learning through the media that he and another fellow retired cop had shot each other to death at a somewhat remote location and that the police found plastic trash bags at the scene reportedly containing evidence from the most recent Gospel Killer murders... Well, that was of concern.

She lit another of the clove cigarettes while shaking

her head. She understood that Short Timer, that old piece of shit, was trying to turn her in. A man she detested, a man whom she almost from the start was planning to kill and eliminate as soon as he was no longer needed, and here he was playing her. Unbelievable.

She closed her eyes in disgust at the thought of him. She almost vomited in her mouth as she remembered him and the times they were together. She remembered his saggy, old man balls that drooped so far down from his sorry excuse of a dick, and oh God, he had gray pubic hairs—gray fucking pubic hairs, for crying out loud!

Here's an idea; how about grabbing a handful of that gut, hoisting it up and then using a magnifying mirror to see that little dick for, like the first time in years, and then removing the fucking gray pubes? Of course, he wouldn't do that, but he had no problem pushing her head down there. Men are pigs—such roll-in-the-mud, cloven-hoofed animals that each richly deserved a date with the butcher.

Angel knew every man had a penis, which meant only one thing. Every man would cheat. It was only a matter of opportunity. Angel never knew for sure if her man had cheated, but she knew he would have sooner or later, and after all, it really didn't matter because either way he had left her. That was just as bad.

She looked down at the ashtray and saw her hand trembling as she put out the cigarette. The ashes soon covered the butt of the cigarette as she stamped it down in the ashtray, but why couldn't these ashes cover up the memories of him? Desperate and painful memories of how he loved her, or at least at one time pretended to, but now loved another.

Just the thought of him being happy with his new, beautiful family…Well, how much was a person expected to withstand? These thoughts were torturing her mind as a key slid into the lock, and she heard the front door open. Tossing the ashes into the shrubs, she went inside where her husband kissed her forehead and remarked how wonderful dinner smelled.

Chapter 39

Driving that evening from Club Fuxx to his office, Mark phoned Yo-Yo and pleaded his case. Something had come up, and he really needed to get right on it. He had told her earlier he would join the family at the lake house later that evening after his meeting, but after the way the meeting ended he knew he had no time to relax. Besides the way his right hand was throbbing after this latest round of fisticuffs, he only wanted a glass of Crown and a handful of Advil and certainly would not have relished the thought of an extra hours drive back to the lake house anyway.

Yo-Yo didn't like it, but there was a certain seriousness in his voice, an earnestness that she recognized. She would have to wait to be with her man. So, after some mild protest at his absence, she relented and assured him she would call him before she went to bed.

As he hung up the phone, he thought of her and the kids, knowing she was worried, knowing she would put that aside in front of the children, knowing she was so right for him. Mark had, from time to time, fantasized that Yo-Yo had magical powers and could look into his mind, as if it were a movie screen, and see their film as it played. That she could watch their love story being shown. That she could see the love story he felt throughout his soul. The love she could express with merely a glance, he would need an entire feature film to show. It would be an epic, and he wanted an audience of only one.

Mark pulled his Charger into the office's parking lot, still dreaming Yo-Yo could somehow sit down inside his mental theatre and with surround sound and IMAX technology, finally see and feel the strength of his love. God, he wanted to be with her then, but he parked and got out of the car, knowing he had work to do.

Once inside his office, Mark checked the clip in his Glock, poured himself a man- sized glass of Crown Royale, cracked open a bottle of Advil, and opened up his Bible to the Book of Numbers. An hour and a half later, he had finished his first reading of Numbers, and upon reflection, he tightened the cap back on the bottle of Crown and placed it inside a cabinet. The Book of Numbers was about the costs of disobeying God, and Mark felt that drinking whiskey, even while reading the good book, probably would be frowned upon.

After putting away the whiskey, Mark got out his notepad and began to read Numbers for the second time that evening. The fourth book of the Bible, situated between Leviticus and Deuteronomy, Numbers told many fascinating stories. Fascinating stories that Mark imagined a serial killer could use for excuses to kill. It told of the people of Israel and their rebellion against God — against God on most high, who had delivered them from slavery in Egypt and who had made a covenant with them at Mount Sinai. How the people of Israel had responded, not with faith and gratitude, but with unbelief and disobedience.

Against this backdrop, Mark wondered if the killer

was perhaps motivated by some feelings of betrayal. He was writing notes and trying to think of these possibilities, possible betrayal scenarios this woman could use as rationale for killing strangers, when he began laughing. The laughter was perhaps aided by the affects of the whiskey as well as the Advil overdose, but sincere nonetheless, as Mark sat there and realized pretty much every woman he had ever known felt betrayed by a man at some point in their lives. Clearly, this wasn't the explosive clue he was seeking. Setting his pen and smirk aside, he picked up the Bible again and continued with his study.

After re-reading in Numbers where Moses sent twelve spies into the land of Canaan to see firsthand and report back with their findings of the land promised to the people of Israel, Mark again picked up his pen and began making notes. The fact that there were twelve spies dispatched was interesting to Mark, as it equaled the number of disciples Jesus had. Also interesting was the fact that two of the spies, Joshua and Caleb, returned telling of the riches of the land and how it was indeed "flowing with milk and honey," while the other spies returned frightened and told how the land was inhabited by fearsome giants. This interested Mark because it showed that a group of people could see the exact same thing and have completely different reactions and opinions. Was this what was happening with the Gospel Killer? Was she seeing something that most people would either approve of or hardly even notice, but yet it be something which would cause her to be filled with a murderous rage? If so, what was it?

Mark set his pen down and resumed reading. He

read where the people of Israel proved fearful and did not invade and take the land promised them by God. For this lost faith, God punished the people by forcing them to wander in the desert for forty years and allowing only their children to enter the Promised Land. Returning again to his notes, Mark wrote "unfaithful" and "punishment." In almost a flow-chart-like drawing, he went back again to betrayal and then added unfaithful and punishment. Had the killer been betrayed by an unfaithful lover and was now seeking punishment on all men?

As he stared at the notepad, Mark thought these ideas might be good for profiling a killer, but he knew he was under the gun, and he needed not generalizations and possible motivations, but he needed to find something to put him onto a singular suspect. What was he missing?

He was thinking of perhaps breaking the Crown out again, thinking perhaps even God wouldn't mind if he attempted to expand his mind with a little help from the whiskey. After all, whiskey was made with ingredients all of which God had made bountiful in this world, and thinking that way, maybe it would really be a form of thanking God if he had another drink.

Pulling the bottle out and setting it on his desk, Mark thought again and left it unopened. Instead, he tried a different tactic. Laying the Bible flat on his desk, Mark took the pages of the entire Book of Numbers between the fingers of his left hand and held them upwards while closing his eyes. Then with his right hand, he felt the pages from Numbers he was holding and picked out a single page and pushed it downward. Then with his eyes still closed, he took his finger and moved it along the page and stopped it on a certain verse.

While he hadn't prayed for divine guidance, he was certainly hoping for a little extra help, and even if this technique was just a shot in the dark, well, it was still at least a shot. Opening his eyes and reading the verse his finger pointed to, Numbers 10:19, Mark quickly felt his new detective method of eye closing and finger delving would probably not lead to the eureka moment he had hoped. The verse read, "And over the host of the tribe of the children of Simeon was Shelumiel the son of Zurishaddan."

Mark guessed a genealogy check probably wouldn't break the case open, so he hung his head downward in a mixture of disappointment and amusement. I mean, come on, for crying out loud; couldn't a white brother catch a break?

And then, he did. Mark's cell rang and picking it up, he saw Yo-Yo was calling. She always provided a break from his worries. He could talk with her and the world seemed a million miles away — a million miles away and so completely unimportant.

Answering the phone, his mood improved at just the sound of her voice. They talked for more than a half hour, and it did both of them wonders. Everyone was safe, and Yo-Yo was in bed calling to wish him good night. She did say how big and scary the bed was and how she was all alone and how wonderful it would be if she had a big strong man there to protect her.

Mark joked that there were probably a lot of guys who would love to apply for that job, but Yo-Yo said she was holding the position open for a special guy — a guy who had just the right experience and qualifications. In fact, she even knew exactly who she wanted, a man who had worked with her before.

Teasingly, Mark asked what was so special about this one particular guy. Yo-Yo answered with a part sigh, part moan, altogether sexy as hell, full body-lingering almost primal sound, and then said that this certain very special man was so, so good with his hands and his mind. And, she added, if memory served correct, he had some other quite capable features as well.

She said it had been almost a week since she and this oh so special man had worked together on their very special private project, and she was afraid they might be falling behind schedule. He was a really, really good worker, she said, but he had been away from the jobsite for a little while, and he needed to come back and get right to work.

Smiling broadly, Mark said into the phone that really, really good workers were in high demand and that maybe this fellow had gone to work somewhere else. Yo-Yo purred that it was true that many others would love to hire him, but that she offered a terrific benefits package, and besides, he always seemed very happy and she knew he really enjoyed his work.

Mark said that from his experience as a detective, workers generally returned to their jobs if they left their tools. Yo-Yo laughed softly that her worker left a couple of tools behind, but that he carried his main one with him. Then she said that this main tool, well, it was something else. It seemed larger and more impressive than other men's tools, and he was able to dig deeper with it, and he always found that just so special spot with his large, impressive tool.

Mark checked his watch and saw it was after 12:30 a.m. He was listening to Yo-Yo cooing into his phone, knowing that he had ingested the Crown and Advil, knowing he was an hour and a half away, but thinking that he could make it in an hour in his Charger. Yo-Yo could read his thoughts, as usual. "Stop being quiet and thinking about how long it will take you to get here,"

More silence followed from his end until she added, "Stay there and take care of your business. Your job here will be waiting for you."

Maybe she was in his mind and watching the screen-play of his movie after all, because she always knew what he was thinking and always kept him on the right track. So, he said good night and told her he would finish things and see her as soon as possible.

He sat there for a minute thinking of her, and then closed the Bible and reopened the Crown. As the drink swirled in his mouth, Mark imagined it was Yo-Yo he was tasting. Soon he began to wonder if it was the whiskey that was making him intoxicated or if he was becoming drunk by her smell—the smell that would waft from her hair as her sun-kissed body lay next to his. Her smell, her taste, her feel, it was all so real for Mark. These things combined in Mark's mind, and as it happened, some impure thoughts followed—graphic, impure thoughts of carnal lust between a man and wife. How far away again was that lake house?

But after a moment, the reality of what he was facing reappeared, and Mark knew he had to stay at the job. Still, it felt odd going back to Bible study so soon after these sexual thoughts and feelings, so Mark placed his Bible back into the desk and again took out the police reports and began to pore through each one yet again.

Poring over the reports led directly to the pour-ing of more Crown Royale and the next thing Mark knew, it was 3:30 a.m. He could recite the details of each murder, and he knew the cases inside and out; he just didn't know how to find the killer. He still did not know how the victims were located or how initial contact between the killer and victims may have taken place. There were no suspicious emails and as for phone records, only dead-ends.

The only similarity in the crimes was that a couple of the victims, Matthew Owens and Marcel Durand, in the weeks before their deaths, had made multiple calls to individual numbers that were found to be out-of-order listings for recently purchased track phones. Mark and the police theorized that the killer purchased the track phones and then disposed of them after the crimes, but even after watching thousands of hours of local Wal-Mart and other retailers' surveillance camera footage, no discoveries were made that could link a face to the purchases. The phones seemed to have not been purchased by the same individual, at least not in the Dallas-Ft. Worth area, and at least not in the days immediately preceding their beginning usage. Even the FBI's investigation into large purchases of multiple track phones throughout the entire southwest proved fruitless.

As the last of the bottle of Crown Royale went over the ice cubes and into Mark's glass, he sat there wondering just who he was seeking? What was he missing? Rodeo cowboys had a saying that there had never been a bull that couldn't be ridden, and Mark always believed there never had been a crime that couldn't be solved, but this case was making him start to reconsider. What was he missing?

The answer to what he was missing this early

morning was sleep, so around 4:15 a.m. his head slipped down to his chest, and he finally caught some much needed shut-eye.

Chapter 40

Around 8:30 a.m., the sounds of the traffic outside his office and the sun poking through the blinds on his windows combined to wake Mark. Never exactly a morning glory kind of guy all full of pep and eagerness to start the new day, this morning would prove especially difficult. Leaning back in his chair and trying to focus his eyes was bad enough, but what in the hell was going on inside his head?

The whiskey was exacting its revenge, and Mark was feeling his age and then some. Why could he drink and stay up all night fifteen years ago with little side effects, and now too much Crown left his body feeling the next morning like a construction site – with too much noise, rumbling, and feeling like a bunch of things needed to be put back in place and nailed down. Slowly rising and stretching his body, Mark considered trying the time-honored hangover cure of the hair of the dog, but since the bottle was empty, he settled instead for pouring water and grounds in the coffee maker.

Staring at the closed police reports on his desk and thinking about their contents while he drank his first cup, Mark glanced up and saw his reflection in the mirror hanging on the wall behind his desk. Damn, had he been abducted? He looked worse than he felt. Finishing the coffee, he walked over to the mirror and looked closely. It's always a sad milestone in anyone's life when they notice and, really for the first time, see themselves aging. When did this happen?

The age in Mark's eyes was now apparent and so were the lines around his bloodshot eyes. Not laugh lines but hard and deepening lines now snaked from the corners of his eyes. The gray on his temples was now invading the rest of his hair and making serious progress. Had those lines and this much gray been there before he took this case?

As he stood there pondering how this case was fucking with his body, his family, and his marriage, he suddenly had a thought that the only thing probably worse at that moment than the way he felt and looked would be his breath. Cupping his hand over his mouth and exhaling, he almost gagged at the smell. What was that rancid odor? Had someone come into his office last night while he slept and taken a shit in his mouth?

If the Gospel Killer was to maintain her pattern, this was the day before she was scheduled to strike again. Even so, Mark's involvement would have to wait until after he brushed his teeth and had a hot shower and shave.

A little more than an hour and a half later, Mark returned to his office from his home where he had undergone his shower and oral "beauty treatment." Ahh, he did love his morning Listerine ritual. Finishing the remains of an Egg McMuffin, he sat back at his desk feeling and looking a lot better, but there was still one thing he needed to do before he could return his concentration to the case.

Remembering the happenings of the previous night at Bubba's and paying heed to Marcus' warning, Mark picked up his phone and called his long time insurance agent, Gary Blackburn, who handled everything for Mark from auto, home and life to surety bonds and business insurance. Gary spent most of his time on the golf course these days it seemed, but luckily, Mark caught him in the office this morning and asked about getting an additional two million dollar life insurance policy. To Gary's surprise, Mark didn't seem at all concerned about the cost of the premiums for such a large policy but only with how fast it would go into effect. Hearing he would need a complete physical beforehand, Mark told him to schedule it as soon as possible.

"Say, uh, is there some kind of problem I should know about?" Gary asked. Mark had always liked Gary, and he didn't necessarily like too many people, but he wasn't in the forthcoming mood this morning.

"I haven't been to a doctor, haven't been diagnosed with anything," he replied. "I just want to get this done, and I need it fast." Gary thought this was strange, but he wasn't in the business of turning down large commissions, so he told Mark he would get back with him later that day after he set the appointment for the physical.

With this taken care of, Mark sat back down at his desk and turned his attention to the case. Before he opened either the Bible or the case files, he decided to check the rewards hotline and see if anything promising might have somehow miraculously come in. The first two calls sounded like disgruntled employees trying to make trouble for their bosses, but the third caller sounded like he was troubled. So hanging up from the hotline, Mark called the number he had taken down from the third caller and dialed up a Mr. Luke Colbert.

This morning, as usual, Luke had skipped his nine a.m. biology lab. He didn't much like either waking early or biology labs, and after all, there was that girl in his study group. She wasn't all that much too look at, and the freshmen fifteen weight gain had turned into the freshmen forty-five, but what the hell, big girls need love too, and she was generous with both her ample body and her test answers. So Luke wasn't worried about class and was playing Xbox in his dorm room when he received Mark's call.

Mark made a small introduction and let Luke know why he was calling. "So tell me about this woman you think might be the Gospel Killer?"

"It's not like I think she's the killer," Luke hesitated and then answered. "It's just I told some friends about her, and they all thought I should call you guys."

Mark was maybe a minute into the conversation and already about to hang up but decided to give it one more try. "Okay then, why do your friends think she might be the killer?"

"They watch a lot of T.V., you know the news and all," Luke replied after loosening up. "Since my name matches one of the Gospel names, they've been on me to be careful about the women I meet."

"You meet a lot of women?"

"I do all right."

"That's good," Mark said, quickly starting to feel contempt for this player wannabe. "But actually, I'm pretty busy, so could you tell me about the woman you called the recording about? Besides just your name, anything else make you think she could be a suspect in these murders?"

"Well, she had tattoos on her arm and back. My friends said that according to the news, that was one big thing, and also her name is Angel. She never told me her last name. We were supposed to meet a couple of days ago, but she stood me up, and it was the same day they found those two old cops dead, you know the ones they say had some kind of evidence about the killer."

Suddenly Mark's contempt diminished and he became very interested in what young Luke had to say. No one had come up with a name yet of the killer, but Mark immediately knew that Angel would fit with the whole case.

"You're sure that it was the same day that the two policemen were found dead?" Mark asked.

"Yeah. I was at the yogurt shop waiting for her when they broke in on the TV and were talking about it."

"What does this woman look like?" Mark asked, feeling energized.

"She's hot. I mean, I don't go just for anybody, at least not till closing time," Luke said, unable to hide his lack of humility. "But, this old girl is strong, probably five seven and a buck twenty-five, I'd say, but strong you know, just tight and muscular. And, she's got like blondish hair, I think."

"You think?"

"Well, I didn't really spend a lot of time looking at her hair, if you know what I mean."

"Yeah, I think I follow you. So how old do you think this woman is?"

"Geez, you know pretty old, at least for me. Guess

probably around maybe thirty-five or so."

"Any chance you got a picture of her?" Mark asked, pushing aside the disdain that had suddenly reemerged.

"No. I usually like to wait until after I nail them and then snap a picture and sort of put their photo up in my gallery, so to speak."

Mark winced. "So where did you meet her?"

"At the dog park," Luke answered, rubbing his dog's head. "I go there pretty much every day with my Lab Cassie, and she was there with her dog Goliath. Man that dog is huge—a big mastiff with this giant head, and that sucker is white as snow. That dog is a pretty fuckin' dog, man."

"So how many other times did you see her?"

"Just once. We went riding on my Kawasaki, and I think it must've got her charged up. Either the bike or me one did - because she got pretty friendly, shall we say."

"Pretty friendly? But you said you hadn't had sex with her yet?"

"Fuck, no. You know, I was trying my best, and we were doing about everything else, but I couldn't get her pants off. Said I had to wait. Said her husband would be working late this week, and we could get together Tuesday. Some shit about making it special for me."

"Tuesday, like as in tomorrow? Mark asked, knowing that Tuesday would be the twenty-seventh day since her last killing and would fit the pattern. "She was planning on seeing you then?"

"Yeah, Tuesday as in tomorrow, but that was before she stood me up this weekend and all. So, guess I won't be hittin' that Tuesday, unless she changes her mind and calls."

Mark believed this could indeed be the killer and almost wished she would call Luke back. He didn't even want to talk to this idiot but needed his information, so he swallowed hard and continued. "I took her phone number down from when you called the rewards hotline; the number you said is not working any longer. Is that the only way you talked with her? Did you ever email her?"

"Yeah, I almost forgot," Luke responded. "How would I get that reward?"

"I've got your information," Mark sighed and answered. "If anything you give us leads to the arrest and conviction of this woman, you got my word you'll get your reward."

"That's good," said a laughing Luke. "Man, can you imagine how much pussy I'd get if I had that kind of bank?"

"What about the email?" Mark asked, not wanting to imagine that sort of thing.

"No, we didn't email," Luke said, brought back from his dreams of riches and the spoils that go with it. "I asked, but she said she couldn't on account of how her husband always checked everything."

"So, if we find this woman, you'd be able and willing to identify her?"

"Fuck, yeah, I'll identify that prick teaser. For a half a million dollars, damn straight."

"What about the tattoos? Your call said they were of a large Angel on her lower back and a strand of barbwire around her arm. Any chance you think they could be fake?"

"I don't know," Luke said. "They looked real to me. I mean, fuck, you know, fake tits, fake hair, fake orgasms, fake tattoos. Why the fuck do I care?"

After hearing this, Mark was wishing he could find the killer and then arrange for her and Luke to have a conjugal visit after the arrest. He managed to hold back his feelings and said, "Before I let you go, is there anything else? Anything about her that was strange or would make her stand out? You know something to go on in trying to find her."

"Believe me, her ass makes her stand out," Luke answered, rubbing Cassie's head. "You could bounce a quarter a foot high off that ass. You know, shit man, I was looking forward to bouncing up in that fine ass."

"So that's it? That's everything you can tell me about this woman?"

"Well, you know there was one weird thing," Luke answered after hesitating again.

"What's that?"

"Well, that day in the dog park when we met, I started coming on to her, but she said I was too young for her, that she could get arrested for being with me. So I showed her my driver's license, showed her I was eighteen, showed her my birthday right on the license and all, and then she just starts laughing."

"Why? Was it a fake license or something?" Mark asked.

"No. And it wasn't just my age, but she started counting the letters of my name on her fingers, of my real name, you know, Lucas Ryan Colbert. She just busts out laughing when she got done at sixteen. Kept laughing and saying sixteen and eighteen, eighteen and sixteen, and about how perfect that was. Wouldn't ever say why, but she sure seemed happy about it for some reason. Like really happy. Kind of weird, huh?"

It did seem a little odd, so Mark wrote it down in his notes and completed the interview with Luke. He left his number in case the young Romeo remembered anything further and again assured Luke he would remember him when it came time to pay out the reward. Mark said good-bye and hung up the phone about the same time it vibrated in his hands with a text message from Gary. It read that the earliest available time for the life insurance physical would be Thursday. Grinning and hoping he would still be alive come Thursday, Mark texted back to make the appointment and to let him know where to go and what time to be there.

With that taken care of, Mark pulled out the Bible from his desk and again opened it to the Book of Numbers. A few minutes later and only partially through with the first chapter, Mark sat the Bible back down on his desk. Something was going on in his mind and not allowing him to concentrate on reading. Mark was thinking of the phone call he had just had with Luke Colbert, thinking of how Luke had told him the woman counted out the letters of his name. Thinking of how Luke said the woman laughed at his age and at the number of letters in his name. Thinking of how the numbers he mentioned, eighteen and sixteen, were after all numbers. Thinking maybe the advice or clue he had received from Nicolas during their last phone call could perhaps actually mean these type numbers and not the Bible's Book of Numbers.

That was it. Mark threw open the Bible and his mind was racing as he quickly searched for what he hoped would be the key to the case—the scripture found in Luke 18:16 which read: "But Jesus called them and said, suffer little children to come unto me, and forbid them not, for of such is the kingdom of God." He leaned back in his chair and considered what he had read; certainly a wonderful verse, but not one his gut felt would be a motivation for multiple murders.

Mark closed his eyes in an effort to focus more clearly on the subject. Luke had said the woman laughed and acted strangely saying the numbers were "perfect." Repeating his age and the number of letters in his name, repeating eighteen and sixteen, sixteen and eighteen over and over again — what was she laughing at?

Then it hit Mark. He had looked up the verse in Luke 18:16, but what about flipping the numbers and checking out Luke 16:18? Quickly turning back a page in his Bible, Mark read the verse: "Whosoever putteth away his wife and marries another, committeth adultery and whosoever marrieth her that is put away from her husband committeth adultery."

His mouth fell open as he realized that divorce and adultery were indeed possible motivations for murder. He scribbled on his pad the question, "Have all the victims been divorced?" It was something to check, but then he thought of Luke Colbert; he was only eighteen, and Mark wondered if he had been married and divorced already? Based on Luke's personal skills and tact displayed during their phone conversation, that was possible but still unlikely, Mark thought.

This thought dampened some of Mark's initial excitement, but his gut still told him that Luke 16:18 would prove important. Sixteen eighteen, sixteen and eighteen, Mark repeated those numbers aloud once and then again. Hearing his own voice triggered something in Mark's subconscious. He had heard or seen those

numbers somewhere recently. But where? Spreading
the police reports out across his desk, Mark picked up
the file for the Luke Jacobsen murder. In less than a
minute, he saw where Kim's husband Luke had been
found murdered in apartment number 1618. Quite a
coincidence and one that whet Mark's appetite.

Grabbing the file for the Stoneleigh Hotel murder,
Mark scanned the report for any listed numbers concerning the killing of Matthew Michaels. There were
several: the room number, the number of sequins and
black fibers discovered on the floor, Michael's home
phone number, the number of wounds to Mr. Michael's
body, the amount his company had paid to rent the
room, the number of calls made on his cell that day.
But the thing that stood out to Mark was reading once
more about the nickel found standing on its edge on the
bedside nightstand. It was the one odd thing, the one
thing that was obviously staged. What did it mean? A
nickel represented the number five, so Mark sat wondering how five fit in this puzzle?

Picking up his Bible again and turning to the Gospel
of Matthew, Mark began reading chapter five, and
within minutes, the puzzle started fitting together
in his mind. Matthew 5:32 read, "But I say unto you,
that whosoever shall put away his wife, saving for the
cause of fornication, causeth her to commit adultery,
and whosoever shall marry her that is divorced committeth adultery." It was almost word for word with
Luke 16:18. When Mark glanced back at the police
report to confirm that the victim had suffered exactly
thirty-two knife wounds, he knew this was more than
coincidence.

Feeling energized like he hadn't in months, Mark

took his laptop and punched into a parallel Bible site. The site allows someone to put in a specific Biblical verse, and within seconds, it shows all other similar verses or references in the Bible. Typing in Luke 16:18, the site immediately displayed Matthew 5:32, Matthew 19:9, and Mark 10:11.

Returning to his Bible, Mark looked up the two new scriptures and found that the content matched, and in fact, each was nearly identical with Luke 16:18 and Matthew 5:32. Writing down the two other verses, Matthew 19:9 and Mark 10:11 on his pad, Mark grabbed for the reports and soon found what he sought. The air conditioning company owner, Matthew Owens, had a nineteen-by-nine inch cross perfectly carved into his chest, and the murderer had killed Marcel Durand with ten knife wounds to his chest, presumably followed postmortem by eleven shallow cuts to his back. The numbers fit, the verses matched. Mark knew this was more than coincidence. Way more.

~~~

Lew the Magician arrived at Bubba's home early to drive him to work but before departing told the old man he needed to talk. Not trusting that even his own home or car were safe from prying FBI ears and eyes, Bubba suggested a walk through the neighborhood. Knowing this cue, the Magician took out two breathing masks from his pocket, the type people sometimes wear outdoors to protect themselves from ragweed or pollen, and handed one to Bubba. Each man put the masks on over their mouths, not worried about allergies, but desiring to speak freely and not allow any law enforcement officers to tape them and read their lips.

On the walk, the Magician said he had an idea how

to handle Mark and the whole situation on Bubba's land in Stephenville but would need a few days. Bubba's arched eyebrows asked the unstated question of what he had in mind.

"Thinking of acid," answered the Magician. "Talked with a guy I know who says that's what the cartels use, a mixture of sulfuric and muriatic acids combined with hot water. Says within twenty-four to forty-eight hours there won't be anything left of the bodies 'cept some fuckin' goo."

Bubba was not used to walking or really to too much physical exertion of any kind, at least not while in the vertical position, so he stopped to catch his breath and leaned against a street sign for support.

"What about the fucking cameras?" he asked. "The cocksucker has 'em strapped to the trees and is watching everything round the clock."

That's why I need a few days to get things together," the Magician answered, keeping his head down. "Gonna use two trucks, one flatbed to haul in a backhoe and a box truck to carry the barrels of acid. Gonna use the backhoe to dig up the bodies real quick, then dump 'em in the barrels and get the box truck on the road back here to a mini warehouse I rented. So, the fucker can call the highway patrol if he wants, but we'll be gone before they can get there."

"What about Witt?" Bubba asked, smiling to himself as he began walking again.

"I'll take care of him myself," the Magician said with an unmistakable gleam in his eye. "And don't worry, 'cause I got a barrel all picked out just for him. And, get this, the mini warehouse I rented, it's in the name Mark Witt." Both men got a good laugh from this.

"Get things set up but clear it with me before you do anything," Bubba ordered, on their way back to the car.

Chapter 41

Almost an hour had passed since Mark made the discovery of how the Bible fit into this case. Yes, he had received help from Nicholas, the original Gospel Killer and a man whose name he didn't yet know, and yes he still certainly did not know how the Bible figured into Nicolas' set of murders, but that worry would wait till another day. For today, Mark was excited and sure he was onto something that would help him find the woman who had stepped in to carry on Nicholas' work.

But what exactly had he discovered? Was the killer divorced or perhaps a second wife married to a divorced man? Mark reasoned that it was more likely the killer was a scorned woman driven to murder by a painful divorce. And if this was the case, she was in good company. Mark figured there were probably hundreds of thousands of divorced women in the Dallas-Ft. Worth metroplex area alone. Each, no doubt, with a laundry list of reasons why she had been wronged in her failed marriage and each a possible suspect capable of reaching her breaking point and using the old Ginsu knife set on some unsuspecting postcoital males. So which one snapped?

Mark was going over the possibilities in his mind, but like the rest of the case, he was finding more frustration than answers. Of the four victims killed by the woman, Mark found only two had been divorced, Luke Jacobsen and Marcel Durand. The others, Matthew Michaels and Matthew Owens, were both still married to their high school sweethearts at the time of their deaths. Worse yet was the fact that of the two women divorced from these men, Marcel Durand's ex-wife lived in France and had never visited the United States and Luke Jacobsen's ex had been killed in an automobile accident four years after their divorce.

Since this rather limited either one's ability to be the murderer, Mark expanded his thoughts and considered the one woman who had married one of these divorced men and had therefore, according to the Bible, been forced into a life of adultery—the woman who had hired him to work on this case, Kim Jacobsen. Kim would not be the first criminal to try and cover their tracks by hiring a private detective to try and appear as if they were very interested in solving the case when that was not their true intent at all. And she had, after all, tried to sidetrack him with her sexual advances on multiple occasions.

So was her real plan to seduce him or to confuse him? Was she an evil criminal genius capable of being an undetected serial killer, or was she just a bored rich whore wanting a hard dick? Thinking back over his time spent with her, he quickly decided she was no genius. And judging from the evidence provided on the sex tapes, as well as her own boastful admissions of her rather enormous sexual appetite, well pretty much even a slut would classify Kim Jacobsen as a whore, so Mark crossed her off the list.

While sitting there thinking of other possibilities and

finding no other immediate good ones, Mark picked up his phone and called Yo-Yo—just a quick call to let her know he was thinking of her and missing his family. She and Cubbie were getting the kids ready to take to the pool; later they were planning a big dinner because Will was coming down after work. "It would be so great, really wonderful, Mark, if you could make it also," she pleaded. He didn't promise but told her to wear something nice because he would try his best to come see her. She pleaded further, causing Mark to give in.

"I love you," he said, sighing. "And okay, yes, I promise I'll come and see you tonight. You happy now? I promise."

As he was closing the phone he smiled and shook his head at what that woman could make him do. He hadn't meant to promise he would make it down there tonight. Hell, who knew what kind of day he had ahead of himself, but he would make it there, because a promise was a promise.

Turning his attention back to the case, he began again to pore over the case files. While doing this Mark thought about the Bible verses regarding divorce and adultery and wondered how those verses helped the killer select her victims. How was she able to find appropriately named men for her task? How had Nicholas, the original Gospel Killer, found the men all named Matthew, Mark, Luke or John?

Mark was making a note to ask Nicholas that very question if he ever called again when his phone rang, startling him. Could it be that Nicholas was calling him at that very moment? Answering the phone he found it was not Nicholas, but rather, his old friend, Detective

John Coleman. Mark had not talked with John for the last few days and had been uncomfortable dealing with him — ever since the first call from Nicholas and getting blackmailed into finding this copycat Gospel Killer before the police did.

While Coleman was telling him of the police's planned media blitz scheduled for that day, Mark was thinking of the four men he had killed during the Carolina Ramirez kidnapping and how their bodies were buried on Bubba Furh's property — along with the headless corpse of Bethany Adams. Mark was thinking if the police found this second Gospel Killer before he did it would prove very bad for him and his family, and now here they were making a concerted effort to let as many people as possible know that tomorrow would be the next date when the killer was expected to try and strike again. He knew this tactic could work for the police - and against him.

When Coleman was finished, Mark tried to concentrate only on the case and not his personal situation. "I think that's a great idea. The public needs to know and hell, maybe we can get lucky."

"What about you?" John asked. "Any new leads or new angles you're working on?"

Mark wanted to tell John about the calls from Nicholas, about his believing he had found the Biblical significance, about the Ramirez kidnapping and his involvement with it, and how that involvement now involved Bubba and the Magician, but he didn't. "Still trying to figure it out. But, say, I know you can't find a connection between any of the victims, but what about their families? Any of the families connected? Even extended family, in some way? There's gotta be a way this woman is finding these guys, all of 'em with just the right names and all."

"Ellis and the FBI boys have been hittin' that hard but nothing concrete yet, just theories. Thinking the killer could be a state or federal worker, or maybe has access to credit files in her job, like working at a bank or credit union, or somewhere like a car dealership that runs credit apps. Hell, maybe she works in a restaurant and sees names from credit card receipts and then follows them."

This interested Mark. "Have you gotten anywhere with that?"

"No, not yet. The victims banked at different places, had all types of credit profiles, and there's no record that any of them sought or got credit from the same place before they were killed. Not even any proof they ate at the same places. Like I said, it's all pretty much still theories at this point. Hell, you know, thinking it might be a federal or government worker, we even checked to see if it might be a cop. But the fingerprints on the items from the bags we found at the scene with your dad and David Vaughn cleared all law enforcement also."

While these facts interested Mark, they did nothing to point him in the right direction.

"But about the families and about Vaughn," John added, almost as an afterthought. "Ron is going to question his daughter this afternoon, to see if she knows anything about him or his acquaintances. Something the wife might not know. Because with the evidence we found at the crime scene, Ellis is convinced that either Vaughn or your dad must've known who the killer is."

"Yeah, the evidence was taken from the murder

scenes and they wound up with it," Mark responded. "No getting around it; that looks bad. And I don't think either one of 'em would make a good lookin' enough transvestite to get a bunch of men hot after them, so I don't think they did it themselves. But I gotta tell you, I'm betting it was Vaughn. You know yourself, if my dad had known who the killer was he damn sure would have come forward for the half million."

"Yeah, that's the way I see it too," John said, echoing his sentiments.

"Well, what about Vaughn? You find any dirt on him yet?"

"Not too much," John said, shrugging his shoulders like a poker player holding a pair of deuces in a Jacks or better game. "The usual stuff. He retired after twenty-five years on the force with less than three thousand dollars in the bank, a bad back, and a pretty serious drinking problem. Spent some time in rehab after he got his security job with the Stoneleigh, came back, and they say was clean."

"You mentioned his wife, but did he have any ex's?" Mark asked, thinking of the Bible verses.

"Yeah, that was one interesting thing about him I didn't know. He was married once before when he was in the Army to a German woman from Frankfurt. But it only lasted a couple of years before they divorced, and then he came back to the states and got remarried. He had been with his wife for the last twenty-seven years."

Twenty-seven years was a long time to carry this kind of hatred, even if she were a Nazi, so Mark figured the German woman had nothing to do with the crimes. He said good-bye to Coleman after asking John to call him if anything came from Ellis' interview with Vaughn's daughter.

Mark got back to work after the call ended. He read aloud the Bible verses, walked around his desk and then read aloud the police reports. He wrote key information on note cards and thumbtacked the cards to the walls. Then he spread out the reports on the floor in chronological order. He tried everything he could think of in an attempt to force his brain, his consciousness, to see what he was missing. Closing his eyes, he tried to imagine he was a divorced woman: distraught, angry, jealous, betrayed, deadly violent, perhaps abused. How would he act? How would a woman conceal these traits within her normal life?

After what turned out to be hours, Mark looked at his watch and saw it was nearly 4:30 p.m. An entire afternoon had vanished as he tried to ascertain how a female serial killer would act, how she would select victims, how she would compromise in her own mind that the Bible sanctioned her actions, how she would educate herself on the ways to avoid detection, and he had really come up with nothing. His brain had not reached the eureka moment he desperately sought; his consciousness had not expanded and put him onto a singular suspect. What was he missing? He was getting closer. His Bible discovery convinced him of that, and his instincts told him that, but he still didn't have a name. What the fuck was he missing?

While sitting there racking his mind over what detail he might be missing, over what clue he could be overlooking, over what piece of the puzzle he was staring at but not seeing, Mark heard a knock on his office door. A louder and more forceful one shook the door a second later. Normally the outer door was open when Mark was in, but after the confrontation at Bubba's the night before and the ominous warning from Marcus that followed, Mark had locked it behind him when he entered.

He was looking through the peephole when the young woman outside knocked for the third time. Mark studied the woman's face through the door. He had seen her somewhere before, and recently, but where? Withdrawing the Glock from his shoulder holster and holding it behind his back with his still good left hand, Mark opened the door and the woman came in without saying a word.

Once inside, the woman — really no more than a girl in perhaps her early twenties — walked straight to a mirror hanging on Mark's wall and began looking at her reflection. Mark thought this was strange, but before he spoke, and while she was finger tousling her hair the woman said, "I know who you are."

"Great. Now who are you?" He asked to the young woman who was still much too wrapped up in her own image to turn away from the mirror.

"Yeah, you're Mark Witt," she continued, over her shoulder. "I've seen you down at the club a couple of times lately. I remember your face; it's a good face."

Mark now recognized the woman; he had seen her dancing at Club Fuxx. This didn't exactly endear her to him. "I think you must be in the wrong place. I didn't call for any private lap dances."

"That's a shame," the woman said, pulling herself away from the mirror and walked over to him smiling. "Cause I could so rock your world. I surely could. You know, when I saw you in the club last night the thing

I liked most about you was your walk. I watched you and could just tell you had some great man legs. And I do love me some man legs, you know the kinda legs with feet on one end and a dick on the other." She reached out to touch him but Mark stepped away.

"Look, I don't know why you're here, but I think you'd better leave," he said while re-holstering his gun.

"Like I said, I'm here because I know you, and because I know who the Gospel Killer is," she said, surprising Mark.

"How do you know who the killer is?" he said after a short pause spent again studying her face.

"Because of Boy," she said, stepping closer with a devilish smile. "You think Beth was the only one fucking him?"

Mark knew that Boy had to mean Boy Russell, the bisexual juggernaut whose relationship with the actual Gospel Killer had gotten both himself and Bethany Adams murdered and whose leaky mouth had given away the location of the four bodies Mark had killed. So when Mark heard the name Boy he officially became interested in what the woman had to say.

"Okay. Say I believe you; then give me a name. Who's the Gospel Killer?"

"You have anything to drink?" she asked, the devilish smile turning to one more flighty. Walking back away from him and heading toward her friend the mirror, she added, "Maybe some Tanqueray?"

"I'm not a bartender, and I'm not real patient either," Mark said following her and placing his left hand on her shoulder. He roughly wheeled her around to face him. "So who's the Gospel Killer?"

Perhaps not yet fearful, but at the very least

concerned, the woman looked at Mark's huge hand on her shoulder. "They say there's some kind of rewar…"

"You'll get the reward if what you say is true. Now tell me what you know."

The woman said her name was Missy, but that her dance name was Mystical, and that she had been seeing Boy for more than a year. She said she knew who the killer was but didn't know his name. "One time we were at Boy's apartment, just hanging out and all. All of a sudden he starts acting like a dick and tells me it's time for me to leave. Said he had someone else coming over and I had to get out. I was pissed, and figured it was that bitch Beth, so I decided to wait in the parking lot and give her some shit—you know, tell her I'd already had what she was about to get and all. But Beth didn't show. Instead this dude did. Knocked on Boy's door and went right in. A couple minutes later they walk out kissing and everything, then get in the guy's BMW and drive away. And here I didn't even know Boy was a fag! But it pissed me off, you now, getting thrown out on account of a dude. Anyways, they never knew, but I followed them to the other guy's house."

Trying to hide his excitement at the possibility that the dancer might be on to something, Mark paused before asking, "Did you get a license plate number?"

"No," Mystical said, exhaling. "I thought of that later, but I was too pissed at the time to think of it."

"How long ago was this?"

"I dunno, maybe a couple of months," she said, shrugging her shoulders.

"Do you remember where you followed them too?" Where the house is?"

"Really, I think it was more like a townhouse."

"Do you remember where the townhouse is?" Mark rephrased.

"Just follow me," said Mystical, the devilish smile returning to illuminate her face. "And remember about that reward."

"Come on and show me," said Mark, flinging open the front door and forgetting to hide his excitement.

Mystical went out first, closely followed by Mark. The brightness of the afternoon sun shone directly into his eyes, affecting his vision. Briefly, he thought he saw a silver glimmer flashing in front of him. Before he could think what it might be, Mark felt the garrote wire tighten around his neck and cut into his flesh. With well-played assistance from Mystical, Lew the Magician had managed to catch Mark off-guard and was now behind him, viciously pulling on the garrote. The wire—the type made famous in the strangulation death scenes of the Godfather movies—was shearing through his skin, cutting off his oxygen supply and jeopardizing his carotid artery. Mark was thrust instantly into a brutal kill-or-be-killed fight for his life.

Hearing only the Magician's grunts from the force of his pulling, while frantically grabbing at the wire in a futile attempt to free himself, Mark was facing a desperate situation. Struggling and being pulled backwards into his office, Mark began swinging his broken right hand violently back over his head, where it crashed repeatedly into the Magician's face but was unable to create any extra breathing room.

While Mystical scrambled to close the office's door to try and avoid detection from any possible witnesses, Mark maintained his senses during this struggle well enough to withdraw his Glock from the shoulder holster he was wearing. Rapidly losing his oxygen, Mark pushed the gun behind his back and fired three shots. The wire didn't loosen as the shots hit directly into the bulletproof vest that the Magician was wearing. Nearing death and almost blacking out, Mark heard the Magician scream at Mystical, "Get the fucking gun away from him."

She rushed over and tried to grab at the gun, but Mark found enough strength to take it and smash the butt of it into her face, sending Mystical bleeding and tumbling away. Seeing he still had the gun, the Magician furiously pushed him forward and with all of his strength began trying to smash Mark's head into a wall. With precious little air left, and with his head now facing downward from being slammed into the wall, Mark saw the Magician's feet. Out of air and not able to free himself, he used the last of his strength and pulled the trigger.

The first shot missed and blasted into the floor, but the second shot ripped through the Magician's right foot. A slight loosening of the wire gave Mark another breath, which he used to fire shots three and four. The bullets tore through the Magician's Kenneth Cole dress oxfords and shred apart his left foot.

Shrieking out in pain and dropping the wire, Lew fell facedown to the floor and began reaching for his own gun. Gasping for breath and reaching to feel the blood spurting from his neck, Mark saw the wounded Magician scrambling to draw his gun. As Mark pushed the Glock towards him to fire a kill shot into the Magician's head, Mystical bull-rushed him and knocked him off balance. The Glock dropped from his hand and

Mystical kicked it away from his reach. Mark showed his appreciation for her involvement by smashing a huge elbow into the stripper's face. Teeth exploded from her mouth and blood gushed downward as she staggered back, flailing her arms before falling over the coffee table to the floor.

Seeing the Magician draw his own gun and start to roll over and fire, Mark leaped on Lew and began wrestling for control of the weapon. Both men were in pain, fatigued and winded, but adrenaline was in overdrive. The Magician fought with all his might and guile, but the younger and better-conditioned Mark struggled and gained control. On top of the Magician's back, Mark pressed his shoulder down into Lew's neck. Then with his right hand pushing down onto the Magician's face, Mark managed to get his left hand under Lew's head until he was able to grab a hold on the Magician's chin. Knowing he was in serious danger, Lew tried desperately to free the gun that he now held in his hand underneath his body, but to no avail. This was one trap the Magician would not escape from. With a single violent and bone-shattering reverse pull of his two hands, Mark snapped Lew's neck.

With the Magician dead, Mystical scrambled to her feet and ran to pick up Mark's Glock, lying on the floor. Mark quickly rolled Lew's body over and grabbed the gun that had been under him. He fired a shot inches from her feet, stopping Mystical. As he got to his feet, he kept the gun trained on the dancer while he retrieved his Glock.

Still keeping the gun aimed at the stripper, Mark looked around and saw his office in complete disarray—chairs tipped over, broken glass strewn across the coffee table, photo and certificate frames knocked from the walls, bullet holes in the floor, blood stains throughout, and a rather large and very dead body lying face down on his carpet. With one hand rubbing his neck, and making sure he could still breathe while staring at the dead Magician, Mark said to the frightened Mystical, "Looks like you bet on the wrong horse."

"It wasn't like that," Mystical said, beginning to cry. "He made me come. He said he would…"

"Shut up," Mark cut her off, in no mood for chivalry. "You're coming with me." Though the dancer had put off finishing her GED, Mystical was no dummy.

"Alright," she answered quickly. "And don't worry, I won't try anything else."

Cutting through traffic, and though his broken right hand was sending constant shock waves of pain throughout his entire body, Mark had only one thought on his mind. Bubba had sent down this order. The Magician would never have tried such a bold move on his own. No, the old man called this shot.

Not that it was a problem, because, after all, Mark had already decided he would have to kill Bubba. He just didn't expect his hand to be forced this soon. Mark had thought things would wait until the case was solved. But sometimes timing and situations change, and a man has to be willing to change the order of his plans. For Mark, the case could wait a couple hours, and besides, why put off a good thing? And killing Bubba would be good. Good for so many people and good for Mark.

So for Bubba, especially for Bubba, Mark would change the order of his plans. He had never before killed a man except in self-defense, but he would make an exception for Bubba Furh. Knowing what he had to do didn't even require any rationalizing for Mark. It was really simple. Bubba had tried to have him killed, so he needed to die. Bubba would continue to pose a very real threat to him and his family, so he needed to die. Bubba knew the darkest of his secrets, and would leverage that knowledge against Mark, so Bubba needed to die. Simple.

With that squared away in his mind, Mark shifted gears and started running through possible scenarios in his mind. Would he catch Bubba off-guard? Or, having not heard back from the Magician, would the old man be prepared? Would he still have any surprises left up his old sleeves?

Bubba had fended off many rivals in his time. The old cat definitely had nine lives, and though he was now aging and weakened, Mark knew better than to discount him. Mark would be prepared. But the fact remained, Bubba was now older, and he was indeed weaker, and now, for the first time in a long time, he was also without the Magician. Mark was confident that today would be the day he had long awaited. Today he would see Bubba dead.

Mark had handcuffed Mystical's hands behind her back earlier when he threw her into his car. Up until this point, she had remained quiet. Not knowing what to expect as they were nearing Club Fuxx, the dancer broke her silence. "You know, I meant what I said about your face and all. You do got a nice face." Getting no response from Mark, she nervously continued, "Yeah, a girl could really like that face. That face and that walk. Hmmm. And your legs, too, your man legs," she laughed, while still spitting blood from her damaged mouth. Exiting off I-35 and turning onto Walnut Hill Lane, they were minutes from the club, and Mark still gave her no response, so Mystical shifted gears.

"I don't know what you're planning to do, but you don't have to kill me," she pleaded. "I won't ever say anything." Mark, checking his rear view mirror, didn't say anything either.

"Look, I can help you!" Mystical said, with desperation born of fear now entering her voice.

"Like you helped the Magician?" Mark asked, glancing over to her as he took a right onto Composite Drive.

"No, nothing like that," Mystical answered, shaking her head. "I'm talking about money. Cash fucking money. Listen, I can make you rich."

"No offense, but don't you think your back would give out on you before you could make me rich?" Mark responded, turning into the Club Fuxx parking lot.

"No, I'm talking about Bubba's money," Mystical continued as he pulled into a parking space. "I know where he keeps it—a bunch of it anyway. It's all buried in metal boxes under his patio." Mark looked at her closely as he got out of his Charger. "I was there when they buried it—plastic coated sheets of hundred dollar bills. There's gotta be millions. We could split it. Then I'll do anything you say, anything you want—anything, anytime, anyplace. Just don't kill me."

"The surveillance cameras for the club, where do they keep all the tapes?" Mark asked, unmoved.

"They're in this little room, like a closet almost, right in the hallway between the Magician's office and Bubba's," she said after a moment of silence.

"I've heard enough of your lies," Mark said before slamming the door. "Stay in the car and keep quiet until I get back and I'll let you live; otherwise I'll be burying your ass under that patio." Watching him walk into the club, Mystical decided to wait in the car.

Entering the club, Mark walked determinedly past the customers and workers and through the velvet curtains towards Bubba's office. He didn't hesitate as he walked down the musky hallway. The time for thinking was over. Drawing his gun and pushing the safety off, he kicked open the office door with his boot. Bubba was sitting behind his desk talking on the phone when Mark burst into his office, startling him. The blood drained from the old man's face as he attempted to reach for a .38 on his desk. Mark raised the Glock while shaking his head no and Bubba's hand stopped.

"Let me call you back," he said feebly into the phone as Mark walked towards him.

Picking up the .38 from the desk and pushing it down the back of his pants, Mark smiled at Bubba. "If you're wondering how this is going to end for you, the answer is badly."

"Just what in the hell do you…"

"Shut the fuck up." Bubba stopped speaking but not thinking. Mark could practically see the wheels turning in the old bastard's head. He remembered his father saying that Bubba always kept a nine-millimeter in his desk drawer so Mark then said, "And keep your hands where I can see them."

"I told Lew to just use a fuckin' gun," Bubba said, placing his hands flat on the desk. "But no, the motherfucker wanted the wire. Wanted it more personal."

"I thought I told you to shut the fuck up?"

Even though he was growing fearful, Bubba hardly slowed down. "But you were better than him. Better than me or him knew." Watching Mark circle the desk, Bubba pleaded, "Listen, I can help you."

"Suddenly, everyone's wantin' to help me," Mark grinned.

Bubba was undeterred. "I can make your dreams come true. You want Marcus' business? I'll give it to you; it's yours. And the Magician is out of the way now, so when I'm gone you can take over everything. You can have it all."

It was almost like on the mountaintop when Jesus was being tempted by Satan, being offered all of the world's kingdoms, all if only he would bow and worship Satan. Jesus refused and discarded Satan by answering his temptations with Bible quotes; Mark would choose a different method to discard of this devil.

Instead of quoting scripture, Mark viciously slammed the palm of his left hand into the old man's throat. Bubba's head flew back and his hands went around his neck as he suddenly battled to breathe. Panicked eyes locked onto Mark.

"You shoulda just shut the fuck up," Mark said, rubbing his own wounded neck. "It's no fun not being able to breathe, is it?"

Bubba was almost convulsing, rocking back and forth trying to catch his breath. Mark offered his pity by tearing away Bubba's oxygen tubes and then backhanding the old man out of his chair and onto the floor, where Bubba's colostomy bag ruptured, spilling waste all around him.

"Death with dignity, huh?" Mark grinned, seeing him

lying there, rolling in a pool of shit and who knows what all else.

"Fuck you!" Bubba gasped, realizing this was indeed not going to end well for him. "Fuck all you Witts! I'll see you all in hell."

Bubba's last words resonated with Mark, breaking through his anger and determination. As he stood there looking down at Bubba, Mark considered for a moment the possibility that he might be throwing away his salvation, throwing away his Savior's promise of eternal life in heaven by committing murder. He stared at the old and feeble man lying there, frightened as he faced death, and this gave Mark pause. Was this really even necessary? After all, without the Magician left to do his dirty work, what threat could Bubba now really pose? As Mark stood there considering these questions, considering the consequences he could be facing, the old man picked an unfortunate time to prove once again to be Bubba.

"You hear me? Fuck you, fuck your daddy, your momma, your wife. Fuck all you to hell." Hearing those words strengthened Mark's resolve to finish the job.

"Say hello to the Magician," he said, pressing his boot down on the old man's throat.

A couple of slight twitches later and Bubba's body lay motionless. Mark kept his boot on Bubba's throat for another minute or so to make sure and then left the office. He quickly went to the surveillance office, grabbed the tape, and then walked down the hall and through the pathetic patrons out the club.

Chapter 42

Moments after Bubba's death, Mark sat in his Charger listening to its engine. He had un-cuffed Mystical, and now she was walking away from him, across the parking lot. As he looked out into the street, he saw cars driving by — cars being driven by smiling people who didn't appear to have a care in the world. He couldn't move. He felt like a tornado was whirling all around him and there was no place to hide.

Two hours ago he had been immersed in the case. Reading the Bible and poring over the police reports, Mark had deciphered the code. He hadn't discovered the actual killer, but he had made progress and his instincts were telling him for the first time he was on the right track. He was feeling optimism, excitement, energy — all only a couple short hours ago. Now, he didn't know what to feel.

What was he supposed to feel? A man had tried to kill him, and that man now lay dead on Mark's office floor. Another man was dead as well, and Mark had killed him too. Both killings were necessary, but why did killing Bubba feel worse? Had he just committed murder? Killing Bubba had to be done, but would God understand it the same way?

The winds of the tornado were strengthening. Mark

took a deep breath as he picked up his cell. He knew he had to call Coleman and tell him what had happened, but first he needed shelter from the winds. Mark dialed the number to the one safe harbor he knew, the one secure place where he could always return. Mark was surprised when Daniel answered Yo-Yo's phone. The reception wasn't clear on the phone, but while talking with Daniel and before asking him to get Yo-Yo, Mark heard what he thought was a dog barking.

"What was that," he asked, still not thinking all together clearly.

"Oh, that's Goliath," laughed Daniel, petting the dog.

"Who's Goliath?"

"He's our neighbor's dog. Mom is dog sitting and brought him down here with her." Snapping back into the present, Mark remembered that Luke Colbert had earlier that day told him he met Angel at the dog park with Goliath, her white mastiff. Of course, this was only a coincidence. Wasn't it?

"Goliath, huh. He sounds big. What kind of dog is it?"

"Oh, he's big, all right! Mom says he's a mastiff." Suddenly, Mark's heart felt like it would pound right out of his chest.

"What color is he?"

"He's white. Biggest and prettiest ole white dog you've ever seen," Daniel said, still with half a head full of Goliath in his hands.

Mark pressed the accelerator down to the floor and roared out of the parking lot. It all instantly fell into place for him, this was his eureka moment; he knew his ex-wife Kellie was the second coming of the Gospel Killer. Mark also knew she was in the same house with

Yo-Yo, Lily and Daniel over an hour away. With his mind exploding, Mark found himself on I-35 racing through cars. He had to get to the lake house as quickly as possible for he knew Yo-Yo was in danger. Kellie probably wouldn't hurt her own son, but Yo-Yo and Lily were different stories.

"Why did you ask what color Goliath is?" Daniel asked, reminding him of the cell phone still in his hand. His son's voice pierced through the worry.

"Oh, no real reason, son," Mark said, trying to sound lighthearted and not frighten Daniel. "But say, could you put Yo-Yo on the phone?"

"Sure, Dad. I'll go get her."

He sat the phone on the kitchen counter top and went to find his stepmother while Mark was experiencing fear like he'd never felt before. His ex-wife was a serial killer and was alone with his family. How was that even possible? Why hadn't he been able to see some type of sign or warning? Mercifully, after what seemed like an eternity, he heard the phone being picked up from the counter.

"Hey you, didn't know you were such a dog lover. What's with all the questions about Goliath?" Mark tensed as he heard it was Kellie. Somehow he managed to hold it together and sound natural.

"Oh, just making small talk with Daniel. Say, is Yo-Yo around?"

"I think she's gone down to the lake with Lily, but Daniel went outside to look for them," Kellie said with a controlled pleasantness. His heart was about to burst through his chest, but he couldn't let on that he knew.

"Geez, my other line is ringing," he finally said, digging his fingers into the steering wheel of his Charger.

"Could you just tell Yo-Yo I'll call her back in a few minutes."

"Sure, I'll let her know," Kellie said cheerfully.

Hanging up the call while blaring his horn for the speed-limit-loving idiots ahead of him to get the hell out of his way, Mark hit speed dial and called Coleman. The detective's ID told him who was calling. "Mark, Kellie is the killer," he blurted out before Mark could say a word.

"I know," Mark practically screamed. "That's what I was calling to tell you, and she's with Yo-Yo and the kids."

"Oh, my God!" were the first words out of the detective's mouth, but then he quickly tried to calm Mark. "Don't worry. They'll be all right. We got SWAT at the house right now about to arrest her."

"They're not at her house," Mark yelled, fishtailing at 105 mph around a Ford pickup. "Oh, goddamn John, I should have told you. I've got so much to tell you. I shoulda told you everything from the beginning. They're at a lake house; take down this address."

"What is it you shoulda told me?" John asked, scrambling for his pen.

The Charger was spitting gravel like a hailstorm as Mark went on the shoulder to pass a Volvo. "That's gotta wait. I'll tell you everything, but it's gotta wait." He quickly gave his friend the address on Nob Hill in Gordon, Texas. "It's west, straight out 20. Get everything you can there, John, and I'll call you back. Right now I gotta get a hold of Yo-Yo."

Coleman assured him he would reach the local authorities and said he'd also call the highway patrol to find Mark on the road and give him an escort. Crossing over Spur 408 onto westbound I-20, Mark ended the call with Coleman while almost simultaneously hitting Yo-Yo's number on the speed dial. He waited impatiently for her to pick up. Finally, the phone was answered on the third ring.

"Just got a text from my hubby," said Kellie, without the pretense of a hello. "He says there's quite a few police at our door looking for me. But judging from the dog questions, I guess you already knew that. That fuckin' Colbert prick."

Mark felt panic-stricken terror as he listened to her. "Kellie, listen, please. Give yourself up," he pleaded after grappling for words. "The police are on their way."

"Really? Well, guess I better hurry things along then," was her cold response.

"Don't hurt anyone else," Mark screamed frantically into the phone. "Please, Kellie!"

All he heard was a chilling laugh before she hung up the phone. As Mark raced along, he repeatedly hit Yo-Yo's number on speed dial, like an NBA star dribbles a basketball, boom, boom, one right after another, but each call went unanswered.

Mark cursed and cried, fearing the worst. He finally gave up trying to get through to Yo-Yo and called Coleman back. Coleman listened to his friend, and then tried to calm Mark by telling him that the police would be at the Nob Hill location in a matter of minutes. While talking with Coleman, Mark saw the flashing lights of a highway patrol cruiser heading eastbound. As he watched, the cruiser did a U-turn in the grassy median ahead of him and then pulled alongside the Charger, giving Mark the signal to follow.

Mark thanked John for the escort, and then in an

almost complete breakdown, asked, "What if she does something to Yo-Yo or Lily? Or what if she hurts Cubbie or Will, or even Daniel?"

"That's not gonna happen," John said, knowing his friend was in emotional danger. "Listen, Ellis got us a helicopter and we'll be airborne in ten minutes. Mark, we're gonna meet you there at the lake, and everything is gonna be fine. You hear me, everyone is going to be fine." When his friend didn't respond, Coleman yelled into the phone, "Mark! Mark are you there?"

Tears were flowing from his eyes enough to almost blur out the flashing lights of the cruiser ahead of him but Mark finally answered. "This is all because of me."

Detective Coleman did not know what to make of that statement, but he knew his friend was in real trouble, so he wanted to keep him talking. "What do you mean? How is it because of you?"

Reality and the fear of the unknown, the fear of what his ex might be doing, and the reality that he was still at least fifty miles from being able to stop it, were waging a battle within Mark but he heard Coleman ask again, "How's it because of you, Mark?"

With that, Mark couldn't hold off any longer. It was time, past time, for a "Come to Jesus meeting" and for Mark to put the whole truth out on the table. Barreling 115 mph down the highway, he started the meeting by telling Coleman about the Bible verses, about his guilt over divorcing Kellie and making her commit adultery by getting remarried, and how he didn't know it was her until the dog barked — the dog that Luke Colbert had told him about that morning on the rewards hotline. Then the meeting got good. Through his tears, Mark told Coleman that he had killed The Magician, killed Bubba, and previously, killed four men during the exchange in the Carolina Ramirez kidnapping. Coleman was shocked enough, but then Mark went on to tell him that he had spoken with the actual Gospel Killer and that Kellie was only a copycat. This was some meeting, even for Jesus.

John was sitting in the back of a sedan between Ellis and another FBI agent as Mark went on and expressed to him how uncontrollably frightened he felt. Even though he heard the pain and terror in Mark's voice, he couldn't respond; he didn't yet want the other two men knowing of Mark's misdeeds. John would need time to sort through what he was hearing. He had been about the law his whole life, but Mark was like a son to him. He would decide how best to handle things later, but right now his only thought was how to best care for Mark.

As a uniformed cop sped Coleman and the two FBI men to an airstrip, the agents were each on their own phones shouting out directives as John fought to control his own fear that seemed to be transferring through the phone. The admissions he had heard were staggering, but this was Mark. He had to do what was right for him, and right now, what was right was for John to protect this man who he loved like a son. John did this by keeping himself engaged and by forcing Mark to concentrate—on something other than the horror they both feared might be taking place at Nob Hill.

John began telling Mark how Ellis had questioned Vaughn's daughter earlier that afternoon. The daughter finally caved and said she suspected her father was having an affair with a friend of hers, a pastor's wife named Kellie. She herself had introduced her father to Kellie, thinking after rehab it would be a good idea for her dad to get involved with a church, and how instead he got involved with the youth minister's wife.

He wasn't getting any response from Mark, but John kept talking. As Mark followed the Cruiser down 20 at now nearly a hundred and twenty-five miles per hour, Coleman began apologizing that he hadn't called an hour or more ago.

"The whole thing was unbelievable. I just wanted to be sure it was Kellie. Turns out she was required to get fingerprinted to obtain her claims adjuster license. We got the fingerprints from the state insurance board and they matched the ones from the bag of evidence found with your dad and Vaughn. By that time, SWAT was ready for the arrest. I was about to call you when you called me."

Coleman and the others were in the helicopter. He didn't know if his friend had heard a single word.

"I'm twenty miles out," he heard Mark say.

John kept talking. Ellis thought Kellie must have used the customer lists from her work with State Farm to select her victims. He said that each of the Matthew, Mark, Luke, and John's only thought they were in "good hands" with the insurance giant.

It was a lame joke, and a horrible time to try any humor, but Coleman didn't know what to say. He was battling his own emotions, fighting them all the while and feeling like he was talking into a dead phone.

After a moment, and hearing no response, John asked, "Mark, Mark, are you still there? You still with me?" More silence followed until Coleman heard the Charger's engine being down-shifted into a lower gear.

"We're here," Mark finally said.

Chapter 43

Just ahead of him, Mark saw the flashing lights of a half dozen squad cars in and around the lake house. Police were attempting to secure the perimeter when Mark, still traveling close to thirty miles per hour, shoved the Charger into park and leaped out of the car. Mark's world was silent now; he saw the swirling lights illuminating the front yard, saw the huge Goliath standing on his back legs at the fence mouthing barks, but he heard nothing. His mind contained only panic.

While he ran full speed towards the house, a uniformed officer tried to stop Mark, but instead got bull-rushed and flew backwards, tumbling head over heels. When two others tried to take up chase, the highway patrolman who had led Mark into the area jumped from his car screaming that Mark was the husband.

The garage door was up and Mark raced through it to enter the home through the door leading to the laundry room. Grabbing the door and slinging it open to rush inside, Mark stopped cold in his tracks and then screamed out in terror. Two police officers were in the room, standing over two dead bodies. Both Cubbie and Will lay dead, a few feet from one another. Will's throat had been slashed and Mark could see

Cubbie had been stabbed several times in the chest.

The highway patrolman who had escorted Mark was trying to follow him into the house when he heard Mark yell, "Where's my wife and kids?"

As he reached the door, he saw the two police officers look to the ground and shake their heads as Mark exploded past them through the kitchen and into the living room. Screaming out Yo-Yo's name, Mark raced down a bedroom hallway until the trailing highway patrolman heard his screams turn to shrieks of horror. On the hallway floor near the kid's bedroom door, Yo-Yo lay face down in a huge pool of blood. A policewoman knelt next to her body as Mark fell to his knees.

Crying in anguish, Mark crawled the last few feet to Yo-Yo and picked her up in his arms. Rolling her body over, Mark could see that she had died from multiple stab wounds to the abdomen and chest. His head sunk into her body. Clutching her tightly and screaming that he was there with her, that he was there with her now, Mark began rocking back and forth until he collapsed backwards into the wall.

From the corner of his eyes, Mark watched as the policemen followed and began to gather behind him in the hall. Spitting out mucus from his mouth, and with eyes clouded by tears, Mark finally became coherent enough to ask about his kids.

"They're not hurt," a police captain said, stepping forward. "They're in the bedroom behind you. We think your wife was protecting them when she was killed. I'm sorry."

Covered in blood, Mark gently laid Yo-Yo aside and stood up. Looking through the bedroom doorway, he saw both Daniel and Lily crying and huddled next to a policewoman who tried to comfort them. Seeing they were unhurt, at least physically, Mark took out his notepad and wrote down the name of Detective John Coleman.

"This man should be here any minute," he said, handing the note to the police captain. "I want you to have him take care of my children."

After the captain read John's name, Mark looked once again at Yo-Yo and then walked down the hallway. The surrounding group of policemen gathered there parted and let him pass. They watched as he followed the same path he had taken while entering. Mark nodded downward as he passed Cubbie and Will and then left the house. His tears were now slowing. Once outside he began running to his Charger. The police watched as he pulled the Glock from his shoulder holster, checked its clip, jumped into the car and sped away.

Chapter 44

The helicopter landed near the lake less than ten minutes after Mark had left. Jumping into a waiting car, Coleman and Ellis arrived at the scene only moments later. Seeing the police presence at the home as they got out of the car, John feared what had happened inside, but even the veteran detective couldn't prepare himself for what he was about to see.

Taking the same route as Mark had upon entering the house, Ellis and John immediately saw the bodies of Cubbie and Will. John began to tremble as he saw Cubbie's lifeless body. He had known him as a young boy. He had seen firsthand the all too frequent cruel treatment he had received. Still, throughout his life, Cubbie had only offered kindness to others. And he had received so little in return. Seeing him again fall victim to an act of violence left Coleman almost unable to move.

Ellis was having a hard time himself, as he saw the effect this was having on John. As they worked together for weeks, Coleman had told countless stories about Mark and Cubbie. Knowing the feelings John had for the Witt family, Ron wondered if he could handle the situation.

"Are you up to this?" he asked, grabbing Coleman's

forearm.

John breathed deeply and nodded his head. Through the house and into the hallway John followed Ellis until he saw Yo-Yo in the hallway. The bloodletting had been huge and the scene was horrific. Seeing Yo-Yo, the most vibrant person imaginable, now in this condition and void of life, forced John to balance himself against the hallway wall.

Glancing back, Ron turned to comfort his friend just as a local police captain was pointing at Yo-Yo.

"Look at her arms and hands. See those cuts; they're defensive wounds. She put up a helluva fight, probably to save those kids," he said to a young officer.

This seemed almost a slight to Ellis and sent him into a rage. He began waving his FBI badge and screaming for everyone to leave. The officers hesitated, which further incensed Ellis. He hurled obscenities at each one in rapid fire until the captain instructed all his officers to go outside. As the captain was leaving, he remembered Mark's request.

"Excuse me, but which one of you is John Coleman?" he asked sheepishly.

John was staring at Yo-Yo when he heard his name. He nodded and the captain handed him the note from Mark. John quickly read it. When he looked up, the captain pointed down the hallway. "They're okay—at least as best as they can be. I've got one of my ladies taking care of them."

John nodded in appreciation. "Where's the man who gave you this?"

"He saw everything and left in a hurry. Didn't say where he was headed."

"So this was Mark's wife?" Ron asked, as the captain

walked away. With tears welling, John managed to nod. "And the two others, did he have two brothers?"

"No, just one," John answered, pushing past Ron. "The other man is Will Evans."

Ellis was asking if the house belonged to Mark and did he know where he could have gone, but John continued down the hall and then pushed open the bedroom door slightly. When he saw the children, John remembered how Mark had honored him by asking him to be the godfather for both. As he looked at the combined fear and emptiness in their eyes, he swallowed hard.

"Give me a minute," he said, turning back to Ron. The policewoman left as he entered. Soon the minute turned into thirty as John sat on the bed holding Lily and Daniel. The tears in his eyes began streaming downward as he answered their questions.

"Is mommy in heaven?" Lily asked.

"Did my mom kill everybody?" Daniel wanted to know.

No child should ever have to ask these questions, and no friend should ever have to answer them. With arms stretched around both children, John did answer the questions though, and the crying of all three became a torrent. As he kissed Lily's forehead and ran his hands through Daniel's hair, John forced himself to gather himself and think of happier times. Thinking again he was their godfather, John remembered how Mark and Cubbie had so much fun with the whole godfather thing — kissing his imaginary ring and calling him, in their fake Italian accents, "John Corleone."

Coleman remembered how in his own best Brando imitation, he would refer to them as his sons, saying that Cubbie was his beloved son Sonny and that Mark was poor Fredo. He remembered how the joke made all three men laugh, as they each knew full well that Cubbie was no hot-blooded Sonny and that Mark himself was the leader and would have been Michael and not the idiot son Fredo.

Laying the children on the bed and telling each not to leave the room because he would be back before they knew it, John finally left the bedroom and sent the policewoman back in. In the hallway, and now with his emotions more under control, Coleman met with Ellis and got up to speed.

Ron had checked with the county and found that the home belonged to Bryan Hart, a Dallas area cab company owner. Ellis had spoken by phone with Bryan, who had told him that Mark's family had been staying at his lake house for the last few weeks because Mark had feared for their safety because of threats made by the Gospel Killer.

After talking to Bryan, Ellis was full of questions, with the biggest being: Had Mark told John he had been in some form of contact with the Gospel Killer? Feeling that he couldn't answer truthfully yet and wanting to protect Mark, Coleman lied to the FBI agent.

After getting negative answers to all his questions, Ellis told Coleman he had put out an APB for Kellie's maroon Acura. Unfortunately, Ellis had not known that the kennel that transported Goliath wouldn't fit into her Acura, so Kellie had borrowed her father's green Toyota Tundra pickup. Additionally, Ellis told Coleman that Mark wasn't answering his phone and asked John if he thought they should put out a bulletin for Mark as well.

"No. Let him go," said a sullen-faced John. "Don't try to find him or stop him. He needs to be the one to finish this."

Ellis arched his eyebrows as he started to ask, "So you think Mark knows where she's…"

"He'd never have left these kids if he didn't know where she was going," answered Coleman, shutting him off midsentence.

Chapter 45

Tearing down the road, Mark realized there were so many things he couldn't explain. Like how Kellie could be the killer and how he knew exactly where she was headed. But as a salmon is born from an egg, along with thousands of others in a small mountain stream, then heads out to the ocean to live its life, and then somehow manages—at a predestined time, along with the thousands of salmon born from the other eggs—to return to that same mountain stream to lay their own eggs and then die, Mark knew Kellie would return to the Eagle's Nest bed and breakfast at Lake Travis. The Eagle's Nest was where Mark had taken Kellie long ago on a weekend trip before their marriage, where he had taken her virginity, where she spoke of so often as the place she became a woman, and it would be the place where Mark would see her become a dead woman.

Turning off his cell signal to avoid possible detection from tower pings, Mark cut south on State Highway 281 to Highway 190, where he headed east. The drive normally would take three to four hours but he would make it in less than two hours and fifteen minutes. Despite the speed, the trip seemed endless for Mark. Flat land hidden by the darkness surrounded him, his head lights the sole figures to cut through the humid night, while Mark drove with tears of grief combined with tears of rage raining from his eyes and falling down his face.

The radio was turned off and the only sounds from the speeding car were Mark's sobbing, as well as screams of anguish and fist punches into either the roof or the dashboard at his thoughts of Yo-Yo and Cubbie. For while he could turn off the radio, turn off his cell, turn off the wipers he occasionally had to use when the wetness from the humidity clung too heavily on the windshields, Mark couldn't turn off his thoughts.

He couldn't stop thinking of Cubbie, of the many times in the past he had seen him beaten, humiliated, taunted, and how each time Mark had tried to stop the abuse and tried to make things better for Cubbie. Now, after seeing him dead on the floor, he knew there was nothing more big brother could do. He couldn't save Cubbie or take his place this time. Cubbie was dead, along with Will, the only person other than Mark and his mother that Cubbie had ever loved, and Mark hadn't been there to stop it.

And while thoughts of Cubbie and Will were prevalent, thoughts of his beautiful Yo-Yo dominated Mark's mind. With one hand on the wheel and the other clutching his shirt that still bore her blood from when he had held her in the hallway floor — from when he held her for the last time on this earth — Mark raced to Lake Travis.

His radar detector alerted him outside Killeen, Texas, and helped him avoid a speeding ticket, but nothing could help him avoid the pain his entire being felt. The finality of her death was overwhelming. The sight of her body lying on the floor, slashed and dead was seared into his mind. He was tortured by thoughts of what her last moments may have been like. He had brought Yo-Yo to that moment. She would still be alive if he had never met her. And he had been the one to tell Kellie where the family was hiding, because she was Daniel's mother. Why hadn't he been there? Why hadn't he realized earlier the killer was Kellie and stopped her before this horrible thing happened? These thoughts and a thousand others bombarded Mark's mind.

At a hundred and five miles an hour, and with these feelings of pain, remorse, grief, anger, and guilt all continuing their rage, Mark looked over at the passenger seat and saw her. Yo-Yo sat beside him. Her hair was up and she was wearing the necklace he had given her for Valentine's Day. She looked so radiant. Mark reached for her, but in reality, she wasn't there. In his eyes, she had only moved. Now, she seemed to be riding outside the car, sitting alongside it in an imaginary seat. The wind blew her hair down and then back, only making her more beautiful. She sat effortlessly in the imaginary seat right outside his car as he drove.

The sight of Yo-Yo made Mark almost forget the road, as he rarely looked ahead. Instead, he focused on her and the wonderful look in her eyes. On her mouth was a slight smirk — the half grin, half smirk he had seen so many times before when she would coerce him into going somewhere he had no interest in going. When from across a room, as he stood in some corner silently wishing he was almost anywhere else in the world, Yo-Yo would stop talking with such and such couple for just a second, and she would scrunch her lips and mouth into that funny and wonderful half smirk, half grin of hers, for him to see and laugh at. It was only for Mark, and it was her way of saying, "Thanks for coming."

As he drove and watched her riding outside the car, Mark faced the realization. She was appearing only in his mind. Despite that, he still wondered if he were seeing her for a reason, wondered if Yo-Yo was visible in his eyes to say "Thanks for coming" on this trip to avenge her death.

Now southbound on I-35, the Charger barreled through Round Rock on the last miles of the journey. Within minutes he was at Lake Travis. Cutting his lights off, Mark pulled into the Eagle's Nest and parked near the owner's office.

Getting out of the car, he grabbed two extra clips from the console and then drew his Glock and started towards cabin number nine. Set away from the others and nearly at the water's edge, cabin nine had been where Mark and Kellie had stayed that weekend years ago. It was where she had experienced her first taste of sexual ecstasy and found it to be intoxicating, and now it was where he intended for her to taste death. Crouched over and slowly walking to the cabin, he saw her father's familiar pickup in the parking lot, recognizing it from the "I serve a Jewish Carpenter" bumper sticker. Not that he needed confirmation; Mark knew she was there.

Approaching the cabin, he saw what appeared to be a glow coming from inside, seeping out under the window blinds. Quietly, he tried to look through one of the side windows but couldn't make it out. As he approached the front of the cabin, Mark switched the gun's safety off and silently stepped onto the small porch. He turned the knob very slowly, and was surprised to find the front door open. Ever so slowly, he pushed on the door. When it creaked slightly, he flung the door open.

Bursting into the room with gun drawn, he was surprised at what he found. The lights were turned off in the small Victorian style cabin but candles were everywhere. In fact, like an airport runway, they lined the floor and created a lit path leading to a four-poster brass bed against the far wall. Seeing no one and no movement in the room, Mark felt along the wall for the light switch.

He would not find it, because just as he knew she would be there, Kellie knew that Mark alone would come looking for her and that he would know exactly where to find her. She had prepared the cabin before hiding outside to watch for him. Now, as he entered the cabin, she followed him inside.

A sudden noise behind Mark caused him to turn just as he got hit with 50,000 volts from a stun gun. Dropping to his knees, Mark tried to fight back against the pain, but a second charge from the gun put him on the floor writhing uncontrollably.

As he fell, Kellie moved quickly, hopping over his body, kicking the gun away from his reach, and then pressing a chloroform-laced rag down on his nose and mouth. About twenty minutes later, a pounding ache from his head forced Mark to first open and then try and focus his eyes. The room was dark and his vision was hazy. His mouth was bound and gagged and he was lying nude on the rose-petal-covered sheets of the cabin's brass bed, with his hands and feet tied to its four posts.

Seeing him awaken, Kellie smiled as she slipped off her satin nightgown, walked over and knelt on the floor next to Mark. Taking a sip from her wine glass, she watched the candlelight dance upon Mark's body. Finishing the wine, she gently stroked his bound body with the back edges of her fingernails. She felt the excitement of seeing her man again, seeing him without clothes, without the ability to resist, without the ability to leave.

Mark tried desperately to free himself, tried to yell or speak, tried to arch his back and literally break apart the bed, but his efforts only made her wetter. Watching his body, seeing his chiseled muscles tighten and strain, feeling the rawness of him with her hands caused Kellie to join Mark in bed, where she lay down on him. Stretching out and spreading her arms, she grabbed Mark's bound wrists and held onto them, while kissing and licking his neck. With him tossing in bed and attempting to push her away, throwing his head violently side to side, Kellie took her arms and began first rubbing and then grabbing and massaging Mark's chest, which in turn made her move her mouth to his ear and lick the outside of it.

"Baby, you feel so good," she whispered. "So good."

With the exception of his penis, Kellie took time to touch and hold every part of Mark's body. It was the touch of a prospector fondling a huge gold nugget—a nugget long dreamed of and which was now in her hands. No amount of Mark's straining mattered. He was in her bed again and he wouldn't leave this time.

After a long while, Kellie rose from the bed and poured herself another glass of wine. Staring in disbelief, Mark watched as she stretched her arms out

and turned around, displaying her nude body for him
like a model on the catwalk. Desperate for his desire,
she wanted him to see the years of effort she had put
into her body. Wanted somehow for Mark to know
that all the work had been just for him, everything she
had done had been for this exact moment, had been
done to make him want her again, as she had always
wanted him.

Still standing and facing him, she held onto the wine
glass with one hand and with the other began to pleasure herself. Wide-eyed with horror, Mark was filled
with rage, but only able to thrash helplessly on the bed
as Kellie began dancing for him in the candlelight. She
was lost in the moment—a moment she had waited
an eternity to enjoy. Pushing two fingers up inside
herself, she shuddered and then asked, "Do you like
it? I waxed it. It's all clean and fresh, and it's all just
for you."

Withdrawing the fingers, she slid them into her
mouth and licked her own juice from them. Mark
closed his eyes, unwilling to watch and unable to
accept what was happening. Afterwards, she set
down the wine glass and picked up the knife she
had used to kill Yo-Yo, Will and Cubbie. Returning
to the bed, she athletically climbed over his body and
sat down on the bed, cross-legged, facing forward
between his legs. Still holding the knife, she stared
at Mark's penis. The wine, the soft rose petals on her
skin, the shadows from the candlelight leaping on
the walls, and his glorious, nude body all combined
to intoxicate her.

Trying ever harder to free himself from the cuffs,
Mark contorted his body with wild movements, but

Kellie only gently touched his inner thighs with the back of her hand. After setting the knife and its flat-edged blade down on his stomach, she took his dick in her hands. As he struggled, she began to stroke the shaft of his dick with a feathery touch. Disappointed to find him not aroused, she continued touching and then gently squeezing his dick.

"Mark, do you remember what the Bible says in First Corinthians, chapter 7 and verse 4?" she said, looking into his eyes. She moved her other hand down onto his balls while he frantically tried to pull the bedposts from the frame. "It says, 'The wife hath not power of her own body, but the husband, and likewise the husband hath not power of his own body, but the wife.'" Clutching his dick tightly, she added, "Do you know what kind of power you've had over me, over my body?" Now rubbing the head and shaft forcefully, she commanded, "Now give me that power over yours."

Sliding her legs back, she lowered her head and took Mark into her mouth. Desperately struggling, over-whelmed with anger and hatred, Mark thrashed on the bed, trying to pull himself away from her mouth. It was no use; she continued to hold the base in her hands, sucking, licking and kissing, and then biting, until she could feel his dick harden. Feeling it become rigid, feeling its veins begin to pop outward from the shaft, Kellie was satisfied she now controlled his body, so she raised herself forward until she slid his dick inside her vagina. Lifting her hands upward, almost to the heavens as if in joyous thanksgiving, she began to ride and grind Mark with slow, deliberate move-ments. She desperately needed to feel every inch of him inside her.

Lowering her head, she clutched Mark's shoulders with her hands as she rhythmically moved forward and back, pushing her pubic bone into his. At this point, perhaps from the lingering effects of the chloroform or perhaps from the emptiness he now felt, for the first time in his life Mark stopped experiencing the desire to fight back. Not able to shake free, not able to push her away, not having been able to prevent this entire horrific night, the fire seemed to extinguish inside Mark and he lay still. Grinding harder against him, almost losing her breath from the excitement of again being with her man, Kellie felt Mark's motionless body and reached down to bite into his neck. Getting no response, she looked into his glazed eyes.

"Come on baby, fuck me!" she demanded. Speeding her pace, she moaned, "Fuck me like you used too. Didn't you used to like to fuck me?" Grinding faster and harder, Kellie felt the warmth building in her lower abdomen, the warmth that preceded orgasm, and she screamed, "Oh goddamn, come on and fuck me. Fuck me like you fucked her."

Hearing "her" and the reference to Yo-Yo penetrated Mark's semiconscious state. He had been almost unwilling to go on, with thoughts and frozen snapshots of his previous life swirling in and out of his mind in an evil and surreal nightmare. But Kellie's screaming command, "Fuck me like you fucked her," caused Mark to try again to grasp reality.

His senses began coming back. He felt the pain in his right hand. He felt the enormity of the evil being perpetrated to him. He heard Kellie's audible moans and quickening breath, and he felt it as she pushed her hips faster and faster into his groin. Then, he saw the cabin's door inch open. In her excitement from subduing Mark, Kellie had forgotten to lock the door behind her. Now, a tiny bit of light shone off the lake and into the room from the door, which was being ever so slowly opened.

Forcefully blinking his eyes in an attempt to clear his blurred vision, Mark focused on the door and saw a dark figure enter the room. Nearing orgasm and furiously grinding into him, Kellie screamed, "Come on, baby. Come on, baby!" All the while Mark concentrated on the dark figure, now moving slowly along the back wall and nearing the bed.

With Kellie's back arched and both hands pushing into Mark's chest as she readied for climax, Mark watched the figure. In the candlelight, he could tell it was wearing a dark ski mask. Now it stepped out from the wall and grabbed something from a nearby windowsill.

Kellie was oblivious to everything except Mark, and tremors began contorting her body and face as she was about to come. Throwing her head and hair back, preparing to allow her body to lose control and give itself completely to ecstasy, Kellie was already experiencing the mental rapture of again making love to her one true husband as the masked figure moved along the bedside right behind her.

Now closer, Mark could see the figure was brandishing something in his hand. It was still dark and he couldn't make out the object. Kellie was seconds away from an eruptive orgasm when Mark saw the figure quickly grab her from behind and smash the object, a bookend, into the side of her head. She had been caught completely off-guard and the blow sent her tumbling off Mark and onto the floor dazed. The figure deftly darted around the bed, and with one additional blow to the back of her head, knocked Kellie unconscious.

Now, the masked figure bent over and checked her pulse, before laying the bookend on the floor. While he checked her pulse, a tiny drop of blood oozed from Kellie's ear, dripping across his finger. The man casually wiped it away on one of her breasts before standing. After rising, he turned and gazed fully on the still bound and nude Mark.

"I must admit I can see how this might drive a girl crazy," he said, flashing a hedonistic smile at Mark. Licking two fingers, he reached down and flicked the head of Mark's still partially aroused dick before adding, "A different time, a different place, who knows... But alas, business before pleasure."

The senses were now completely back. Mark didn't know why or how the figure was here, but he knew from the voice that this was the man he had spoken with on the phone. He knew this was the Gospel Killer. Mark once again strained to free himself, as Nicholas sat down on the bed beside him and patted his leg.

"There, there. I'm not here to hurt you," he soothed. As Nicholas stood to turn on the lamp sitting on the nightstand, Mark could see that he was wearing a dark grey rain suit and leather gloves, in addition to his ski mask. After switching the light on, Nicholas walked to the foot of the bed and faced Mark.

"I suppose, as a gentleman, I really should introduce myself, but for obvious reasons that is not a good idea, so let's just go with the Gospel Killer. And let me begin by saying how terrible I feel about what happened to your family. It was horrific, such an unnecessary waste of life."

"Now I know you must have so many questions," Nicholas continued, with Mark's eyes glued to him, "but I probably ought to hurry, since I really am not sure how long your lover here will remain unconscious. So, regarding how I came to arrive here, I had a GPS tracking system placed some time ago under your passenger side, back wheel well, and I have been monitoring your movements ever since. Consequently, I have known about your lake house retreat all along, and tonight when I heard on my police scanner about the crime there and how they were now seeking your ex-wife, well naturally, I wanted to help so I followed you. And speaking of that, you drive like a maniac," he laughingly added.

With that said, Nicholas returned to the nightstand, picked up the wine bottle and took a drink. "Geez," he said, reacting in horror. "The bitch led you here to have her celebration of all celebrations, and she brings a six dollar bottle of wine? No wonder you divorced her."

Shaking his head in amazement at the awful wine choice, Nicholas took great care to wipe away any possible DNA he may have left on the bottle before returning it to the nightstand. "But enough about that. The reason I'm here tonight Mark, is you. It's very important to me that you are able to get past this evening and the tragedy of losing your wife and brother. You see, I have great plans for you. I can't imagine things being as fun without you pursuing me."

While saying this, his eyes fixated longingly on Mark's taught muscles straining to break free. However, the sound of Kellie's moans distracted his lust and he looked down to see her body start to slowly move.

He knew she would soon be regaining consciousness.

"How is she when she first awakens?" he asked mischievously as he returned his eyes to Mark. "I'm guessing she'll be a mother bear tonight."

Mark strained harder than ever to free himself, but the effort only made Nicholas smile even more. "You are a fighter, aren't you? And that's precisely why I can't tell you how I do what I do. How I create my mural of life and death. How and why it is men are deliriously happy to be with me one minute and the very next moment they are dead. And it's why I mustn't say why it is I pick men named Matthew, Mark, Luke, and John, or how I select them. Where would be the fun in that? In telling a fighter where to fight, or in this case where to look?

Kellie's moans were becoming stronger. As Nicholas watched her, she tried to blink. She would soon be awake. He Returned his attention to the bed and placed a hand on Mark's chest.

"I must hurry. She'll be awake any moment. Mark, do you understand?" The fierce anger on Mark's face showed he wasn't in an understanding mood. "Over these last few weeks, I've come to respect the fact that no one except you can properly challenge me. Only you can push me to reach the level needed for the everlasting fame my gifts deserve. It's why I sat in the parking lot tonight for so long. When you didn't appear, I became frightened. I had to come inside to offer my assistance. It's why I protected you, protected us, here tonight. Don't you see that? Only you can truly challenge me, and now I need you to challenge yourself—to survive this night and to again pursue me. God knows I've given you so many reasons to want to kill me. And he also knows all the reasons I want to see you try. Will you do that for me, Mark?"

Now sitting up, Kellie attempted to roll into an all-fours position while shaking the cobwebs from her head. Watching her, Nicholas pulled a serrated-edge knife from his jacket and sliced away the rope tying Mark's left hand to the bedpost. Mark stared at Nicholas and then at Kellie, noticing that her moans were less frequent and her movements more coordinated. Shaking his hand free, Mark pulled out the gag stuffed inside his mouth before beginning to furiously work to free his other hand.

Retreating from the bed, Nicholas made his way across the room. Reopening the front door, he slowly looked outside to see if anyone was nearby. Seeing that there wasn't, he turned back to Mark.

"Good luck, my friend," he said, leaving and closing the door just as Kellie was rising to her feet.

Soon she recovered the knife which had been knocked from her hand, and now glanced around the room, trying to clear her head.

"What happened? Was there some…is there someone else here?" she asked.

Mark had managed to free both hands. Sitting up in bed, he now worked feverishly to untie his feet from the bed.

"Fuck! Stop trying to get away," Kellie cried, and then lunged at him with the knife, slicing deeply into his right forearm. "Stop leaving me."

As Kellie began to draw the knife back for another attack, Mark smashed his left fist into her face, sending her stumbling backwards into a wall. With one foot now untied and with blood spurting from his cut, Mark ripped away the ropes from his other foot. He scrambled from the bed just as Kellie leaped on it, wildly swinging at him with the outstretched knife.

Mark backed away from Kellie, clutching his bleeding, throbbing forearm and scanning the room for possible weapons. He saw his gun on the floor across the room, but Kellie blocked his path to it. Seeing the lamp and wine bottle on the nightstand, he inched towards them, but following his eyes, Kellie reached the nightstand first, knocking the lamp to the floor and breaking all but its base into a hundred pieces. As she grabbed the wine bottle, Mark backed away towards the wall. Smiling, Kellie stepped towards him, the knife in one hand and the wine bottle in the other.

Taking a drink, Kellie pulled the bottle from her lips, tilted it downward and let the wine flow out and escape. The wine covered her nude body, and she appeared to glisten in the candlelight.

"Right here in this room was the first place I ever tasted wine," she said, tossing the now empty bottle back on the bed. "I tasted so many things for the first time here, right here with you."

Mark was not the nostalgic type and he was tired of playing defense. Surveying the situation, Mark sought an opportunity to get at Kellie and take the knife away. With eyes glued to her, he inched closer, holding his battered right arm and hand outward towards her.

Sensing his aggression, Kellie tightened her grip on the knife. "Before this goes any further, I want to tell you my plan wasn't ever about killing women, but I hope you understand that I had to kill Yo-Yo. I had to kill her to have you. You would have never been mine again as long as she was alive. I'm sorry that Cubbie was there and got caught up in things, but Yo-Yo, she had to die."

Thinking of his beautiful Yo-Yo and how Kellie had murdered her drove Mark past the edge. He took a giant step towards Kellie and threw a bone-crunching left hook into her ribcage while grabbing for the knife with his injured right hand. The blow sent her reeling into the corner wall, but she stayed on her feet and the two of them wrestled for control of the knife. Kellie's hand had become slick from the wine that had cascaded down it, and she was able to pull the knife away from Mark before he could grasp it with his good left hand.

Next, still alongside her and in no mood for defensive actions, Mark head-butted Kellie and sent her reeling backwards. Lunging towards her, he grabbed for her throat just as she plunged the blade into his stomach. Mark then slammed her head back into the wall and tried to strangle her for several seconds before he realized she had stabbed him. As he looked down at his abdomen, he saw both her hands on the knife that she continued to push into him. Blood gushed from the wound, and Mark instinctively let go of her neck and grabbed her hands. Engulfing her hands and the knife's handle with his own huge hands, Mark tried desperately to pull the blade from his body. This time it was his own blood that made Kellie's hands and the knife slippery, causing Mark to lose his grip. Breaths were getting difficult and his strength was evaporating.

"Why are you making me do this?" he heard the now crying Kellie say, before he could try again to get the knife from her. "I didn't want to hurt you. Stop fighting me."

The pain from the knife's blade being driven further into his stomach was excruciating, but Mark wasn't ready to stop fighting. Out of the corner of his eye he saw a small mirror hanging on the wall. Before he could even form a thought, Mark drove his fist into the mirror. Small shards of glass fell to the floor while several larger, jagged pieces of the mirror clung inside its frame. With what he thought might have been his last breath, Mark grabbed one of the biggest pieces of glass and ripped it away from the broken mirror.

Seeing this, Kellie let go of the knife and tried to escape, but Mark grabbed a fistful of her hair and held tight. The last image Kellie saw was her frightened reflection in the mirrored glass as Mark drove the jagged glass deep into her neck. She dropped to the floor where each heartbeat caused blood to gush from her gaping wound. Within seconds she lay dead.

Mark collapsed to one knee on the floor next to Kellie. Summoning all his strength, he gripped the knife and with one forceful and quick movement pulled it out of his body. More blood flooded out, appearing darker, almost black in color. The color told Mark his kidneys had been punctured and he knew he was in serious trouble. Staggering to his feet, he looked for a phone to call 9-1-1.

Mark had found his pants and was reaching into his pockets for his cell when he heard a car door slam and an engine roar to life outside in the parking lot. He dropped his pants and before they hit the floor, he heard tires spitting gravel out in the lot. Reaching down and picking up his Glock from the floor, Mark rushed outside in time to see a masked driver racing a BMW 535 past cabin number nine.

Nicholas had hidden beside the cabin and watched the struggle between Mark and Kellie through a window. The room was by then well lit and Nicholas had stayed and watched the final outcome. It would prove a costly mistake. He was less than fifty yards past the cabin when the first shot struck him in the back of the shoulder. Shots two and three blew out the remainder of the BMW's back window while shot four tore through the driver's seat and into his back. Shot five exploded the rear view mirror at the exact time Nicholas lost control and smashed into a parked Ford F-150 pickup.

Porch lights from occupied nearby cabins were coming on as Mark walked towards the BMW to fire the kill shot into Nicholas. Each step became slower and more deliberate because of Mark's loss of blood. The car door opened and a leg stepped from the car and onto the gravel parking lot. Mark raised the gun, but nearing the back bumper his nude body gave out and he fell to the ground unconscious under the lone parking lot streetlight.

Chapter 46

Three people sat in the room without saying a word. If not for the incessant beeping of the medical equipment, the entire room would have been silent. John, his wife Jackie, and Ron Ellis were holding a bedside vigil for Mark, who lay sedated in room 1209 of Austin's Seton Northwest Hospital.

The three didn't speak, but each person sat there thinking of the events which had led them to this hospital room. The room may have been a sterile medical environment, but it certainly wasn't devoid of emotion. John and Jackie sat next to each other holding hands in a fruitless battle to somehow fight against overwhelming despair. A quick glance from John towards her showed the two were sharing a feeling, as if they were halfway to scaling a huge mountain, when from above, they hear a huge and terrifying noise. An avalanche has started and with nowhere to hide, they are left to only be able to reach out and touch one another. It would have to be enough.

Ellis sat across the room with his elbows on his knees and with his hands running through his thinning hair. He had many questions he hoped to get answered, but at that moment he was there showing his friendship for John and his respect for Mark.

It had been almost nineteen hours since police took the call of shots fired at the Eagle's Nest bed and breakfast and EMS professionals had transported Mark almost immediately after that. Within an hour, the scene had been secured. Kellie's dead body was seen through the open door of cabin number nine and Mark's identity was discovered there as well from his driver's license, which was found inside the wallet in his pants pocket. Calls to Mark's next of kin went unanswered, but shortly afterwards Ellis got word from a friend in the Austin FBI's office telling him of the situation. An hour after the call, Ron, John, and Jackie boarded the agency's helicopter and rushed to Austin. They had been at Mark's bedside ever since.

Tears welled in John's eyes, and when he looked up at the clock on the wall it was as if he was attempting to see through a heavy mist. He couldn't make out the time; not that it mattered. He had tried also to listen when the surgeon had come in to check on Mark but couldn't make those words out either. He heard the doctor talk of a lacerated kidney and of a large intestine that had been severed during the attack. He knew the doctor said that when the intestine had been cut, it had spilled out its contents into Mark's abdomen and that the risk of infection was great.

The doctor had warned that an infection could be very dangerous. John heard the words, he tried to understand, but it didn't register. These words, these dire words said in such a solemn tone, could just not be true. Yo-Yo, Cubbie, and Will had died; John simply could not allow for the possibility that Mark wouldn't make it. John had tried to pray for Mark to be given strength. He knew those words would mean something, but each time John tried he would break down after saying, "Dear God…" That would have to be enough.

During the day, there had been numerous times when Mark made various moaning and distressful sounds from the bed. Frequently his eyes, though closed, appeared under their lids to be darting back and forth. The group had become almost accustomed to these brief reactions from Mark—reactions of a man unable to awaken from a nightmare or in Mark's case, awaken from his reality. When Mark finally did awaken and ask, "Where am I?" all three in the room were surprised.

"You're in the hospital, Mark," said Jackie, rushing to his side and grabbing his hand. "But it's all right; you're going to be fine. We're here with you, and everything's going to be fine."

Mark tilted his head and saw Ellis at the foot of his bed and John on the opposite side from Jackie. The large Coleman, squeezing between machines and tubes, put his hand on Mark's shoulder and tried to talk, but the emotions were too great and his words remained inside.

"Do you remember what happened?" Ellis asked after a hesitation.

Mark closed his eyes again and slowly nodded yes. "Where are my kids?"

"Lily and Daniel are both with Yo-Yo's parents," Jackie answered. "Her parents came to…they came to the…" Tears stopped her words and Jackie turned away from Mark before completely breaking down.

A nurse entered the room to check Mark's vitals. Finding him awake would have normally been an occasion to try to say something cheerful, but when she saw Jackie sobbing and sensed the mood, instead, the nurse kept her head down while quickly finishing her business and leaving. John had walked around the bed to console Jackie.

"Say, I need to talk to Mark," he said after the nurse left. "Can you give us a minute?"

Ellis nodded and escorted Jackie into the hallway. Coleman pulled up a chair next to the bed and took Mark's left hand in his own. "The doctor's say you might not make it. It all depends on how much you want to live."

Mark didn't say a word, but his eyes revealed his feelings. They showed a man who down to his very soul had no interest in living. A man who had endured all the pain he could handle and who only wanted someone to mercifully pull the wires and tubes from his body and let him die.

Coleman wouldn't stand for it and squeezed Mark's hand as hard as he could. "Get that shit out of your mind. Those kids lost their mother; they're not gonna lose you too. You hear me?" After getting no response, Coleman yelled, "Goddammit, they're going to their mother and uncle's funerals; they're not going to yours. Not now. Not fuckin' now."

Thinking of his family caused Mark's hollow eyes to moisten. Tears soon streamed down his face. "Did they see Yo-Yo and Cubbie, or Will? Did they see their bodies?"

"No. The bodies were gone before Lily or Daniel left the bedroom. They know what happened, but they didn't see it." The tears continued for Mark as Coleman added, "We're going to take care of those kids.

Whatever they need. Whatever you need. We're gonna get through this; all of us together."

Those words helped Mark regain his resolve. He didn't want to live, but this wasn't about him. It was about Lily and Daniel. His actions had threatened and hurt them, and now he would have to protect them. Mark had gotten the message and now nodded and squeezed John's hand in return. It was an unspoken but meaningful "thank you" from one friend to another. This signal, this silent nod and squeezing of his hand, greatly helped John.

"Listen, I need to tell you some things before Ellis and Jackie get back in here. I have to say some things and they have to stay just between us."

"All right."

"To start with, fuck Bubba Furh. He's dead and he's gonna rot in hell. So let him, and don't ever tell anyone you killed him. You understand? His death is gonna be swept away. Nobody wants a murder investigation. Nobody wants to pull that thread and see what unwinds when they start looking into why you or anyone else would have wanted him dead. That onion has too many layers and a whole lot of people would get real scared. So trust me just let it go, or else you'll wind up with a whole other set of problems. It's going to be ruled either an accidental death or a death by natural causes so don't start feeling guilty and go and admit something nobody wants to hear."

"John, you're a homicide detective. You can't be telling…"

"Fuck homicide. I'm not talking as a detective; I'm your friend."

Mark hesitated, looking to the ceiling as if for guidance. "I can't let you be an accessory to anything I've done."

"Stop that shit! Stop worrying about me. You got those kids to worry about. They're all that matters now!

His tears had temporarily stopped, but after hearing this, Mark began tearing up again, his eyes about to betray him for so many different reasons. The thought of his friend turning his back on his police career and telling him these things in order to try to protect him, thoughts of Yo-Yo, thoughts of Cubbie and Will, and of course, thoughts of Lily and Daniel, these thoughts combined to hurt far worse than the injuries that he had suffered. He wondered, really wondered, if he could endure this hurt when John stood up and blasted the palm of his hand into the wall. The noise vibrated through the room and turned Mark's attention back to John.

"Son, with what's happened, you'll never be what you were; you'll never be that man again. And I'm sorry about that, but you gotta find a way to still be your kid's father. You gotta be that man again."

The tears were again streaming down and Mark began biting his lips in a wasted attempt to make them stop. Coleman returned to his bedside and took his hand, causing Mark to look at him and give a nod of acknowledgement that he would try again to be a father for his children.

Seeing this, and needing to push back his own tears, Coleman went back to business. "And listen, don't worry about the Magician. That was a clean kill, and besides, believe me, nobody is too upset about him being dead either. I only hope you saw to it that he has to have a closed casket."

Mark's tears slowed as he listening to his friend. "Now, about the four bodies buried in Stephenville; that never happened. That never fucking happened. Understand?"

Mark's face showed that no, he didn't understand; he didn't understand at all.

John sat back in the chair and leaned in towards Mark. "We found the GPS tracker in your back wheel well," he said in almost a whisper. "The guy you shot in the parking lot was the Gospel Killer, wasn't it?"

"Yeah, it was him," Mark answered, having difficulty speaking. "He followed me there. Is he dead?"

"Yeah. He's got to be," John said, sighing.

"Got to be?" questioned Mark, lifting his head from the pillow.

"We haven't found him yet. But he lost a lot of blood. He managed to get out of the parking lot where you shot him and flagged down a car. The driver of the car, a guy named Eugene Wilson, probably stopped to try to help a wounded man and got knifed to death for it. A couple hours later we found Wilson's car abandoned near the UT campus. It was full of blood. The lab confirmed it was the same blood that we found in the BMW next to where you were found."

"Do you have a name?" Mark asked.

"We think so," Coleman answered. "The BMW was registered to a Nicholas D. Claxton of Dallas. We haven't been able to get ahold of him, but the car hasn't been reported as stolen."

Mark thought for a moment and then remembered one of his conversations with the Gospel Killer. "This Claxton, does he have a record? You could check the prints from his car because the Gospel Killer has a record. He all but told me that he did during one of his phone calls."

"That's the shit," John said, shaking his head. "They say there wasn't a single print in the car. Nowhere. Can you believe it? Not a print, not a fiber, nothing. It's like a ghost had been driving it. Fucker had to have driven it all the way to Austin wearing some type of plastic suit and gloves."

"He had a rain suit on," Mark said, nodding.

"Ellis has got his guys digging up everything they can on this Nicholas Claxton," John said, pacing around the room. "They say he comes from money, big money. Father started a cable television company in Pennsylvania in the seventies and sold it to Time Warner in the nineties for something crazy like a couple hundred million dollars. Supposedly since then dear old dad has parlayed that money into a real fortune."

Mark didn't respond, so Coleman continued. "The family claims they disowned Nicholas more than ten years ago because of some kind of major problem he had in prep school. Turns out they paid the other kid's families off, sealed the records, and claim they haven't seen or spoken to Nicholas since. They say they don't know where he's at or what he's been up to. At least that's their story. But get this; the dean of the prep school, the guy who managed to keep the mysterious problem hush-hush, was murdered about a year after Nicholas left school. "

Mark still stared at the ceiling. "But it doesn't matter even if the family is lying," Coleman added. "Because the truth is their fucked up son was the Gospel Killer and now he's dead."

Coleman patted Mark's leg. "Hey, I need to go and

get Jackie and Ellis. I'll leave you alone for a minute, but you remember what I've said, all right? It's important and it's all for the best. It's the way it's got to be."

After a brief hesitation, Mark looked at John and nodded as Coleman was leaving the room. Alone now, Mark resumed staring a hole in the ceiling. What else was there to do? Grief constricted him. He felt a suffocating pressure on his chest as he thought of his dead Yo-Yo. He could never have explained how he was weighed down by a crippling, tormented anguish on one hand, and on the other hand felt empty and more hollow than ever before. It was if the world was closed to him now and he was destined to be held prisoner to the dark thoughts of the prior evening.

Mark was a man of serious thoughts—pent-up thoughts and emotions that defined much of his being—yet he was not a man to verbalize these feelings. He had never lain on a shrink's couch and moaned of his troubles. That was beneath him. Besides, Yo-Yo could read him so well he seldom had to actually speak of his demons.

Above all, Mark was not a talker, but a doer. He was a man of action, so now he would have to survive his injuries and then find a way to act like both a father and mother to Lily and Daniel. Could he do it? He wasn't sure; he honestly just wasn't sure.

In fact, lying there that night, about the only thing Mark was sure of as Ellis and the Colemans came back into his room, was that if the Gospel Killer was somehow still alive, he was going to find that motherfucker and kill him.

The End

www.ingramcontent.com/pod-product-compliance
Lightning Source LLC
Chambersburg PA
CBHW070751280626
47162CB00016B/64